30p

GW00454903

*Sc*

YF

# PRIVATE ACCOUNTS

By the same author

THE NATURAL ORDER

# PRIVATE
# ACCOUNTS

## URSULA
## BENTLEY

**SECKER & WARBURG**
**LONDON**

First published in England 1986 by
Martin Secker & Warburg Limited
54 Poland Street, London WIV 3DF

British Library Cataloguing in Publication Data
Bentley, Ursula
    Private accounts : a novel.
    I. Title
    823'.914[F]    PR6052.E/

    ISBN 0-436-04021-2

Photoset in 10/12 pt Plantin by Deltatype, Ellesmere Port
Printed in Great Britain by
Billing & Sons Ltd, Worcester

To Veronica, Max, Evelyne, Ernst,
Barbara, Ron and the Groupies

# CHAPTER

# ONE

"PHILIP, where are my ankle weights? I have to work off that fruit cake I ate on the plane."

"In the trunk. Can't it wait till we get to the apartment, BJ?"

"Oh my God, my legs are somewhat swollen. They probably wouldn't fit anyhow. I guess I'll just put my feet up. Could you move further into the corner please? Thank you."

As the taxi sped at twenty-two miles an hour from Zürich airport to the city, BJ lay down with her head on Philip's awesome thighs and raised her legs so that her feet touched the roof just in front of Philip's face. The taxi driver shot out of his slouch in amazement as BJ's ankles appeared in his rear-view mirror. He fired off a round of Swiss German at them. Philip removed his glasses, wiped them and put them back on.

"You'd better sit up, BJ. The driver seems to think we're contravening some sort of immorality act."

BJ giggled, but remained where she was. "It may be my last chance. From what I've heard about the Swiss I feel like I'm going into – like – a Betty Ford Rehabilitation Center or something. I mean the Swiss have this thing about fresh air and yoghurt and going to bed early and stuff, don't they? We should be in real good shape when we leave. And all that snow and sunshine. No wonder they yodel all the time."

"Zürich was built on a swamp," said Philip.

"Really? I hope they did a good job."

"I think one can be sure of that."

"Yeah. That's what's so attractive about their image, like they have all this sophisticated technology and money and so forth, but basically I guess the people are real healthy and in tune with their environment."

The taxi driver turned round. "What address you want, please?" He looked askance at BJ's feet.

"Keltenstrasse," said Philip.

"To ze clinic?"

"No. What clinic?"

"Bircher Benner Clinic. Iz very famous. For the muesli. Iz right there in Keltenstrasse. I tink perhaps your wife is ill."

"That's an explanation I hadn't thought of."

"Please, she must sit up. I get problems wiv Polizei."

"How do we get into the apartment?" said BJ. "Is the key under the mat?"

"No. The Institute is sending someone to hand it over."

"How nice of them to get us an apartment."

"It's all part of the service, I understand."

"Please, madam," begged the driver.

"Okay." BJ sighed and sat up. "I guess the police have nothing else to do around here." She frowned at the back of the driver's head. "By the way, talking of immorality – do you happen to know if Swiss men are routinely circumcised, Philip?"

"No. I don't." He paused. "Why?"

BJ laughed and squeezed his knee. "Just routine research."

She looked out of the window and was pleased by the leafy cityscape. All the well-behaved automobiles looked new, and at intersections the traffic was directed by young ladies in dazzling orange raincoats and cowboy hats, who signalled their wishes with swoops of their illuminated sticks, as if miming I-LOVE-YOU in Swan Lake. The few policemen had exceptionally neat bottoms, done up in spotlessly laundered grey uniforms and blinding white accoutrements.

"I guess the Swiss are somewhat straight where sex is concerned," mused BJ. "It should be an ideal atmosphere for work."

The village of Eglikon lies approximately thirty miles to the north of Zürich, at the foot of a wooded hump in the landscape called the Irchel. As BJ and Philip drove to their apartment in the city, a willowy blonde with yoghurt and early nights written all over her set out on

2

horseback up the Irchel and into the woods. It had been a dry autumn, and leaves had already fallen in abundance from the deciduous trees, so that the thin November sun penetrated easily between the taller firs. It glinted off Kirstin's long hair, the black flanks of Pinot Gloire, and the steaming piles of his calling-cards. The paths swept symmetrically this way and that through the quiet woods as if laid out with the aid of a spirograph.

Kirstin's mood was rueful as she trotted along them. She had the feeling of the last day of the holidays, as her husband was due home from a business trip the following evening. It was no coincidence that she chose to spend the last day with Pinot Gloire. Max disapproved of her riding. He resented the horse's evident dislike of himself, although it was an attitude he almost welcomed in the rest of The Village, who shared it. He had also become impatient of the disfiguring contusions and broken bones that Kirstin regularly came home with, which interfered with their love-life. She knew he thought she did it on purpose, to give her excuses a more authentic ring than that of the traditional headache. Kirstin dreaded more arguments of this nature, so she kept Pinot on a tight rein, talking to him and pointing out the autumnal changes in the trees, and the new red and white notices warning of a fresh outbreak of rabies. The only sound was the occasional plop of a pine cone as a bird broke from cover.

Kirstin put Max out of her mind. There was still twenty-four hours before he came home. She and Pinot could canter through the healing solitude of the woods all afternoon, and again tomorrow. For her the woods were indeed botanical replicas of the unconscious, as claimed by professors of fairytales and experts on collective myth. But into this unconscious she cheerfully escaped, as into memories of childhood.

Today the sun drew mushroomy vapours from the undergrowth, which mingled with the sharp fragrance of wood fires drifting up from the village. She slowed Pinot to a walk and took off her jacket. Pinot pricked his ears, and then flattened them.

Suddenly the searing scream of military jets ripped through the sky and was gone. A herd of deer lumbered out of the trees across their path. Pinot reared in fright.

The taxi driver took BJ and Philip to a quiet residential street up a steep hill. Just beyond their house the street disappeared into woods. The large old houses were interspersed with luxury low-rise apartments, now for the most part empty, the gnomes having abandoned the telex for their weekend retreats in the mountains.

Their apartment was on the first floor of a house in chalet style. The

3

interior was filled with haut-bourgeois fittings – spindly Gobelin chairs, a grand piano, large tapestries of overweight seraglios cavorting in thickets, and innumerable console tables with knobbly gilt legs.

BJ was somewhat awestruck, but she managed not to show it in the presence of the female graduate student who had been sent by the Institute to hand over the key. The girl was a husky type from Montana. BJ fell in a few paces behind her and Philip as they toured the premises. It behoved her, she thought, to maintain a low profile around Philip's colleagues, and it usually suited her, too, as they quickly lapsed into the jargon of astrophysics. But they had come to Zürich so that Philip could spend his sabbatical at the Institute and write up a paper on gravity waves that he hoped would have Cal. Tech. and Harvard and one or two other places grovelling for his services. This was, for the moment, his world, and BJ was not comfortable in worlds which she did not bestride. So when they went out into the garden Philip discussed the view from a proprietorial location in the middle of the lawn, while BJ strolled around the perimeter pretending interest in the shrubs. The girl was more than a match for Philip's beef-fed dimensions. The two of them dominated the lawn like a couple of Vigeland sculptures. BJ was agreeably aware that while Philip and the girl talked their eyes followed her every move.

"It's kinda quiet," the girl was saying. "We chose it for that reason. There's an old lady underneath you and a dentist at the top, so you shouldn't be bothered at all."

"It's perfect," said BJ. "Just like I imagined."

"Oh, before I forget, the secretary told me to give you this copy of the house rules." She took out a wadge of paper from her pocket and handed it to BJ. "It's like when you can use the washer, and when you have to clean the stairs, and stuff like that."

"In that case it's for you, Philip."

They laughed. Philip dug his hands deeper into his pockets.

BJ signed. "Okay, what is all this?" She looked over the list. "Listen to this, Philip. 'No baths after 22 hours. No telephone calls after 21 hours. Washing machine to be cleaned after each use.' " She flipped through the pages. "Is this some kind of joke?"

"Nope," said the girl, chewing her gum – with glee, BJ thought.

"Is this an annex to the clinic, or what?"

"Nope. It's like that everywhere. You're lucky, you won't have much competition for the facilities with two singles. A friend of mine only gets the washing machine once a month, and she has two kids."

4

"I don't believe it."

The girl smiled and shrugged. She exchanged a glance with Philip, as if to establish with him a conspiracy of indifference to domestic hassles.

"Well," she said, "I'll leave you now. If there's any problem just call. See you on Monday, Phil."

"Philip," BJ corrected her.

"Oh. Pardon me." The girl gave Philip a smile of sympathy for his little-woman problems.

"What a bitch," said BJ, just before the girl was out of earshot. "Dyke, I shouldn't wonder."

"She seemed friendly enough to me," said Philip.

"To you. Exactly. She must think I'm just the traditional female appendage. She obviously has no idea of my professional credentials."

"How could she? You made no effort to talk to her."

"Why should I have to? It's the assumption that makes me so mad."

"Don't get mad, BJ. It weakens your argument."

"Huh."

They walked back to the house. At the side was a door labelled 'Kindereingang'. BJ looked at it, puzzled, because it was the same size as the adults' entrance.

"Let's take a nap," said Philip as they let themselves into the house. "Then afterwards we can go downtown for dinner."

"Okay." BJ groaned inwardly. Their naps were usually preceded by a complete run-through of the *Hindu Art of Love* and she was too tired. "By the way, do you think they're real picky about these house rules? I mean, I expected something along these lines, but this – " She waved the list – "approaches comical exaggeration."

"The Swiss aren't famous for their sense of humour," said Philip. "I would stick to the spirit, if not the letter."

"After the nap," said BJ, "we have to discuss our respective workspace." She stood in the hallway of the apartment, looking anxiously towards the living area, which somehow or other would have to yield the equivalent of two studies. "I really can't relax until I've done my first sales pitch." She hoped that Philip would take her literally and forgo the nap, but he did not respond.

BJ was anxious about her own success in Europe. She represented a data resources company that specialized in trade-related software. Considering what she had heard about Europe's clapped-out economy, out-moded industry, Marie Antoinette-type attitudes to the workforce, derelict ideas and effete management, it was reassuring that Switzerland, at least, seemed to have its act together. Her first impressions were of discreet affluence, and if all sections of society were as precisely regulated as the apartment-dweller, it pointed to a level of organization that would make her work in the business sector that much easier.

But the problem of breaking into the market was formidable. BJ called on the spirit of Walter Raleigh to be her aid, for the service she was selling would have to make as much impact on Europe as the potato if the continent – and BJ – were to survive.

As she lay in the bracken where Pinot Gloire had tossed her, Kirstin could not help wondering if his gelding operation had been performed correctly. True, he had been startled by the deer and the screaming jet, but they were both such regular features of life that he should by now be able to encounter them without having hysterics and bolting. Apart from the excruciating pain in her ribs, it was not unpleasant lying there, the sun warming her bruises. The earth beneath her still trembled as the offending deer lumbered away through the trees. But an accident was exactly what she had hoped to avoid in view of Max's imminent return. She must get home and try to conceal the evidence. Max had been in Poland for three weeks, he would expect to go straight from the airport to the bedroom – if she was lucky. On one occasion he had stopped on the way home and turned the BMW off the road to a local authority hut deep in the woods. The hut was one of several that could be hired for leisure activities, as he had reminded her with a smile, so the car would not arouse suspicion. Besides, she could not lie around sunbathing while Pinot was on the loose: by now he was no doubt ripping up freshly planted saplings on the edge of the wood.

Kirstin pricked up her ears. She thought she heard a scooter coming from the direction of the village. The woods were closed to general traffic, and she did not think officials of the forestry department went around on Yamahas. If the driver were bold enough to defy a ban on traffic there was no knowing what he might be capable of. In her vulnerable position, the prospect of meeting a man alone suddenly made the sunny seclusion of the woods rather sinister. Trust Pinot to run off just when she needed him. Furthermore, her injuries would prevent her defending herself, if it should come to that. Kirstin was not a nervous type, but if the tabloids were to be believed, the scooter had become the favoured steed of youthful muggers and pouncers on women alone. And a few weeks before, a woman had been attacked in the car-park of the local tavern. Admittedly, the victim had been German, a visiting retired midwife and grandmother of four, but The Village had been far from convinced that her attacker had knowingly gone for a foreigner; they feared that it was just a happy coincidence. Under the headline "Urban Terrorism Takes to the Hills" the local paper had brought Eglikon to the attention of the general public for the first time since the war, when an English bomber had accidentally wiped out the General Purpose Hall.

As the scooter approached, Kirstin struggled to her feet. If she were already lying down no judge, official or casual, could be expected to decide that she was not Asking For It. But as she stood up the pain in her ribs took her breath away and the woods dissolved before her eyes into a swirl of sickly green and yellow miasmas. As they cleared she hobbled off down the path in the same direction as the scooter, forgetting in her panic that she should be going back to the village, which was in the other direction. She tried to adopt a casual air as the scooter gained on her, dying to turn round, but knowing that to do so would also be Asking For It. Her stomach revolted as she realized that the scooter had slowed down and was coasting along behind her. But after a few minutes she could not go any further without pausing for breath. As she stopped the scooter drew alongside.

Kirstin's smile, always as spontaneous as a traffic light, flashed with relief and pleasure. Grinning from whiskery ear to ear was her neighbour, Herr Umberg. He was pulling a small trailer piled with logs behind the scooter.

"Afternoon, Frau Baumann. Did I give you a fright?"

He looked rather nervous himself, and Kirstin wondered if the logs had just fallen off one of the many piles of same that the Forestry Department heaped by the side of the path.

"No, no, not at all. I was just – er – looking for my horse."

"Ah. I wondered why you'd be up here by yourself. Did the brute throw you again? I always said he had a mean streak."

"No he hasn't, honestly. It's just that he doesn't like men. I'd better go and find him before he meets up with any."

"Herr Baumann still away, is he?"

"Yes."

"Excuse me being nosey, but you know the wife has to stay in bed a lot and she can't help noticing the comings and goings at your house."

"He's been in Poland for three weeks. There's a very big contract on offer. I'm so curious to know if he's landed it."

"Huh. I read these communist countries can't pay their bills."

"Oh, the Soviet Union underwrites really big deals."

"He ought not to leave a lovely young woman like you alone so much, Frau Baumann. Why can't he work in Switzerland?"

"Well, he specializes in ships' engines and we're not exactly seafaring folk, are we? Anyway, the industry's so depressed he's lucky to sell concessions to have the stuff made abroad."

"It ought not to be allowed. It's taking the bread out of the mouths of our own people."

Kirstin sighed. She was used to acting as Max's liaison officer in the village, but resented having to excuse him for the state of the Swiss economy as a whole.

"But he's not 'our people', is he?" She referred to the fact that Max was German, but instantly regretted it, knowing that she must sound like Ruth amidst the alien corn.

"Huh. I suppose he owes his loyalty to Humbel Brothers before the country he's living in."

"That's unfair, Herr Umberg. Humbels is full of Swiss doing exactly the same thing. Anyway, Max has applied for citizenship."

"Oh yes?" Herr Umberg leaned forward to pat Kirstin's arm. And then squeeze it a bit. Kirstin went rigid. It was a routine she was familiar with – the otherwise law-abiding husband taking advantage of sudden seclusion to touch her up – but she had never expected it from this quarter. But then she never expected it from any quarter, and decided, not for the first time, that she must be extremely naive. "It's a pity you haven't got any kiddies, then, isn't it? A little soldier or two to push up front. It all helps. I hope I'm not speaking out of turn, Frau, but the wife always wondered if there was something wrong as you'd bought such a big house. She thought you'd be starting a family."

Kirstin blushed. "It's complicated."

"Because they can do marvellous things these days you know, with lasers and whatnot. Perhaps I should get Frau Umberg looked at. It might not be too late!"

He laughed till the tears filled the troughs under his eyes. Kirstin's smile flickered, the batteries fading.

Herr Umberg pulled himself together. "Just my joke, Frau. No offence, eh?"

"Of course not. But I really must be going."

"Right. Tell you what, hop on the back. I'll give you a lift."

"But – " She was about to point out that he had been going away from the village, but could not resist the prospect of a ride in view of her injuries. At least she would know where his hands were, although it was definitely the lesser of two evils. Herr Umberg had bought his vehicle quite recently, inspired by a film from the French-speaking

8

region about a lovable old duffer who had acquired one in his dotage and gone around having adventures on it. Herr Umberg already had a tractor and a station wagon, but he clearly fancied himself on the scooter, perhaps because of the association with young tearaways. He certainly drove like one. She climbed on the back and hugged Herr Umberg tightly round the waist as they roared away, her ribs and the logs rattling in unison.

They found Pinot grazing happily in the Umbergs' vegetable garden which, like most of the plots on the outskirts of the village, was dug out of the hillside and unfenced. The horse stood ominously still as they approached, and when they came up to him he butted Herr Umberg squarely in the chest, sending him crashing into the knobbly stalks of his own Brussels sprouts.

"Oh dear," said Kirstin, helping him up. "I'm so sorry, Herr Umberg. He's really awful with men."

"Jealous, I suppose." He was trying to sound jolly, but eyed the horse with loathing, leaving Pinot in no doubt of his fate if left to Herr Umberg.

"I think I'd better get him back to the stables. He's due for his roll in the mud and he knows it. Thank you for the lift, Herr Umberg."

"My pleasure." He walked with her to the road. "By the way, you haven't heard from the Gemeinde about the new houses, have you? I thought they would have made a decision by now."

"No. To tell you the truth I haven't been paying much attention to the subject. We knew those plots were building land when we moved in."

"You didn't go and inspect the plans, then?"

"No."

"That's a great pity, Frau. You'll be affected, you know. They're going to bring a road right between our two properties."

"What? Pinot, stop it!" The horse was trampling through the jumbo dahlias in the Umbergs' front garden.

"Perhaps they've withdrawn the plans. I wrote and objected right away. In no uncertain terms, I can tell you. I can't understand why we haven't heard."

"Oh dear. Well, I hope it did the trick. Look, I really have to go now, Herr Umberg. If I hear anything I'll let you know."

Kirstin waved goodbye, gingerly, and led Pinot off down the hill towards the main street. The steep red roofs of the village, clustered in a dip between sloping hills, were thrown into picturebook relief by the giant cranes that dangled over them, marking the sites of the new pizzeria, the extension to the kindergarten and a batch of semi-

9

detached concrete family homes.

It being late on Saturday afternoon, Eglikon was fairly zinging with activity. Gardening is forbidden on Sundays, and householders were hurrying to finish urgent pruning and lifting of cabbages for winter storage. Along the village street, where half-timbered farmhouses still predominated, neighbours were conscientiously sweeping leaves into each other's territory. Some of them had taken time off to lean on their brooms and chat, in what appeared to Kirstin to be extremely earnest tones. On Saturdays at this time the air was usually filled with the cheerful badinage of workers anticipating their day of rest, when only leisure activities, voting and shooting were permitted. But when she greeted them, with her ready smile, there was no answering surge of polite pleasure, only a solemn "Gruezzi, Frau Baumann" and a half-smile that suggested pity for her obvious ignorance of what had happened. Could something have happened in Eglikon?

Then she noticed, at the other end of the village, the orange-and-white-striped car of the police commandant. It was parked outside the Pagliaccis' house, a run-down building of four farm workers' apartments. As she walked past, Herr Schulthess, the commandant, came out and got into the car. He greeted Kirstin briefly before driving off.

Kirstin began to feel uncomfortable. The Pagliaccis were of mixed race, the mother being Swiss, but the large brood seemed to have inherited the Latin temperament undiluted, and Kirstin was afraid that one of them had got into trouble with the law. In Winterthur, the nearest big town and seat of Humbel Brothers, there had been several outbreaks of window-smashing, graffiti-spraying and mugging, and the town had a sufficiently unfair share of punk teenagers and alternative wholewheat pacifists to make it a magnet for lively youngsters from a village like Eglikon.

On the other hand, Herr Schulthess had not left with a young Pagliacci handcuffed to his wrist. Kirstin's curiosity mounted.

She turned off down a side road to the stables and delivered Pinot gratefully to the care of a stable-boy. On the other side of the road was the home of her friend Geraldine, an English woman married to a Swiss and now bearing the name of Hengartner. Kirstin had been attracted to her not only by the prospect of practising her English, but because they had arrived in Eglikon at about the same time, starting the trend for ripping out interiors, installing low-flush sanitation and hot-air ovens, and restoring façades to previously unknown glory. The plaster between the beams of Geraldine's ex-farmhouse was now a tasteful Crushed Shortbread, and old railway sleepers staggered artily around the large enclosure.

As Kirstin dithered, wondering whether it would be all right to call just before supper, Geraldine opened an upper window and yelled at her to go over. She was grinning and excited. Kirstin made her way with difficulty up the garden path, which was strewn with plastic tractors, mounds of mottled weeds, and banana skins.

Geraldine met her at the front door.

"Am I disturbing?" asked Kirstin.

"Very. But not me. Come in, come in. You obviously haven't heard."

"No. Is something afoot?"

"I'll say. Rosa Pagliacci's been attacked."

Geraldine's small features were lit up with excitement, but the way in which she hugged herself to stop the trembling, even her knees pressed together, suggested that she was not entirely happy with this development.

"Are you sure? This is terrible newses."

"Of course I'm sure. Would I make it up?"

"Excuse me, but Fraulein Pagliacci is – how can I say – "

"Kirstin! You mean just because she's half Italian and goes around in split-crutch motorcycle leathers she must have been asking for it. Racist!"

"No, no. You know me, I am no racist at all." In fact she always did everything in her power, like voting occasionally, to better the lot of guest workers. But it was true that the idea of Fraulein Pagliacci as the victim of crime needed some adjustment. "But are you knowing what happened exactly?"

"Well I don't know the details. It was only at lunchtime. But I presume – *It*. She'd just gone into the woods to check her Dad's beehives."

"Oh dear. Is she wounded?"

"Don't know. The grapevine was caught napping. Come in, do. This calls for a drink."

Kirstin followed Geraldine into the kitchen, stepping over discarded coats and accessories that led right through the house and out to the garden where screams and verbal abuse indicated the children at play. A large cardboard guineapiggery and the overweight mongrel took up the rest of the space. The luxury rustic interior had been quickly turned into what Geraldine called Early Doglover. In the kitchen the flat surfaces were covered with the weekend shop, open tins of dog food stood next to antique coffee grinders and apothecaries' bottles. It typified the blend of culture and crud that Kirstin thought peculiarly English.

Geraldine removed a box of wine from the table.

"Oops! I should have put these away. It gives the right impression to casual callers."

She carried the box out, then came back with one of the bottles and poured them both a glass, clearing a space among the rubble on the table. She sat down, and got up again to remove a boiled sweet from her bottom.

"Cheers. That's better." She tossed her sleek mousy hair out of her eyes. "I must say I got quite a fit of shivers when I heard. I mean, two cases in as many months. It amounts to an epidemic. Well a rash, anyway."

"I wonder," said Kirstin. "Now you will call me racist again, but could it perhaps be one of ze workers who are building here? Zis perhaps explains why it has started recently and not before."

"Not the Swiss supervisors, you mean, but the hired hands? Honestly, Kirstin, there you go again. You're determined to involve a working-class alien somewhere along the line, aren't you?"

"No, no. It is not because zey are foreign. But when workers are away from their own country and their family almost ze whole year – I don't know."

"Umm. If they're obliged to spend their nights in Eglikon as well as their days you may well be right. Actually I never thought about what they do with them at night. Is there some kind of Soweto on the outskirts of Winterthur where they're locked up?"

"Of course no. But is logical zat it is someone new in the willage, no?"

"Like us, you mean?"

"No, no. So new we are not."

"How true." Geraldine sighed and looked down at her stomach, scooping up the loose flesh in one hand. "Look at that. I'm literally turning into an old bag. Where was Max, by the way?"

"Max? In Poland. Until tomorrow night. Why? Surely you are not suspecting Max?"

"He's a foreign worker." Geraldine smiled.

"You are making ze joke."

"All right. If he was in Poland I suppose that does rule him out. It's a pity he didn't stay away longer. I was going to ask you if you wanted to come to Zürich with me on Tuesday, when I go for my German class. There's an exhibition of nineteenth-century Estonian flatirons I think you should see."

"All right, I will come. Is your German teacher a good one?"

"Yes, frightfully. German, but he's awfully nice otherwise. Oops. Sorry."

"It is all right. I am so used zat people do not like Max. But I am sad when everyone is tinking it is because he is German. It is nutting to do. His mudder is a real lady, and his brudder is a Green. Zey are having six childrens."

"Yes, you said. I wonder what went wrong with Max, then? Oh dear, there I go again. Actually I don't dislike Max at all, it's just that he never gives anything away – you know – like a petrol pump."

Geraldine's nine-year-old ran into the kitchen.

"Can we have some ice cream, Mummy?"

"In this weather? Say hello, please. Kirstin is not a decoy duck."

"Hello Kirstin."

"Hello Rachel."

Rachel took some lollies out of the freezer and dashed out again. "By the way," said Geraldine, "what does 'umgezüglet' mean? Frau Schurzenegger said her daughter had just done it."

"To move ze house."

"Oh. How boring. It's a wonderful word – sounds as if one had won the pools and been raped by Cesare Borgia on the same day."

"I do not tink you would like to be raped, Geraldine. Even by Cesare Borgia."

"My dear, the state I'm in, anyone prepared to rape me will receive a complete set of cast-iron saucepans as an added bonus."

"It is a pity it is not Cesare at work in Eglikon. You might fulfil your fantasy."

"Hardly. He was probably only four feet high. One would have to stand him on a chair to get a good fit. Well, you would. Though actually you look as if you've already been done. I gather Pinot's been standing on your face again. Would you like to borrow a yashmak?"

"No tank you. Perhaps by tomorrow ze bruises will be going."

"They'll be like inkstains by then. Everybody will assume Max has finally taken his gloves off and let you have it. It would make a lot of people jolly happy to have some evidence for their opinion of him."

"Please, Geraldine."

"Sorry, sorry. I keep forgetting you're in love with him. Well, who wouldn't?" She glanced sidelong at Kirstin, hoping for some comment, but Kirstin was fiddling with her boot. "I suppose we should all take self-defence lessons now."

"Are you frightened, Geraldine?"

"Who, me? It would make my day. No, joking apart, it's really you I'm worried about. You're always going around by yourself, everybody knows that. And you'd certainly be my choice if I were that way inclined."

"You are exaggerating I think. If your theory is true, I would have been ze first case."

"Perhaps he's just practising."

"Then you should also be careful."

"I will be."

"So you are frightened?"

"Well it makes sense, doesn't it? I'm sure it's just one of the farmers whose vitamin deficiency has got out of hand, but still. They eat far too many potatoes."

"One can live alone by potatoes. I read it. Zey contain all the body desires."

"Really?"

"Personally I tink it is all a storm in a T-shirt. I do not believe it is one of our neighbours who has just now lost his onions. People are not changing so quick."

"But of course they do. Rapists, anyway. If they started in Kindergarten they could be weeded out, couldn't they? Something must set them off."

"Nutting ever happens in Eglikon."

"It suits me that way. I'm always so tired."

"You are not looking vell, Geraldine. Are you all right?"

"So-so."

"Let me take the baby sometimes. Zen you can rest."

"Thanks. I suppose you'll be going away for Christmas, New Year and February as usual?"

"Yes, I hope. But just now I was talking to Herr Umberg. He tinks there may be trouble about ze new houses zat are to be built next to us. I did not have time to discuss wiv him, but he says there is coming a road between our houses."

"A motorway?"

"I do not know. But if there is to be trouble I better stay at home."

"Who's the builder?"

"Roggenburger."

"Oh-oh. You might as well forget it. They're the construction industry's equivalent of a right-wing death squad. And of course the sun shines out of their bums as far as the Gemeinde is concerned."

"Zen you tink is no use to protest?"

"I wouldn't say that. There's no evidence for the fact that one can stop the spread of concrete, but one knows oneself in the attempt, like the Boy on the Burning – hang on."

14

The telephone was ringing. Geraldine took her wineglass with her into the hall to answer it.

"Hello. Hengartner . . . Yes . . . Yes . . . Yes . . . Goodbye." She came back, a wry smile on her face. "That was Max. He wants to know if and when you are going home."

"Max?" Kirstin jumped up. "But he was to come home first tomorrow."

"Try to conceal your enthusiasm, love. And sit down. He's not a soufflé. At least finish your wine."

"Did he sound – "

"In a good mood? I don't know. He always sounds as if he's ordering office supplies when he talks to me, so it's hard to tell."

"Oh dear. Now I shall have to cook dinner."

"Pretend it's your birthday. Get him to take you out. I'd ask you round here but I'm sure Max would rather go back to Poland for dinner. Anyway we're going out."

"Oh?"

"Yes, it is noteworthy, isn't it? We haven't been out since the baby was born. It'll be my first ketchup-free meal for fourteen months."

"Where are you going?"

"To Zürich. A candlelit dinner for two. Then we'll probably end up at that medieval stew where there's a piano player, and I'll get drunk and start singing 'Hee-ee who would valiant bee, Let him come hither.' I suppose it's hardly surprising Peter doesn't take me out more often."

"I wish you a nice evening. Ow!" Kirstin clutched at her ribs as she stood up.

"What's the matter?"

"Only a few bruises, I tink. But zey are becoming stiff."

"You should go to Dr Huber. He'll still be up, it's only five-thirty."

"No, no. It is nutting."

Kirstin hurried into the hall for her jacket, hoping that Geraldine had not noticed the hot and cold flushes and sickening palpitations that racked her at the mention of the doctor. Together with, she supposed, two or three hundred of his other patients, she was madly in love with him.

Geraldine walked with her down the garden path, absent-mindedly picking up debris. It was getting dark and the street lamps were on.

"Do be careful, Kirstin. Though I know it's gratuitous advice. Like telling someone to be careful in shark-infested waters."

"Do not vorry. Enjoy yourself tonight."

"Same to you. Honestly, after what's happened round here it will be a relief to go into the city again and remind oneself what civilization is all about."

Geraldine waved and stood watching for a moment as Kirstin hobbled off to meet her mate.

BJ awoke dazed from her nap. It was dark outside and Philip had evidently been up for some time: all the lights were on. She squinted at him over the billowing feather bed as he rummaged through the luggage for clean pants. The fleeting thought that they forgo dinner in favour of sleep she abandoned with a sigh. Philip's powerful structure needed regular sustenance. At times she felt like the stoker on the *Queen Mary*.

After her shower, and a short workout to break down enough fat to fuel the trip into the city, she felt better.

They set off down the hill clasped together for warmth against the chill November evening. It was a posture BJ was not entirely comfortable with, as their different heights meant that her head was in danger of snapping off at the base, besides the additional hazard of being steered through dogshit and lamp-posts. But she suffered gladly: it was good to be seen to be loved when others walked alone.

They quickly arrived at an intersection where well-oiled trams flashed and farted up and down the hill. There were a few closed shops on the corners. They went to the tram stop and studied the ticket dispenser with its columns of coloured knobs and helpful map of the pricing zones, and decided to walk.

"I guess there'll be shops open in the city," said BJ. "We have to get food for tomorrow."

"Maybe not. I know everything closes at four o'clock on Saturdays."

"You're kidding!"

"And lunchtime, I think."

"I don't believe it. What about women who work?"

"Maybe there aren't any."

"Come on. There was a woman driving the tram that just went by." BJ looked around her, as well as she could with her neck in Philip's armpit, at the staid bourgeois villas with their lace curtains and polished shutters. "I feel like I should be wearing a bustle, and smelling salts. Perhaps I should turn up for appointments in drag."

Philip smiled and hugged her tighter. "You didn't come here on the Tardis, BJ. You'll have a great time. Just because people like to eat at lunchtime doesn't mean they're retarded in other ways. It's a more traditional society. People like to get together with their families for meals."

16

"They do?" BJ frowned. Rushing home to be with one's family was a habit she had thought confined to Ernest Borgnine and Cary Grant, and other heroes of black and white movies.

As they walked they discussed their gastronomic fantasies for the evening, for BJ was as interested in food as in maintaining her size 8 figure, an anomaly that turned every day into a marathon of decision making. But tonight hunger had made her conscience deliciously clear.

Nearing the city centre they found themselves part of a large crowd of mostly young and aggressively trendy people. The majority wore monkey jackets and jeans and had long scarves wound around close-cropped heads. There was a curious acrid smell in the air, which BJ thought might be fireworks, and she wondered if they had hit some national festival. The suspicion was fanned when a police car and ambulance honked down the hill, a *sine qua non*, she thought, of public festivities.

They followed the crowds down to an open plaza beside the river, where there was a large tram terminal. But the few trams stopped at the terminal were dark and empty, and the crowds quickly dispersed over the bridge that led towards the central station, or down a street beside the river.

BJ and Philip were soon standing alone, speechless with amazement. Further downriver, swilling out over a picturesque stone bridge and the streets on either side, was a full-scale riot. Orange smoke hung over the shifting mob, riot squads in Darth Vader helmets ran around like hysterical sheepdogs, taking random swipes at the small groups that tried to break away.

"Philip!" BJ's tone was severe. "What the fuck is going on?"

"How should I know? Just some student trouble, I guess."

"Don't you know? So much for not coming here on the Tardis. It looks like Chicago in the sixties."

BJ had not been in Chicago in the sixties, but it had gone down in her historical memory alongside the storming of the Bastille and the Battle of Lexington.

A plain van drove up nearby and deposited another detachment of riot police. They thundered off towards the trouble area, one of them knocked BJ's shoulder-bag to the ground and dropped his truncheon. His fury, behind the plastic windshield, was clearly fearful. He shouted in her face, gesticulating to the effect that she should, at the very least, be elsewhere.

"Well, fuck you too!" BJ shouted after him. Philip restrained her as she prepared to chase after him with her anti-rape kit.

17

"BJ, for Chrissakes stop swearing. You might get arrested."

"Is swearing a crime round here?"

"Who knows? But it's dumb to provoke the police when they're jumpy anyhow."

"But it's okay for them to provoke me, huh?"

"BJ, we're in a volatile aggression situation. Logic is temporarily suspended, except it's dictating we get out of here as soon as possible."

"What about dinner?"

"Is it really necessary? Think of the pounds you're shedding."

"I can't think. I'm so hungry I feel like I swallowed a pair of scissors."

"Let's go down that street over there. I remember from when I was here in June. There are lots of restaurants down there."

"Hopefully we can find out what's going on. This is outrageous."

They headed off down a street that ran parallel to the river. The first restaurant they came to was closed. A man in a green butcher's apron was hastily pulling down shutters at the window. In fact all along the narrow street men in aprons were rolling the shutters down, and in some cases nailing wooden ones up. They walked despondently along holding hands, stepping over broken glass from shops whose owners had failed to take precautions. Security alarms wailed unremarked. The few people who passed hurried by with their heads down. From time to time groups of demonstrators dashed across their path and into a side street. BJ noted that their average age was around thirty-five, and their less-than-sprightly movements, and the way they crouched to look back at the pursuing police, knees cracking, was a pathetic pastiche of children playing cowboys and indians. "Bang-bang, you shot me down," she sang to herself, and was so intent on watching the demonstrators that she veered round a corner straight into the vizor of a stray policeman. Both of them were so startled that Philip only just saved her from being clubbed to death like a baby seal. Or so it seemed to the shattered BJ, whom Philip led up an alley and into a large courtyard.

She was not too shattered to notice that the restaurant on the corner was still open. They peered through the window at the alluring cosiness within – rough-hewn tables set with mountainous dripping candles. But no customers. A waiter was standing at the door smoking. Philip asked if they were open. The man, presumably on a full stomach, grinned.

"Sorry. Chiuso."

"Would you happen to know where we could get something to eat?"

"Sure. Milano!" He laughed and went inside, shutting the massive wooden door in their faces.

"Well what are we supposed to do now?" BJ demanded.

"How should I know?"

A detachment of demonstrators charged up the alley yelling – or yodelling, BJ could not be sure. She grabbed Philip's arm and ran for cover in the entrance of a closed cinema, stumbling into a couple huddled together. The woman shrieked.

"Hey, watch it – we haven't been introduced."

She spoke in English.

"I'm sorry," said BJ. "Look, do you happen to know what's going on round here? We just got here from the States and quite frankly I'm wondering if we got on the right plane."

"I don't blame you," said the woman. "I had no idea about all this, either. I really should listen to the news occasionally. I was so looking forward to a quiet dinner. Ouch!" They all ducked as a Pepsi Light can hit the window of the cinema. "It's so annoying."

"Yeah, we were kinda hoping to eat too."

"We're like those characters in *The Discreet Charm of the Bourgeoisie*, aren't we? Looking for a five-star meal in the middle of a national emergency."

"You're half right," said BJ, meaning that the woman and her portly bearded husband were, to judge by appearances, irredeemably bourgeois.

"Peter says it's just some students creating about the money being spent on the opera house. I hope you don't think this happens all the time. It must be the planets on the rampage again. I mean, there's a sex-maniac in our village all of a sudden, and nothing ever happens in Eglikon usually. We'll have to keep a lookout for lionesses whelping in the streets and whatnot."

"Our fates lie in ourselves, not in our stars," murmured Philip, who stood with his hands deep in his pockets at BJ's side on the step. The woman's husband was in a similar pose at her side.

She laughed. "That's what you think. I can tell you're new here."

"What," said BJ darkly, "do you mean?"

"Just my joke."

The woman teetered on the edge of the step, peering down towards the bridge where the crowds confronting the police shifted aimlessly.

"It is rather like wartime, isn't it?" she said. "At least it gets people talking to each other. If you can hear yourself speak over the crash of social barriers, that is."

Or the chattering of teeth, BJ observed. The woman's jaw was vibrating and her eyes darted around the scene in confused alarm. BJ was amused by her terror and smiled, aware of the superior resilience that had been bred into her as a result of growing up in a society where someone was shot every thirty-three minutes.

"I guess this does somewhat spoil your vacation," she said.

"Oh we're not on holiday. We live here. Peter's Swiss."

Her husband smiled and muttered something in his native tongue into his wife's ear.

"We're here for a year," said BJ. "I hope what we've seen tonight isn't typical. It's the last thing I expected in Switzerland."

"Well, quite. What with the forty-six hour week and digesting the fondue, I mean the population's usually comatose by Saturday night."

"Because I'm in business and social disturbances are bad for confidence."

"Oh yes? Is that why you two are here?" She smiled at Philip, evidently embarrassed by his silence.

"Not exactly. My husband's on sabbatical. He's a physicist."

"At the ETH?"

Philip nodded. "Uh-huh."

The woman raised one eyebrow, signalling some inner comment on Philip's granite-like demeanour. "What are you doing over here then? I thought the States was the white-hot crucible of creative science these days."

"He has a project to write up," said BJ. "He thought a change of scene would help him to get his ideas clarified. That's right, isn't it, Philip?"

"Uh-huh."

The woman drew nearer to BJ and spoke out of the corner of her mouth. "Doesn't he mind you talking about him as if he was deaf and dumb?"

"Oh no. He's not comfortable discussing his work with – let's say – unbelievers. That's all."

"Has he got a Great Work on the go then? Like Mr Casaubon in *Middlemarch*."

"I wouldn't know about that. I don't read books usually."

"What! Good Lord, how weird. I'm not sure I believe you. What do you do, say, in the bath?"

"I masturbate."

The woman fell off the step. Philip and Peter kindly helped her up.

"BJ – " said Philip.

"Now Philip. I've told you, if I embarrass you, just walk away."

"That's not a bad idea. There's nothing to be achieved staying here."

Just then three rioters ran up the alley, pursued by six or seven troops. They caught up with one of the young men just in front of the cinema, and the starving foursome were obliged to watch as he was dusted up and hauled back down the alley. The sound of shattering plate-glass from a neighbouring street marked the progress of his comrades.

"Not a whiff of an East German accent," remarked the woman.

BJ put her hands to her stomach. "I don't feel so good. You're right, Philip, let's go."

"We too," said the woman. "We'll just go home, I think. I don't feel like moonlight and roses any more. Honestly, what a waste of a baby-sitter."

"You have kids?" said BJ.

"Yes. Three."

"Uh-huh." It figured. The woman's mousy, Beatle-era hairstyle and pink-a-dink lipstick put her in a caste with which BJ usually did not associate. She also wore fresh pink-a-dink nail varnish, and BJ surmised that she was on her annual night off from the mind-numbing routines of child-rearing. Nonetheless, given the circumstances, BJ experienced slight annoyance that the woman did not overlook her own lack of qualifications as BJ's associate and invite them home for a hot meal. "Do you live nearby?"

"No. In the country. But actually I come into Zürich every week for my German lesson, so we could meet if you like. I don't suppose you know anyone over here yet."

"Is it a good school? I should take classes also."

"Well, I've been going for three years and I can just about order sausage and chips. But perhaps I'm not very bright."

"Uh-huh."

"It's called the Carnaby Club, I regret to say. Come on Tuesday afternoon, two to five, if you can take it."

"I might just do that."

"See you then. Bye!"

They hurried away, and BJ and Philip began the long trek back to their apartment.

The village street was deserted as Kirstin hurried home. The mist made her cough, which hurt her chest, but she dared not slacken her pace. The drawn curtains, dark alleys and cadaverous hulk of the unfinished pizzeria under its brooding cranes formed a suitably sinister setting for the emergence of a rapist from the shadows. Bloody gurgles would go unnoticed as Eglikoners settled round the television for an evening of beer, sport and folk-singing. Outside the Pagliaccis' a number of Lancias and Fiats were illegally parked, presumably belonging to friends and relations who had come to commiserate with the family misfortune.

Kirstin hurried on. Max would never forgive the disruption to his schedule were she to get herself raped. Perhaps it was ridiculous to stay married to a man who rendered daily life into a network of pitfalls for her.

She had been warned. Kirstin's parents had always been dubious about Max's potential for becoming a fun-loving family man. They had spoken of the hottest fires burning up first, molten passions cooling in the light of experience, and basically he was German, wasn't he, and what was the matter with her when there were so many eligible Swiss, and did he intend to learn the dialect? Of course not, and she needn't imagine that speaking 'Schriffdeutsch' in bed was going to keep the said fires aglow. Her mother prophesied that it would kill her father, and vice versa. What would he tell the male voice choir? Surely it was enough that the Germans had bought up the Ticino when ruined farmhouses were going cheap, not to mention clogging up the motorways in the rush to trample native Swiss to death in the battle for the ski lift, without robbing them of their only daughter in their old age? Kirstin's mother had been forty-six at the time.

Kirstin had been shocked by their racism, which up till then had only shown its positive side, like refusing to set foot out of their native land even for weddings and funerals. She had told them that their prejudice brought them lower than gas-chamber manufacturers or match-bearers for the Spanish Inquisition. But they had been right. The fires had died down, exposing the molten parts cooled into elegant but indisputably metallic bonds.

The Umbergs never closed their shutters, and Kirstin could see Herr Umberg slumped over the kitchen table snoring.

As she let herself in at the front door she heard the imperial fanfare that announced the evening news. Their interior was now so thoroughly open plan that from the door of the small hallway she could see Max's Mig-22 grey head at rest on the back of the rawhide sofa in the far corner of the house. He had a beer in his hand. On the television screen were pictures of some Asians being shot through the head by other Asians. That was a relief. It was the kind of spectacle that induced in Max a feeling of well-being.

When the news had finished she went up to him and bent down to

22

kiss his cheek. Her long hair slithered over his tweedy shoulder like a
shoal of angel-fish. When she stood up he carefully picked off the hair
that still clung to him.

"There you are at last. Where have you been?"

"At Geraldine's."

"Not all day you haven't. I called earlier and there was no reply."

"Why, when did you get back?"

"Around eleven-thirty."

"Oh. I must just have missed you. I'm sorry. Did you get the
contract?"

"Yes. Twenty-four pumping stations."

"That's absolutely wonderful, Max. Congratulations."

"I thought you'd be pleased."

Kirstin was drawing the curtains, but turned round to check the
expression that accompanied his remark.

"What have you done to your face?" said Max, frowning. "Have
you come off that damned horse again?"

"Yes, briefly. But it wasn't his fault. I don't exercise him enough,
that's why he gets restless."

"It's a pity you don't have the same consideration for me. You put
off his castration for far too long. It was no kindness."

"I'm sure you would have liked to help."

"Spare me your sarcasm, Kirstin. It doesn't suit you."

"Seriously, we could have done with some help. The vet was very
young and inexperienced. I'm wondering if he did it right. When he
arrived he was expecting to deliver a calf. We could have done with
another man to control Pinot during the operation."

Max paled a little. "You know I don't want anything to do with that
animal. Horses are quite stupid, actually. Your friend Geraldine was a
nurse. You should have got her to go along."

"Poor Geraldine. She seemed better today, but she hasn't been well
for the last few months."

"Another one on the way, I suppose. Is this one for you?"

"You can joke about it, but I think she would do that for me if I
were so desperate."

"How desperate are you? Is there some kind of Richter scale for
these things?"

"Please, Max. I haven't tried to change your mind, have I?"

"No. But as you cry every time we have sex, I can't help wondering
if you've really reconciled yourself to the idea."

"I do not."

"Every time you're awake you do."

23

"I can't help it, Max. I feel I'm getting old and – "

"Of course you're not getting old!" He jumped up from the sofa and went to get himself another drink. "You're not even in the prime of life yet. I hope." He turned the television off and sank back onto the sofa. "It's always the same, isn't it? I go away, leaving you in complete freedom to fulfil yourself in any way you like – you could even sleep all day if you wanted to. And then I come home physically and mentally exhausted, looking forward to a bit of comfort and relaxation, and what do I find? A wife who has been dividing her time being beaten up by a horse and slobbering over other people's babies. It can't go on."

"What do you suggest?"

"Why should I have to suggest things for you to do? You're intelligent – everyone says so."

"But you don't want me to get a job, Max."

"Of course not. Then you would have two jobs and be even more exhausted than I am. There are lots of other things you could be doing."

"Like what?"

"Well . . . I don't know. You could teach riding. If you're so keen on children that would probably slake your thirst for them. Blind children. What about teaching blind children? That would be rewarding, wouldn't it?"

"But you don't even like me riding Pinot Gloire."

"You see, you reject every suggestion."

"No, Max. But I do think I'm more realistic than you are."

"You what?" Max smiled, as one would at a child who threatens to cut one in half with a sword.

"About some things. You perhaps don't realize that here one has to have proper qualifications just to deliver meals on wheels. And people are queuing up to do it. Just to pass the time."

"That's all having children is – filling in time. Quite a futile activity, really."

"Then everything is."

"Yes, in one sense everything is. But somebody has to pay the bills. Look, do you think we could discuss this some other time? I have needs of my own, you know. Like food and sleep. I'm off to Romania in the morning for three weeks."

He leant back, crossed his long legs and closed his eyes.

Kirstin studied his handsome face for a moment, wondering how he managed to maintain such an even tan in places like Romania and Poland, and what his reaction would be if she unravelled his legs and kicked him in the balls. Such thoughts had become quite frequent of

24

late, together with dreams in which Max fell into the hands of the inexperienced vet. She supposed they sprang from a far from unconscious urge to make sure that if she could not have his children nobody else could either. The urge was always accompanied by guilt. Max's face in repose lacked only the furry ear-warmers to closely resemble the death mask of a Venetian doge. It raised comparable feelings of the bearer's dignity, and the respect owing to it.

Kirstin admitted that from the depths of Max's tunnel vision she must appear exasperating, and that he would long to come home to a high-powered intellectual female who was content to stay at home filling the freezer with gourmet snacks, and boning up on Comecon and metal fatigue to fit herself for his conversation. But the instinct to protect him from the consequences of his fantasies always stifled the desire to propel him into them. She always ended up feeling sorry for him when he had been mean to her, sorry for his need to conceal the soft, vulnerable parts of his humanity as one would a webbed foot.

While Max ate heartily after his refreshing nap, Kirstin sat with him at the table crumbling wholewheat crackers, and told him about the attack on Fraulein Pagliacci.

Max was unperturbed. "There were no witnesses, I suppose?"

"I don't know, but it won't be long before we find out. Everyone's talking about it."

"It's a measure of Eglikon's otherwise good moral health that such a minor incident can create such a stir."

"Minor incident! And what about that German lady? She had to go to hospital for shock."

"For two hours. She'd have been the same if someone had pinched her bottom."

"But Fraulein Pagliacci might be pregnant. How can you call that a minor incident?"

"You're just jealous, Kirstin. If that happened to you your problems would be solved. Perhaps you should go around being less careful."

"You wouldn't mind?"

"It's an amusing idea."

"You find the strangest things pleasurable, Max."

"I wish I knew what you found pleasurable, my dear. Apart from cotton underwear and peppermint liqueurs."

"Isn't that enough?"

Max followed her into the kitchen as she cleared the table and lolled against the counter, sipping Jack Daniels and watching her bottom as she washed the dishes.

Presently he came up behind her, pressed her up against the sink and fumbled with the zip of her jeans. She shrieked.

"What's the matter?"

"I'm sorry. It's my ribs. I think I may have broken one."

He sighed. "There's always some excuse, isn't there?"

"I'm sorry, but it really hurts."

"Would you like me to put you in a splint? I don't want to appear unsympathetic."

"No thank you."

"I'll go to bed, then. You don't mind, do you? Don't take all night with the dishes. I might as well get some sleep if I can't have anything else. I hope your ribs aren't going to rattle all night."

When he had gone Kirstin reflected on Max's knack of wanting sex when it was least convenient, like when she had a cake in the oven, or had just settled down with an exciting new book on the Hittites. It was always a wordless affair, so that they could both pretend afterwards that it had never happened. She wondered what normal husbands and wives talked about in bed. Frau and Dr Huber, for example. She stood at the end of their bed and listened to their cosy chatter about building a pergola over the barbecue pit, the latest blood feud in the Kindergarten commission, the effect of martial law in Turkey on their planned getaway weekend touring the harems. Kirstin replaced the Frau Doctor in the bed and started kissing her husband, rubbing her long hair over his bare skin while he fondled her breasts, which according to Max were impossible to find in the dark, but being a doctor he would have an advantage and would anyway be too civilized to have a thing about breasts. He would arouse her with skilful hands and let her kiss him from head to foot and caress him with her hair, like Mary Magdalen and Jesus –

She grasped a packet of Dishlav for support as the waves of gratification throbbed through her.

Afterwards she went into the living-room with the glasses, and as she plumped up the cushions where Max had sat, it occurred to her that if someone as undersexed as she was – according to Max – was so easily aroused, it was surprising that rape was not more common among those at the other end of the spectrum. Perhaps she would be able to help the Eglikon Ripper if he were to reveal himself to her. She might be able to persuade him that his crime lay in externalizing his self-hatred. This translated itself into a vision of herself standing in a shaft of sunlight in the woods, her cool hand on the rapist's brow as he repentantly tucked his penis back down his Y-fronts, tears of gratitude splashing onto the carpet of autumn leaves.

She yelped with laughter.

Overhead, Max banged on the floor with the heel of his Adidas sneakers.

As they trailed up the hill BJ was voluble on the subject of the riot, the steepness of the terrain, the absence of 24-hour supermarkets, Philip's selfishness in bringing her to a country which, it seemed, even Macdonald's Hamburgers had not discovered, and how was she going to cope, with access to the washing machine only one day a week? She hinted that she might even go home early, like in the morning.

"As you wish," snapped Philip.

BJ was stunned into silence. She had a horrible feeling she might cry if she opened her mouth. Philip's encircling arm had gone limp and she released herself from it and dragged along behind him for a while. But when they had walked up out of the city proper, past the Institute where Philip would be working, and the modern hospital, and they were again in the lush residential street near the apartment, Philip stopped and waited for her. In a mindless access of *esprit de corps* she allowed herself to be clamped once more to his bosom.

Further along the street they were overtaken by a young man in a long grey coat. BJ's hunting instincts were alerted. The young man's rear presented a unity of casual elegance that made her agog to see the front. She urged Philip to quicken his pace so that she could keep the young man in sight. The quarry turned into a house a few doors down from their own. A light came on in the upstairs apartment. As they approached it BJ said.

"You go on ahead, Philip. That young man is still up. I'm going to ask him if he can't give us some provisions to see us through until the stores open."

"You are not, BJ. People over here won't go for that spontaneous stuff. It looks cheap."

"To hell with that. We're both starving, Philip. I'm just obeying my wifely instincts for putting bread on the table."

"BJ!" Philip looked meaningfully into her eyes, knowing only too well which instincts she was obeying.

"Go on home now, Philip. I'll be right over."

She watched as he walked meaningfully on to their own gate and waited until he was safely inside the house before turning, with slight trepidation, towards the young man's. She pressed the buzzer – twice. The name "von Arx" was neatly handwritten beside it. Nothing happened, but she waited patiently. She already knew that he was the type who did not mind keeping people waiting, it was part of the

27

attraction. In the course of her sales work BJ manipulated people all day long, so it was a change to be humiliated occasionally in her time off.

Eventually the door was pulled open and the young man, already changed into a short robe, stared at her from large, deadly serious blue eyes. He kept one hand on the door and supported himself with elaborate weariness against the frame with the other.

"Guten Abend."

BJ assumed her I-am-not-a-mugger smile. "Oh. Darf ich etwas – "

"It's okay. I speak English. What do you want?"

"Food. We just got here from the States and all the stores were closed. Then we went downtown and all the restaurants were closed. I guess you know about that. We followed you back."

"You were following me?"

"Don't worry, it was just from back down the hill. We're at 52."

"Isn't it rather late to be knocking on doors?"

"Yes, but I wouldn't have bothered you if we weren't absolutely starved. From your appearance I guessed you were somewhat sophisticated and probably well travelled and that therefore you might speak English." She smiled. "You see, I was right, wasn't I?"

"You have a very fertile imagination."

"Don't mention that word. Fertile, I mean. May I come in?"

"Okay. But just for a few minutes. I am tired."

"Sure."

He preceded her up the stairs, leaping two at a time. His well-turned legs were pale and slender, she thought she would have been proud of them herself.

The interior of the apartment produced a momentary awe. The dull stuccoed shell of the house had not prepared her for what a few miles of Berber carpet, knocked-through archways and back-lit Chinese altarcloths could do to a place. There was very little else in the living area, apart from a couple of armless leather chairs, a pencil sketch of an egg, and two floor-to-ceiling stereo speakers. Through an archway was a somewhat more homey area, evidently used for a study/dining-room. At one end was a perspex dining-table, and at the other a Victorian partner desk covered with papers. The walls in this area were lined with neat bookshelves full of coffee-table glossies, dictionaries, textbooks and tatty paperback French novels. BJ looked around for a conversational handle to grasp, in vain. The apartment did not anticipate the presence of those in need of such handles.

"Please – " The young man made a slightly helpless gesture. "Sit down. I will get the things. I suppose you want coffee."

"Yes, that would be very nice. May I look around?"

"Okay, but please don't disturb anything."

While he was in the kitchen BJ looked at the books, searching for clues to the young man's preferences, but the only ones she found in English were on subjects like fourteenth-century Flemish cloisonné, and Kampuchean temple carving.

"You have excellent taste," she remarked when he came in with the coffee.

He looked up and smiled, suddenly relaxed.

At that moment BJ fell in love, with the fatal gravity of a penny falling down a well.

"I'm glad we can agree about something. I'm Michael, by the way."

"Hello, Michael. I'm BJ Berkeley."

"Mich-hyle," he corrected her.

"Sorry. Mick-hyle. Is there any reason we shouldn't agree about things?"

"Well, you're American, aren't you?"

"Jeez." BJ hung her head in mock shame. "Yes, I am. So what? We're not all mass murderers, you know."

"Perhaps not."

"I like your enthusiasm."

"Frankly, America is not so popular in Europe right now. You might experience some . . . er – "

"Flak? Terrific. That's all I need. I'm in sales."

"Oh my God. An American saleswoman."

"Now Michael! Don't worry, you're not a potential customer."

"Who's 'we', by the way?"

"My husband. He's a physicist. Do you approve?"

"What's his field?"

"Gravity waves – I think. I should know, I type his manuscripts."

"I should like to meet him."

"Would you? Okay. But I don't think you'd get along at all well."

It could be, of course, that Michael was homosexual, among other things. In fact it was almost certain, given his slender build and a stimulating aura of taboo that emanated from him. BJ was fascinated by the twilight world of deviation, anarchy, drop-outs and anti-authoritarian defiance in general. It was to this world that Michael belonged, she decided, made the more enticing in his case by the visual refinement of his appearance and surroundings.

"I get along with most people," he said lightly.

"I'm sure. What's your work, Michael?"

"Lots of different things. A little journalism, I edit a poetry

29

magazine, translations, that kind of thing. I don't have a regular job."

"No, you wouldn't." She smiled. "Perhaps you could help me with my German. I'm going to try and sell in the language."

"I should use English if I were you."

"It's okay, Michael, I don't want to invade your space."

"Good. I wish you luck with your job. It won't be easy, I think."

"Thanks. To tell you the truth I was somewhat disturbed by the riot we got into in the city this evening. Is this country on the verge of revolution?"

"I do not think so. It started because of the opera house. Some young people thought there was too much money spent on bourgeois culture and not enough on them."

"Well, I sympathize with the kids. On the other hand, disturbances like this are very bad for sales. What I deal in has to be seen as a long-term investment and in this kind of climate the confidence of the business community is bound to be shaken up."

"As St Augustine put it, O Lord, make me pure – but not yet. You support the revolution, but it is not convenient for you at the moment."

"That's right. But there are lots of ways of supporting the revolution, Michael. I'm re-distributing wealth in my own way."

"Of course." He looked at his watch. "We will have to discuss this another time. I am tired now."

"That's too bad."

He seemed anxious for her to be gone. BJ sighed. It was an anxiety that might well spring from experience at a later date, but at that point was somewhat overdone. He lit a cigarette and took up a stance in the middle of the room that instantly translated his slim body into a Way Out sign.

"Please – " He indicated his watch again, his smiles fading quickly on top of one another.

"Okay, I'll go." He fetched her coat and the groceries. "There is just one more thing you can do for me, Michael."

"What?"

"I have to go into town on Tuesday. I'll have fixed up a couple of appointments by then. Could you come with me on the tram? I'm somewhat nervous around public transportation. Like I said, I really don't want to invade your space, but if it's not asking too much I'd appreciate it."

"All right. In the morning. I could manage that, I think."

"Thanks. You're sweet."

"I'll meet you at the tram stop at nine."

"Oh. Couldn't we walk there together?"

"I'm sorry, I never walk with people."

Michael came with her to the front door. As she turned to say goodbye she stood up close to him, studying his skin, which was of a creamy golden density that toned exactly with his burnished locks. And yet he had been brought up without the benefit of daily Porterhouse steaks, gallons of milk, and freshly Saran-wrapped bumper vegetables that, as an American, had been her advantage.

"May I say something, Michael?"

"What?"

"I think we'd be beautiful lovers."

Accustomed, as she anticipated, to weathering the unexpected with panache, Michael only drew a quick breath and registered a tiny shock wave at the edge of his nostril.

"With whom?" he said.

BJ laughed. "Now Michael!"

When she got home she was still smiling at the memory of his calculated non-reaction. It was tantamount to an acceptance of her proposal.

Philip had gone to bed and was snoring, so BJ made a midnight feast for herself on the food that Michael had given her – black bread, salami, striped cheese and kiwi fruit. Her good mood fuelled her appetite, although she kept a mental note of the calories so that she could work them off in the morning.

Now that she had fallen in love and the week ahead was charted for productive incident, BJ was thinking more positively about the whole venture. BJ was lost without a full schedule, but now, what with her work and Michael, the immediate future was full of potential, of markers to help her through the unknown wastes all around. It was not just public transportation that made her nervous, it was the whole idea of going down that hill and facing a new world of people acting according to laws and customs she was unfamiliar with. But her mind dwelt principally on Michael.

"Beautiful body," she murmured, with a satisfied belch.

# CHAPTER

# TWO

As Max was going to Romania he did not leave for work at half-past five on Monday morning as usual, and was at home packing when the letter from the Gemeinde arrived.

The sight of the long envelope stamped with the escutcheo of Eglikon made Kirstin's pulse race even before she connected it with the planned new houses and the road that was worrying Herr Umberg. The local authority never wrote offering one the chance of winning a Toyota, or a once-only discount on bun-warmers. It was always a bill – or worse, an indisputable command to purchase regulation mailboxes, install mains drainage, or pre-sort the garbage. Kirstin already foresaw the doomed expenditure of energy and agony that was to be endured before the housing project was, inevitably, completed.

The letter stated that the building commission of the Kanton of Zürich had approved plans for the four new double houses in the field adjacent to the Baumann – Umberg territory, and approval for the compulsory purchase of, and compensation for, the Baumann – Umberg parcels for an access road between the Baumann – Umberg plots.

Kirstin went hot and cold with anger at the Olympian effrontery of the authorities, and the fact that she had not thought of viewing the plans. She had failed to foresee that the new houses, which she had known were to come, would involve driving a public highway between themselves and the Umbergs. Max's head would revolve at the complete failure of her powers of divination. She cocked her ear up the stairs to ascertain that he was well occupied. He was packing to the strains of Richard Strauss's *A Hero's Life* on his new compact disc.

Kirstin hurried over with the letter to the Umbergs', but Herr Umberg was already on his way to her, and they met in the disputed territory. Herr Umberg's letter shook in his hand.

"You see, Frau Baumann? What did I tell you? You know what this means, don't you?"

"Yes, I think so. Not that I can believe it. Show me where the road is going to go exactly."

"Right where we're standing. You see they're calling this titty footpath an 'existing street'. That's the excuse."

Kirstin tried to calm down enough to assess the potential damage objectively. The Umbergs' house and their own were the last two properties on the right-hand side of the road that led out of the village up the hill towards the woods. The other side of the road was cultivated with maize, now burnt stubble. Their large plots were unfenced, but a narrow trodden path separated them and meandered across the grassy hillside where the offending houses were to be built.

"Now you see," said Herr Umberg, straddling the footpath, "they're going to bring the road right through the raspberries, the rabbit shed and the apples. They'll slice a bit off your garden too. The raspberries are the wife's running-away money, you know. A cash crop, straight to Hero." He named a jam and tinned-vegetable giant.

"It's such a cheek. You'd think if one's land was going to be pinched one would be informed beforehand."

"You have been now. That's why you should have gone to look at the plans, Frau Baumann."

"I know, I know. Oh God, I wish I had, I suppose I just assumed they'd make a side road further up the hill."

She looked at her watch. Max would shortly have to be conveyed to the airport.

"They can't do that if the houses are going to have access from the front. Anyhow the land further up is Gemeinde property, part of the forest. It's got to be kept intact for future generations, hasn't it?"

The Umbergs had no children. Kirstin could see that his tears of rage sprang from genuine passion.

"Oh dear, what a ridiculous project just for four houses. Why can't they at least make a wiggle in the road so that it doesn't go through your raspberries?"

"Because they don't make architects with wiggles in them. You'd lose more land yourself if they did that. We have to pay for the bloody road as well, you know."

"So I understand. That's the last straw, it really is. How on earth do they justify that?"

"Well it counts as an improvement, doesn't it? Turning this footpath into a four-lane motorway, I mean, you're supposed to be grateful."

Kirstin was about to surmise that it probably would not be as bad as that, but Herr Umberg was not in a logical mood. "Honestly, it's no wonder people sometimes get round to slashing priceless art works, is it? One feels so helpless. It is Roggenburgers' project, isn't it?"

"Naturally. They went around in the sixties buying up odd plots all over the place. No one in the village could afford to buy more land then. We didn't have a doctor here in those days." He snorted.

Kirstin blushed, assuming as usual that every time someone mentioned the doctor it was with a view to tricking her into betraying her shameful passion.

"Oh I don't think a place like Eglikon is such a goldmine for him."

"Don't you believe it, Frau. He's so busy you'd have to wait a week to get a bullet removed."

"Yes, well I must be going unfortunately. I have to take my husband to the airport."

"Off again, is he? He ought to be ashamed of himself leaving a lovely young woman like you alone so often."

"Yes, so you've said. But it isn't by his choice, Herr Umberg," said Kirstin, sounding more confident than she felt. She walked back towards the road.

"We still have a chance to protest, you know. It says in the letter. You will write, won't you, Frau Baumann? It's us against them. There's no one else involved."

"I'll speak to Max right away. I'm sure when he realizes he'll have to pay he'll take up the cause all right."

But Max was as unperturbed about the rape of the landscape as of Fraulein Pagliacci. Kirstin explained the situation to him on the way to the airport, carefully omitting the fact that she had already missed one opportunity of doing anything about it.

Max bent his ear reluctantly away from the purr of the BMW's Jetronic fuel-injection system.

"When you're in business, Kirstin, you're not so anxious to squash schemes that provide employment."

"I know, I thought of that myself. But there must be exceptions.

34

You could say the same thing about drug smuggling. And this scheme is so small it wouldn't employ anybody for very long. Besides, we'll have to pay for it. The Gemeinde considers it's an improvement."

"Then it probably is. I'm against public spending. I don't object to paying."

"So you have no objections?"

"Look, I'm playing squash with one of Roggenburger's district managers when I get back. I'll have a word with him about it, if you like. At least you would know how determined they are to go through with it."

"I wouldn't do that."

"Why not?"

"Well, you may lose your squash partner. If he suspects that his firm may become involved in litigation with you later on he will begin to distance himself from you. You know what Roggenburger's henchmen are like – kamikaze pilots."

Max frowned. His idea of the changing-room chat had had a remarkably different power base – a comradely exchange of information between persons of equal note. The notion that he might be discreetly dropped as a result, like someone who has lost his job, was as alarming as the ring of truth. But he did not see how Kirstin could have insights into the behaviour of Roggenburger's district managers that were denied to him.

"That's nonsense, Kirstin. However, if you're already so overawed by the opposition I hardly think you're the right person to lead a crusade against them. I should drop it. It will only mean aggravation for you."

"For me. I suppose you are afraid it might create difficulties about your citizenship."

"Of course not. Do you think I would let such trivial considerations influence my behaviour?"

She did not reply.

"No, Kirstin. You're the one who objects to the scheme, so it's entirely up to you. Well, it will give you something to do, won't it?"

With the afternoon postal delivery there arrived a questionnaire from the kantonal criminal police department, concerning the whereabouts of Eglikoners on the day Fraulein Pagliacci was undone.

BJ's week had started well with a leafy jog with Philip in the woods behind the house. Somewhat urban woods of limited extent, with neat grassy clearings for recreation, plentiful brown and white signposts for the short-hop rambler, and dissected by several major thorough-fares.

On the way home they bought some croissants and ate four each for breakfast, with dollops of butter and mascarpone cheese.

BJ ate with a cheerful appetite, for her programme for the day was tightly packed: before lunch there was a business appointment with a firm specializing in abattoirs for hot countries. For the afternoon a three-hour German class was scheduled, which would leave just enough time for a little gourmet shopping before meeting Philip for dinner. The shops she had glimpsed on the trip into the city had given her second thoughts about Europe's clapped-out economy.

BJ tried hard not to train binoculars on the corner round which Michael must come, if he were coming. The suspense was exhausting, but when he did appear it was despair rather than elation that she experienced. Michael's casual dark clothes were a perfect foil for the harmony of his Aryan looks. BJ thought gloomily about the irreconcilable facts of her English ears, Lithuanian legs, French breasts, Canary Island hips and Irish bottom. Only the most strenuous programme of exercise would minimize her mongrel irregularities.

They said hello, and Michael at once began to show her how to use the ticket dispenser. BJ kept up a polite stream of respectful "Ohs" as he talked, his eyes slithering discreetly in the direction of her knees, an unexpected but very welcome development.

"Aren't you afraid of getting rheumatism in your legs?" said Michael.

"No. Why?" She looked down to where a pleasing stretch of flawless leg tapered into an ankle as delicate as a tulip stalk.

"Nothing. I suppose you know what you are doing."

"Sure. This is a business suit." She displayed it as discreetly as possible without actually twirling on one foot.

A woman standing in the line, who evidently understood English, also looked critically at BJ's legs. She was well-groomed and touches of gold flashed from her ears, wrists and boots. BJ guessed that the woman sent her directoire panties to be dry cleaned and that she and Michael concurred in finding BJ's skirt too short and her appearance altogether unsuitable for local conditions. BJ was plunged into depression. Appearances were so important in sales.

Michael noticed that she was on the verge of tears and spoke in a kindly tone.

"Look, don't worry. You look fine."

"No I don't. I know what you were trying to tell me."

"You do? I hope you are always so perceptive."

The tram arrived and Michael motioned her to get in first. She was so depressed that she found it difficult to talk about the American rôle in the latest disturbances in Guatemala, which he started in on as soon as they were sitting down.

They both alighted at the tram depot by the bridge over the Limmat, from where she and Philip had had their first sight of the riot. But now it was only piebald ducks that ran amok, shrieking and swirling in sucked streams over the bridge. The large crowds were cheerful and orderly. Downriver, in a distant shimmer, the Alps added a touch of Olympian indifference to the scene which BJ could have done without.

"The mountains are so clear, it must be Föhn," said Michael.

"What's that?"

"It's a warm wind that makes everyone a bit crazy, but don't worry. It does not affect foreigners. At least not at first."

"I don't believe in all that pseudo-scientific crap. One has a personal body rhythm, of course. Like this morning I dropped three eggs, so I guess mine is in a trough right now."

"That was the Föhn. You were lucky not to break the legs upon getting up."

"Oh baloney!"

"Here comes my tram. Goodbye. I wish you a pleasant stay in Switzerland." He shook her hand, smiling. "Look!" He pointed behind her. "Watch out for that Number 8 tram. It's a killer."

"What? Hey – where the – "

BJ looked in vain for a Number 8 tram, possibly with a Pershing missile on the front, but could make out nothing in the general confusion of clanging trams, snapping doors and jostling crowds. When she turned back, Michael had gone.

She swallowed hard, fighting back tears. Michael had clearly wanted her to understand that there was no room in his life for her, and that just because he was the first person she met after the plane touched down, did not mean they had to be friends. She stared blindly at the picturesque view of the old city with its superstructure of builders' cranes, and the mountains beyond.

What a bitter thing it was to be alone in a strange city and knowing no one, not a soul. Europe was a bust, foreign travel a crushing disappointment. There was only one constant value in her life and that was work. Today would be a disaster because of her skirt, but once kitted out in the Now look for Zürich, the business community had better batten down the hatches. If she did well she might even merit an article in the company jounal, *PIS News*.

But then, so what? That was not what she wanted either. Her mood dissected would reveal an ordinary case of homesickness. BJ was disgusted with herself. She had always despised location dependancy, having been married to a bad case of it for eight years. But there it was. Instead of the bridge and the swirling birds BJ saw Park Street in Boston, down which she would walk to meet her boss, Foster, on the Common at lunchtime. Foster jogged instead of eating lunch. He had a beautiful body, which BJ got the benefit of most Wednesday afternoons at his pied-à-terre in the shadow of the Prudential building, when he had time. Foster had been transferred to the West Coast, otherwise she was sure she would have found some excuse to stay in Boston and not come to Europe at all. She might have been walking down Park Street at that moment, with a chocolate chip ice-cream from Bailey's instead of lunch, before meeting Foster by the pond.

BJ's tram arrived. It was full of old ladies. The woman across the aisle from BJ was talking loudly to herself. Over the bulging shopping-bag that pinned her to the seat she delivered an abusive monologue on some subject that BJ had no clue to. A few of the old ladies turned and stared at her, as did BJ. A basket case, she thought. Interesting.

The woman's voice and gestures were becoming more insistent. BJ smiled at her. She sympathized with the woman, who was obviously retarded, or a social outcast of some kind. BJ guessed she was inveighing against a landlord, or the tax office.

Then she noticed that the more she smiled at her the more angry the woman became. BJ glanced around the tram. The other old ladies were beginning to look at her, and then at each other. BJ was sure she heard the word *Italienerin* and she realized that she, BJ, was the object of the abuse. Why, she had no idea. What local convention could she possibly have broken sitting quietly on a tram? Perhaps it was a seat reserved for the handicapped, or she had placed her purse un-hygienically on the seat, instead of holding it within her own germ field on her lap. She sought for clues in the immediate area, feeling herself go red, and sweat breaking out behind the knees. She tried indicating by gestures that she did not understand what the woman was saying, that she was well brought-up and that if she had offended it was through ignorance. The tram was unconvinced. Almost everybody was now speaking to their neighbour, re-hashing their favourite xenophobic anecdote. BJ was almost in tears. The only thing to do was to get off the tram before she succumbed.

As BJ stepped into the aisle beside her, the woman went purple and yacked at a bearded man sitting behind her. The man looked kindly at BJ and started to speak to her in Italian.

"Er – non parliamo – " said BJ.

"Oh, you are English?" said the man, relieved.

"American. Can you please tell me what this crazy woman is saying? I guess I've offended her in some way, but I really have no idea how."

The man drew a sharp breath and clasped his hands together between his knees, before making procrastinating gestures with them.

He had large, sad eyes of a startling pistachio green, which BJ suspected might be due to tinted contact lenses. His body had a pampered look. He wore a suit, and seemed in perfect control of himself, flipping with ease from one language to the other.

"It's difficult to translate," he said.

"Oh come on, I'm sure it's not beyond you. Did I sit in the wrong seat, or what?"

"No, no. It's something you did with your hand – scratching, or something like that."

"So what? Was I sitting under a sign that forbids it?"

"No, no. Oh dear. I think she misunderstood what you were doing. What were you doing? I could not see."

"Just pulling my skirt down, I guess."

"Ah. You see, she thought you were pulling it up."

"What! She couldn't even see what I was doing."

"She took a guess. The Swiss have much fantasy."

His irony was lost on BJ. "You mean she thought I was masturbating?" Now knowing herself to be morally, culturally, intellectually, philosophically, socially and ethically towering over the seated woman, BJ pulled herself up. "You fucking bitch. It's obvious that your imagination is as crude as your country is pathetic. Will you please tell her that? I have to get off."

He leapt up. "Alas, I too."

BJ kept her burning eye on the woman as she walked down the tram, followed by her translator. "Do you think she understood?"

"The tone of voice – yes, certainly. Please – " He rang the bell for BJ.

"I sure hope so."

They stood on the sidewalk so that BJ could keep her eye on the woman as the tram filled up and moved off again. "So damned insulting. Was she crazy? She should be put away. I should have

39

socked her in the eye, the bitch, the absolute fucking bitch." She was shaking all over.

"Yes, wasn't she," he murmured. "I apologize for this incident very much."

"Why, are you with the tourist board?"

"No, no. But I am ashamed of my – alas – compatriot."

"It's not your fault. You were a great help. And don't take any notice of what I said about your country. That was all horseshit, I just wanted to make her mad." BJ rummaged through her purse for the cigarettes. "She looked pretty shaken at the end there, don't you think?"

"Definitely."

"Yeah, well I hope it teaches her to keep her mouth shut on the tram in future because I tell you if she ever meets up with my husband she'll be in real trouble." She tried to light up, but the flame and the cigarette were wobbling out of control. The man held the cigarette steady in BJ's mouth and applied the light to it, then took the burnt-out match to a trash-can. BJ had mastered the first calming puffs and managed a brief smile.

"You know, I really appreciate your helping me out back there, with that fat bitch, I mean do I sound just awful the way I've been talking about her? I guess I do, but you know what it's like, when I get mad I just open my mouth and all this garbage comes out. You know, you have this sense of group hostility, and it's bad enough in your own language, but in a foreign language it's a real bitch, it really is. I'm afraid I didn't deal with it very well. Did I?" She dropped her cigarette and stepped on it. The man gently manoeuvred her so that he could stand on the stub.

"You must not take this incident too serious. She was not right in the head, this woman. Some Swiss are very in-bred. We are a strange mountain people."

BJ nodded seriously. "Maybe. But the entire tram seemed to be behind her. I didn't notice anyone trying to shut her up exactly."

"It's a free country. Free speech and so on." He shrugged and smiled, looking over BJ's shoulder as if they were being watched. "Are you all right, now? May I direct you somewhere?"

"Just point me in the right direction. I've taken up enough of your time already. I really appreciate it. Here's the address."

Despite her words, BJ was not anxious to part company with him at all. It would have been nice to adjourn to one of the sidewalk cafés and talk for an hour or two – BJ rarely talked for less. But besides the fact of her pressing appointment, she sensed that the man would expect more.

He gave her clear directions to the venue of her appointment. As he did so, BJ looked him over. He was somewhat soft, but his tan went down under the collar and out at the wrists and looked natural. It was probably the product of some expensive outdoor activity, like Club Méditerranée, or gun-running. On reflection, he would not be unacceptable as a sexual partner, but of more interest as a business contact. BJ deftly found her card without interrupting the conversation, and gave it to him.

"This is just a hunch. I have no idea what you do, but you or an acquaintance might just be interested in our product one of these days. Of course, you don't have to tell me your business."

"I don't mind. I have interests in furniture – office furniture mainly. But I am not directly involved. And I breed turtles. Also not directly."

"You don't breed turtles in that suit."

"No, that project is not here in Switzerland. I live in St Gallen. I am only visiting Zürich at the moment." He was looking at her card, fascinated. "This is wonderful. Public Information Systems. That covers a broad spectrum. I also like your name. B.J. de Witt Berkeley. This is wonderful."

Why? thought BJ. "We're in trade-related software. Would that be of interest to you at all?"

"I do not think to me personally. But you could contact the head office. I shall give you my card also." He got it out playfully. "I shall write the name of the director on the back."

"Thank you. Now I'd really better go. Goodbye, and thanks again for your help, Herr Tosch."

"Ah! This is very good. You remember my name at once. You are most professional, like all Americans. I congratulate you and wish you luck."

In shaking hands he covered hers with both his own. BJ withdrew as quickly as possible. He really was amazingly fresh. But with interests in office furniture and turtles it might even be worth sleeping with him if that was the price of getting hold of his contacts. "Would it be appropriate to call on you some time? I should enjoy a trip into the country."

"Alas!" He shrugged. "I am rarely at home." He took her by the elbow and lowered his voice. "You see, I am divorced and my former wife thinks that the settlement was very unfair, and that she is entitled to the child support she would have had if she had children, as I was the one who refused to have children. Then she can have the children. Don't you think this is crazy?"

"I sure do. I never heard of anything so unreasonable. But what has it got to do with my visiting you in the country?"

He thought for a moment. "Well you see, my wife follows me everywhere. I must move around all the time."

"I see." That was typical, of course. Whenever a man wanted to score with you he always found it necessary to put down his wife. BJ despised that approach, and never took seriously anyone who used it, which was one reason why her sex life was so dull.

They shook hands for the fourth time, and BJ hurried off down the Bahnhofstrasse, studying the card Herr Tosch had given her. It gave only the name, Frederick Tosch, and an address in Kanton St Gallen. She put it away carefully.

Along the Bahnhofstrasse flags of the kantons in primary colours fluttered high above the road, the pelts of mink coats fresh from storage ruffled in the breeze, jersey skirts clung to thin Swiss legs. Several of the buildings were obscured by scaffolding, and Italian workers with sculpted brown bodies. One of them waved at BJ and said something syrupy in Italian which made BJ feel good. She had always found construction workers sexually exciting: evidently it was mutual.

The jerky kaleidoscope images of the city echoed BJ's inner turmoil. It was good to be a little nervous before an interview, but not actually sticky and stuttering. She ought not to have smoked, it lingered on the breath. Under pretence of looking at Cartier's window display, she whisked out her Gold Spot oral spray. In a flash an assistant was peering at her from behind the jewellery. "Shit, does this look like a Molotov cocktail?" She squirted some Gold Spot on the window before moving on.

Fortunately for BJ, Herr Gut, who interviewed her, was the type with whom she could deal – 50ish, good condition, conservative dresser, a conformist by choice rather than cringing ineptitude for anything else, sexually active, and with a sense of humour, fun even. BJ deduced these facts from Herr Gut's suit.

His eyes twinkled as he welcomed her into the office. He sat her down and brought her a cup of coffee, talking all the time in a deep, chunky dialect of Swiss German that seemed to trail after him like a cement-mixer. BJ was anxious to get down to her moment of truth and her few words of German. She adopted an expression of pleasant seriousness, so as to be ready when he was.

Presently he did sit down behind the desk, holding a folder. He cleared his throat and began to read in High German at a steady pace.

"Sehr geehrter Herr Dr Hisham Abdul Wahhab Mohiyiddin al Jazeyeri: betrifft Ihre Reklamation betreffend – "

"Wait a minute, wait a minute," protested BJ. "Sie haben ein Fehler gemacht, glaube ich."

Herr Gut looked up, delighted. "Ah! You wish already to speak the English? Okay!" He giggled. "But I not very good."

"No, wait. I'm not a secretary. Whatever gave you that impression? I'm sales representative for Public Information Systems Incorporated. Here's my card."

"Oh? You are the American lady who telephone yesterday?"

"Yes."

"Excuse me. Excuse me very much. I am apologizing. No, you do not look like secretary, and your Swiss German is terrible!" He rocked with laughter. "What are you selling?" He tossed his folder away and leaned over the desk, hands clasped energetically.

Well, thought BJ, that's something. He's delighted I'm not the secretary, that way he feels freer to respond to me as a sexual option. She had often noticed how the men she interviewed in the course of her work would make contingency passes at her even if their schedules were too crowded to pursue her at the time. It made BJ feel like a cocoa future at times, but she accepted it as a fact of sales life.

"I'm sorry if I'm not as familiar with your operations as I would like to be, but quite frankly the applications of our service are so broad I'm confident that whatever your problems are we can work out an appropriate package."

BJ spoke in precise, mellifluous tones, laying out the brochures from her briefcase in careful order on Herr Gut's desk. He picked one up for inspection, but BJ took it away from him and returned it to its place. "Later!" she snapped, before resuming her hypnotic delivery.

Herr Gut sighed and looked at his watch. "Yes, but make it short, please. I like to go home at the weekend." He laughed noisily.

BJ bristled, took a deep breath and began. "Ich möchte zuerst fragen allgemein was Sie – "

"Ach!" He screwed up his face and made an impatient gesture with his hand. "Speak English, please. I understand much better."

"Okay." You Swiss turd, she added to herself. "As you may have gathered from our telephone conversation, I represent a company that offers a wide range of services based on trade statistics from all over the world. These services include analytic software, simulation and forecasting models and a wide range of information packages designed to serve the import-export sector. Shall I repeat that?"

A look of incipient confusion had passed over Herr Gut's crinkled face. "No. Proceed."

"It would help me a lot if you could give me a broad outline of a particular problem area you're dealing with right now. Like, what were you working on as I walked in the door? Then I could show you how our services could help in a specific case."

"Please, just get on with it. I am not here to help you."

"Okay, okay. The really outstanding feature of our system is that it is based on a collection of trade-related data that is unique in the world."

"Where do you get all this data? From the CIA?"

"No, absolutely not."

"Good. They always get things wrong."

"How do you mean?"

"Well – alzo – " He fluffed. "Take Iran. The CIA did not know about the revolution until the shooting was already."

"That's true. But apparently the Shah didn't either, so you can't blame the CIA for being a little confused. May I go on?"

He shrugged.

"We have a comprehensive range of international data series. We use government sources, naturally, but we also have agents all round the world whose sole purpose is to collate and validate data from public and private sources and enter it into the system within hours, rather than days." She paused. And don't tell me your crummy little slaughtering-machine business already has something like that at its disposal or I'll throw up.

This thought had apparently occurred to Herr Gut also, as he cast a sneering glance over the brochures that he was not yet allowed to handle, and allowed BJ to swing into her Sesame Street interpretation of the capabilities of the information service. Herr Gut was the type who would like to toy knowledgeably with graphics of cash flow and return on assets, but it normally paid to go the Sesame Street road first, to give the client confidence that he could handle the concepts involved.

"Now." She handed him the first brochure on the left. "This will give you some idea of the kind of information available and alternative presentation formats. So you're basically in the meat business, so you're interested in dietary trends, right?"

"Oh sure."

BJ ground her teeth. "Turn to page 48 and you'll see a breakdown of topics covered in our series relating to your field. Now, you could ask, perhaps, for a diagrammatic interpretation of the worldwide distribution of food shibboleths and slaughtering regulations. Or a

44

New Zealand meat producer, for example, who wanted to find new markets, would be able to see at a glance if there were any places where lamb is a protected species."

"Sure," giggled Herr Gut. "Up there!" He jerked his thumb towards the ceiling and collapsed with laughter over the desk.

Sweat broke out on BJ's face, cleavage and inner thighs. She began to wonder if Herr Gut were not some kind of retard, the loony illegitimate son of the corporate president especially installed to weed out faint-hearted sales persons. There was no point in going into the wonders of the analytical systems available, but she could not leave without tossing a few chips onto the PIS jubilee feature, a series on international terrorism.

This was an exciting new departure for PIS, and it had proved highly successful in the States, where executives had an increasingly sensible fear of having their noses slit, or their legs blown off as soon as they set foot off their native land. BJ felt herself skilled at exploiting this fear, and thoroughly enjoyed it, as her sympathies were, by and large, with the terrorists.

"Well, I can see I've taken up too much of your time already, Herr Gut, but I would ask you to bear with me a moment longer while I draw your attention to a small but significant new service we offer to our special clients in the business community."

Herr Gut wiped the tears from his eyes as he took the glossy flier BJ handed to him, but she was grimly pleased to see that he soon sobered.

"This is a unique series exclusive to our firm, which has been produced in response to the increased need for information on terrorist activities of all kinds. In it you will find analyses of the major terrorist groups, their methods, location, contacts, present and potential targets, long-term goals, and detailed advice on how to minimize the risk of becoming a victim, a critical assessment of security firms that offer an advisory service, a breakdown of the various insurance schemes, behind-the-scenes information on the cases that have come up so far and an updated guide to the political and strategical stand on terrorism of various key governments around the world. We also have a section on global taboos and etiquette."

BJ was slightly encouraged to see that Herr Gut showed some interest in this item, lingering over the photographs of executions in the Sudan.

Having finished the presentation she relaxed and smiled at Herr Gut, encouraging him to rifle at his leisure now she was through. "Are you puzzling over something? Perhaps I could translate something for you."

He laughed. "Into what?"

Fuck him. So much for making the effort to learn the language. She would just like to see him trying to get his pants ironed in Mobile, Alabama.

Herr Gut finished looking at the pictures and slapped the flier on the table. "I think this does not concern us, Mrs Berkeley. We do not have so many people overseas and we can get information if we want it. Thank you for coming. Very nice."

"Oh. Are you sure? Numbers are not the most important factor, are they? Wouldn't you feel just awful if something happened to one of your people and you could have prevented it if you'd known more about the situation?"

Herr Gut wrenched off his glasses and looked at BJ seriously. "Mrs Berkeley, I understand you sell this kind of thing good in US because US so – 'isoliert'. Everyone want to know what goes on in other countries. But here – we know already. This kind of thing – no good. I wish you luck, but – " he shrugged " – I don't think you will have."

"Well. I see. Okay." BJ got up. "Thank you for giving me so much of your time, Herr Gut. I appreciate it. If you don't mind I'll leave these." She put on his desk a selection of brochures and sample materials in a luxurious polyvinyl folder. "If you do have second thoughts please call me. By the way, I must just mention that anyone using our system over here need not concern themselves about delivery. You could access TIMNET twenty-four hours a day. And we do have automatic translation facilities. You could designate almost any language you want."

"Swiss German?"

"Well, no. Not at the moment."

"Very special language, Swiss German. It was used by the Allies to send messages during the war, you know."

"Oh yeah? I'm surprised we won. Look, Herr Gut, if you have no objection I'll phone in a couple of days to see if you haven't thought it over and – "

"As you wish." Herr Gut was twinkling again. "You here long?"

"For a year, I think." Worse luck. "My husband is at the Eidge–Eidge–"

"Eidgenossischetechnischehochschule."

"Yeah."

"How you like Zürich?"

What, thought BJ, was the German for sodding awful?

"It's okay," she said.

"Many great people were here – Lenin, Einstein, Solzhenitsyn."

"I wonder why they didn't stay."

"It's too expensive!" He laughed again.

"Yeah," said BJ. "Well, goodbye."

She managed to smile at the secretaries, but as soon as she was alone in the lift a grimness descended that was more than mere disappointment and depression. The man was a bastard, a total bastard, coming on so friendly and then turning round and practically kicking her out of the office when her realized she was resisting the sexual pressures he was putting on her and intended to stick to business. And how pathetic had been his attempt at the end of the interview to reestablish some kind of rapport, the patronizing turd. Selling in Europe was going to be a pain in the arse.

As BJ walked out into the quixotic sunshine, she instinctively tensed her bottom to get the optimum friction factor out of the short walk back to the Bahnhofstrasse.

## To: Scrubbing-out Department,

Building Commission,
Zürich.

Dear Sirs: re Sectional Plan 125PBG Gemeinde Eglikon.

We are in receipt of the above plan for four new double houses and approach road, and wish to state our categorical objections to the latter. Not only would this thoroughfare mean the destruction of some rare boletus satanas toadstools, but the pollution and nuisance factor arising from continuous traffic would constitute an irreversible impoverishment of the immediate environs and the character of our properties.   We beg your consideration.

With friendly greetings,

*Max Baumann*
*Kirstin Baumann*

The language school was situated on the third floor of a grubby tenement building in a dull street behind Zürich's main station. A smell of farted French fries drifted up the stairwell from the restaurant next door. BJ was late and skipped up the stairs three at a time, skidded on the highly-polished linoleum and all but crawled into the reception hall, clutching her knee. She sat down underneath a poster of Land's End, cursing.

A dapper elderly gentleman popped his head out of an office. His face crumpled with concern.

"Oh dear, another one," he said. "Are you hurt?"

"I sure am. I hope you guys have a good lawyer."

The man laughed merrily. "Unfortunately the stairs are the responsibility of the owner of the building."

"And they're Ciba-Geigy, I suppose, so forget it."

The man shrugged. "It might be worth a try. But you know what lawyers are like. You would have to prove that at the time of the accident you were not knowingly and wantonly using the stairs for some purpose other than the one for which they were intended."

"Well, you seem to have got the Swiss sorted out."

"Not the Swiss, dear lady. That's just big guys, as you would put it, versus little guys. You and I are little guys, I fear."

Speak, thought BJ, for yourself.

"Are you Mrs Berkeley, by the way?"

"Yes."

"Oh good. You're with Otto, my dear. Come, let me help you."

He tenderly helped BJ to her feet and half carried her into a classroom.

The long table was already packed tight with people of many lands. She recognized the woman they had met during the riot whose name, it emerged, was Geraldine. She was sitting between a seven-foot African woman in a scarlet turban and tent, and a podgy adolescent from East Timor.

As BJ sat down, between an elderly Hungarian woman and a beautiful Egyptian boy, the students grudgingly squeezed themselves closer together.

"So," said Otto the teacher, "another American." He was a tall, worried-looking young man, with a face of already disintegrating distinction that reminded her of Michael. "Have you studied German before?"

"Yes, I did two courses in college." She thought it wise not to say how many times.

"Well if we're lucky it won't show."

The group giggled. BJ sensed a groundswell of anti-American solidarity among them, which Otto proceeded to exploit to the full.

The exercise of the day was to put sentences like "As-Johannes-and-Petra-were-in-the-vicinity-of-the-cinema-they-ordered-tickets-for-

48

the-pop-concert" into the conditional tense. In between fiercely correcting their answers many remarks were made, unchallenged, by Otto about American isolationism, colonial expansion, economic blackmail and the disgraceful treatment of the Navajo Indians. BJ was too tired to argue. She concentrated on protecting her country's honour by getting her answers right, which clearly annoyed Otto, who was very impatient with everyone except the coloured students.

Geraldine took every opportunity to relate some anecdote involving her children and, studying her, BJ wondered if it were possible to grow like one's progeny as well as one's pets. There was something of the pout of the spoilt toddler about the pink-a-dink mouth.

When the class broke up, Geraldine made a point of cornering Otto for a chat, in order to demonstrate, BJ decided, her relative intimacy with Otto, and her superior rank in the class's pecking order. BJ was amazed that Geraldine's need to exercise her atrophying sexual charms was so blatant. But a rapid assessment of Geraldine's body with its pot belly and shrunken breasts made her desperation perfectly understandable. But if BJ were to benefit from the class to the full, it was desirable to put Geraldine in her place as soon as possible. She waited until Geraldine was pulling on a baggy sweater before touching Otto lightly on the arm.

"Excuse me, I don't know if you can stand to accept a compliment from an American, but I just wanted to say that I think you're very, very good." She spoke in a low voice and transfixed him with her trusting Doris Day gaze.

Otto was confused. "Oh. Thank you." He paused. "Actually, your German is not too bad."

Geraldine glowered at them. "Are you coming, Otto? I'm sorry, BJ, I can't stop now. We have an appointment."

"We are only going for a drink," said Otto.

"I have some time to kill," said BJ. "Do you mind if I join you?"

"Please do," said Otto, before Geraldine could object.

They went around the corner to a grotty, cheerful tavern full of off-duty workers and their bespectacled molls. The walls were decorated with plastic fruits and garlic, and lurid prints of mountain pastures.

The ladies allowed Otto to choose the wine. There was an embarrassed pause after this piece of business had been taken care of.

Geraldine was sulking and kept looking towards the door. BJ decided it was time to flatter Geraldine into shape. She looked seriously at Geraldine's body.

"Have you ever tried to do something about your pot?" she asked. "It's a shame, because otherwise you have a really nice body. Your legs are still good and your skin is phenomenal. You should try working out with weights if you're pushed for time, it's by far the most productive method. I honestly think you should consider it, because you could really look fantastic with a relatively small investment of energy."

"What?"

"I was just wondering if you'd like to do something about your pot belly. Presumably it comes from having kids. Don't you think Geraldine would look fantastic if she did something about her stomach, Otto?"

Otto opened and closed his mouth several times before replying. "I've never thought about it. I think she looks fine."

"What the hell does it matter to you what my figure's like?" said Geraldine. "Did you get this idea in a jacuzzi encounter group, or what?"

"Now wait a minute. You're getting hostile. But that's okay. I'm sorry if I upset you, but I didn't think an intelligent person like yourself would get upset by an honest discussion of an obvious fact. But why be embarrassed about it?"

"Why else would you bring it up in mixed company if you didn't want to embarrass me?"

"Mixed company? Oh my. I get it." BJ nodded. "Listen, I'm sorry. I didn't realize I was getting into your sexual identity. It was dumb of me. I should have realized that being holed up with the kids all day, and restricted opportunities for self-development and so on, you would be sensitive in that area. I'm sorry."

Geraldine's mouth twitched. She stared at BJ, at the crest of some wave of emotion that could not decide which way to fall. Then she started laughing, and poured some more wine into BJ's glass. "Honest to God, out of the mouths of babes and Americans. You're a scream. Have a peanut. Have two." She went off into more peels of laughter.

BJ was confused by her behaviour, but put it down to a nervous self-consciousness that it would be kind to ignore.

Then Geraldine suddenly stopped laughing and sighed. "You're quite right, of course. My body is a major slum-clearance area. You should see my belly-button. I have a bath with the baby usually, and his favourite trick is seeing how many Playmobil people he can stuff into it. It's like Clytaemnestra's tomb, it's awful."

BJ clutched the edge of the table for support as the image was hauled before her eyes.

"You'll love Kirstin. She's got a terrific figure. I'm unworthy to fill her vol-au-vents."

At Otto's prompting the conversation turned to Algerian cinema. BJ was not surprised that the discussion revealed Geraldine as blinkered right-wing, and Otto as loony left. Geraldine thought films about exploited peasants were tedious propaganda, whereas they moved Otto to tears.

The discussion was getting quite lively when Geraldine suddenly leapt up and waved to a blonde woman who had just come in. Her willowy elegance caused BJ's inside to lurch with respectful envy. The woman's intensely red mouth flashed incessant smiles under the necessities of introduction. Geraldine glowed with pride at having introduced such an ornament to the group.

Kirstin accepted some wine but refused a cigarette. "I was smoking once, but my husband does not like," she explained.

"If I could give up smoking and do such a good job keeping in shape as you, Kirstin, I'd do it," said BJ. "You have an astonishing body."

"See," said Geraldine.

"Excuse me?" Kirstin looked to Otto for guidance, on the assumption that she had misunderstood BJ's remark.

Otto, who had been breaking a lot of swizzle sticks since Kirstin joined them, pulled himself together and spoke to her in German.

Geraldine asked BJ about her work. When she found out that BJ was in international trade statistics she said, "Oh you must come to Winterthur and ply your wares at Humbel Brothers. They're a huge concern. Everyone for miles around works for Humbel Brothers. My husband does, so does Kirstin's."

"And what does Humbel Brothers produce?"

"You name it – railway engines, hip joints, fighter-bombers."

"Are you sure?"

"Of course!"

"Then I shall certainly investigate it. How does one get to this mountain village? I don't have an automobile right now."

"Winterthur is not a mountain village. Honestly, not everyone in Switzerland lives in a hayloft over the goats, you know."

"I'm sorry. Are there trains?"

"No, you just tie a hunk of black bread in a spotted handkerchief, sling it over your shoulder and start walking. Honestly! Of course there are trains. About every twenty minutes. Though I usually come in the car because Kirstin and I really do live in a village. With all mod. cons. Everything except AIDS, in fact."

As they talked BJ found that she could not keep her eyes off Kirstin, a condition afflicting almost everyone in the restaurant. She was flustered to realize that the attraction was potentially sexual in

51

nature. There was something about Kirstin's pliant manner and eagerness to please that cried out to be taken advantage of. BJ had never had an affair with a woman before, but from the evidence of feminist novels and articles on How-To in *Cosmopolitan*, she gathered that it was *de rigueur* for today's woman.

Kirstin apologized for speaking in German. "I am sorry, but my English is not so good."

"It's fine," BJ assured her. "Tell me, Kirstin, do you work at all?" Kirstin's body alone justified her existence as far as BJ was concerned, but she felt it appropriate to be aware of Kirstin's commitments if she was going to become one of them.

"No, no. I make only ze household, really. Is a problem to work here in Switzerland. Ze veek is long – forty-four hours at least."

"Not counting tea-breaks," added Geraldine. "Or lunch."

"My husband does not like zat I vork."

BJ smiled. "You're always talking about your husband, Kirstin. Are you in love with him, or what?"

"No," said Kirstin cheerfully. Then, realizing what she had said, she blushed up through her hair and down to the waist.

"Why does everyone get so embarrassed by a common truth?" said BJ.

Otto shrugged, and again talked to Kirstin in German.

"Just lay off the subject of her husband," said Geraldine, sotto voce. "Take my word for it, he's a killer. Figuratively speaking, as far as I know. She has to put up with an awful lot."

"Oh come on. Nobody has to put up with anything these days. And there's really no need to do this big sister protective thing with Kirstin, is there? I suggest you save that for the kids and let the grown-ups speak for themselves."

"You call yourself a grown-up?"

"Okay, Geraldine, just cut that out, okay? I have a somewhat low tolerance for that kind of crap, you know, I work in a man's world and – okay, let's go."

Kirstin and Otto had stood up.

They made their farewells outside. Kirstin was delighted to know that BJ planned to go out to Winterthur, and offered to transport her any time she wished to visit Geraldine.

"We must make for BJ a tea, Geraldine, no?"

"Oh crikey, yes."

Otto asked, in a coy voice, if he could come too. Kirstin laughed, meaning no.

BJ walked with Otto to the tram stop.

"You know," she said, "Geraldine is the most aggressive English person I ever met. I'm accustomed to being regarded as a threat by other women – particularly women like Geraldine who've made compromises with their personhood for reasons of security. But I never met someone whose hostility was so uncontrollable. I suspect it's going to be extremely difficult to co-exist with her in the classroom situation."

Otto trembled at the prospect.

# CHAPTER

# THREE

KIRSTIN was reading the letter from the Building Commission alone in her kitchen. The palpitations brought on by the sight of an escutcheon on the envelope had been more severe then ever, as she had known that her letter would arrive late, but hoped against hope that the Scrubbing-Out department practised a little humanitarian laxity in such matters. The lurches of anger and dread that set in when she had read it were not so much because their objections had been overruled, but because Max would find out that she had, again, blundered. She should have applied for an extension of the expiry period in view of the fact that Max had been away the whole time. It was just another example of the galloping incompetence that had afflicted her since her marriage: eggs broke in her hand, she drove off with her handbag on top of the car on average once a month, regularly forgot to buy brickettes for the barbecue, and it all added up, Max said, to the fact that she was cracking up. Geraldine thought he was doing a *Gaslight* job on her, hoping to convince her she was unstable so that he could put her away and inherit her money. Kirstin denied this absolutely, but it was true that Max's opinion had become a self-fulfilling prophecy. It had got to the stage where, if a fuse went, she would sit in the dark until Max came home, or do something like turn the mattress over, which she could do by touch.

Passing through the living-room it occurred to her that a little alchohol was a traditional remedy for the vapours.

Kirstin opened the cocktail cabinet. The sight of all those handsome, manly bottles, their labels glinting with hints of fun after dark, gave her pause. It certainly would look bad if she were found hitting the Cherry Heering at ninies – a morning break known elsewhere as elevenses. But she felt that she might pass out unless her circulation got an instant boost so she took a small crystal glass. It was cold in her hand, and clinked discreetly against her wedding ring. Of course, this was how alcoholics got started – using some crisis as an excuse to steady the nerves with drink. Until the "crisis" was only losing the egg-whisk, or forgetting the cat's birthday.

The doorbell rang. Kirstin put down the glass in a panic and, as she closed the cabinet, thought she saw her guardian angel's tail feathers disappearing round a corner.

Herr Schulthess, the police commandant, stood on the doorstep. He held a clipboard in one hand, as if he had come to read the meter.

"Frau Baumann?"

"Yes."

"Schulthess. I hope I'm not disturbing you." He produced his identity card, but Kirstin was too confused to take in more than the frog-eyed stare of the photograph. He put it away quickly. "I would like to ask you a few questions related to the recent attacks in the village." He looked bored, as if he had been to several hundred households already that morning.

"Oh dear. Come in."

Herr Schulthess was large and menacing. He stood among the sunlit domestic sundries in the hall like an iron maiden, emanating unspeakable terror. What if he were the rapist himself? He was certainly free to roam. In her mind she was already gazing up at Max's cross face from the mortuary table as she led Herr Schulthess into the living-room and offered him a choice of coffee, tea or mineral water. He chose coffee and she went off to get it, peeping out at him every twenty seconds to make sure he still had his clothes on. After bringing in the tray she flopped down in an armchair with a sigh of doomed resignation. It was difficult to keep her eyes off his crutch; it seemed the most likely place to look for clues.

He urged her to relax.

"All right."

He turned to his clipboard. "Have you any children, Frau Baumann?"

"No." He must have known that already.

"What do you do all day, then? It's a bit boring, isn't it?"

"No, not at all. Well, actually, yes. But it's not me who doesn't want them."

"Your husband's against it, is he?"

"Well – yes."

"Why's that?"

"Oh – for many reasons. All of them good ones. He's concerned about energy conservation."

"His own?"

"No. You know – dwindling resources, and so on. And he travels so much. He thinks he wouldn't have time to give a child due care and attention."

"Yes, he does travel a lot. Trouble is, at this rate all the responsible people like your husband will die out, and the irresponsible ones will take over. What then, eh?"

"I suppose they'll resort to cannibalism. It won't be my problem, will it?"

"You sound rather bitter, Frau Baumann. You don't agree with your husband about this one, do you? Do you fight about it?"

"No." Kirstin's press-button blush flooded up, not only because she was lying, but because she suddenly saw what Herr Schulthess was getting at: trying to establish Max's home life as fraught with the kind of frustrations liable to drive a man to indiscriminate rape. So Max really was under suspicion. Sweat broke out on her face. She stared at Herr Schulthess, feeling like a wartime resistance worker whose slip of the tongue would send thousands to their death.

"Now then, Frau Baumann, I have a photokit impression of the culprit here that I'd like you to look at. You're aware of the two attacks that have taken place, are you?"

"Oh yes. I filled in the questionnaire." She took the photokit and burst out laughing.

"What's funny, Frau Baumann?"

"If he looks like that I'm surprised he stopped at rape."

"The evidence was rather confused."

"So it seems." She laughed again, and then shuddered.

"You take the matter very lightly, Frau Baumann. It hasn't got you worried, then?"

"Not particularly. I don't often walk around on foot, if you see what I mean, so I don't think of myself as vulnerable."

"What do you walk around on?"

"The horse, usually."

"Ah. You ride a lot."

"Yes."

"On the Irchel?"

"Er . . . yes."

"Why do you hesitate, Frau Baumann? You seem very nervous. What's the matter? Haven't you paid your TV licence?"

"No – yes. I have paid it. That's not the reason I'm nervous today."

"Got your period?"

Kirstin gasped at his audacity. She nodded, shocked into lying.

"Wait a minute." He put down the clipboard and went to the cocktail cabinet and came back with a small glass of kirsch and the bottle, which he put on the table. "Drink that up – no, don't argue. It'll help you relax." He doodled on his notes until she had taken several swigs. "Now is there any reason why you didn't want to tell me about your rides on the Irchel, Frau Baumann? Do you meet a lover? You can talk to me in confidence, you know. It won't get back to your husband through me."

"I'm not Madame Bovary, Herr Schulthess. I just like horses." She took another swig of kirsch, peering into the glass for some clue as to why her brain seemed to be parting like the Red Sea.

"If you wander around the neighbourhood by yourself at the moment, Frau Baumann, you'll be an easy target. It's your duty to be careful."

"I do not wander, I gallop."

"Don't forget Fraulein Pagliacci was pulled from a moped."

"Oh yes? That would be hard to prove."

"She was chased into the woods."

"Really? By what?"

"A car."

"With a man in it?"

"Yes, Frau Baumann."

"Why didn't she just stop?"

"Is that what you'd do?"

"I think so. For one thing the woods are closed to traffic."

"That's why she thought he was just having a lark."

"She must have known him then."

"Very likely."

"Then why is the photokit so cockeyed?"

"The other woman gave a different description."

"Then Fraulein Pagliacci must have deliberately given a false description. Is that possible? Why would she want to do that?"

"I should like to know. It would be a serious matter. Let's assume she didn't."

"Are you also officially forbidding me to ride on the Irchel at the moment?"

"No. I can't do that. Who else has forbidden you to?"

"My husband. I didn't take any notice, of course."

"Why not? It's sensible advice, Frau Baumann."

"Yes, but Max isn't worried about me, he's worried about the publicity. He's such a chauvinist I'm sure he'd think it was no more than I deserved. He despises women, you see. He really does. Oh dear, that's not what I mean. It's just that we're not very well suited. Oh dear, where's the coffee?"

"Here."

"Where?" She struggled to heave the coffee pot back into focus. She felt tears massing in a lump behind her nose. "Now I suppose you've got the information you wanted."

"What do you mean, Frau Baumann?"

"I suppose you think Max must have done it, now."

"Because you have personal problems? My dear Frau Baumann, I would have to arrest the entire village. One needs much harder evidence than that. But do take his advice from now on. Although there is no reason to suppose our man will strike only in the woods, it's just as well to keep away from isolated situations."

"But I have to exercise the horse, there isn't much choice. Should I take him shopping in Zürich?"

"I'll leave that to you. Let's hope this is just a temporary phenomenon."

"Is that likely?"

"It happens. Sometimes if a man is under a lot of stress it can come out in this way. And if his situation gets better he may regret it and stop. Sometimes men don't at all realize the effect on the victim, you know."

"Poor darlings."

"I'm sure you know that there are some men who think it's what women really want."

"Why, is that what men really want, too?"

"I'll have to think about that one. You're very aggressive, Frau Baumann. Are you under a lot of stress at the moment?"

"Ah-ha. I see you're changing your tack. Do you think I could have done it?"

"It hadn't occurred to me."

"What has?" She bit her lip and hid behind the coffee cup. The coffee and kirsch were engaged in a deadly slugging match in her stomach, which she expected to end shortly in her passing out.

"Just a couple more questions, Frau Baumann. Your husband filled in the questionnaire for the criminal division, but unfortunately he didn't put down what he was doing on the days in question. Can you remember? The 17th August and the more recent one on the 2nd November. Have you any record of what you were doing on those days, that might jog your memory about your husband's movements?"

"I don't know. Wait a minute." She stumbled into the kitchen and picked up her *Impressionist Women Painters* day-book. The first occasion was an ordinary workday, and the second was the Saturday Max had come home from Poland. She absent-mindedly put the day-book in the bread bin before going back to Herr Schulthess.

"No, I can't find anything. Why don't you ask him yourself?"

"We are. There'll be someone there this morning."

"Oh." She went cold. If Max were being questioned at work he must be a prime suspect. "I have to say, Herr Schulthess, that you are out of your mind if you suspect Max. He's not the type at all. You've been in Eglikon quite a while, you must know how law-abiding he is."

"Five speeding offences, nine parking violations and one fine for riding a bicycle without a licence."

"Well that's not going to bring civilization to its knees, is it? Why don't you ask me some sensible questions instead of getting me upset about my husband?"

"Such as?"

"Well . . . I don't know. Like, whether I've seen anyone behaving suspiciously – things like that."

"Have you?"

"Let me think. I've seen some strange men around the place recently."

"Wearing paint-spattered overalls, no doubt. They were probably from the building sites. We've gone into that."

"I can't remember what they were wearing."

"Then there's not much point my questioning you about them, is there?"

"But are the police actually doing anything? I mean it could even be a policeman, couldn't it?"

"If you think that, I'm not surprised you were nervous when I came in."

"Exactly. How was I to know you weren't the rapist?"

"How do you know now?"

"Excuse me?" Kirstin frowned and found herself shivering. She was confused. She could not decide if he was a fool, or a ferret of the first water.

"I know the public likes to fantasize about police corruption, Frau

59

Baumann. It helps them accept levels of crime that they might otherwise find frightening if they thought that the police were doing their best. Now, you didn't actually see anyone behaving suspiciously, did you?"

"I passed a young man on a moped in the woods once. I think he wore one earring."

"I don't think earrings have been mentioned. All right, that's all. Just remember to stay clear of lonely areas if you can."

"But if everybody does that he'll just go somewhere else."

"Perhaps, but we don't want to feed him like a dragon, do we? You talk as if we're mean to make things difficult for him, Frau Baumann. Most of the people in the village take a rather different view."

When Herr Schulthess had gone Kirstin went back into the living-room, holding her head. Her skull had shrunk; all the effervescence had suddenly drained out of her as at the pulling of a plug, leaving her shivering and damp and aghast at the comments that had shot out of her like air pellets while she had been intoxicated. She staggered to her chair and put her face in her hands, peeping out through the fingers at the spot on the sofa where Herr Schulthess had sat. Herr Schulthess's presence had polluted the atmosphere of her home: there was no spray that could purge the ether of the impression made on it by an event of such magnitude.

The fact of his presence was actually more immediate and horrible than the business he had come on. Kirstin's instincts totally rejected the idea of Max as the rapist, but on reflection she could see that there were things about Max that, instincts apart, pointed directly to his fitness for rape: he did seem to despise women, he did have frustrations at work, he had recently hit forty, he had a taste for bizarre sexual practices, such as wanting to do it in an armchair while watching *Jeux Sans Frontières*, and it was just possible that one of those parking tickets had sent him over the edge. It did not fit with the image that she and everyone else had of him – of being lofty in body and mind, incapable of stooping so low – but she could not rest until she heard his reassurances for herself.

The phone in Max's office rang for five minutes, then there was difficulty locating him, so that by the time he came on the line she had forgotten why she called. When she heard the disappointment in his voice she felt, as usual, that she ought to order a couple of engine casings to justify the disruption to his schedule.

"Max, I'm sorry to bother you, but I was so upset this morning. There was a policeman here. You know, Herr Schulthess, the commandant."

"Yes. There was one here too. So?"

"He wanted to know what you were doing on the days the attacks took place. I remembered the 2nd November, because it was the day you came home from Poland. But you said you came home in the morning, and I didn't see you until the evening. How was it you came home in the morning, Max? Isn't that rather unusual?"

Max's python-like sigh came down the line. "As a matter of fact I did get back the evening before. I spent the night in a hotel at the airport as it was so late. Any more questions? Are you thinking of taking up police work, Kirstin?"

"No."

"Have you called the electrician yet?"

"No."

"Have you filled in your passport renewal form?"

"No."

"See if you can't accomplish those mindless tasks by tonight, Kirstin."

"All right."

He rang off.

Kirstin stared unseeing at the rotting sprouts in the Umbergs' garden. Her stomach had gone into a nosedive as she realized that Max had been at home alone during the rape of Fraulein Pagliacci.

BJ was fascinated to note that everyone who got onto the train took off their outer coat and hung it up on the hook provided. She took off her own jacket reluctantly, because it was a suit she had bought the day before at Löw, a haunt of crowned heads.

A few days before she had called Kirstin and suggested that she – and Geraldine if absolutely necessary – should meet her at Winterthur station. Her research suggested that this visit should be highly productive. Humbel Brothers, where she had scheduled her appointment, was, as Geraldine had claimed, an industrial giant with operations all over the world. The heavy metal image of its products did not quite fit into her preconception of Swiss industry, in which little old men in woolly hats and bifocals were bent over watches in workshops carved out of knotty tree-trunks. But BJ learned fast. Her researches had also shown that the Swiss were right behind Coca-Cola on the export bandwagon, which was exactly the area where her company's information services could be the most use. She had been encouraged by the Nestlé baby food scandal, which allegedly resulted in widespread infant mortality in the Third World. Such hicks in public relations were liable to create the kind of nervousness that would make businesses more receptive to the services of information analysts.

Relaxing from the hassle of catching the train she reached for her cigarettes. The man sitting opposite tapped her on the hand and pointed to the No Smoking sign.

"Fuck," muttered BJ.

The man giggled. BJ did not know that middle-aged men could giggle. But she had been in Switzerland long enough to know that she would be thrown off the moving train if she disobeyed the sign. Philip also objected to her smoking, but one could not start deferring to one's husband's preferences, or who knows where it would end.

BJ's attention was drawn to a small human drama in the next compartment. A young man had a stud through his nostril, a razor-blade through one earlobe, skinny legs and a plastic jacket lined with orange fun fur. He wore cowboy boots and looked about twelve-and-a-half. He sat with his hands in his jacket pockets, his face inscrutable. It remained so when the ticket inspector came round and asked for his non-existent ticket. During the inspector's well-spittled tirade against his anti-social behaviour, the young man merely produced some kind of identity card. His cool defiance won BJ's admiration. It was touching in view of his fragile physique. If it were not for the razor-blade, BJ imagined that he might well be the type that would appeal to Michael – vulnerable, yet defiant, a body scarcely formed in the image of a man, yet perfect in every detail.

BJ's thoughts dwelt pleasantly on a conjunction of this young man's body and Michael's. After the inspector had moved on she closed her eyes to give her daydream more privacy.

Too soon the train slowed down to a rhythmic chunt, orchestrating BJ's fluttering orgasms as she came round from her reverie. BJ blinked as the houses blotted out the sun. Now, damn it, her panties were wet. It might not show, but it would affect her concentration. And where her skin had been hot it was blown cold and clammy as the doors were opened on the still-moving train and a draught whistled up her skirt. She regretted now that she had arranged to have lunch with Kirstin and Geraldine before the appointment: she was not in the mood to deal with Geraldine's rôle-related aggression.

It was a great relief to see Kirstin standing alone on the platform. They shook hands.

"Hi. Where's Geraldine?"

"She is not feeling well today. We will go later this afternoon, for the tea."

"Good. Wonderful."

Geraldine's absence would give her the opportunity to put out feelers in the matter of herself and Kirstin. BJ was of an age where the urgency of fulfilling sexual ambitions was beginning to press, and foreign travel was an appropriate opportunity for collecting experiences. It might even be a pleasant one, with someone as physically perfect and biddable as Kirstin. BJ was used to the submissive stuff in her heterosexual life: a rôle reversal was in order. The idea of having a lover buried in The Country appealed also. It accentuated her rôle as tycoon at play. She understood that although Winterthur was an industrial town, Kirstin and Geraldine lived outside it in The Country. She was anxious to confirm this, as the journey between Zürich and Winterthur revealed few stretches unspoiled by housing development, gravel pits or electricity pylons. BJ had never seen a concrete house before coming to Switzerland: it was certainly a shock to see them in The Country.

BJ was somewhat pleased with her first sight of Winterthur. It was a compact, bustling town with a certain amount of vestigial Disneyland charm. The time it took for them to walk over to the main thoroughfare was easily charted by exchange of information about their respective journeys. Kirstin apologized for her appearance, she had been in such a hurry. BJ assured her that there was no need, that she was the type where a little windswept scruff merely added a sexy lure to the underlying perfection. She was tempted to dwell on the theme, as it would give some indication of Kirstin's reaction to the idea of BJ's interest in her body.

But Kirstin seemed distracted as well as dishevelled, and her obvious preoccupation made BJ wonder if her husband, the so-called beast, Max Baumann, had been giving her a hard time.

BJ valiantly kept up a running commentary on the shops, the construction work that choked the narrow street, the crêpe-sellers and the occasional off-key street entertainers singing American hits of the sixties. BJ was starving and attempted to enter every eatery they came to, but Kirstin always said there was a much nicer place with tablecloths further on.

"Tablecloths. Oh-oh."

She followed Kirstin eagerly to the place with tablecloths. It was faintly demi-monde, carpeted and upholstered in cerise velvet, and full of businessmen whose eyes fell out and bounced along the carpet after Kirstin as she edged her way through to a table in a dark corner. The tablecloth and silver cutlery glimmered of intimacy.

BJ's spirits somewhat sank as she took in the details: she was the type who would get the tablecloth stuck in her purse and take the whole thing with her when she went to the bathroom.

A low gasp from Kirstin distracted her. "What's wrong, Kirstin?"

"Nutting. I only am recognizing someone over there."

"Oh? Who?"

"My doctor, actually."

"So what? Did he just order you to stay in bed for a month?"

At the word "bed" Kirstin blushed.

"No, no. I am not afraid. But zis morning I am asking an appointment already. He must tink I cannot keep away from him."

"Well, where is he?"

"Please do not stare at him. He is sitting under ze small barrel on ze vall. Now he has seen us. Ay, ay, ay."

"I hope it doesn't fall on him. He looks cute."

The doctor was a boyish-looking man in his early forties, with a ready smile. He had regular, Marlboro man features, a jaw lightly clenched when not in use, and eyebrows drawn together as if to play down the aura of joie-de-vivre given off by his general vigour. He was sitting with two other men in grey suits and blue ties.

BJ felt the vibrations from the doctor's well-endowed body and guessed at once the reason for Kirstin's confusion. Lust. BJ was sympathetic. Personally she did not respond to types like the doctor, who had everything in the shop window, so to speak. She thought he would turn in a pretty routine performance for her taste. But still, he and Kirstin together complemented each other in looks and condition on the scale BJ used to rate the rateable. BJ took pleasure in imagining the union of Kirstin and her doctor. It would be pretty natural and healthy and would probably make both of them feel good.

She turned to Kirstin with a knowing smile, offering her a cigarette, which, to her surprise, was accepted.

"Listen, Kirstin, I think I understand the problem, okay? I think he's very attractive. I hope you get together, I really do."

"Of what are you talking, BJ?"

"You know – your friend over there. I think he's very attractive, and you obviously do too, so I hope you get to sleep with him, that's all."

Kirstin gasped and looked around to see if anyone was listening. "Please do not say zis – please!"

"Oh? Oh. I get it. You've already slept with him. I'm sorry – "

"No! Also not. I do not want to. Let us please talk of someting else, *please*."

"Okay. Sure. Listen, have I come on a bad day for you? You seem a little tense." BJ knew that doctors slept with their patients all the time, it could not be that suggestion alone which had caused Kirstin to get so upset.

Kirstin blew smoke inexpertly in BJ's direction. As she had taken the last cigarette, BJ motioned discreetly to the waitress to bring some more. This gesture gave her a little thrill of protectiveness towards Kirstin – the Provider. Of cigarettes, of sex – the one was a suitably phallic forerunner of the other.

"Yes, you are right. Today is not so good for me." Her troubled face was mobile with sadness as she concentrated on turning the cigarette tip round and round in the ashtray.

"Do you want to talk about it?"

"It is wery difficult."

"Well, think of it this way. I'm a complete stranger, really, and likely to remain so." Unless we end up in bed under Plan A, reflected BJ. "So you can trust me if you want."

"I would like to talk of it, BJ, but it is a question of the marriage bond. You, I am sure, would not be saying bad tings of your husband before me."

"Oh sure I would. I think that's all crap, anyhow – unswerving loyalty no matter what and all that. Of course, Philip and I are pretty open about everything and when it comes right down to it he doesn't do anything that I'd be ashamed to talk about. But if he beat me up, or anything, I'd talk about it. With my feet, probably."

Kirstin smiled. "Max does not beat me. He is a pacifist."

"Sweetheart, don't believe it. There are some areas where no man is a pacifist. This Max character sounds to me like the type who'd get a real kick out of whipping you occasionally."

"BJ, I must tell you, I tink you are crazy."

"That's okay. People tell me that all the time. I just say what I think, that's all."

"But your husband – does he vip you occasionally, as you say?"

"Philip? Oh no. On my, no. No, Philip and I are real good friends. We have an arrangement that's somewhat commercial in nature, but – oh no, that kind of thing would be quite inappropriate for Philip and me."

"But I tink most husbands and vives are good friends."

"Yeah. That's the trouble, see – oh, thank you." The waitress handed them menu cards, firing off a round of Swiss German in BJ's direction.

"She says, do you know you must have lunch – not coffee only."

"Okay, okay, I want lunch. Isn't that typical? Does she think I'm

65

Turkish, or something? Do I look Turkish? I mean, have you ever seen a blonde Turk?"

"Yes. Actually, I think Kemal Ataturk was blond."

"Who's that?"

"He was a famous leader."

"Oh. Well I'm sorry if I overreacted. I guess I'm a bit sensitive because of what happened on the tram the other day. Did I tell you about it?"

"Yes," said Kirstin, a little too eagerly, BJ thought.

"Yes, well the Swiss have this thing about telling you what to do all the time, don't they?"

"Zey are nervous in Zürich, perhaps, because of the riots. But anyway, it is always vorse than here. Zürich is a stuffed-up town in some vays. It is full of stuffed-up people."

"Yes. Your vocabulary is excellent, Kirstin. But here's me going on about myself as usual. Tell me about yourself, Kirstin. Quite frankly, I'm somewhat fascinated by you."

"Me? I tink you must be making ze joke. Why do you say these tings? Is it not because it is making you more fascinating, actually?"

"Huh? Oh no. Oh God, no. I'm really quite dull. I guess I must seem patronizing, and if so I'm sorry, but I was quite sincere. I am genuinely interested in you, Kirstin."

"But I am just a housewife. You – you are full of courage like a man. You go to the offices of Humbel Brudders and Aluswiss and Sprüngli and so, and you make men wiv important jobs listen to you. Zis I could not do. I am imagining if you go to my husband, for example, in his office. He would not be so nice, I tink. No, no, you are full of courage."

"God, I'm dying to meet your husband. As a matter of fact I could very well go call on him quite legitimately. What's his business?"

"Marine engineering. But no, please, BJ, if he tinks I have sent you he vill be very angry."

"Don't worry. I'll make it quite clear it was my idea."

"He vill not believe you."

"Jesus, you are scared of him, aren't you? What does he do to you? Come on, you're hiding something interesting there, aren't you, Kirstin?"

"No! No. But he must alvays vork so hard, and he is having big responsibilities. He vill not give you a charming reception."

"Uh-huh. Well, I guess I know what you mean. On the other hand, if I considered that he was a legitimate potential sale, you wouldn't expect me to give that up, would you?"

66

"No. But I don't tink he is buying stuff from you. Honestly."

"We'll see."

Kirstin had whetted BJ's appetite to meet Max Baumann, and plans for an eyeball-to-eyeball with him began to form. Even if she did not sell him anything, which seemed likely, it would prove to Kirstin that BJ had – why not? – balls. BJ was beginning to fill in the scenario that would culminate in sleeping with Kirstin, and what more natural preamble than proving herself to be of equal weight with the dreaded M. Baumann? BJ did feel herself superior to Kirstin. Her brownie points, however, were balanced by Kirstin's sophistication, her ease in restaurants with tablecloths, and very probably, her intelligence. Considering she had not lived in an English-speaking country, Kirstin had a command of the language that was impressive. BJ, despite the oft-repeated German 1 and 2, still felt lost for words when speaking German. She remained unconvinced that German was a real language, used by millions daily, rather than a kind of Lego for grown-ups that had to be assembled with laborious exactitude each time.

The waitress brought BJ's cordon bleu, a huge slab of veal that flapped over either side of the plate, the hot cheese inside dripping towards the tablecloth, but just air-cooled in time to be arrested in an arty droplet. BJ's mouth ran with saliva. Five hundred, six hundred calories – but what the hell?

Kirstin was brought a plate of paper-thin smoked beef with a baby gherkin in the middle. BJ's saliva turned to ashes. No wonder Kirstin was thin, and BJ had to spend every waking minute fighting flab.

"You should be eating this," she said. "I'm so fat. It's disgusting." She pushed the plate away.

"No, of course you are not fat. Usually I eat a lot, but today, I told you, it does not go vell wiv me."

"You didn't say why."

Kirstin gave a little smile and a shrug, letting her eye slither for a second on to the doctor's table, where he was taking a glass of black tea.

"Zis morning vas terrible. First of all I became a letter from ze Building Commission. There is to be built a road troo our garden and ze neighbours, and I vas sending my reclamations too late."

"Oh. Well, that happens." BJ was not surprised. Despite the fact that the Swiss voted for something every other week, she had decided that their freedoms were everywhere in chains. "A good lawyer could fix it."

"And zen, what vas vorse, ze police commandant of Eglikon came to wisit me."

"And all for the sake of my little nut tree," murmured BJ. "Sorry, go on."

"His wisit made me wery much afraid."

"Why? Though personally I would be shit-scared to be cornered in my apartment by a policeman. In the States anyway, they're considered educationally sub-normal. That's an exaggeration, but you know this image you get on TV where this young guy about six-foot five is standing there with his hands on his hips, with these short sleeves showing his muscles." She demonstrated the pose. "Beautiful body with all these shiny medals and guns and stuff, and he stands there saying, 'Yes, ma'am, no ma'am, glad to help you, ma'am.' That's all bullshit. I mean they're dangerous, seriously. Is that why you were scared?"

"Oh no, I tink the Swiss police are not criminals themselves."

"Well, neither are all American police: there are one or two good apples. As a matter of fact, there was this just divine patrolman in Cohasset – Oh well, I guess you don't want to know about that. I just know I'd rather deal with a criminal. At least they're not under the protection of the law."

"I am sorry, I am not believing you. I tink if you are frightened you go to ze police at once, just like me. No, I was not afraid of the policeman. He was asking questions because of ze rape zat was in our willage recently."

"Oh. That. In the States someone is raped on the hour every hour, so I guess you've been lucky up to now."

"He was asking me where I go, and what I do all ze day."

"Uh-huh. Trying to show that if you get it, you were asking for it."

"Yes. And – " Kirstin's chin trembled " – he vant to know also where Max was at zat time."

"Max the B – ? Oh. Wow. Did the victim identify Max?"

"No! Fraulein Pagliacci say she did not recognize ze man. Her mudder says zat she remembers nutting, only zat he tore her underwashes."

"I'll bet. I guess Eglikon's a real one-cat town. You'd think it would be a doddle to find the guy."

"Yes."

"What's interesting is – " BJ broke off to shake hands with the doctor, who had to pass their table on his way out. Kirstin was thrown into a seizure, introducing BJ to him in High German, which confused them all as the doctor spoke English and wanted to show it off. He crushed BJ's hand and spoke of his joy in meeting her. He really was very cute. Within seconds he was gone, leaving Kirstin in a

68

state that might have been justified had she been run over by an express train, but which to BJ seemed overdone.

"What's interesting is," she repeated, returning to the subject of the rape by way of calming Kirstin down, "why she didn't remember anything. Was she badly hurt?"

"No. Bruises only."

"It sounds to me as if she did recognize him. A married man, maybe? That's the usual reason people's memories fail in a case like that."

Kirstin had paled. "Why would a married man need to do such a ting?"

"Rape is a crime of violence. It has to do with repressed conflicts, I guess. If he were married it could explain why the victim didn't want to give him away. Nobody likes to be responsible for breaking up a marriage."

"Excuse me, I must go to ze bartroom."

"Okay. Are you all right?"

"Yes." Kirstin put her hand to her mouth as she hurried away.

Perhaps she's pregnant, thought BJ. She wondered how Max would react to a baby. He did not sound like the type who would rush home to give it a bedtime bottle.

When Kirstin came back BJ summoned the waitress for the bill. She smiled knowingly at Kirstin.

"I guess there's something important you haven't told me yet," she said.

Kirstin looked startled. "How are you knowing?"

"I'm not. It's just a hunch."

Suddenly Kirstin burst into tears, rushed outside and collapsed over the hood of the nearest BMW.

BJ followed her, feeling slightly annoyed. Her appointment was only a half-hour off, and if Kirstin were pregnant it would make a sexual relationship with her sufficiently unlikely as not to justify sacrificing a business appointment for her. She also prayed fervently that Kirstin's crisis would not disable her for driving the car, as BJ was relying on her for transport to Humbel Brothers. She patted Kirstin anxiously.

"Hey, what's the problem?"

Kirstin tried to pull herself together. BJ provided the handkerchiefs. As they talked she prised Kirstin off the BMW, and guided her through the streets in what she hoped was the direction of Kirstin's car.

"Are you not tinking it a problem zat Max is ze rapist?" said Kirstin.

"Huh? Is that all you're worried about? I thought you said Fraulein whatever-her-name-is didn't recognize the man?"

"She did not say. But perhaps she did, and is saying nutting to protect me, like you say. And also I found out zat Max was alone in ze house at ze time. He says."

"No alibi. Wow. Still, that doesn't prove anything. Do you have any other reason to suspect him? I mean, has he ever come home with his pants open and bits of fir tree stuck to his clothing?"

"No."

"Then I suggest you forget it. What's happening is, you're projecting your own fear of Max and turning it around, like, syllogism-wise, that he is therefore someone to be feared, i.e. the rapist. I have an idea that if Max were feeling anti-social he'd work it out through more conventional channels like prostitutes. Your businessmen have a number of discreet services available to them through certain hotels – students with a cash-flow problem – that sort of thing."

"You really tink Max would go to a prostitute?"

"Hell, I don't know. I'm just saying that if he's a sophisticated guy it's a lot more feasible than his jumping some kid from behind a tree."

Kirstin sighed. "It's true zat I do not tink I am good at sex any more."

"Maybe not with Max. He's obviously brainwashed you into this pose of being inadequate, because it makes him feel comfortable. You should . . . er . . . experiment. Try it again with someone totally different." She squeezed Kirstin's arm and smiled. They had arrived at the parkhouse. "Here, give me the ticket. I'll get it."

"You I tink are wery vise, BJ. You must be wery good at sex. Your husband is a lucky man."

"Well now, listen – " Fortunately, BJ had to break off to pay the ticket, so she had a chance to think of a suitable reply. She had flustered visions of Kirstin ringing Philip at work to find out what BJ did in bed. She doubted that he would endorse her image as the Julia Child of sex. "Actually, if I seem conversant with your problem, it's because I share it to some extent. Though with Philip and I it's more a question of our equal weight in other areas that tends to inhibit. He's also somewhat conventional. There has to be an element of outrage for sex to work properly."

"But I am not outrageous like you, BJ."

"I'm sure it will rub off."

BJ took her arm as they went in to find the car.

BJ was impressed by the size and complexity of Humbel Brothers. Her appointment, Herr Winkler, had an office on the fifteenth floor of a black glass high-rise, which commanded an excellent view of the station shunting-yard. He had spent four years as manager of a chemical company in North Carolina, the fleshpots of which were still vivid enough to make him receptive to Americana in general – blonde, leggy Americana, so much the better.

Herr Winkler was reluctant to discuss his product, or end markets, but from the interest he showed in the political risk model and the defense data bank, she deduced that he was in weaponry of some kind. She therefore waxed lyrical about the system's ability to forecast global conflicts and imploding social order, while Herr Winkler browsed through the literature. BJ was riding high by the time she came to the terrorism service.

By a stroke of luck, two of the company's employees had that week been kidnapped in Panama. Herr Winkler studied the flier with interest, lingering over a photograph of a diplomatic corpse.

"A cousin of my wife's," he explained.

Holy shit, it's my lucky day, thought BJ, cursing the fact that Kirstin was waiting to take her to Geraldine's. Herr Winkler was as ready for a little mutual ego-stroking in the senior personnel lounge as she was; she read the signs like a familiar flight-departure board.

Herr Winkler accompanied her to the elevator. He made jovial enquiries about whether Ho Jos still sold Rocky Road ice cream, and how many million Big Macs had been sold when she left. Had he not been so cute, BJ might have found his nostalgia for North Carolina offensively phoney, and his use of it to soften her up an abuse of American friendliness. As it was she felt with every word her Americanness crowning her like the spikes on the statue of Liberty. How sweet it was to be standing in the flow of the current of respect that should, but usually did not, pass from little, unimportant countries to the magnet of great big powerful ones. Since coming to Europe she had seemed to be apologizing for her country every day: she felt like claiming expenses from the State Department. Her waking hours were spent defending American imperialism, street violence, television violence, drug-taking among grade-school kids, junk food, sex scandals in Congress and bubblegum. There was clearly a conspiracy among the media to present the States as unwholesome.

But Herr Winkler had restored her sense of might being right, and the naivety of inveighing against the balance of power. Herr Winkler knew that, having experienced the immensity of the States for himself. Herr Winkler was going to buy from her, having experienced her professional performance for himself. Things were definitely looking up, was BJ's dominant sensation as the elevator doors closed on Herr Winkler's jokey "Mzzzzzzzz Berkeley."


Rachel, Geraldine's nine-year-old, held the guinea pig up to BJ's nose.

"You know, they were only invented in 1935," she said.

"By whom?"

"Dunno."

She put it back in the cage, which was in the corner of Geraldine's living-room. Its body twitched incessantly, as if plugged in to an electric shock machine.

"Frankly," said BJ, "they're just rats, as far as I'm concerned."

"I agree," said Geraldine from the sofa. "They smell like month-old hostages, too."

"Geraldine!" Kirstin looked embarrassed. The drama of the American hostages in Iran was still a talking-point, although contestants in quiz shows were already getting the numbers involved, the date, and even the country, wrong.

"That's okay," said BJ. "I'm not sensitive about that. I guess we're lucky to have been let off so lightly."

"Lightly?"

"Sure. Those people in Iran had been oppressed for a long time. If you take the lid off there's going to be a helluva head of steam."

"Does gloating over mutilated bodies come under your head of steam theory?"

"Oh. That. That was unfortunate. I guess our guys did worse things in Vietnam."

"Which makes it all right."

"That's a somewhat simplistic interpretation of my opinion. I just mean that we have to stop being surprised when we get a dose of our own medicine."

"It's a pity you're not Jewish, BJ. They could use your resignation to the pursuit of vengeance."

"It's just human nature."

"It's not my nature."

"Well you're not a repressed minority – majority, in the case of Iran."

"But that's exactly what women are according to you, isn't it? Mothers, anyway."

"Do we have to get into that again? Your kids are neat, Geraldine. I like them, really."

"I'm overwhelmed."

BJ returned, reluctantly, to the fireplace grouping. She registered the fact that her visit did not rate lighting the fire. It was no doubt an unconscious omission on Geraldine's part, but BJ considered that the unconscious sent messages of ringing clarity through such gestures, whereas conscious actions were often designed to deceive. BJ tried to keep herself free from that kind of deception, in which most people were enmeshed, and she often felt compelled to take a few liberating slashes at other people's mesh, to see if it hid anything worth revealing.

So when Geraldine asked her if she would ever have children – pathetically soon – she had replied, "No. I don't need that kind of prop for my ego."

"It's self-supporting, is it?"

"If you like."

"Doesn't your husband mind?"

"He respects my wishes. I might reconsider when I'm around forty, but not unless we could afford to have someone take care of it at least eight hours a day. I need that kind of space for myself, or the kid would suffer."

"I'd get this person to look after it full time. And have it to start with."

"Yeah. Right." Had not Geraldine looked as grey as concrete on a builder's pallete, BJ would have expanded further on the negative aspects of motherhood so evident in her. Probably Geraldine was pregnant again; women always looked like they had radiation sickness for the first few months. "Perhaps I should call a cab to take me to the station, Kirstin. You obviously want to go home. You've been looking at your watch all the time."

Kirstin blushed. "Have I? I'm sorry."

"That's okay. Does the old man give you a hard time if you're not in the kitchen when he comes home?"

"No, no," said Kirstin.

"Yes, yes," said Geraldine.

"I also like to be home ven he comes from vork. It is normal, I tink."

"I tell you what," said BJ, "why don't I go with you back to your place now? Geraldine looks somewhat tired anyhow, you could be at

73

your post when he arrives, and I could get to meet him. I'm dying to meet him after all you two have said about him. And it would be useful if I'm going to approach him in a business situation. He might even offer to drive me to the train station while you fix dinner. I could give him a little pre-sales patter."

BJ was laughing. Geraldine and Kirstin were not. Kirstin's horrified gaze appealed to Geraldine for help.

"She's trying to say," said Geraldine, "that Max is usually in a filthy mood when he comes home and it will be even filthier if there's someone there and he can't be natural."

"No, no," said Kirstin.

"Yes, yes," said Geraldine.

"Oh. I get it. He's one of those guys whose contempt for his wife contaminates everyone she associates with."

"Yes, exactly."

"No, no," said Kirstin. One of the children dashed in and dragged her out to see what they had done to her car.

BJ and Geraldine looked at each other suspiciously, toying with the unwelcome prospect of agreeing with each other about something.

"I guess you know this Max character quite well," said BJ.

Geraldine screwed up her face. "Nobody really knows him. He has such self-control, such self-discipline, one can't even imagine him having bodily functions."

"Do they have many friends?"

"They used to have. But if they were friends of hers they were having to dinner Max always got a headache after the salad and went to bed. Mind you, he likes to serve Bulgarian grand crus, so it's not surprising. I don't think he ever did bring his friends home. He takes sporting pals out to a restaurant occasionally. They socialize in the village a bit. Of course, it's so unusual for Max to cross anyone's threshold they boast about it for weeks afterwards. It's ridiculous. Everyone thinks Max is a pill, but his rarity value is enormous. I mean, even I fall for it. If he walked in here now I'd be hopping about like a jackrabbit trying to find things to please him."

That, thought BJ, is because of your slave mentality. She was amused at the idea of whole villages grovelling to Max. It was a pity she would not see Geraldine's face when she learned how very differently BJ dealt with him.

"I've decided to call a cab," she said as Kirstin came back into the room.

Kirstin looked pained. "Please, BJ, I am taking you to ze station as I promised."

74

"Okay," said BJ. "If you're sure." It was actually quite agreeable to have Kirstin sweat for the privilege of giving her a ride.

As they were getting their coats the girls hurtled down the stairs tearing the bemused baby limb from limb.

"Mummy, Mummy it's my turn to feed him, it is, it is!" shouted Claudia, trampling on BJ's feet in the narrow hall.

Geraldine roughly pulled the baby away and pushed Claudia hard so that she fell over. "Shut up you spoilt brat. Neither of you feeds him if you behave like that. Get upstairs both of you, of you'll get it on your bottoms."

Quite right, thought BJ, but too late.

The girls started arguing their case. Geraldine got hold of Rachel by the neck of her pullover and booted her towards the stairs. They both ran up crying. The baby started to yell. Geraldine joggled him up and down, obliging him to choose between screaming and breathing. He quietened down, suddenly fascinated by BJ, who was adjusting the matching foulard of her 90% slub silk blouse.

BJ thought it would be appropriate to show some interest in the baby, by way of proving that she could be gracious to the opposition even if Geraldine could not. She moved closer to the baby's face, which was mottled like a tie-n-dye T-shirt from crying.

"Hi, little man," she said, in her best Wizard of Oz voice. "Are you awl better now?"

The baby laughed a deep, ominous laugh. Two truncheons of glistening green snot dangled from his nostrils. BJ thought she would throw up. Then he swiped BJ full on the nose. His hand had recently been in contact with some evil-smelling, viscous substance like rancid moisturizer.

"Shit," said BJ. "What did the little turd have to do that for?"

"Oh dear, he's always doing that. It's no use smacking him back, he just thinks it's a game."

"Perhaps you should use an implement. Excuse me, I have to go to the bathroom now."

There was another tense moment when she came out and had to manoeuvre past Geraldine to get to the door. The baby had been well satisfied with BJ's reaction and lunged at her, giggling itself into hiccoughs as BJ ducked and dodged its flailing hand. Even Kirstin thought it was funny. The goodbyes were brief.

BJ did not say anything as they drove away. Kirstin, after all, was Geraldine's friend. She might be incapable of appreciating the cause of Geraldine's hostility – the realization that her bargain with security had not paid off. Her hostility could be unconscious: living in

75

Switzerland might have lulled her into acceptance of the economic enslavement of women. She would never have gotten away with it in the States: social pressures would have forced her out of the home. Geraldine was fininshed, and had been when she had her first child. BJ was renewed in her resolve never to let that happen to her.

After dealing with Geraldine in her own mind, BJ felt calmer. But Kirstin still had to be put in the picture.

"Did Geraldine have a profession before she was married?"

"Yes. She was a nurse."

"Oh? Couldn't she do that part-time? She needs to get away from those kids, although she would never admit it."

"That would be very tiring, I tink. Jonathan is only eight months."

"And Geraldine is only – what? Thirty-five?"

"Yes, I tink, about."

"She can't put it off forever. Shaking off the kids, I mean."

"But she does not want to. She is happy."

"Bullshit. She looks terrible."

"She is not so vell at ze moment. This I already tell you."

"Another kid on the way, I guess."

Kirstin said nothing. But when they stopped at a parking meter outside the station, she switched off the engine and sat tossing the keys between her narrow, unvarnished fingers and looking away from BJ towards the Augustan entry to the station. "I would also be happy to have children," she said.

"But you're different. That's okay for you, I can see that."

"Why is it different? Because I can do nutting else? Is zis what you are tinking?"

"No. No. Wait a minute. You are right, it looks like a double standard. But Geraldine gives the impression she did not make a free choice. That's the difference. God, I've never met anyone whose envy was so explicit. It made me feel good, actually. Now, I don't intend to socialize much with Geraldine – for her own well-being primarily – but she's very much mistaken if she thinks her sarcasm and so forth makes me question my own assumptions."

"You tink she envies you?"

"Sure. Didn't you get that? It's clear."

"I do not tink so. Geraldine does not like businesses. She would not be doing what you do, even if she could."

"Maybe. But she sure envies the freedom that goes with it. She can't bear anyone who is honest enough to say that looking after kids is a pain in the arse."

"You talk like my husband."

76

"I'm sure I'll love him"

"But you are unusual, BJ, because your job is unusual. If Geraldine started again with the nursing, it would only be more work, not more freedom."

"But it would give her some self-respect. Though I don't know. You could be right. Nursing is just one of those jobs that extends female servitude into the public sphere. I'm not surprised Geraldine chose it."

"I cannot agree. Helping people, this is the most important thing. Dr Huber, for example. He is a very happy person."

"Not because he's helping people. Money and self-fulfillment are what motivate people, Kirstin."

"No, no, he really cares for his patients."

"Shit, there's my train. I have to run." BJ climbed out of the car. "Listen, Kirstin, go home and talk to your husband. He sounds like the kind of guy who could put you straight about a few things." She slammed the door. "Thanks for the ride. I'll call you."

**To: Scrubbing-Out Department,**

Building Commission,
Zürich.

Very honourable Sirs:

We are in receipt of your letter of December 3rd in which it is stated that our objections to the new road adjoining our property in Eglikon are invalid on technical grounds. We are deeply distressed by this development, and hope after clarifying the circumstances in which this miscalculation arose you will be able to reconsider your decision on humanitarian grounds.

We received your letter on Monday, November 4th, on which date the three week period for lodging objections began. Unfortunately, my husband had just left for a business trip to Romania, Hungary and Czechoslovakia, which was to last three weeks. He returned on Sunday 24th in the late afternoon. I considered that an objection from me alone would be invalid, as we are joint owners. Upon my husband's return the letter was duly signed by both of us, by which time the last collection from Eglikon had already been made. There remained the possibility of driving to Winterthur where there is a later collection, but, in the course of unloading my husband's luggage from the car, it was discovered that one of the rear light bulbs was not working, thus rendering the car illegal to drive. The bicycle is on permanent loan to an elderly widow in the next village who had to give up driving as a result of falling from a ladder while collecting plums. The other possible means of transport, the horse, was suffering from thrush. We therefore had no choice but to hold the letter until Monday, November 25th, thus just missing the expiry date.

It is our sincere hope that you will appreciate the unavoidable nature of the delay. Furthermore, we would ask you to consider the injustice of an individual's being penalized in the private sphere as the result of the circumstance of his being engaged in serving the interests of our country in the public sphere. In other words, if my husband had not been on a vital export mission he would have been able to deal with the matter promptly. We hope that you will be able to take this aspect of the matter into consideration when reconsidering your decision.

Yours very respectfully,

*Kirstin Baumann*

Max did not know about this letter.

# CHAPTER

# FOUR

MAX sank exhausted into the front seat of his Air Force blue BMW, bending his long body into foetal comfort around the steering column.

Driving gravely out of the car-park, he returned the nods and twitches of other homebound employees on a scale according to status. For Annalie Schumacher, a rising star in spare parts who spoke five languages, he brought his left hand into play to put some warmth into his response. Part of him was attracted by Annalie, but he was put off by her impenetrable – so far – veneer of professionalism. Max was rather intrigued by Annalie's immunity to his powers of intimidation – the willed glazing over of the pale blue eyes, rather short-sighted eyes as it happened. He often put small fry in a fright while merely focusing on them. Max knew well enough that he could turn his electrifying powers into pure gold when the circumstances were right, which usually meant when he was well away from Kirstin and the haunts of her ubiquitous relatives. So even if he thought that Annalie would have dropped her knickers for him as for a god, he did not think he would take advantage of it.

Fraulein Schumacher and her ilk were consciously new women anyway, women who were somehow evolving into a new sex altogether, something vigorous and sleek and self-congratulatory that removed them entirely from the ranks of females that Max had been used to ploughing. So why was she wearing nostalgia stockings with seams up the back and little black arrows rising upwards along the calf? They could certainly not assist her in her work at Humbel Brothers. But still, Max had no intention of pursuing the ambiguity to see if it might lead anywhere: for example, bed.

He had enough problems of that kind already. On his last trip to Prague he had ended up in bed with the hotel receptionist, a petite, smiling girl with blank brown eyes and dark hair which was flicked up into a kind of rigid drainage channel round the shoulders. She was politely suggestive, again in a rather distant, professional way. Max was quite willing. He assumed there was some kind of kudos attached to it for her – the affluent Western businessman, his redolence of private wealth, throw-away razor-blades and his freedom to breathe the same air as Elton John and Joan Armatrading.

Max understood Elena's vague, glamorized view of the West, and that he represented it to her. Her image of him corresponded pretty closely with his own. And he was always on the lookout for no-mess alternatives to the fading lure of Kirstin's limp, reproachful body.

But now there was mess. Elena had telephoned his office. It suggested a serious, misguided ruthlessness that small people often displayed. Elena wanted a job in Switzerland, complete with work permit and temporary accommodation. She had sounded very professional about that, too. How dangerously ambiguous profession-alism in women was turning out to be. How right he had been when he assumed she took a vague, glamorized view of him. She spoke as if he must live between a chocolate magnate on one side and a Zürich gnome on the other, and had only to throw a hint over the garden fence while they were all out mowing the lawn and the thing would be arranged.

He was furious with himself for falling into such a trap, although it was not clear from Elena's textbook German exactly what sanctions she had in mind if the job was not forthcoming. If she informed Humbel Brothers of their sexual relations he did not think it would seriously prejudice his position. If she informed Kirstin, would that be so terrible? Even if Kirstin used it as an excuse to seek a divorce, he understood that adultery was considered a lot less serious than pawning the silver as grounds for same these days.

By comparison with this nagging mess, the visit from the police was a minor irritation. They had sent a very junior detective with prominent ears who seemed to personify the frivolity of the enquiry. Max was amused by Kirstin's suspicion that he was the Eglikon Ripper. It might be even more amusing to foster the belief – start acting illogically, make the odd unexplained disappearance. It would make a good story at the Lions, or with his cycling pals, his gymnastics partners and his skiing friends. It was no wonder that Kirstin wanted a family: he was away so much, what with one thing and another. But it would be very unfair on the child to deliberately bring it into a home where the father was part-time. Max coddled this thought, as he often did when Kirstin's wishes began to acquire the patina of reasonableness under the constant friction of his objections.

A scene of relative devastation met his eyes when he arrived home. The duvets still hung from the upstairs window, a tray of dirty coffee cups stood on the counter, there was no dinner brewing, no Kirstin, and the cat had not been fed.

Cursing, he searched for the cat-food. He slid the contents upright into a glass fruit dish and put it on the floor. After initial excitement the cat sat back, upset, to contemplate the turdy obelisk dripping with jelly.

The front door slammed and Kirstin came into the kitchen.

"Oh Max, you've fed the cat."

"I know. I feel quite sick."

"That's so kind of you. Thank you."

"How about feeding me? Where have you been?"

"To the station in Winterthur. I had to take BJ to her train. You know, the American woman I met with Geraldine."

"Why couldn't Geraldine take her?"

"It's difficult at this time of day. The children have to be bathed and fed and things."

"It's just as well we don't have any at times, isn't it?"

Kirstin started to take meat and tomatoes out of the refrigerator. "Geraldine isn't well at the moment."

"So you said. She'll probably have half a dozen with you to look after them."

The knife with which Kirstin was cutting beef into strips slowed on its way through the gummy fibres. She wondered why meat did not bleed.

Max was standing at her elbow. "Jesus," he said, "now what's the matter?"

"Nothing."

"If you cry for nothing you must be having a nervous breakdown. You should go to the doctor."

"I am. Tomorrow."

"I'm surprised you even contemplated having children when your nerves are so delicate."

Kirstin lifted the knife in both hands and brought it down with a shattering crack onto the chopping board. "Why do you always go on about children! It drives me crazy!"

"All right, all right. I wasn't aware that I did. I just think you'd be happier if you were more realistic."

"Like you, you mean. Happy Max."

"Don't talk drivel, Kirstin. Being happy is something for children. You shouldn't expect it."

"I don't any more."

"Oh, I see. You mean you've gone off me, so you want children to fill the vacuum."

"Is that so unreasonable? You don't even want me for sex any more."

"That's not true."

The truth was that he was embarrassed to hear the word sex on Kirstin's lips. It was quite natural to bang up an unresisting body, but a major upheaval to talk about it in daylight in the presence of meat and tomatoes. It was especially uncharacteristic of Kirstin, who in the early days of their marriage had vomited when presented with a Paradise Island vibrator kit, which she had taken at first glance for a hairdrier. She must have been talking to someone, presumably the American woman. There were plenty of liberated women in Switzerland, but an American one would probably have a more proselytizing mouth.

"You're being very aggressive, Kirstin. You've obviously been got at by someone. I just hope this person knows what they're messing with."

"I can draw my own conclusions, even if I do talk to other people."

"I don't like you discussing our private affairs with other people, Kirstin. You understand what I mean?"

Max's voice had slid into the tone he used for making dogs drop slippers. Kirstin's hair bristled. She recognized the opening manoeuvres of his Svengali act. Perhaps he was the rapist after all: a compulsion to subdue women must be part of their stock-in-trade. But he was too fastidious. At least the Max she knew was too fastidious. She had never even found a pair of sticky underpants in his laundry basket. But that was only the Max she knew –

She jumped as Max's right arm clamped around her waist, pinioning her to the sink. His long fingers deftly turned off the tap without releasing pressure on her body. Kirstin held her breath and placed her hands flat on the draining-board. Max put his left arm across her breasts and pulled her back against him, pressing his fingers into her right shoulder so that his chainlink watch-strap dug into the skin over her collar-bone.

"You see," Max said in her ear, catching parts of it in his mouth, "I do want you very much. Very much, Kirstin."

It must have something to do with watching that knife slice through the unresisting lean brownish meat, the slices keeling over into limp huddles, faintly glistening, like vulvas. Or perhaps it was the thought of Kirstin harbouring thoughts of sex so unexpectedly, as if on slicing a peach one finds repulsive, fascinating little maggots waving their phallic pinheads in the air, inviting destruction. He did not particularly like the creature of instinct he became on these occasions – he was too attached to his image as Business Man – but Kirstin would go on co-operating, yielding, keeling over. It would take a saint not to invest the tiny output of energy required to set her in motion.

But after a few minutes preliminary nuzzling, Max noticed that Kirstin was not yielding. Her body was as stiff as a telegraph pole and seemed stuck fast to the sink, like a trick coin glued to the pavement to enrage acquisitive passers-by.

"What's the matter with you? Why don't you turn round?" Kirstin said nothing. "That's right, you complain that I don't want you and turn your back when I do."

"That's not what I said. I said you didn't want me. Me."

"But I do. Is there anybody else here? For Christ's sake turn round. Come on."

"Don't. Stop it."

"Don't what? What's got into you? What rubbish have you been reading?"

"Let go, Max. I don't want to."

"Christ." Out of the corner of his eye Max observed a male figure, with a dog, walking down the path beside the house. He let Kirstin go. He deduced that it would be as well not to acquire a reputation for domestic violence when everyone was out looking for a rapist. He stared after the figure until the crunch of hiking boots on gravel had faded.

Kirstin was trembling. She turned back to the stove and put the cooking plate on under the onions. Max watched her in silence. Then he asked if she wanted a drink.

"No, thank you."

"I don't think I could eat that stuff now."

"Why?"

"I just don't fancy it."

"You'll be hungry later."

83

"I'll make myself a sandwich." This was a skill Max had acquired during a stolen weekend with an American croupier in Constance. Boredom and indigestion had cut short the affair, but he had kept a taste for liverwurst, gherkin, banana and bacon sandwiches, on rye.

"You're sure?"

"Yes."

Max watched in silent amazement as Kirstin shot the fatty onions and tomatoes into the bin and dropped the meat onto the remains of the cat's Whiskas.

"What a waste. What did you do that for?"

"I don't know. But I feel better for it."

"That's very childish, Kirstin."

Max watched her now brisk movements in mild confusion. She seemed positively jaunty now. It was an attitude that anyway jollied his desire to death. But he could not quite understand what was going on. Some kind of petticoat revolution, no doubt: the American woman must have quite a sales pitch to have got to Kirstin so fast. It was irritating, as if she was in the grip of a spirit medium. If this sort of thing went on he would obviously have to have a word with the American woman.

"And how long do you intend to keep this up?"

"What, Max?"

"This – this denying me my rights." He tried to sound jocular.

"The legal minimum is twice a month. You've had that already, last Sunday."

"I see." He continued to smile, with difficulty harnessing the underlying yelp. "Well, if we're going to co-habit on that sort of basis I suppose you'll be moving into your own bedroom."

"All right."

Max keeled round into the living-room to get his drink.

Of course, she would not go through with it, and if she did it would not make a marked difference in their sex life, but he did not like the idea of meter-readers or delivery men being made aware of their marital arrangements. They might assume it was Kirstin's decision, instead of correctly diagnosing the rôle Max's provocation had played in the affair.

While standing at the cocktail cabinet pouring his Campari, Max found himself thinking of the police commandant's visit to Kirstin that morning. He sat down and stared at the blank television, or rather at the silhouette of his body that was imposed on the charcoal-grey glass. Images of Abraham Lincoln similarly relaxed in marble on his riverside monument flickered briefly. It was odd that Kirstin had not mentioned the police again. Perhaps the female chat with the American woman had riveted her attention onto her sexual identity and led to a casting off of other more trivial concerns, like whether her husband had raped two women.

A gurgle of frustration escaped from him. There he was, pre-occupied day and night with the world's most sophisticated diesel systems, as at home with a four-stroke engine as with a foreign finance minister, the trivia of his day embracing minor matters like delivery dates, penalty clauses, barter deals in commodities worth millions: his competence extended to almost every area of human endeavour.

And there was Kirstin, with nothing to do but push the Hoover round, and whose productivity extended to home-made Christmas presents which saved money that would have been better spent circulating in the economy.

He began to think more positively about Annalie Schumacher, even about the American woman. Why on earth had he married for money and sex when he could have had his own emancipated PR manageress who would be delighted to take the initiative in bed and dress up in scarlet frillies, as well as being able to discuss turbocharging and investment trends? Kirstin had thrown herself at him. Sex, money and the improved prospect for a Niederlassungsbewilligung had clouded his judgment at the time. Max poured himself another Campari, waiting for Kirstin to finish in the kitchen. As he waited his resentment waxed. What a way to spend an evening, discussing with your frigid wife why she thinks you might be the local rapist. He could have been down at the Hallenbad doing his eighty lengths. Unfortunately he had now had too many Camparis. On an empty stomach, too. Fancy Kirstin chucking the dinner out. It was tantamount to a declaration of war. Should their unequal weight prevent him from taking her on, he wondered. The David and Goliath outlines of the situation bothered him, though, because he could not actually remember who had won.

When she finally came out of the kitchen Kirstin made straight for the door, but Max caught her round the waist.

"Well," he said, "aren't you going to interrogate me? Apply something to the soles of my feet?"

"No. Can't we just forget what I said on the phone? I just panicked, it was stupid. He made me drink Kirsch, darling, I didn't know what I was saying."

"But people tell the truth when they're drunk, darling. Why do you think he gave you the stuff?"

"Then give me the bottle and ask me again."

85

"There wouldn't be much point in that. If you'd made up your mind to deny everything you could presumably stick to it, even under the influence."

"You're the one under the influence at the moment, darling."

"Am I darling? Is it so surprising, darling, when my wife calls me at work accusing me of being a rapist, and at home behaves as though I am one? You'll be changing the locks next."

"No, I won't."

"Then why do you want your own bedroom?"

"I – I don't. Wasn't that your idea?"

"You snapped at the chance fast enough."

"Well it has nothing to do with the police."

"What has it got to do with then?"

Kirstin fidgeted in her seat. The subject had moved in from the woods to the bedroom but was still set about with snares. She sighed.

"You aren't interested. It's the old story."

"Which one?"

"Well, can't you imagine that it's very painful to sleep with someone who – "

"Rapes young women?"

"No, no. I mean . . . you know I want children. I mean sleeping with someone who doesn't."

"Doesn't what?"

"Want them. That's all I can think about."

"Well I hope you don't think you were disguising your thoughts."

"No, probably not. Max, I'm awfully tired."

"Ah yes, I forgot about your harrowing interview with the police."

"It was really silly of me to suspect you."

"However, just to prove that your faith in me was justified – " He produced a sheet of yellow paper from his jacket and handed it to her. "It's an account of my movements on the night of the crime. The one when I wasn't home, anyway. I gave it to the police. I thought it would be of even greater interest to you."

Kirstin read the prosaic list of activities anxiously: consultation with A. Schumacher over an open sandwich at the Garden Hotel, lift with A. Schumacher to BMW garage, Seen, to pick up car after service, test drive to airport, drink in the Bye-Bye Bar, followed by short swim at the Hallenbad, Winterthur. A somewhat hectic evening, but well within Max's range. On the Saturday he claimed to have gone to the public sauna in Henngart.

Kirstin lolled forward over her knees, laughing with relief.

"Oh Max, thank God you showed me this, you don't know how

worried I've been. I know it was stupid, but – oh, I'm so happy."

She had slithered off the sofa and over to Max's knee. Her delicate hands made little scratchy clutches up and down his leg, her hot cheek producing a warm tingling patch on his inner thigh, like rheumatism cream. Her abandoned movements had undone the top buttons of her blouse, leading the eye to the gentle, shadowy breasts below.

Soon her hot and bothered body was wrapped around his leg, her head nudging his zip fastener.

He prised her off his leg and round his neck, biting her still-apologizing lips.

Kirstin's blue eyeball caught the rays of the street lamp, further heightening the ecstasy in her eye as it passed close to his own on its way to being buried in his neck. She started to rip his clothes off. A shirt button tinkled into the ashtray. In between the tugging and unzipping and levering of shoes and socks off Max's unhelpfully long feet, Kirstin kissed each part of him as it was revealed, being moved to the heights of abasement by the gooseflesh on his suddenly air-cooled skin. Dear God, she's so bad at it, thought Max, remembering a similar scene with Fyleen McDuffy, the croupier. But sensations were ricocheting through him which obliterated all images but that of the pulsating welcome inside Kirstin's pale body. They tumbled onto the carpet.

Afterwards Max fell asleep on the floor and Kirstin lay throbbing blissfully beside him. After some time she noticed that the leg that was hooked by the foot between Max's thighs was mottled with cold, or impeded circulation, or both. She was reluctant to release it. The gracefulness of his resting limbs moved her to forget her numb foot, and the fact which often worried her at this point, that Max was already forty and the maintenance of his svelte outline was a matter of much sweaty toil, and would entail yet more and more sweaty toil with every year that passed. But now his body was flattered by the light and dark into sculptored pallor, like a coil of party sausage, and she could only sigh in silent worship.

Her leg was paralysed up to the hip. She tried to wriggle her toes unobtrusively. Max stirred, rolling back onto her, crushing one lung and moving the tourniquet further up her leg. He reached for her hand and pulled her arm around him. Kirstin applied her lips to the nearest bit of flesh in tearful gratitude. It was an unthinking gesture of affection that meant more than all the rest. They lay like that for a while, but Max, once stirred, could not lie still for long. He gave her her arm back and sat up, rubbing his face. Kirstin put a hand on his back.

"Kiss me," she demanded.

He looked down at her, smiling – not even condescending for once – and obligingly lay full length on top of her and administered a fairly complicated kiss. Kirstin ecstatically craddled his soggy penis between her thighs.

"I'm going to have a shower," said Max.

"All right. I love you."

Max stood up and stretched and Kirstin sat up. She felt something stuck to her shoulder and took it off. It was the list Max had shown her.

"Look." She held it up. "I'll keep this as a kind of talisman in case I'm ever tempted to suspect you of capital crimes in the future."

Max picked up his scattered clothes. "I wouldn't bother. I just made it up. I did all those things some time around then, but I couldn't remember exactly. I was quite pleased with it, though. It looks pretty convincing, doesn't it?"

He went out, leaving Kirstin sitting on the floor staring at the piece of paper as if it were his severed ear just come in the post.

After her triumph at Humbel Brothers, and the ensuing tension chez Geraldine, BJ was exhausted. The last stretch of vertical slope before the apartment had never seemed steeper, and when she arrived home she went straight into the bedroom to lie down.

She had scarcely closed her eyes when Philip came crashing into the apartment, calling her name. His body language had only to be heard to know that something had occurred which would require her immediate response. She groaned and hid under the covers, but Philip ripped them away and sat down on the bed. He dropped a folder onto her chest.

"There you are, BJ. Start reading. It's finished."

"Oh. Your paper? That's wonderful, honey. I'll read it later. I'm somewhat tired."

"Aren't you even going to look at it?"

"Oh. Okay." She dragged herself into a sitting position and squinted at the title. " 'Spacetime quantification of gravity waves: Black holes, quantification of radiative perturbations and the possibility of transits into deep space.' Wow. Are you expecting me to type this, Philip?"

"You always have. It's the only way I can be sure you'll read it."

"Uh-huh." She flipped through the substantial manuscript, dreading the frustrations involved in deciphering the arcane text and counting spaces for the doodles to be inserted afterwards. "You made real good time writing it up, honey. It looks – great."

"It is."

Out of the corner of her eye she could see that Philip had taken off his glasses in a masterful manner, and they were followed by his shoes and socks. Soon all six foot five of his powerful and relatively hairless person was revealed. His contours reminded BJ of Japanese wrestlers, and the idea of being tossed around like a rag doll by one made her faint away.

Philip leaped into bed and cuddled up. "I love you, BJ."

"I know, honey, but –"

"Are you too tired?"

"Frankly, yes."

"Just relax. I'll do it."

It occurred to BJ that if he loved her he could show it by letting her get to sleep.

But nothing could deter him from giving her the works. Within seconds she was being crushed, spindled, folded, swivelled like a centrifugal lettuce drier, tossed up and down and wrapped around her own neck. Having come, and gone, several times, the longing for sleep began to paralyse her from within. She glanced at the digital clock as she flew over Philip's shoulder into the pillow. 6.30. Being familiar with the routine she anticipated relief quite shortly. But she had reckoned without the spur which finishing the paper had given to Philip's efforts. 6.44. 6.59.

This is ridiculous, she thought, as they swung into the bucking bronco segment. Amnesty International should know about this.

But relief was not yet in sight. 7.14. 7.32.

It was ten to eight when the end came. Philip at once slumped into an exhausted torpor across her. She managed to crawl out, but his arms closed round her again like automatic doors.

"I love you," he repeated.

"Uh-huh."

"I was going to take you out to dinner, but I guess you're too tired right now. We can make it tomorrow night instead."

"No we can't. Michael is coming for dinner."

Philip's body became ominously still. "Who's Michael?"

"You know, Philip. Our neighbor."

"The blond gay?"

"You don't know that for sure. Just because his body is somewhat slight."

"He weighs about as much as my left leg."

"That's nothing to be proud of. Michael says Americans are

inefficiently large. They've passed the point of equilibrium between mass and energy – sort of like prehistoric monsters."

Philip did not say anything, but after a moment he got up quietly and went out.

BJ could not sleep. It was clear that Philip's adolescent jealousy of Michael was going to make for a somewhat fraught evening.

# CHAPTER

# FIVE

THERE were only two other patients in the waiting room besides Kirstin, a doleful farmer in non-matching tweeds, and a miserable-looking young woman in tight jeans. From time to time the patients would surreptitiously glance at each other, hoping to glimpse a clue to the other's disease.

Kirstin shifted on the hard seat, read an article on the best diet for hypertension, and tried to think of excuses for leaving before her turn came. She already knew that her irregular periods were due to over-production of prolactin, because her mother had taken her to a specialist at sixteen. Would Dr Huber be able to tell from the whites of her eyes, or the deposits in her fingernails, that she had already undergone treatment? It was wrong to be wasting his time. He would expose her as a fraud and there would be an end to consummating her fantasies about Dr Huber. She laughed to herself, looking round the sterile sanctity of the doctor's office, at BJ's idea of telling him, instead of a string of lies about her periods, that she found him very attractive and she would like to sleep with him because she was sure it would be beautiful. In fact the idea now made her feel dizzy with embarrassment. Surely everyone sitting across the doctor's desk must feel as she did – six years old and in the presence of their first teacher. On the other hand, if she were very ill and he had to visit her at home –

She jumped up and snatched a copy of *Schweizer Familie* and applied herself to an article on buying ski boots for pre-school children.

Presently Fraulein Schupisser, the doctor's receptionist, called both the other patients together, leaving Kirstin alone. The Fraulein left the door open so that she could keep an eye on Kirstin. Under her invigilation Kirstin's escape was impossible: her resemblance to a fourteenth-century madonna was too awe-inspiring – the same long, crinkled ginger hair, mean eyes, sagging head, and the expression of one smelling rotten fish.

Some more patients arrived and another twenty minutes passed before Dr Huber himself came out with the young mother, chatting with her about the preparation of carrot broth for the baby. Kirstin's blood ran cold at the imminence of her turn.

After handing over the young mother to Fraulein Schupisser he whacked open the door of the waiting-room and stood looking round, rubbing his hands.

"Now then, who's for the high jump? Frau Baumann? Come along then. I hope you haven't had to wait too long. I've been on the phone most of the afternoon. Patients are getting too lazy to walk down here nowadays. I don't suppose you walked, did you?"

"No, I came on the bike."

"Not the horse?"

"Oh no, he doesn't like to be kept waiting."

"And he'd leave piles of shit all over the garden to express his feelings."

"Yes, probably."

"To tell you the truth I know nothing about horses. I'm a city lad myself. Sit down, sit down." They were now in the consulting room. "Well, what's the problem, Frau Baumann?"

"Er – it's my periods, doctor."

"Oh yes. What's wrong with them?"

"They're so irregular. I haven't had one for three months. And I feel so irritable and tired all the time."

"You've done a pregnancy test?"

"Pardon?"

"A pregnancy test. That's the first thing to eliminate if your period is late, isn't it?"

"Oh. Yes. I mean, no. I'm not pregnant."

Kirstin clutched her handbag soggily. She had not thought of having the test because Max personally inserted at least four suppositories every time as well as using a condom himself, so she was reasonably sure she could not be pregnant. She felt like the run-off from a detergent factory afterwards, but what price peace of mind, as Max put it.

"If you're not pregnant, I suppose you want to be, is that it? How long have you been married now?"

"Six years."

"Umm. And are you worried about the fact that you haven't conceived?"

"Not exactly, no. We . . . er . . . we haven't decided whether to have children yet."

"I see. Well, in that case I'd stop worrying about your periods. When you do decide, we can do something about it, but meanwhile I suggest you relax and enjoy yourself."

"It isn't a sign that something's wrong, then?"

"Probably not. It's not uncommon. You're probably producing too much prolactin."

"Oh really? What's that?"

"It's the hormone that suppresses your period when you're breast feeding."

"I see. Why aren't I producing milk, then?"

"Because you haven't got a baby sucking blue murder every three hours I should think. Get your husband to have a go, you'll probably start pumping it out in no time."

"I'm afraid he would be sick. Anyway, he says he can never find my breasts in the dark." Dr Huber's eyes swivelled lightly over the area in question. "Do you think I'm too thin, doctor?"

"Eh? No, not at all. It doesn't matter how thin you are if you're healthy. You'd have to watch out if you were pregnant, that's all, to make sure the little bugger gets enough nutrients."

"Oh I would do anything if I were pregnant."

"Oh-oh. You do want a baby, then?"

"To be quite honest, yes. But my husband doesn't."

"Ah. Here we go again."

"What do you think I should do, doctor? Or can't you advise me on a matter like that?"

The doctor swung round in his chair and frowned at Kirstin. He put down the calendar he had been fiddling with and picked up a ball-point pen attached to a rubber sucker by a chain, swinging the sucker round the pen and back again as he talked.

"Now tell me the truth, Frau Baumann. Are you really worried about your periods per se, or are you thinking that if you were in proper working order you would have more chance of a little accident?"

"The latter," said Kirstin. Really, how could one help loving a man who put such terrific ideas into one's head.

"I thought so." The muscles in his jaw twitched more violently as he prepared to get serious. "Now of course it's not my job to help you get pregnant against your husband's wishes." He laughed. "It's happened to me five times, so you can imagine how I feel. However," he sobered, "you just tell me what you really want and I'll do my best to help you. You're the customer. Of course, if your husband came along wanting a vasectomy, I'd have to keep him happy, too."

"I don't think even that would make him happy. But for myself, I must say, I would very much like children."

"Umm. You have to ask yourself if you want them so much you're prepared to be a one-parent family in a case like this. You see, I've seen it happen so many times – the wife has a baby, thinking it will bring them together, and for a few months before the baby can walk it's all right, and then as soon as it gets to the stage of stuffing Dad's cigarettes up the cat's bum, Dad gets fed up and goes off to South America. Figuratively speaking, usually. Of course, it can happen the other way round, too. Now I've no idea what would happen in your case, Frau Baumann, but I'm just warning you that if you want me to help you, you must be aware of the possible consequences. It's no joke, you know, having children. It's a commitment for life."

"I know. But a lack of commitment for life is also no joke, Doctor."

"Umm." He finally stopped fidgeting and leaned across the desk with clasped hands, studying her.

Dr Huber was assessing her chances of bringing it off. He was not often confronted with such a flawless case of the human body: he guessed that unless she was a religious, klepto- or other variety of maniac she had a good chance of hanging on to Herr Baumann whatever she did. He would not be surprised if she were a bit of a damp squib in bed, she was a bit too genteel. But there would be a queue of men ringed round the house willing to take the risk. It was her thinness that gave her that virginal, violatable air. Today she was wearing some dark thing that draped her long body elegantly. It would be like slipping the robes from the innocent flesh of a cloistered Infanta....

He pushed his swivel chair violently into the filing cabinet behind him, rattling the pickled embryo that stood on it.

"Frau Baumann, I think you should see a gynaecologist and have a proper examination. Infertility is a subject for a specialist, really. Do you go to one already?"

"Oh no. I think it's bad enough coming to – I mean – "

94

"I see. You'd rather have as few people as possible mucking about with you? That's perfectly understandable." Promising, too. "I still think you should consider it, though. There might be some obstruction that's not visible at first glance. Do you have pain during intercourse?"

"Sometimes, yes." But she had always ascribed it to the pressure of squashed suppositories.

"Well, in that case, perhaps I'll just have a little look."

"Pardon?"

"Just a routine examination. You can take your clothes off while I fetch Fraulein Schupisser."

This turn of events took them both by surprise. Kirstin undressed in agonies of modesty behind the shower curtain.

Fraulein Schupisser drew it back with grim delight, and motioned Kirstin to lie down on the examining table while she got the stirrups out and put Kirstin's legs into position. Vague thoughts of Nazi medical atrocities occurred to both of them. Fraulein Schupisser lowered her eyelids still further to veil an anxious survey of Kirstin's body for defects.

"Just relax," she cautioned.

Outside it had gone dark and light snow was falling. Dr Huber flicked on the fluorescent lights as he charged into the room and set about donning his plastic gloves. He looked theatrically out of the window and up at the blackening sky as he fumbled among the implements. He picked up a small cement-mixer and homed in on Kirstin's brightly-lit vagina.

"Just relax," he said. "It won't hurt."

"Are you sure?"

"Well, I've never tried it myself, but not many patients pass out. Now then – "

"Ow!"

"Just relax," advised Fraulein Schupisser, smiling at the film of perspiration that had broken out on the patient's face.

"Were you trained in South America?" said Kirstin weakly.

Dr Huber laughed. "The white mouse is just going in now, Frau Baumann. There. Is that comfortable?"

"Yes, it's terrific."

"Relax!" ordered Fraulein Schupisser. "Well, keep breathing, anyhow."

"That's right, take deep breaths – in – out – so. Hmm, what's the matter with this thing – "

"Ow."

"Sorry. That's better." He left the cement-mixer dangling in place while he looked for another implement. "Soon be over." He hummed as he worked. "Looks as if the skiing accidents will start early this year. Do you ski, Frau Baumann?"

"Yes, I love it. That's one thing my husband and I have in common. I don't know why we never go together. Though actually I do. He got bored with downhill. He likes to go ski touring, but it's too strenuous for me."

"Where do you go then?"

"I have a cousin who owns a hotel in Bergün. I go there during the sport weeks to help out with the children and so on. You know how busy it gets. Ow." He had just removed the implements.

"Now for a quick look at the tummy."

Fraulein Schupisser pulled up Kirstin's petticoat. The doctor gouged his powerful fingers into her abdomen.

"Does that hurt?"

"Yes, but I think that's because you're pressing so hard."

"Oh, sorry. That?"

"No."

"Good. You can get dressed now, Frau Baumann. Thank you, Fraulein Schupisser." He leaped up to open the door for Fraulein Schupisser, and, more particularly, to close it after her. Then he returned to tidying the implements. "You can get dressed now, Frau Baumann."

"Yes, I heard you. But I don't know if I can walk to the cubicle."

"You are joking, aren't you? You do look a bit pale."

"I'm probably all right."

"I'll help you down." He lifted her firmly by the waist but, as when heaving on an empty case one had thought was full, the surprise of her lightness nearly shot her through the window behind him. They both emitted alarmed noises and he quickly dropped her.

Laughing and pink with confusion and with a freshly sprained toe, Kirstin limped over to put her clothes on. Dr Huber sat down at his desk and started to write on a filing card.

The doctor motioned her to sit down again when she was dressed and thrust a wad of temperature charts at her.

"You'll need a basal thermometer," he said. "Now be sure to take your temperature before you get out of bed in the morning. Don't go for a wee first, or anything."

"All right."

Kirstin examined the charts in awe, handling them as she might the Dead Sea Scrolls. How exciting it would be to tune in to her body every morning and to know when that little egg, that little fifty per cent of her Stefan or Andrea, was on its way. It made the pregnancy seem certain.

She looked up at the doctor, smiling with gratitude, but was cut by his expression. It seemed that the sand of the doctorial egg-timer had run out and he was impatient for her to be gone. Or was it that the sight of the charts had stirred some muddy waters of his own married life? Dismayed at having upset him and anxious to get home with her booty and read the small print, she got up quickly.

"No, don't go yet." His jaw was twitching again as he pushed her back into her seat.

Kirstin sat mute. Now I'm for it, she thought. He's seen through the deception. Perhaps the other doctor left some kind of calling card in my vagina, like ringing ducks.

For some moments the doctor stared at his blotter. He cleared his throat several times.

At last he said, "So you'd recommend Bergün for a family holiday, would you?"

"What? Oh yes. The skiing isn't too difficult. In fact it's too easy for some people."

"That won't bother me at the moment. I've got rheumatism in the knee. I have to give up skiing for the present."

He clasped a hand on the knee in question and they both looked at it for a minute.

"But there's an indoor pool," said Kirstin. "Very quiet, usually. I often go there when there isn't time to ski."

"Oh yes?" He continued to look at his leg, but Kirstin modestly turned away.

The compact, muscular limb disturbed her. Max had rather thin, egret's legs. Steel hinges, he called them, but to her they were more like bent vanilla pods. Powerful intimations were reaching her from the doctor's aura. The jolly medical Father Christmas was gone, but she declined to analyse what had taken its place. The Doctor Huber who was possibly conceiving fantasies of his own was very different from the one who figured in hers. She stood up.

"Well, thank you, Doctor. Your other patients must be getting restless."

"What? Oh." He went to open the door for her, apparently back to normal. "Now bring the charts along after your next period and we'll see what's going on. If you haven't had one by next Easter you'd better come anyway. Otherwise we might see you in Bergün, eh? I might give it a try if you recommend it so highly. The thing is I'd told the

97

boys there'd be no sports holiday this year because they were such little beasts on the summer holiday. But I always give in in the end."

"Where did you go for the summer holiday?"

"Camping in Norway. Yes, well it was my wife's idea. She says she must go where there's water and as it rained every day she enjoyed it enormously."

"Don't you like camping, Doctor?"

"I don't mind it. To be fair, I don't think camping in a soggy field in a tent designed for the Hunchback of Notre Dame is really giving it a fair trial. Goodbye, Frau Baumann. Have a nice evening."

"Thank you. You too."

Patients were spilling out of the waiting-room and swarming round the reception desk when they came out. Embarrassed, Kirstin hurried away, forgetting to say goodbye to Fraulein Schupisser.

As soon as she had gone, the doctor's mood of introspection returned. He stood at Fraulein Schupisser's desk studying Kirstin's file. Then he made a couple of notes and handed it to her. He was making for the waiting-room when she called him back.

"Excuse me, Doctor, but is this right what you've written for Frau Baumann? The medication, I mean."

"What?"

"You've put 90dl Codipront." She named a universal cough linctus. "That's what she had in February and she's been here twice since then."

"Show me." He snatched the file and studied it. "Well, I repeated the prescription, didn't I?"

"But I thought she came about her periods."

For a moment he looked at the file, then dropped it on the desk.

"Fraulein Schupisser, who is the doctor here?"

Fraulein Schupisser gasped, and sank under the tidal wave of humiliation and hurt feelings that swept over her.

When the last patient had gone Dr Huber went into his room and shut the door. The disappointment was keen. Fraulein Schupisser hung about for a while, hoping for an apology so that she could forgive him and still the clamouring for revenge.

The door of the doctor's room remained shut. Fraulein Schupisser put her ear against it. There was complete silence. Could he possibly have passed out? What an opportunity for mouth-to-mouth resuscitation. But in the stillness of the empty surgery the slump of the doctor's powerful body into a heap on the polished linoleum would not have gone unnoticed.

Reluctantly she put on her coat and walked slowly down to the post office to wait for the bus, looking over her shoulder from time to time to see if the doctor had revived and come running after her.

The initial ferment of hurt pride was channelling into a stream of consciousness that she could control and attempt to anaesthetize. Always an avid consumer of hospital romances and profound admirer of her own employer, Fraulein Schupisser had a leftist resentment of the affluent in general, at least until she should be called upon to join them. An illicit conjunction of them was doubly affronting. She had imagined often enough that Dr Huber would one day take her by the arm in a lull between urine tests and tell her how good she was at her job, and how he could not understand why more good-looking young professionals were not beating a path to her door. Her imagination sometimes extended to the point where Dr Huber leant longingly towards her lips, but drew back, pricked by the horns of an ethical dilemma. Fraulein Schupisser thought it would be very romantic to be on the horns of an ethical dilemma. But not with Frau Baumann.

Until this incident she had thought the doctor would be the last person to become infatuated by a pretty face, and the first to see that Fraulein Schupisser had attractions far more profound than looks – punctuality, orderliness, a real flair for anticipating the demand for surgical supplies. Even now she was prepared to forgive him because she recognized his superior virtues. But not Frau Baumann.

The scene there was clear to Fraulein Schupisser's mind. Not content with nature's gifts, and those of money, status and a sexy, though German, husband, that idle Hausfrau had to use up the surplus libido not absorbed by having the children she was probably too selfish to conceive by carrying on with Dr Huber. Had she not rushed out of the surgery flushed with guilt, but smiling like a cat with the cream, leaving the doctor in such a state that he, the most congenial of men, had been momentarily turned into a snarling beast? Such a liaison held dangers that positively called upon Fraulein Schupisser's civil courage. There was Frau Huber and their five sons. And there was Frau Baumann's respectable, though German, husband.

Cogs in Fraulein Schupisser's mind began to turn.

# CHAPTER

# SIX

BJ WAS chopping water chestnuts.

Philip sat at the kitchen table, pregnant with a silence that had afflicted him since she had mentioned that Michael was coming to dinner.

"Are you going to change, Philip?"

"Nope."

"Uh-huh."

BJ's heart squelched with dread at the coming encounter between Philip's polyester checkered trousers, in two shades of plankton green, and Michael's discerning eye. Worse, Philip had put on weight since coming to Zürich, and the weight hoisted the trouser legs up to show his legs and short spotted socks. She feared that Michael might be unable to eat his dinner.

"How do you know he likes Chinese food?"

"I don't. But Michael has a very cosmopolitan background. I'm sure he'll be receptive to new dishes."

"You're going to a lot of trouble."

"No more than usual when we have guests."

"He's your guest, not mine."

"That's a somewhat hostile observation, Philip. If you didn't want him to come you should have said."

"Not much point in that if you'd already invited him."

"I'd have cancelled."

BJ started on the zucchini, flushes of misery careering up and down her nervous system. It should have been Chinese okra, but she had reckoned without the scarcity of such commodities in Switzerland.

The time had come for a bit of stir-frying in her wok substitute. They ate Chinese often, but Philip had blown a fuse when she suggested bringing her wok. Without it, the rug was pulled from under her culinary feet. So many of the props that had sustained her back home, she now realized, were gone from under her feet: her mother, weekends at the Berkeley beach house in Maine, steady sales, Foster . . .

Philip fixed his eye on BJ's neat bottom as she fretted over the dinner. For the last time, he told himself, he was resisting the impulse to tell BJ that he was tired of entertaining her boyfriends at his board under the pretence that he did not know what they were, that he was fed up with living in a marriage that was only open on one side and that she had better do something about it or he would be obliged to take steps. This flirtation of hers with the gay next door was particularly provoking as he had hoped that getting BJ away from Foster would result in her turning to him for the sex, companionship and moral support which she had been getting from the first days of her marriage elsewhere.

Philip's visions of their enforced intimacy, BJ's enlightenment as to his ability to fulfil all her fantasies himself given the chance, and her possible reconciliation to the idea of continuing the Berkeley dynasty into the seventh generation, had quickly faded. He loved BJ, that was why he had married her. Why she had married him was once again puzzling him.

Ten minutes frizzled by before BJ noticed that Philip hadn't said anything. It was not a record for their household, but the necessity of softening him up was more urgent than usual. It was now 6.20. Michael was due at 7. The table had to be set and the salad tossed. It was not Chinese, but BJ could not eat dinner without salad. Or dessert. In addition to Sub Gum Won Ton soup, Bong-Bong Chicken, Beef and Water Chestnut Fun Goh, Braised Bean Curd, Happy Smile New Year Cake, Fried Walnuts, Caul Fat Shrimp rolls and Fried Peanuts with onion and garlic, she was serving Boston Cream Pie to finish up. No harm in impressing on Michael that the States had a culture of its own.

"I don't suppose you've read my paper yet, have you BJ?"

"Not yet. I'm busy right now, Philip."

"You're always busy, BJ."

"For Chrissakes, why not? What's the point of leaving chunks of one's life under-utilized? If you can suggest a way I can usefully re-schedule my program to be more productive I'll listen, but otherwise would you please go set the table."

"I will not."

"Okay."

There was a pause. BJ tried to keep her tears of rage from splashing into the soup.

"You always come through for other people, BJ. Never for me."

"Philip, this dog-in-the-manger attitude has no place in our relationship. You're homesick, that's all. I know, I've been through it too."

"No, not homesick. Lonely, BJ. Lonely."

BJ ground her teeth. Trust Philip to throw his jealousy into the works disguised as Personal Crisis.

"Philip, I can't deal with that now. Can we discuss it later, please?"

"After I throw myself off the bridge or before?"

BJ finally turned round.

"After."

For a moment they held each other's gaze.

"You know, Philip, you're behaving like a little kid who threatens to hold his breath until he gets what he wants."

"Some die, BJ."

"For Chrissakes will you stop feeling sorry for yourself. It's one of those self-fulfilling prophecies, you know. Pretty soon you'll be as pathetic as you're trying to appear."

"You've got a wicked tongue, BJ. Haven't you ever wondered why I'm your only friend?"

"No. That's bullshit, I have hundreds of friends. I think you should see a shrink, Philip, but in the meantime would you please do the table?"

"You would like me to set the table?"

"Yes, I would like that very much, Philip."

"Very well."

As soon as he had closed the door, to keep the smells in, BJ turned back grimly to decorating the Happy New Year Cake. She was fuming, going over in her mind all the other Poor Philip scenes from their marriage.

After a while she noticed that the apartment was silent. A ghastly thought struck her. There was a balcony outside the dining-room. With a thirty-foot drop onto a patio. A vision sprang to mind of Philip's body smashed onto the flagstones, tortoiseshell glasses pressed into the bone, spotted-socked feet crooked into a pathetic angle. She rushed to the door. Poor Philip. Of course he felt lost and lonely here, she should have been more sensitive. And what in hell would she really do without him?

On the other hand . . .

She paused in the hall. What would she do without him? Go back to the States and make contact with Foster again. Perhaps even marry Foster, now that his divorce had come through. Take up a new job, a studio apartment on Beacon Hill . . . Perhaps she would be interfering with Philip's personal freedom by trying to stop him. And then Michael would arrive and there would be a highly dramatic scene over the discovery of the body, which Michael would thrill to, being European and knowing how to make the most of death and stuff.

For a moment BJ stood indecisive. In her heart she knew she only wanted Philip to die for an hour or so, to get her revenge for his screwing up the evening. She thought of his family, and more particularly of the family firm, an old-established cat-food manufacturer that had recently overtaken its rivals in a national poll. There would be no future for BJ in Uncle Remus Inc. if anything happened to Philip in mysterious circumstances.

She went quickly into the dining-room. The French windows were open, letting whiffs of evening fog creep around the walnut furniture. BJ went white. Where was Philip, then? She rushed onto the balcony, calling his name, peering down into the darkened patio, which fortunately looked empty. She came in and pushed open the heavy sliding doors into the living-room, revealing Philip. He was standing in the middle of the room, his head lightly brushing the bottom of the chandelier, all two hundred and fifty pounds stranded in a pose of unhappy confusion. Among the dinky furniture he looked like a creature out of its element, dismayed by gravity.

"Oh, thank God. There you are." She flung her arms around him and felt herself being slowly crushed against his chest. "I'm sorry, Philip. We'll talk things out later, okay?"

Philip took his glasses off and carefully laid them on the piano. He started to kiss her.

"You're mine, BJ," he murmured.

"Sure, honey, sure. Okay, that's enough now. I have to go back to the kitchen."

"Let's go to bed."

"What? What about Michael?"

"Put him off."

"I can't."

"If you love me, you'll put him off."

"But he'll be here in ten minutes."

"I see." Philip released her and put on his glasses. "Then there's nothing more to say."

"This is fucking blackmail, Philip."

"No, it's an ultimatum."

"Or what?"

"Or we split up."

"What?"

"We'll talk about it later. You have to get back to the kitchen."

"I'll put Michael off."

"No, you have to get back to the kitchen. I'll do the table."

"Philip, what's the matter with you?"

"We'll discuss it later."

"Oh, fuck you."

BJ went back into the kitchen and slammed the door so hard a glass drawer full of split peas popped out and crashed to the ground. She kicked the pieces into the corner and went back to the dinner, no longer concentrating, her mind spinning at the prospect of being forcibly split up from Philip. The image of herself and Foster installed in their bijou on Beacon Hill tormented her. It had come to her mind in magazine format, as it would no doubt feature in an Alternative Lifestyles series in *Good Housekeeping*, such a clarion call would it be to the concept of the childless working couple.

But the outlines of a quite different fate were forming also, where she would be slumming it in a dilapidated three-family in Somerville, where the car tires would be slashed regularly by teenage drug addicts, the summer air thick with the smells of melted tar and cheap grass, and liberated women in smocks and hairy armpits would call her "sister" on the street and try and interest her in Women Only square dances and soy bean co-operatives. BJ's soul, to her conscious shame, grew faint and cried out to be saved from such a fate. In fact, it was a matter of such urgency that she be saved from it that she too began to curse the fact that she had invited Michael to dinner.

Moreover he was punctual. The doorbell rang just as she was checking the table.

"Hello," he said, "these are for you." He handed her a bunch of pink gladioli in a perfunctory manner.

"Oh Michael, I appreciate that very, very much." She squeezed his arm. "It's great that you can show your feelings like this."

"Listen, it's normal round here – "

"Now don't get embarrassed, Michael. They're so phallic it's ridiculous." She lightly stroked the fleshy buds. "You'd better come and meet Philip, or I don't know what."

She took him by the hand and led him into the living-room. Philip was at his desk, ostentatiously playing with his Commodore 64. He stood up and hoisted his trousers, a habit that made BJ feel ill. His concrete face warned against any attempt to soften him up.

BJ introduced them. Philip returned to his work.

BJ swished back the nets to show Michael their view of the fog and they bantered for a while about the famous health food clinic next door until it was time to sit down and wait for Philip to fail to offer them all a drink. BJ pre-empted this non-event by offering drinks herself, which finally got Philip to his feet. But when they were clunking ice around their glasses, silence, which BJ felt she had been fighting off like squids, tentacles, gripped them.

"This is very embarrassing," said BJ. "I can see you're embarrassed, Michael."

He shrugged. "No. Why?"

"Well, you're probably not accustomed to being embarrassed socially. I am."

Michael smiled. "I cannot imagine that you are ever lost for words, BJ."

"No, well maybe not."

"BJ is like Nature," said Philip. "She abhors a vacuum, but she's not fussy what she fills it with."

"That's not fair, Philip. I don't talk just for the sake of it. I'm genuinely interested in people, but if I try to express that interest they quite often take offence. For example, the other day I got talking to this Turkish guy in the swimming pool about the Cyprus situation. I was explaining that the West sort of naturally inclines to the Greek cause, not just because Greek civilization was so fantastic and the Turks hadn't contributed anything in that way, but more, that the Turks have this reputation for sadism and bestiality, and really obscene kinds of decadence. Well, for no reason at all this guy got real mad and started on about Vietnam and stuff like that, and tried to hold my head under the water, so I was obliged to get out of the pool."

"Perhaps it was his menses," said Michael. "Men have them too, you know, in a different way."

"I'm sure Turks do," said BJ. "Well, if you'll excuse me I have to go to the kitchen. Philip, why don't you tell Michael about your paper while I'm gone? I'm sure he'd be interested."

"Yes, indeed," said Michael.

"BJ will you stop trying to wind me up like a Barbie doll. I can decide for myself what I want to talk about."

"But I would really be interested," said Michael.

"See."

"Why?" said Philip. "You don't even know what it's about."

"Oh yes I do. BJ told me. It's about gravity waves. Is that right?"

His intonation was quaintly irregular as he said this and he looked at Philip in a trusting I-am-willing-to-be-taught way that BJ thought really charming. BJ could see that Philip was going to allow himself to be drawn on the subject, so she went cheerfully back to the kitchen.

When she went back to call them to table she stopped at the door for a minute to observe them. Philip was droning on about electric-dipole radiation and the conservation of momentum in the flat voice he lectured in, which made it sound like he was talking from inside a mailbox. Michael was smoking attentively. Stranded together in the middle of the fake Louis XIV chairs, she was reminded of French films she used to see in college, where people talked about life and stuff at dinner parties, and went out and committed suicide afterwards, usually to a background of Satie or a leaking trumpet.

They both sprang up like spotted deer as soon as she called them to the table and there was a nice fluster of anticipation that goes through a group before sitting down to dinner. It did not last beyond the soup. Michael was reduced to admiring the tablemats, in between feigning real interest in astrophysics. BJ attempted to pick up his enthusiasm.

"You mean," said Michael, "you get one row of these little things flying along up here – " He waved his finger like an electrical pulse. "And another row down here – "

"Yes," giggled BJ. "And these little fellahs get tired and – "

" – fall down on top of these little ones – "

" – and these little ones go up here – "

" – and take their place – "

" – until they get tired too."

They both giggled and whooped themselves out of breath.

"Right," said Philip.

"How do they avoid bumping into each other?" asked Michael, wiping the tears from his eyes.

"They don't," said Philip.

"Does it hurt?" said BJ.

"Of course not."

"Oh now how can you be sure?" said Michael. "Atoms are human too."

"You know," said BJ, "one thing that's always worried me, is that if our bodies are made of atoms, why don't they float away from each other?"

"Particle bonding. Haven't you ever wondered why the atoms of an aircraft don't float away from each other?"

"Jesus," said Michael, "don't even talk about it. I have no idea why they don't float away from each other."

"Ignorance isn't always bliss, is it?" said Philip.

BJ was observing her husband through an increasingly fuzzy glow of candlelight, smoke and shrimp-roll steam. Her nerves had slumped to a pleasant torpor seeing Michael so relaxed and apparently enjoying himself, though she knew he must be secretly heaving with boredom. Through the fuzz she was aware of Philip fuelling himself with bread roll, Burgundy, stir-fried peanuts, in a constant cycle. This consumption of surplus food frightened her. She could imagine Philip's cells multiplying like yeast. It seemed to exonerate her from siding with Michael in making fun of his work, at the same time knowing she would regret it in the morning.

"Ah," sighed Michael. "Shiva and the dancing atoms. Tell me, Philip, does your work give you the feeling for – how do you say – the blueprints of existence?"

"The Tao and all that? Not specially. I'm in the business of revealing facts, not mysteries."

"What's your problem at the moment?"

"It's confidential."

"Oh really? Then what are you doing over here? Why aren't you locked up in Stanford Research Laboratories?"

"A, I don't work for Stanford Research Laboratories. B, I came here for the skiing."

"I thought you came here to work with Huytens?" said BJ.

"It sounds better."

"I didn't know your work was so confidential, Philip," said BJ. "You're just being a spoilsport."

"You've never shown any interest in it till now, BJ."

"True. But you can't say that about Michael."

"Please, please," said Michael, "if Philip does not wish to discuss his work that is okay. We will change the subject."

"But I don't want to now," said BJ. "You know, Michael, Philip once told me he sometimes gets so excited about his work it's better than orgasm."

"No, really?" Michael snatched another cigarette, presumably to steady his nerves at the idea of Philip in orgasm.

"Why don't you go ahead and describe me having an orgasm, BJ," said Philip, "so that we can have an even better idea?"

"Okay, Philip, okay. Let's drop it."

"It's a little late for that, BJ." He pushed back his chair, which fell over. "I can see I'm in the way here. I'm going to bed."

"For Chrissakes, Philip, don't be a dog in the – "

But he had already slammed the door behind him.

BJ stared at the door for a minute and then burst into tears.

Michael came round the table and put his hands limply on her shoulders. "I'm sorry, BJ."

"Don't be." She grabbed one of his hands, and then the rest of him, crying hotly into the top of his trousers. He patted her until she calmed down, occasionally looking at his watch.

"Listen," he said at last, when she finally released him to blow her nose, "I think I had better go now. You go and make it up with Philip, and tell him sorry from me too, okay? I think that's the best thing to do."

"No – no." She shook her head violently. "It's no good. You don't understand. Philip wants to split up anyway. He told me just before you arrived."

"That's nice."

"He's eaten up with jealousy about us. It's so uncivilized. I just don't know what's got into him."

"Well, he loves you I think."

"No he doesn't. He eats too much to love anybody."

"This I do not understand."

"It doesn't matter. Oh Michael, what a godsend you are." She jumped up and flung herself around his neck. "Oh God, how awful I must look. Do I look awful?"

"No, of course not, but – "

"Then kiss me. Kiss me, damn it!"

"Er – " Lightly stirred by BJ's desperation he yielded to the pressure that was bearing his lips down on hers.

"Oh Michael." Sated with kissing she pressed her head against his chest. "I worship you, you know that. Let me go down on you, you're used to that, aren't you? Come on – "

"No! Wait – what are you doing?" He wriggled and laughed, pushing her hands away. "What's the hurry? Here – I mean – please, it's impossible."

"Okay, don't panic. I won't rush you. Come, let's sit down."

"No, I really think I should be going. Philip – "

"Forget him. It's over between us."

"Oh of course it isn't. Just a quarrel. You musn't do anything that would really finish it, BJ. Listen, I don't want to be responsible for that."

108

"Don't worry, you wouldn't be. My sex life is my own affair, it has nothing to do with Philip. He as good as told me he wants a divorce."

"Are you sure he meant it?"

"Oh yes. He wants to change the basis of our relationship, but he's trying to do it under threat and I'm just not buying it. He was a father-figure, you know. I don't need one any more."

"That may be, but it doesn't mean he thinks of you as a daughter. I don't think so."

"Yes he does. Listen, I know I shouldn't have made fun of his work like that, but on the other hand he has never shown anything but contempt for mine. He thinks I'd be better off breeding Philip Ensign Berkeleys junior. He's still got this all-American thing about Motherhood. I keep telling him if he'd only sleep with his mother he'd get over it, but I guess she's a bit old now. The vagina dries up after a certain age, doesn't it? So you can't make a smooth entry. By the way, I think your shoes are really elegant."

"Thank you. Did you sleep with your father then?"

"Huh? Actually, no. He has a heart problem. I wouldn't want to overstimulate him. But I considered it. I probably should have done, and I might never have married Philip."

"Or anyone else."

"So what? I only did it to make it easier to get an apartment. It really pisses me off that if I'd waited a few years I wouldn't have had to, but you know, a few years ago Boston was like Saudi Arabia for a woman."

"Saudi women have their own banks now."

"They do? Well, that's just glorified clerical work. That's no big deal. Are you feeling more relaxed now? We could go over to your place."

"Actually I am quite comfortable here."

He did not look it. BJ had him pinioned in the corner of the hard sofa so that he had to crook his hand back at an excruciating angle to flick his cigarette ash.

"But I want to make love to you, Michael."

He twitched all over. "Listen – please stop being so pushy. It's so American. I'm not used to it."

"Oh-oh. Whenever you're upset with me you call me American, as if it's the biggest insult you can think of. Look, I'm not going to put napalm down your pants, I just want to caress you a little. I'm aware of your sexual preferences. Come, let me show you. I'm really quite good at it. Foster said I was – "

"Don't touch me! Stop it! What are you doing?"

"Okay, take it easy, you'll wake Philip. Why are you so defensive, Michael? I told you my skills in that area are somewhat better than average. Foster said – "

"I don't care what Foster said. Please control yourself, or I am going immediately."

"I see. Uh-huh."

"What do you see?"

Michael had escaped from the sofa and was casting round with trembling hand for a cigarette.

"You're nervous about your ability to respond. Of course. I understand that. But you know there's no need to be like that with me, Michael, though I feel it's not inappropriate at this point to mention that smoking has a deleterious effect on the haemoglobin and anything that affects the health generally tends to diminish one's sexual energy. Though I have to say it's never affected me, and Foster smoked and he never had any trouble getting an erection."

"Will you stop telling me always of this Foster! What do I care about his erections?"

"Oh. I get it. You're jealous of Foster. But I'm not in love with Foster any more, Michael. I'm in love with you. Let me prove it. Would it help if I took my clothes off?"

"No! If you take your clothes off I am definitely leaving."

"Actually that figures. I would expect you to find clothing more erotic. I thought you'd like this dress, it's pure silk. I got it at Löw. They have such elegant clothing."

"Yes, it's very nice."

"Michael, Michael." BJ took his face between her hands and smiled up at him. "I got it for you. I got it because I knew you'd like it. Everything I do now is with you in mind. I'm at your disposal. Forget about Foster. I did, as soon as I met you. If you'll just let me make love to you you'll be able to believe it. Please, it could be so beautiful."

"BJ, it's not that I don't want to make love to you – "

"I know."

"But not now. I am too exhausted now."

"Okay. Yes, emotion is exhausting, isn't it? When?"

"When? Oh, I don't know." He looked at his watch.

"Does it have the date on that thing?"

"Yes. It's American. Now you can laugh at me."

"That's neat. Fost – Sorry. I promise I won't mention him again. Honestly, it's just habit."

"Yes, that's clear. Is this what Philip is working on?" He had edged away from BJ in the direction of the desk.

"Yes. But Michael, I know you're an intellectual. There's no need to make a big thing about being interested in Philip's work in order to impress me."

"I thought I could fool you."

"No, you can't. I understand you so well, Michael."

"Yes, of course. But is Philip's work really so secret?"

"I'm sure it isn't. It's just academic jealousy that makes him pretend it's important. It's such a pathetically narrow world, academia. I'll be happy to disassociate myself from it."

"Now, BJ, you know it won't come to that."

"Yes, it will. I've made up my mind."

"Your pride is hurt, that's all."

"Maybe. But as it holds me together I'd better take care of it."

"I really must go now."

"Okay. By the way, I have to go to St Gallen next week for an appointment. I was wondering if you'd like to come too. I'm going to see a guy I met on a tram in Zürich. He's fascinating, a sort of millionaire drop-out. He breeds turtles. I'll bet he has a gorgeous home and I'm sure he'd be just delighted to meet you."

"You want me to drive you, is that it?"

"I can take the train. But it could be a somewhat agreeable experience for both of us."

"Are you going for the whole day? The night also?"

"Now, Michael, you're terrible! I only met the guy once."

BJ's spirits rose. At least Michael had not turned the idea down like a bedspread. She wanted very much to introduce Michael to Herr Tosch, whom she assumed was bored as the rich are bored, that is, in need of erotic diversion. BJ assumed that Herr Tosch was rich enough and old enough to have got beyond heterosexual titillation by now. Michael's presence would lend a desirable piquancy to the encounter. It had been quite an achievement to track down Herr Tosch since he had saved her from lynching on the tram, and get him to commit himself to an appointment. BJ was anxious that the meeting be very, very special.

"All right," said Michael. He got out his diary. "There's some business I can do in St Gallen. But I will drive you only. I cannot stay with you."

"Okay. I guess that's better than nothing."

BJ went down to the front gate with him, blowing kisses after his hurrying figure. Her mood was jubilant. It had been raining during the evening and she joyously breathed in the musky churchyard odours of the box trees around the house as she went back inside. She had not done botany in school, so she assumed it was European tomcat she was smelling, but since it invested the place where Michael was it reeked magic.

BJ went upstairs two at a time, straight to her desk, where she indulged the thrill of entering Michael's name beside that of Frederick Tosch in her appointments book. She flipped back through the pages, then sat down and started counting.

Suddenly she felt faint. She had just calculated that it was five weeks since her last period. She dashed into the bathroom and found her diaphragm, filled it with water and watched to see if there were any holes. It seemed to be all right. She stripped off and stood on the bathroom stool to examine herself in the mirror. Her inner thighs, as usual, were a source of torment. Fortunately Michael had an artist-type sensibility and would not necessarily be repulsed by them. BJ had learnt in Art Appreciation that when Picasso was real pissed he would order his housekeeper to lift her skirt, and a few moments contemplation of her podgy thighs would put him right back on form. BJ knew that, not being an artist, she was not obliged to appreciate this kind of aesthetic, but Michael would know exactly what theories of monumental plasticity Picasso extracted from fat thighs.

Everything else seemed to be in order. She turned round to view the rear. Her eye riveted on the area behind her knee. A tiny purple line, as if scratched with a mapping pen, wriggled down from the joint.

With a gasp of horror BJ jumped off the stool, sat down and grabbed her leg for closer inspection. She could not believe it, and burst into tears. How could Nature be so unfair, after all those years of exercise, massage, and eating enough of the right nutrients to bring an entire family of starving Africans to maturity? She thought of Geraldine's belly-button and burst into more anguished sobs. It had begun – degeneration, disfigurement, the break-up of the perfect body into a bunch of malfunctioning organs barely held together by blotchy skin. She must not be pregnant. It was unthinkable.

Cursing, she realized that she had left her woman's guide to herself at home. This indispensable volume, besides providing information such as how to locate the clitoris, and the joyful awakening experienced by mothers of ten who finally admitted to being gay, also gave routine gynaecological data. It was as well to be sure.

BJ got on the phone and dictated a telegram. "To: Mrs Dorothy Kurowski, 10942 East Abbot Street, Malden, Massachusetts. Please send our bodies ourselves."

In view of the heavy snow that had fallen while Kirstin was at the doctor's she decided to walk the bicycle to Geraldine's house. In the quiet street asters were beginning to blacken and rot in all the gardens. As she walked past the odd mixture of concrete, chalet and half-timbered houses she let her mind dwell on the time, perhaps next year, when she too would now be at home in the kitchen feeding little Stefan or Andrea apple and yoghurt mush for tea. Max would no doubt have left by then, but, being honest, what a relief it would be not to have to dread the crunch of his BMW on the driveway every night.

Turning into the main street she saw two familiar men standing on the steps of the Sonnenhof. One was Herr Umberg, and the other, she recognized with a slight frisson of dread, was Herr Schulthess, the police commandant. It was not raping weather, so she wondered what developments there could have been.

Herr Schulthess got into his car and drove off before Kirstin reached them, but Herr Umberg started walking towards her.

"Hello, there, Frau Baumann. You want to be careful you don't damage your kidneys with all the riding you do."

"Don't worry. I always wear thermal underwear round my kidneys when I'm riding."

"So did the wife. Now look at her. She always prays that she won't last another winter, but she always does."

"Well, she won't one of these – I mean, you should take her to some warm place in the winter."

"She won't stir out of Eglikon, Frau Baumann. But guess where I'm going in February."

"I've no idea."

"South America. Brazil."

"That's – that's very adventurous of you, Herr Umberg."

"I'm going on a package tour, mind, not striking out into the jungle on my own. In fact I've no intention of getting as far as the jungle. I'm going to stay where the women are. The women they have down there, excuse me, but they're fabulous. Absolutely fabulous."

"Yes, so I understand. Perhaps you won't want to come back, Herr Umberg."

"I'm sure I won't. But the wife needs me, you see. Mind you, this Roggenburger business is enough to make you emigrate. Did you write?"

"Yes, but unfortunately it arrived too late."

"Oh. You'll have another chance."

"Really?" Bugger, she thought.

"Look, can you spare a minute? I've written a letter, too, but the last one didn't do any good. Perhaps I didn't write it properly. Can you just come and check it for me?"

"I'm sorry, I've got an appointment."

"Please. It won't take long. I'll push the bike."

"Oh all right."

Kirstin was actually quite glad to stay out of the lowly realm of Christmas puddings and female chat for a while longer. Christmas was a painful subject, as the absence of her own little wide-eyed wondering consumer was more marked than usual.

Nonetheless, she was a little nervous about going into Herr Umberg's house alone. She kept up a bright conversation about Frau Umberg's gout at first, but as they turned away from the main street and up the hill where the houses were spaced increasingly far apart, conversation petered out. Standing at Herr Umberg's back door she looked over at her own flat-faced grey house, longing to go home and curl up with the instructions on her temperature charts.

Kirstin had never been inside the Umbergs' house. She stepped into a narrow passage with chipped plaster on the walls. A mildewed carpet was laid over buckled linoleum.

The parlour was a pleasant surprise: the wood panelling was original, and there was a delicate grey tiled oven with impressions like snowflakes on the tiles. The red acrylic sofa jarred, but the atmosphere was cosy. The oven gave out a smothering heat. She sat down at the corner table and unwound her scarf.

"Is your wife at home, Herr Umberg?"

"Yes, she's upstairs having a rest. She has to take a lot of painkillers, you know. It makes her sleepy all the time."

"Oh dear. I wonder if it would be possible to get help with the cleaning."

"I do all that. It's not in bad shape, is it? Now, I'll just fetch the letter." He brought some papers over from the sideboard and sat down beside her. He spread large ground plans on the table.

"Look, I had photocopies made of the plans."

"Yes, that's right. Who owns this bit?" She pointed to a blank square numbered E151 that lay between the Umbergs' raspberries and the doomed footpath.

"Roggenburger."

"Oh." Roggenburger, whose name sounded in the ears of the hapless landowner like the knock of Nazi stormtroopers on the Night of the Long Knives. "We're surrounded by them. I didn't realize they owned all these plots."

"And having to pay for it! That's what sticks in my gullet."

"They'd make you pay for your own tumbril."

"Didn't your husband have anything to say about that?"

"Unfortunately I think Max is not keen to get involved in disputes like this until he gets his citizenship. Though I hardly think the government only wants cowards and pushovers to qualify for a Swiss passport. And he plays squash with one of Roggenburger's engineers, so he's inclined to think they must be right."

"You don't get on well with your old man, do you, Frau Baumann?"

Kirstin laughed nervously. Herr Umberg's thigh had moved alongside her own. "He thinks I get worked up about nothing, that's all. He's rather given up on this, because it will just make trouble for him."

Herr Umberg's mottled face clouded over and his head trembled as he looked at the plans.

"Are you saying you're going to give up, Frau Baumann?"

"No, not at all. But I must admit I didn't realize we were already surrounded on all sides by Roggenburger. I'm afraid Max will definitely think it's a lost cause."

"If you give up, it will be."

"I'll do what I can." He looked so forlorn, as much the picture of shrivelled strength as a Bog Person recovered from the slime, that she was moved to put her hand over his.

"I'd still like to send the letter." He looked at her meekly. "Will you look at it?"

"Of course."

"Thanks. Here it is. I'll just go and make us both Café Fertig before you go. You'd like that wouldn't you? It'll warm you up."

"Thank you." She was already sweating like a foundry worker, but anything to put a distance between them.

Herr Umberg's letter started with a horticultural history of the surrounding area and went on to accuse the district planners of conspiring to kill his wife at long distance and drive him to suicide. It finished with libellous accusations of corruption and graft and some colourful slurs on the likely inhabitants of the new houses. Kirstin could well imagine the amused indifference with which the letter would be read by the official in the Scrubbing-Out Department, safe in his office in Zürich with a wife and two statistically pure children at home in their own new house in somebody's former field. She wrote a draft which retained the major points in reasonably strong language, but without accusing the authorities of plotting serious crimes.

By the time she had finished Herr Umberg had been out of the room for some time. It was twenty past five. She decided to go and chivvy him along a little. There was a thundering crash from above, presumably Frau Umberg getting up.

Kirstin went out of the parlour towards the kitchen. The kitchen door stood open. Opposite, against the wall, was an old-fashioned bath tub on rusty legs and on an ugly painted buffet the coffee stood ready in an electric percolator. The table was covered with a laminated cloth. It was a depressing, grotty room, that spoke of the nastiness of rural poverty, the poverty of lead sinks and naked light bulbs and the smell of damp walls and primitive sewage pits. Kirstin thought of the hundreds of her ancestors for whom this had been the reality of country life. After all, people were right to want three-fold insulation for the central heating and outdoor conversation pits.

She pushed the door open. There was no one there. How annoying of Herr Umberg to go off on some business of his own while she had been toiling over his prose.

Another door under the stairs stood open. Perhaps he had just gone to fetch the schnapps. Overhead Frau Umberg's leaden footsteps were approaching the top of the stairs. Kirstin called to Herr Umberg. She could hear him behind the open door, making peculiar noises, as if he were having an attack of some kind. Concerned, she went and pushed the door open. It was a lavatory and his back was towards her, but through the gap in his legs she saw a squirt of his semen and heard the faint plop as it landed in the water. Herr Umberg heard her gasp and turned round.

Kirstin found that her jaw was partially paralysed when she tried to speak. "Ex – ex – excuse me. I g – go."

"No, wait, Frau Baumann. Let me talk to you. Come, don't go now." Pulling up his trousers with one hand he ran towards her and grabbed her arm.

Kirstin shrieked.

"Frau Baumann? Is that you?" From the top of the stairs Frau Umberg was leaning down to see who it was. "Don't rush off, Frau Baumann, it's so seldom we have visitors."

"Good evening, Frau Umberg. I – I'm so sorry, I have to go. Goodbye. Goodbye."

She ran through the house and outside, grabbed her bicycle and pedalled recklessly down the snowy street. At the bottom she fell off, squashing the foot that had not been damaged by Dr Huber.

Outside Geraldine's house she let the bicycle fall in an aggressive heap by the front doorstep. Geraldine had seen her coming and opened the door.

"Hello. What's up?"

"Someting terrible happened."

Geraldine's eyes lit up. "Did he get you then?"

"No, no. Not ze Ripper. But, oh, I am feeling terrible. Please may I have some of your sherry? Look, I am shaking."

"Of course. Go and sit by the fire. The children are out the back so you can speak freely."

"Tank you."

She went into the living-room and flopped into a chair by the fire. Geraldine quickly brought a tray with the bottle of sherry and two glasses, and made herself comfortable.

"Go on, then. Don't keep me in suspense. What happened?"

"Well, I was just now by Herr Umberg, to help him with a letter about ze road. Then he go out and I go looking what he is doing and I see him in ze WC doing – zis, you know – "

"Jerking off? Honestly, Kirstin, that's just the effect you have on people. Do try to be more sophisticated."

"Oh Geraldine, you never take anyting serious. I tell you it was horrible for me. I was being really frightened."

"Okay, sorry. Yes, I suppose you would be. I spoke out of pique because you hadn't been the victim of a major crime."

"I am sorry, I am not going to get myself killed to amuse you."

"It wouldn't amuse me, you know that. But it could have been worse. It's lucky you didn't have the horse with you, Herr Umberg might have relieved himself in him instead of the lavatory."

"No!"

"Of course. That sort of thing happens all the time in the country. Didn't you read about that farmer who sued a chap for having sex with his prize Simantelle? Admittedly the cow was a basket case afterwards, but I daresay that was because it was one of those hysterical French types."

"Yes, now I remember it. But that does not mean it is common, I tink. But what is ze matter wiv zis willage today? First ze Ripper, and now Herr Umberg."

"Oh rubbish, there's nothing wrong with Herr Umberg. He's just a randy old man whose wife is past it. His behaviour is perfectly healthy. Hey, *shteefeli abziehe!*"

Rachel and a little friend had just come in at the french window and were running through the room in their snowy gumboots.

"Can we have some sausages, Mummy? We're making a fire."

"No."

"Thanks." They ran into the kitchen and out again with the sausages.

Geraldine sighed as they slammed the door. "The trouble with kids is, they're like strains of malaria. Whatever you do to squash them they become immune to it after a while." She yawned. "I must be getting old. I can't seem to get worked up about all these sex maniacs in the least."

"Do you vorry about becoming old, Geraldine?"

"Well, I am thirty-five. Not exactly drying out like a tobacco leaf, but on the way."

"No, you are still a pretty woman – only a bit dick around ze vaist. You are not having waricose weins, or so, are you?"

"Only in the vagina. Fate has been kind in that respect."

"You know, I tink BJ is affecting you. Her love of beautiful bodies has made you vorry now about yours."

"Oh yes? She must have affected you, too. Before we met her you would not have made these sharp little observations, my dear."

"Perhaps."

"Oh blast, there's Peter. I should have started dinner. Now he'll stuff himself with cheese. Hello, darling. Kirstin thinks Herr Umberg's got Ripper's syndrome. She caught him jerking off in the loo."

"Surely not."

Geraldine's large, bearded husband sat down wearily beside her on the sofa. He had spent the last three days entertaining a delegation from Bulgaria who were supposed to be interested in buying his firm's industrial meat-freezing equipment. They had certainly been interested in three full meals a day at the firm's expense, but it had proved impossible to get them off the subject of the World Cup and onto meat freezing. After a day like today he quite fancied a spot of rape himself.

"Don't think so much about it, Kirstin," he said. "Look, stand up. I'll show you a karate throw you can use in an emergency."

"Tank you, but I damaged my toe at ze doctor's zis afternoon."

Geraldine frowned. "That's rather unusual, isn't it?"

"Is it? But anyway, I have to go now. Max will be home soon."

"Give him my regards. How's business?"

"He does not say. He finds so much travelling in these Communist countries wery tiring. He is not in a good temper."

"That's funny," said Geraldine. "Staying at home has the same effect."

They went with her to the front door. Peter picked up her bike and dusted off the snow.

"Now remember," said Geraldine, "if you meet the Ripper keep looking him in the eyes. It puts them off. A social worker in Liverpool told me that."

"And if he wears glasses? There is always reflection. One cannot see the eyes."

"I'm quite sure he doesn't wear glasses."

"Why?"

"Well – it's rough work. The chances of their coming off in the struggle and getting trodden on are terrific. No one would take the risk with the price of replacements round here."

"They would have to be in a very logical mood," said Peter. "One would have to doubt it."

"Who else wears glasses apart from Peter and Dr Huber?" said Kirstin.

"Dr Huber. Of course! It's probably him. That would explain why his victims have remained silent. Everyone loves Dr Huber."

"I do not," said Kirstin, turning away.

"No, all right. Everyone else, then."

"You two should go in the house. It is snowing again."

But they nonetheless waited until she was out of the gate and walking the bicycle towards the main street.

Peter put his arms round Geraldine and she leant back against him.

"You know," she said, "that image of Kirstin between the Sonnenhof and the lime tree, waving, it looked horribly like one of those Victorian narrative paintings. *The Last Hours of Kirstin Baumann.* I hope we haven't been too glib about all this. She seems to have hurt her foot, she wouldn't be able to run away."

"You ladies are getting paranoid. You'll be demanding police escorts next."

"Not me. No one would even use me for target practice."

"How are you feeling?"

"About the same. Please don't keep asking me, sweetheart."

# CHAPTER

# SEVEN

MICHAEL had instructed BJ to wait for him by the car. As she waited, she glanced up at his apartment, wondering why he had never allowed her in since the first evening. Of course, Michael was anxious to keep his private life to himself. Probably because he did not want to spoil his image with her as a sophisticated upper-class person. His friends might be of a somewhat underworld caste, who had been picked out for their artistic or sensuous qualities. He might think they would disestablish him in the bourgeois/academic milieu that BJ inhabited. She had somehow failed to convey to Michael her fascination and respect for sub-cultures, misfits, drug addicts, drop-outs, sexual deviants and the underground generally. But she could work on it during the drive to St Gallen. She smiled, remembering the "business" Michael claimed to have in St Gallen. It was a lover, of course. BJ thought Michael had lovers in most of the major cities of Europe, and quite a few with places in The Country.

When Michael appeared BJ was disappointed to note that his clothing – old cords and a brown sweater – did not indicate his reserving the option to spend the day with an avant-garde millionaire. In fact he seemed to have taken pains to emphasize his rôle as delivery man. He smiled at BJ.

"You look nice today," he said.

"Thank you. Do you like this jacket? I like padded shoulders, they balance the bulges low down."

"You have no bulges, BJ."

"Huh. At the moment perhaps not. It may be a different story a few months from now. I have to talk to you, Michael."

"Well, we have an hour or so."

"Please don't rub it in, Michael. It really pisses me off."

"Rub what in?"

"The fact you turned down my invitation."

"But I am taking you, aren't I? What do you want?"

"Okay, I'm grateful. Let's go."

While Michael concentrated on driving out of the city BJ told him all about Herr Tosch, the circumstances in which they had met, everything else that had happened that day, and most of what had happened since. When they were at last on the highway she paused for breath, wondering how to bring up the subject that was most on her mind.

"So," he said, relaxing, "we will be there in a half hour."

"There you go again, looking forward to the moment when you can dump me."

"Please, BJ. You say always things that are better not said."

"That's a matter of opinion."

"Why can't you just relax? For you everything must be intense and exceptional. It makes me nervous."

"I'm sorry."

"Don't get upset, now. Just cool off a little, okay?"

"I'm sorry. I'm just a fucking bore, is what you mean, right?"

"No, not at all. But here we have an example of what I mean. Why can't we talk of something else? like – "

"Yes? Like what?"

"I don't know. The Middle East – or the Middle West. I don't care. Something important."

BJ began to cry. "I'm sorry, Michael. I'm so unhappy. I may be pregnant. I can't think of anything important."

"Oh? You are going to have a baby? This is wonderful. Congratulations."

"No, I'm not going to have a baby. I just said I might be pregnant."

"I don't understand. You want to get rid of it?"

"Of course. Kids would mess up my life totally. Work is my life."

"What is so important about your work? Anyone could do it."

"Anyone could have kids. It's important to me."

He shrugged. "If you think you cannot cope  . . ."

"Of course I could, if I wanted to."

121

"Then what are you afraid of? It is so boring to be selfish always. Anyway, you would be lucky to get an abortion here."

"Why? I thought Europe was pretty sophisticated about these things. Surely the threat to my emotional health –"

He laughed. "No chance. You are in good health and married. That's it."

"But listen, Michael, this is serious. Are you saying that I would just have to have it? This is ridiculous. Supposing I threaten to throw myself off a bridge?"

He shrugged.

"Supposing I threaten to throw the kid off a bridge?"

"Then you get arrested."

"But this is an outrage. Why should I have to put up with this? I took precautions."

"Don't panic. There is a women's group in Zürich which might be able to help."

"I'd pay any price."

"Why not have the baby and have it adopted? Then you would at least experience the birth."

"Philip would never agree to it. And why should I want to experience the birth, for God's sake? It hurts. Shit. Don't forget that was Eve's punishment for lifting the apple. 'Go forth and bear your kids in pain' and all that macho shit."

"It doesn't always hurt. A friend of mine said it was like a big orgasm."

"A friend of mine said it was like shitting a football."

"Oh."

"I guess it varies."

"Yes. But you know, you are a very sensual person, BJ. I'm surprised you don't want to experience a pregnancy. My friend said it was the most sexually erotic experience she had ever had. She wanted to make love all the time, she was so aware of her body."

"You'd better believe it."

"Pregnant women can be beautiful. That big, smooth sphere, and the way it makes the head and shoulders appear so fragile and vulnerable. It's very moving."

"Oh yeah?"

BJ reflected. Images of herself reclining on a wicker chaise longue in the garden, the folds of her Greek cotton maternity gown brushing Michael's knee as he sat at her feet and appreciatively touched up her swollen stomach. It might be one way to get him into bed, if he was turned on by that sort of thing . . .

"Michael, I wish the fucking thing was yours. I could really get something out of having a kid with you."

"But surely, Philip would be very happy."

"Oh Philip. He'll make such a fool of himself about it. I can see him now, weighing it ten times a day and calculating its growth potential on the computer."

"It could be fun."

"Fuck."

Michael sighed. "BJ, may I say to you something?"

"Sure. What?"

She sat up expectantly. Now, perhaps, he would be moved to make her an offer.

"BJ, do you realize that practically every other word you use is 'fuck' or 'cunt' or something like that?"

"It is?" BJ's face fell. "Shit, I'm sorry."


As BJ had come to expect, the historic city of St Gallen was a dodgem track of roadworks and building sites, but he navigated their way through it with practised cool.

About ten minutes out of the city they were again in a rural landscape. They followed a narrow winding road uphill, past a large ornamental pond on which a porticoed summerhouse had been built at the end of a jetty.

"Hey, that's cute." She pointed to the summerhouse.

"Yes. Like out of Chekhov."

"Yeah. In fact the whole area is somewhat Norwegian in character."

"Strongly Norwegian."

"It's a pity it's so near the city."

"But BJ, if you go much further you will be in Germany already. You Americans have too much land. You don't realize the rest of the world has to fight for just a little bit."

"Those rules don't affect the rich, Michael. They make their own rules everywhere. I mean, Jesus, look at this place. It could be some solar-heated dream bubble in Colorado, or Brasilia or anywhere." She hoped the slightly sour note of her comment concealed the disappointment that this haunt of the rich should be such a far cry from the gracious pseudo-colonial mansion she had expected. "Oh, God, I just know it's going to be full of those ten-thousand dollar camping chairs you can never get out of. I keep forgetting they have no arms and end up on the floor."

They were parked on a neatly asymmetrical driveway outside a collection of perspex rhomboids gouged into the hillside and linked by semi-underground arcades. The rhomboids were supported from the front by giant girders. In the middle of the amoeba-shaped lawn in front of this assemblage a couple of pieces of elongated knobby brass were entwined on a black pedestal.

"Well," said Michael, "I wish you luck finding the front door. Goodbye."

"Arsehole. Shit – sorry. You're not leaving until I find it."

"Okay. But here is your friend, I think."

Herr Tosch had appeared from one of the rhomboids and approached them, rubbing his hands together and smiling.

"Michael, there's no need to overdo this 'friend' bit. I only talked to the guy for ten minutes at a tram stop. He's no threat to you, believe me."

Michael had no chance to reply as Herr Tosch was upon them, but he made an exasperated noise which BJ interpreted as frustration at having revealed his jealousy.

Herr Tosch shook them both warmly by the hand. BJ introduced Michael and they exchanged a few neutral words in German. Then Michael turned to her.

"Okay, have a nice day you two."

He waved as he got into the car. Then he put his foot to the floor and headed back towards Zürich.

BJ watched him go in the grip of sudden panic. How could she get through the day alone with this soft-spoken bespectacled gnome in his unreal, materials-oriented house. As she allowed him to carry her back-breaking cases of sales data inside, never had she felt less faith in her product, less conviction that the businessman would find the PIS systems an invaluable aid to decision-making.

She skidded across the marble floor behind Herr Tosch, into a living area under a rhomboid, and sank dispiritedly into a leather bean bag.

"I hope you don't mind if I take my shoes off, Frederick. May I put my feet on the table? I'll put my shoes on again before I make the presentation." She glanced at the coffee table. "Oh dear, you have one of those. Oh well."

"I am sorry, I have difficulty understanding you sometimes. Don't you like the coffee table?"

"Huh? Oh – it's okay, but you know it's one of those fad things that are basically so unaesthetic that you can only sell them over-priced." She put her feet up, carefully placing a copy of *Bilanz* underneath them on the cross-section of fossilized redwood they had been discussing. "What's the elevation here? I feel somewhat dizzy."

"The elevation? Let me think. About two thousand feet. Not enough to cause shortage of oxygen I think."

"Maybe it's enough to affect low blood pressure, though. Mine's very low – 110 over 65."

"Good heavens. You had better have some coffee."

"That would be nice. Who the – what the –" Someone had spoken – a woman's voice.

BJ sat up and stared. From another conversation area behind the grand piano a tall pregnant woman was waddling towards them. She was dressed in a gaudy Indian smock, her bare feet, soiled and bony, flapped in disfiguring brown sandals and she smiled at them with such prominent teeth that BJ's every instinct cried out to grab the paperweight and knock them back into place. The woman came towards BJ and held out her hand.

"This is Frau Ruesch, BJ, a friend of mine. She has just kindly offered to make the coffee. And some appetizers? Or do you rather not spoil your appetite?"

"That depends if you've prepared anything special, Frederick."

"Oh no. I hope you don't mind, but I have reserved for lunch in the town."

"Oh. In that case I'll take anything."

Frau Ruesch let off a hospitable-sounding round of Swiss German and humped off to the kitchen.

"What is she doing here?" said BJ.

"Frau Ruesch? She is the wife of a former employee who ran off with another woman about two months ago. We think he might be in Finland chopping trees. It's the season and he took his hard hat. But anyway, there were many debts and she was evicted, so I offered her to stay here for a time."

"That's amazing. Do you do that sort of thing a lot? I'm not surprised your wife walked out."

"It depends. I have place for many people here. But Frau Ruesch came after my wife left."

BJ put her feet up again. "I guess that takes care of your sexual needs for the time being."

"Sex? With Frau Ruesch?" He laughed. "Oh no. In her condition –"

"Come on, Frederick. That's nothing these days. Pregnancy is a deeply sensual experience. Some women feel like making love all the time."

"Really? But don't you think that would be cheating a little bit?

Then what would I do with her afterwards? Just get rid of her?"

"I don't think it would make any difference to her position afterwards. In the meantime she'd probably be glad to do you a favour. See, you're this rich boss man, quite a glamorous figure from her point of view. She looks like she has good peasant blood in those sandals, she'd probably think you had every right to ask."

"I see. Droit de Seigneur, and so on?"

"How's that? Well anyhow, let's say she falls in love with you. That could happen even without sex."

"You are very perceptive, BJ. I'm so glad you came."

"That's okay."

"Are you feeling any better now?"

"A little."

He sat down on the other side of the coffee trunk, carefully picked up a magazine and put it down again.

"Listen," he said, "I don't want you to become the wrong impression about my wife. You must think now that I am a very cruel person. But the fact is my wife is an alcoholic. That is why I did not agree to have children. She even allowed her poodle to become run over, so you can imagine how much more dangerous it would be to let her in charge of children."

"How did that happen?"

"She was standing looking into a shop window in Zürich – just where the road was dug up for building work. And a lorry came backwards round the corner straight over him. Apparently he was barking very much, but as usual she took no notice."

"Yuch."

"Yes. She was having to go to the hospital a few days for shock."

"I'm not surprised. I wouldn't even like to see a kid run over if I was standing right there."

"It certainly didn't help her drinking problem. Are you feeling better now?"

"Yes, much."

"You have kept your promise?" He smiled and pointed to the bulging attaché cases that BJ had put down beside the bean bag. "Perhaps we can do business first, and then it will be time for lunch."

BJ laughed. "You're real sweet, Frederick. It's obvious you want to get down to pleasure as soon as possible, but you don't want to cheat me out of the chance of a sale. I appreciate that. But if you want we can go to bed now. The presentation can wait."

Again Herr Tosch looked slightly puzzled. Then he smiled and readjusted his glasses.

"You are most kind, but I am really curious to see you – in action."

"Okay."

BJ at once became very serious and removed the tray of coffee things onto the concrete hearth, and covered the coffee table with literature. The astute commentator on human behaviour and ferret of personal weakness disappeared, and an air of the dedicated kindergarten teacher descended on her as she began the presentation.

BJ had researched Herr Tosch thoroughly, and was able to guide him swiftly to the econometric models that would be of most interest to someone with such diverse pursuits as office furniture and turtles. The turtles were bred in the Philippines, so he also showed a healthy interest in the political risk forecasts.

BJ was enjoying herself. Herr Tosch seemed to assume her place among the elite of those who kept the cash tills ringing round the world, thus allowing people like Philip and Michael, with useless academic talents, to function. This sense that the men in her life were kept, like mistresses, by her and those of her ilk, gave a thrill of domination to their relationship, although she was careful not to discuss this aspect of things with the men in question for fear of crippling their psyches.

"I must congratulate you on your professionalism, BJ," said Herr Tosch when she had finished. "You really know your subject."

"So how about a sale? I can cut the crap with you, Frederick."

"Thank you, thank you. I appreciate your directness. The only trouble is the price: $26,000 for the basic package. This is a lot of money in time of recession. And information becomes so quickly out of date."

"True, but don't forget it's being continuously updated."

"And then I would have to buy a computer."

"No, only an outlet. Perhaps you're not aware how cheap they are these days. You could get one for as little as 2000 francs – probably less than you paid for this redwood junk."

"Well, I will certainly consider it seriously. It will give me an excuse to meet with you again, no?"

"Sure. But as regards mutual pleasure, I suggest you take up your option on that pretty fast. I think I may be pregnant."

"Ah. Congratulations. You will also have to work fast then."

As if acting on her hint, he jumped up. "And now I would like to show you something before we go to lunch. You are, I think, one woman who would be interested. It's my laboratory."

"Your laboratory? Wow. Like Dr Jekyll and Mr Hyde? Let's go."

"I hope you will not be bored. It is my passion."

"I'm never bored by passion."

Intrigued, BJ followed Herr Tosch down into the spacious cellars, past the ski room, the wash room, the atomic shelter room, the drying room, the bicycle room, the lawnmower room and the luggage room.

BJ had difficulty controlling her amusement during the tour of the laboratory. It was full of such clearly phallic symbols. Herr Tosch was a frustrated petrologist, and had caused to be built a number of piston cylinders for heating samples of rock, in order to find out what happened to them. The fat, smooth metal cylinders contained a narrow heating chamber into which a powdered sample was fed in a long piston, and Herr Tosch suggestively demonstrated the insertion and withdrawal of the piston on a couple of cylinders not in use. BJ politely kept up a line of scientific enquiries, since he seemed happier dealing in symbols.

"And does Frau Ruesch help you with this stuff?" asked BJ, after allowing Herr Tosch a decent interval to get a panegyric on the secret life of silicates off his chest.

"Yes, she controls the temperatures and records the data for the samples and so on. Well, thank you for being so patient. But now we must go to lunch."

The only thing that BJ found inconsistent about the incident, reflecting on it as Herr Tosch ushered her into his old-fashioned Porsche, was why he had done the laboratory guide before lunch and not after. In the fuzz of post-prandial intoxication, the business with the erotic cylinders could have led naturally to the real thing.

Time was getting on. It was past one o'clock when they reached the restaurant. Allowing perhaps two hours for a leisurely meal, the afternoon would be nearly gone by the time they had finished, and any hope of a civilized seduction back at the luxury fishtank would be gone with it. From the surreptitious glances at his watch, and the non-sequiturs that could not be attributed to linguistic misunderstandings alone, she realized that she was losing Herr Tosch's attention. Having manoeuvred her into a situation where he was unable to get at her he was projecting his annoyance with himself onto her. It occurred to her that she should not have told him about the pregnancy. His chivalrous attitude to sexual relations with Frau Ruesch in the same condition was no doubt a hangover from the peasant mores of his education, but it almost certainly meant he would be even more circumspect in her case as there was the extra hazard of actually bayoneting the Berkeley heir to death at a delicate stage. "Are you all right, BJ? Perhaps not feeling so well again? You are unusually quiet."

"Well, I gathered you aren't interested in Eritrean batik, and as I

128

can't think of anything else to talk about right now I thought I'd just shut up." She gulped back a knot of tears.

"I am apologizing if I seem not attentive. I will tell you why later. But otherwise you are all right?"

"No, I'm not. I feel fat and ugly and repulsive. Well, I guess I am fat and ugly and repulsive. And please don't tell me I have a pretty face – that always means by implication that the body's a bust."

"All right, then I won't say anything."

His eagerness to oblige verged on downright rudeness, thought BJ.

Herr Tosch had other things on his mind. "Excuse me, don't look round now, but I am trying to get a good look at that man sitting by the window with a woman in a yellow striped knickerbockers. Just very quietly look."

BJ swivelled her eyes towards the couple. "Oh. The one with the red flower hanging into his wine glass?"

"The begonia, yes. He has not yet noticed, he is too fascinated by the lady. Shall I tell you why I am so fascinated also? Because I know this man, and I have never before seen him smiling. I cannot get used – it looks ridiculous, a bit."

"The friendly shark. Do you know that little poem? 'Said the shark to the flying fish over the phone, Come and join me tonight, I am dining –' Oh well. Wait a minute, I have to put my glasses on before I can get a good look."

"Please be discreet. The lady is not his wife."

"Here let's see. Oh-Oh. Is that right? Yes, it is. Holy shit. That's interesting."

"You know him too?"

"I'm pretty sure. His name is Max Baumann, right? He probably doesn't recognize me. I only saw him in his car as I was leaving my friend's house. His wife is a close friend of mine. I'm not at all surprised to see him with someone else."

"Let us not jump to conclusions. It could be a perfectly innocent business lunch."

"Uh-huh. Well it won't be for long. Look at the way he's blushing. Boy, I wish Kirstin could see him now. I don't suppose she's seen him like that since he got his residence permit. I wonder if I should say anything to her."

"No, don't. You don't know for sure that they are having an affair, and his boss is the uncle of his wife, so you could make a lot of trouble for them."

"That wouldn't be such a bad idea. He's a real bastard, actually, but they seem to have this bondage-type relationship which she enjoys, so I guess it would be better not to interfere. You know she's so scared of him she actually suspected he'd been doing the rapes that have occurred in their village. It's just projection in my opinion."

"Oh? I have not read of this."

"It's only a teenager and a middle-aged woman who have been attacked."

"You are very detached."

"Oh well. There are a lot worse fates than rape, I guess. Rape has been put in the limelight by the women's movement, mainly for political reasons. I mean, the same feminist who objects to rape on behalf of her victimized sisters would probably be quite happy to castrate all wolf-whistlers, so – you know. Some women are born victims, anyhow. I'm afraid Kirstin is one of them."

"You talk as if you were safe from attack. Are you never afraid?"

"Not really. For one thing I travel mostly by car, and for another I don't go places alone with people I haven't checked out."

"You came to see me. You did not know I would not be alone."

"I didn't know I would be. I hoped my friend Michael would stay."

"Ah." He smiled. "So you have heard about the terrible murders around here?"

"I beg your pardon?" BJ abruptly put down her fork and felt the mass of risotto al funghi in her stomach scatter and re-form like points in a kaleidoscope. "What murders?"

Herr Tosch sighed. "Teenagers. Little girls. The usual psychotic pattern. Not all in the last week, of course."

"Has it been going on for long then?"

"It comes and goes. I don't mean just in this town. But in the area generally. But there are always unsolved murders, I suppose, in most densely populated areas."

"Yuch. That's terrible. But to tell you the truth," said BJ, neatly pouring off excess salad dressing into an empty glass, "I'm somewhat fascinated by the phenomenon of personal violence as a political statement. It may not be conscious, of course, but I'm sure if one analyzed the pattern it would amount to an interesting reflection of political repression in a society. You only have to look at the States to see that. In many cases it's bad enough to give rise to organized resistance, but if it's only the guys at the bottom of the heap who get the effects of it then it comes out like that – impersonal violence against other individuals. Don't you think so?"

"Yes, I'm sure this theory is well documented. But as I am at the top of the heap it is difficult for me to comment. Is that another reason why you thought you would be safe with me?"

"Frankly, yes. But listen, I don't go around worrying about stuff like that. If anything happened I guess my family would be quite philosophical about it. Well, perhaps not my mother, but mothers generally have a hard time being rational."

Herr Tosch laughed. "It would certainly take at least two strong men to overpower you, BJ. Will you take dessert?"

"I've eaten too much already. If they have Black Forest Cake, yes. This wine is delicious." She drained her glass. Her cheeks and ears were burning. As her nerves were anaesthetized one by one her awareness of the good things around her flooded in – the bourgeois comfort of the room, the food, Herr Tosch's admiration, the independence that allowed her to be there in the first place, the probable sale, her own physical charisma, which she felt to be drawing the envy and desire of every man in the restaurant towards her. Even Max Baumann, she noted, was stealing glances at her. She felt how good it was to be herself.

Herr Tosch was relaxed now also. Perhaps it was enough that she had won his respect and enslaved his imagination. Michael would probably be very upset if she had a sexual relationship with Herr Tosch and might even ignore her for a while. It was not worth that, as Michael was the real quarry.

The Black Forest Cake was brought. Herr Tosch asked if she would like coffee.

"No thank you. Umm. This looks really delicious." She examined it from all angles, nudging at the layers of cream and cherries with her fork, as if seeking some kind of personal relationship with it before consumption. "Actually I think I ought to be going when I've finished this. You've been very generous with your time already."

She relished his look of disappointment.

"No. Why? I know it is late to finish lunch, but I was hoping you would return with me and we could talk about your experiences in America. I mean your business experiences. I was there as a student, you know, and I am always so happy to meet Americans."

"Oh, well –"

"Listen, I was thinking it would be nice if we asked those two also. I will have to speak to him before they leave, and they are just getting now the bill."

"Max Baumann you mean?" This was an interesting turn of events.

"We could open a bottle of good wine, light the fire. It could be nice, don't you think? A little happening, as you would say."

"Uh-huh."

BJ felt a vague unease about this little happening. Could it be that

131

Herr Tosch could only be turned on by group sex? Or by yellow striped knickerbockers. They might well have suggested the idea to him, in which case she would be paired off with the iron businessman, Max Baumann. She looked towards the couple. As she did so she noticed Max glance at Herr Tosch with what she interpreted as a conspiratorial smile. The look suggested a sinister interpretation to BJ. Supposing it was a put-up job? If they knew each other in their business life it was not at all improbable that they shared a taste for diversion from it. Some such arrangement might be a regular feature of Herr Tosch's life. The girl might even be a party to it. No wonder they were laughing.

"What do you say? I have to speak to him now or he will be gone." His look pleaded with her to say yes. "If you are worried about getting back to Zürich I'm sure they would take you in the car. At least as far as Winterthur. Max loves to impress people with his car."

"Thanks, but the fact is I don't feel so good again."

"Oh."

"It must be the fu – pregnancy."

"Oh. Yes. I had forgotten about that."

You sure had, thought BJ, still shaken from the detection of the plot. Herr Tosch's disappointment could not possibly be explained by his having been cheated out of an innocent fireside chat-cum-travelogue.

Max and the young woman came up to them and were introduced by Herr Tosch. BJ was on the point of saying something to Max about Kirstin, but as he heard BJ's name, and realized who she was, his mask of joviality dropped away like a lump of plaster, revealing a look of threatening suspicion that quite took the words from her mouth. She reserved them for a later occasion, making a mental note to ensure that one should arise. Herr Tosch had clearly not told Max the identity of his proposed playmate. Whatever they were saying to each other in German, Max's displeasure had dispersed the atmosphere where further pleasantries were appropriate. Shortly after saying hello they said goodbye.

Despite his disappointment, Herr Tosch's knee-jerk politeness was unaffected. He kissed BJ's hand and wished her many sales, and even offered to accompany her to carry the attaché case when she told him she intended to do some shopping.

"No thanks. It would be so boring for you. I couldn't really enjoy it. And I'm sure you have lots to do."

"Yes. Well, goodbye, BJ. I look forward to hearing from you. Thank you for the visit."

"Likewise the lunch. Listen, I'm sorry if I ballsed up your plans, there, but you know that Baumann guy really isn't my type, and anyway I haven't outgrown one-on-one encounters yet. It's ridiculous, but now I feel guilty about not playing along. You're right, it could have been fun."

"I'm sorry, I do not fully understand you."

"You know, this micro-orgy you had planned for this afternoon. I overreacted. I should have agreed to it. I panicked, actually, it's as simple as that. I'm sorry."

"Please, BJ, what are you saying? Please don't go around saying things like that about me."

"Of course I won't."

"I did not plan anything. Truly, I was just feeling sociable."

"Sure. Okay."

It was natural that Herr Tosch should deny everything as it had not come off, but BJ was sure of her facts. Why else had he crammed the lab. visit into the slot before lunch, if not to clear the way for any orgy afterwards? And the idea that someone like Max Baumann could trigger merely social ripples was of course ridiculous.

After a short walk in the old town BJ gave up the idea of shopping and turned towards the station. The sidewalks were too narrow: she kept knee-capping passers-by with her attaché case. Normally it would have given her some satisfaction to practise her vocabulary of abuse on the people who scolded her for carrying such an object on a public street, but she found that her adrenalin had been exhausted for the day. Then an earnest young man who spoke English came up and said that God was looking for her, at which point she threw in the towel and made for the station.

As the train drew out BJ leant wearily against the window. A man sitting opposite to her looked askance, and knowing that he was about to tell her to sit up straight so as not to break the glass with her head if the train should come to a sudden halt, she closed her eyes and feigned a coma, just as the last letters of ST GALLEN slipped out of her sight.

The image of Max Baumann's hostile face stayed before her eyes. The problem of why she had allowed him to intimidate her did not easily resolve itself: people like Kirstin would never be free if even their emancipated sisters could not stand up to the enemy. Cries of "Chicken!" haunted her as she recalled the paralysing effect of Max's gimlet eye.

In the semi-conscious miasma of images that competed with it, the lettering of ST GALLEN dominated. Then she remembered Herr Tosch talking about the murders.

An appropriate revenge suggested itself. Why not cast suspicion on Max? Anonymously, of course. There was certainly something fishy about his presence in St Gallen with the yellow knickerbockers, and while she did not for a minute suspect him of murder herself it would serve the bastard right if the police made his life difficult for a while. And while they were doing so she would try and fix her business appointment with him, so that she could enjoy the effects of it for herself.

# CHAPTER

# EIGHT

**To: Fr. Kirstin Baumann, Eglikon.**

Highly respected Frau Baumann:

We are in receipt of your letter of 14 ult. in which you request that your failure to lodge objections to the Sectional Plan 125 PBG Gemeinde Eglikon be set aside on humanitarian grounds.

We regret that by a vote of 6:2 it has been decided that your appeal not be granted.

Enclosed please find a bill for 360SF for the transaction.

With friendly greetings,

*The Scrubbing-Out Department.*

**To: Criminal Police Commando, St Gallen**

To whom it may concern:

With reference to recent capital crimes in the St Gallen/Schaffhausen area, I suggest that a Herr Max Baumann (Im Graben 99011 Eglikon) should be investigated. He is frequently in the area, and is well known to have sadistic tendencies and domestic problems. For the sake of his wife, I would urge discretion.

Yours truly,

*A Concerned Citizen.*

## To: Max Baumann, Humbel Brothers, Winterthur.

Highly respected Herr Baumann:

You will no doubt be very surprised to hear from me, as you do not know me, but although we are strangers – at least I have only met you twice – I write as a friend with your interest at heart and the welfare of the community in mind. What I have to say will probably be very annoying to you, and that is why I have put off writing, but now I have consulted the pendulum and it has told me to get on with it.

I have reason to believe that your wife and Dr Ernst Huber are lovers. Unfortunately I am unable to go into details but their behaviour leaves me in no doubt that they are up to something. I thought it would be a good idea if you sorted this out with your wife before it got too serious. I have not yet informed Frau Huber of my suspicions as, with due respect, I think your wife is the guilty party. Up to now Dr Huber has always been a devoted husband and father. I need not remind you about his five delightful sons and what a lot of damage would be caused if this affair got out of hand.

Needless to say I have not informed Dr Huber that I am writing to you, and it would be a good thing if you did not bring it up with him. Being a man, you probably can sympathize with his position.

Lastly I should explain that I am concealing my identity only because I do not want to be accused of betraying professional confidences.

With friendly greetings,

*A Well-Wisher.*

**To Herr Max Baumann, Humbel Brothers, Switzerland.**

Hello Comrade: greetings from Prague! I am so disappointed not to hear from you. Have you forgotten your spring chicken? Spring is coming and birds will soon be on the wing – one way or another.

*Your devoted Elena.*

**To: Herr Max Baumann, Humbel Brothers, Switzerland:**

REGRET TO INFORM YOU THAT ORDER FOR GAS TURBINE PUMPING STATIONS No:685324 CANCELLED DUE TO CHANGES IN GOVERNMENT POLICY. LETTER FOLLOWS.

*Wlodzimierz Wrzaszczyk,*
*Ministry of Foreign Trade and Marine Economy*

# CHAPTER

# NINE

APART FROM the notion of five sons being delightful, Max had no reason to doubt the truth of Fraulein Schupisser's letter, which was on his desk one Monday morning. It took him about ten seconds to deduce the identity of the "well-wisher".

After reading the letter he tried to concentrate on the subject of the Fraulein, her motives, opportunities and trustworthiness, in order to put off for as long as possible thinking about the contents. He also wanted to bring under control his racing pulse and the initial instinct to storm into the secretary's office and hoof the word-processor through the window. Max was unused to being confused and he was anxious to sort out his thoughts before someone came in and found him in anything less than perfect control. He practised a few of the concentration exercises he had learnt at night school in order to help him lecture to his East European customers.

Feeling slightly calmer he returned to his desk and to calculating a payment scheme for the sale of five controllable-pitch propellers to the Albanian navy. The work began to clear his mind. His initial reaction had been shock at not reacting more glibly to the news. He had never considered that Kirstin had the guts to have an affair: he would have been less surprised to learn that Mother Theresa of Calcutta was having an affair with her doctor. In a way it was good news. It would make straight the path to Annalie Schumacher, who seemed quite keen on him, besides frequently asking him over to her studio apartment for sex. Although Annalie was so rigid about separating work from pleasure he could not quite make her out. He would have thought a woman in love would have somewhat less control over herself, that she would be continually thinking up endearing little queries about foreign exchange rates or piston casings in order to come and see him. As it was, he was obliged, as now, to call her himself if he wanted to see her. It seemed like a good idea to take her into his confidence about Fraulein Schupisser's letter. One reason for her rather unflattering self-control might be the assumption that there was no future in the relationship as he was married. If he could raise hope in that direction she might be less secretive about her actual feelings for him. Besides, he had to talk to someone: his attitude to the new situation needed to acquire the irrevocability of public statement.

While he was waiting for her he rehearsed in his mind how best to make the fact of Kirstin's infidelity sound like good news. Try as he might, he could not feel as positive about it as he intended to sound to Annalie Schumacher. Of course, there was a natural element of sentimentality in his reaction, of regret for the time when Kirstin's beauty had inflamed his blood and his prospects for residential qualification. There was also an element of sheer disbelief. Was it some devious rite of passage laid on by Kirstin's hormones to provoke him into giving her a child and re-possessing her in that way in the eyes of society? If so, her hormones were going to be disappointed. He looked forward to seeing her reaction when he told her that he was moving in with Annalie Schumacher and her passion for another man left him completely unmoved. It might even have been true if she had taken up with a nameless stud. But Dr Huber was a prominent member of the community, a pure-blooded Swiss, a captain in the army, and in receipt of a good income - better than Max's – besides inherited wealth from the sanitary equipment business. Max was troubled by the idea that, all things considered, Dr Huber had the right to nobble Kirstin, a kind of *droit de docteur* rarely exercised, but inherent in the absurd servile respect that doctors commanded, at least among women. He felt not unlike a Germanic chieftain of old who was well in command of his own territory, but obliged to offer his woman to any passing marauder who had more cooking pots and *comitates* than he did.

There was a knock on the door. Max smoothed his hair and prepared to smile, but it was only the secretary, Frau Enge, a small, timid woman whom he had chosen for her potential for failing to distract him from his work.

"What is it, Frau Enge?"

"Just some more mail, Herr Baumann." She handed it to him. "And er –"

"And what?"

"There is a person waiting to see you now."

"What person?"

"That policeman." She blushed. "He says it won't take long."

"Jesus. You'd better send him in. Oh, and I've sent a message for Fraulein Schumacher to come up. Could you please apologise for me and say I'll be available in half an hour."

"Yes, of course."

Frau Enge went out, and a moment later the young punk who had previously interviewed Max came in. They shook hands and Max ungraciously asked him to sit down. "I'd have thought you would have graduated to traffic duty by now," he said.

"Very droll, Herr Baumann. But traffic's a different department."

"I see. Well, what do you want this time?"

"Just wanted to check up on a few dates, Herr Baumann. I understand you were in St Gallen on January 5th?"

"Yes. So?"

"May I ask you what you were doing there?"

"May I ask you who was raped there on January 5th?"

"Nobody that we know of."

"Murdered?"

"No."

"Kidnapped? Tarred and feathered?"

"I don't know. I don't have the statistics with me."

"Then why do you have to know what I was doing there?"

"I can find out from other sources if you are unwilling to co-operate." He rose to go.

"Oh sit down, for God's sake. It makes me nervous, you jumping up and down like a cork."

"You're nervous, Herr Baumann?"

"Of course not. I've had a trying morning, that's all."

"But it's only eight-thirty."

"I rise at five-fifteen."

"May I ask what you do between getting up at five-fifteen and coming to work?"

"In summer I jog. In winter I rape snow ploughs."

"You seem to have rape on the brain, Herr Baumann."

"Only when I'm with you." Max was pleased with the course of the conversation so far.

"I see. Well if you'll just give me the name and address of the firm you visited in St Gallen, I'll be on my way."

"Wettstein AG. I saw a Herr Sonderegger."

"And did you come straight back to the office?"

"No. I had lunch with a colleague who accompanied me."

"Could I have his name?"

"Annalie Schumacher."

"And is she in the building at the moment?"

"Yes. Second floor. Third right when you come out of the lift."

"Do you often have to go to St Gallen, Herr Baumann?"

"No."

"Was that the only occasion within the last year?"

"No."

"Do you know people there? Did you meet anyone else while you were there?"

"No – yes. On the last occasion I met an acquaintance, Frederick Tosch, at lunchtime in The Old Grapes."

"I see."

"Is that all?"

The young punk was lost in thought for a few moments, so that Max had to repeat the question.

"Sorry," he said. "It's like this. I'd be obliged if you would come down to the station and clarify a few points in your previous statement. And would you have any objection to having your fingerprints electronically recorded?"

"I most certainly would."

"It would be very unpleasant if we had to get a court order."

"Oh – very well. What an infernal waste of time."

"We're actually wasting less time this way."

"Don't expect me to be grateful."

Max strode ahead of the young punk and got into his own car. On the drive into Winterthur he mentally drafted a vitriolic letter or two to the police commissioners on the subject of harassing innocent citizens. Or rather, innocent aliens. He cursed. Despite his anxiety for a residence permit, Max had been reluctant to change his passport. He considered that the Second World War should have signalled the end of passports, and the beginnings of world brotherhood. He had originally thought of Switzerland as a little pocket of brotherly freedom where one could practise the principles which would eventually ripple out over the entire globe. But in fact it was more like a fortified Shangri-La whose defences were being continually strengthened against the ravening hordes fighting to get in. He had only recently decided to settle for Shangri-La.

Shortly after Max had left for police headquarters, Frau Enge took delivery of the telex from the Polish Ministry of Foreign Trade and Marine Economy. Flustered, she took it into Max's office and left it on his desk, thinking that he had only gone to the bathroom. She returned to her typewriter, for show only. It was impossible to concentrate until the impact of the telex on Max's steely bosom had been weathered. She was embarrassed in advance for his inability to show the slightest emotion in the face of such a humiliating blow. Frau Enge, who wrote romantic paperbacks as a hobby, sighed, reflecting that the tree that will not bend with the wind will be felled by its wrath. And besides the reversal in Max's personal fortune which the cancellation signalled, there was the worrying fact that thousands of families in the area relied on Max and his colleagues to bring home the bacon, and they were getting pretty desperate for new sources.

When Max did not reappear, Frau Enge could bear it no longer. Someone had to be told. She took the telex in to Max's boss, Herr Waldvogel, placing it discreetly on the desk and withdrawing.

In her overwrought state she failed to notice that she had also picked up the postcard from Prague and put it on Herr Waldvogel's desk under the telex.

Max was at the traffic lights by the municipal baths when he realized to his annoyance that he did not know where they were going. The young punk was behind him and Max signalled to him to overtake.

They drove to an office building set back in guileless pleasantry behind a gravel drive and flower beds set with violent magenta and kumquat orange pansies. He recognized the place with relief. He knew the building by sight as he had come to a neighbouring office to get his bicycle licence. Max had done his military service in Germany, a rigorous programme in those days, but still, it had not prepared him for interrogation in some underground bunker that would have disappeared when one came along with a left-wing reporter to find it again. One never knows, although Max knew a couple of senior police officers socially through the handball club and they seemed quite normal. The humdrum surroundings further reassured him that it was all a fuss about nothing that was beneath his serious engagement. He consequently tried to adopt an air of Olympic detachment as he followed the young punk, hoping he looked like a building inspector.

On the second floor he was shown into a room and asked to wait for a few moments. It was a bare room furnished with a table, a few chairs and a filing cabinet. A girl he recognized from Eglikon was sitting by the window. She was wearing motor-cycle leathers and pale blue dancing shoes and chewing gum, the movement of her jaw regularly wriggling her close-cropped scalp. She looked blankly at Max as he sat down.

"Hello," he said. "You're from Eglikon, aren't you? I'm afraid I've forgotten your name."

"Rosa Pagliacci. You live up by the Umbergs, don't you?"

"That's right. Baumann." He shook her hand and sat down again in the furthest corner of the room.

"What do they want you for, then?" she asked.

"I've no idea. Just routine, I suppose. What about you?"

"I'm supposed to be looking at some pictures. They put me in here about an hour ago. I'm fed up."

"I see. Were you the girl who was attacked?"

"Yes. Do they suspect you?"

"I hardly think so, or they wouldn't have put me in here with you, would they? I suppose they're just checking all able-bodied males."

Fraulein Pagliacci snorted. "Well this one wasn't. He couldn't screw a fly to the wall. He crashed his car into me bike and I was so dazed I couldn't use my self-defence. I could've finished him if I had."

"You know perfectly well who it is, don't you? Why don't you tell them, for God's sake? Good God, what a ridiculous situation."

"Hey, steady on. I didn't say I knew him."

"But you do, don't you?"

"No."

"I don't believe you."

"Suit yourself." Fraulein Pagliacci's gum-chewing had speeded up to an angry yap. Her beautiful half-Italian eyes were troubled. For a few minutes she chewed and sighed and cast sidelong, anxious glances at Max. Then she said, "Well, what do you expect? I can't turn him over to the police at his age, can I? I can't be responsible for that. He'll be dead soon, probably. Well, we all will, won't we? Nothing really matters."

"Your philosophy does you credit, Fraulein, but why the fu– , I mean, why report it in the first place if you intended to protect him?"

"I didn't intend to. It was my stupid mother. I told her I had to have a day-after pill quick, and I suppose I did look a bit mauled about."

"But you didn't tell her the identity of your attacker?"

"No. Not her. Well I was confused, wasn't I? Old Umberg was in a

143

right state afterwards, blubbering and whatnot. He offered me fifty francs not to say anything. I ask you! Kept going on about his wife. I just couldn't do it."

"If you ask me he's a totally unscrupulous operator – raping young women and then using his wife's illness to play on their sympathies. And what about the other woman? Or women. Who knows where it will end?"

"Look, I'm not in the security business. That's their job." She jerked a derogatory head towards the door.

"But you don't mind if the police work it out for themselves. That way your conscience will be clear and the problem removed. What loony sentimentality."

She shrugged. "It's their job. I hate the police. Do you know what they did to my boyfriend?"

"No." Nor was he sure he wanted to. From the vicious look on her face he imagined the youth dangling by a wire hook through the back of the neck at the very least.

"They were doing spot checks on the motorway and he got hauled in for a broken indicator, and they deliberately delayed him so long he missed the Rolling Stones concert in Basel!" Tears of rage trembled at the memory.

"I see. This is a revenge tragedy, is it? Whatever your motives, Fraulein, you could still be prosecuted for deliberately protecting a criminal. Hadn't you thought of that?"

"Eh?" She clearly had not. "Surely I can do what I like with my own crime?"

"Of course not. How can you be so stupid? He's a danger to society, not just to you."

"Well – I'll just say I was too shocked to notice what he looked like. I'll say I just blotted it out. Well, that's what I've said anyway."

"On oath?"

"Well, *you* shop him then!"

"How can I? I have no evidence."

"So? You're his neighbour, you could say he's been acting suspiciously. You could make an anonymous telephone call. Speak through the wrong end of a vermicelli squeezer. Then they'll pull him in and examine his semen and things."

Max took a sharp breath to reply, but remained silent. Fraulein Pagliacci's grasp of the grubby end of the business had arrested his indignation with an image of Herr Umberg, shackled and probably blubbering for his wife, taken to some basement interrogation chamber and made to squirt a sample into a police test-tube. He told himself that it was no more than justice, but the image upset him. He, Max, was getting old. He was not sure that he could live with his conscience either if he led the police to Herr Umberg.

Anger at being placed in such a dilemma began to dominate the internal conflict: anger at Fraulein Pagliacci, principally, for allowing him to become so involved, anger at Herr Umberg for being protected by his senility, anger at getting old.

"It's all your fault," he shouted at her. "Why don't you have the guts to take the consequences of your stupidity?"

"Will you stop shouting! They'll hear."

"That's your problem. I've got nothing to hide." Except Annalie Schumacher. He started worrying again. Supposing she got to hear about the police interest in him? Although there was not a shred of truth in it, the fastidious Annalie might decide that even the shadow left a stain. He wanted to rush back to the office and overwhelm her with his innocence and general niceness. The frustration of hanging around was extreme. He got up and went to the door and looked up and down the corridor. An unidentified person strolled past and smiled and disappeared into another office.

"God damn it, how long are we going to have to wait here?"

"Don't get excited, it'll make them more suspicious."

"Of what? I'm innocent. And I don't need advice from you, thank you."

"Suit yourself."

They ground their jaws for a few minutes in silence.

"Do you suppose they've forgotten us?" said Fraulein Pagliacci.

"No. They probably intend to keep us here so long that I get frustrated enough to rape you anyway, and then they can stick the whole thing on me."

She giggled. "If you gave me some warning it might not be necessary."

Max looked at her suspiciously. Was she a decoy set by the police to trap him? From the inane way she was grinning at him and trying to make her two centimetres of hair dangle alluringly over one eye, he rather thought not.

He tried to make his eyes glaze over with their usefully frosty menace. "I think you had better watch what you are saying, young lady."

"Suit yourself. But it would be a laugh, wouldn't it, if they came in and found us banging away on the rug out of sheer boredom. Well, I mean, it could happen, couldn't it? They don't even give you any magazines like they do at the doctor's."

"Do you think that would be the result if the doctor did not provide magazines?"

Fraulein Pagliacci laughed till the tears ran and eventually slumped into her seat, whooping and wiping her face on her sleeve. "You're all right, you know, Herr Baumann. Quite a laugh in fact." He grunted. "But still, you'd better be watching what you say round here as well. They've probably got the place wired up."

"Concealed microphones? Don't be fanciful, Fraulein. You must watch too much television."

"I wouldn't be surprised, though. Why do you think they got us in here together? To see if you were the bloke they're looking for, of course. If you were, I'd probably break down and beg to be let out, wouldn't I?"

"Ridiculous. It was just coincidence."

"Suit yourself."

"You watch too much television."

"Will you shut up! You have no idea how much television I watch!"

"I'm sorry."

"You think just because I'm a woman I'm an idiot."

"Not necessarily." He thought it better to conciliate her. It would be no joke if she tried to put some of her fantasies into practice. "But it seems to me there is nowhere in this room to conceal microphones."

She shrugged. "What about the filing cabinet?"

"Go and have a look, then."

She sauntered over and tried all the drawers, then looked behind the cabinet. "There are no wires coming out."

"Of course there aren't. Haven't you ever heard of batteries? They'd hardly leave wires for us to trip over. Try the drawers in the table." She might have a point. One never knew.

"Nothing here."

"Behind the curtains?"

"No."

"Well, there's no point in looking. They could be using something the size of a pinhead these days."

"Get away!" She threw herself back in the chair. "Oh boring, boring. Fancy missing school for this."

"Are you still at school? You look about twenty-five."

"Thanks." She blushed. "Only for a few more weeks, though. Then I'll be – available."

"Hadn't you better watch what you're saying?"

"Oh, yes. The cunning bastards." She sat up, alarmed. "We didn't mention any names, did we?"

"I don't think so. But you admitted knowing who did it."

"Yes, I did, didn't I. Oh the cunning bastards! What will happen? Will I have to go on trial?"

"Yes, I should think so."

"Oh no. Now what will happen? I'm so fed up. I want to go home. I want my mum." She burst into hysterical sobs, producing a large tie-'n-dye cloth to press to her face.

Max slithered over to the seat beside her and put his arm round her shoulders. "There, there. Calm down. Of course the place isn't bugged. I'm sure it's illegal. And anyway, the case isn't important enough. You'll just have to make a clean breast of it. Herr – you know – he'll be well taken care of. There's nothing to worry about. The police will be only too glad to close the case I'm sure. There, there."

She was gasping and gulping convulsively, her lips drawn back over her lower teeth in a gesture that reminded him of a two-year-old nephew in a similar abandoned state after having had his Smarties confiscated in a public restaurant. He directed Fraulein Pagliacci towards his chest, murmuring reassurances and patting her face and head. It was an odd collection of surfaces, the horsey roughness of her hair, the hot twisting protruberances of ear, the soft pulsating spaces of her neck. He felt the dreaded thrust of desire for the body in his arms, and the panic increased with the need to put a space between himself and temptation.

He tried standing up, but without his support she fell off the chair onto the floor and assumed a foetal convulsion. He grabbed hold of some of the overlapping leather scales of her jacket and tried hauling her to her feet.

"Now stop this, Fraulein, or I'll have to get someone to deal with you. Stop it!" He shook her hard.

"Excuse me –"

The young punk and a policewoman had come in unnoticed and, acting with the swiftness of a golden retriever, the young man was prising Max off Fraulein Pagliacci and into a stranglehold.

The shock brought Fraulein Pagliacci to her senses. She jumped up and went for the young punk. "Get off!" The policewoman attempted to restrain her. "Leave him alone! What are you doing?"

"Wasn't he attacking you?"

"No, he was just trying to be nice."

"That's how it starts very often," said the policewoman, eyeing Max coldly.

"Jealous?" said Fraulein Pagliacci.

"That's enough of that, Fraulein."

The young punk released Max reluctantly.

"You'd better get yourself a lawyer," said Max darkly to him, as he dusted himself off.

"I wouldn't overreact if I were you, Herr Baumann. The circumstances were quite sufficient to justify suspicion."

"There were no circumstances. This young woman had become hysterical and I was just trying to calm her down."

"Why had she become hysterical?" asked the policewoman.

"Because of the intolerable stress of being kept waiting in this hole, of course. She's scarcely more than a child. She should never have been brought here alone."

"She volunteered. Her mother is working."

"Then you should have chosen a time when she wasn't."

The policewoman and the young punk eyed each other. "The delay was unavoidable. I'm very sorry if it caused the young lady any stress." The shade of a police torture scandal, as it might appear in the pages of the local tabloid, softened her tone.

"We can arrange for a car to take the young lady home," offered the young punk.

"No thanks."

"Are you sure you're all right?"

"Yes."

"You can go now then," said the policewoman. "If you like." She smiled. "Have a nice afternoon."

"Huh! What about the pictures?"

Again the two of them exchanged a glance.

"Another time," said the policewoman. "You're too upset now."

"Huh." Fraulein Pagliacci stormed out without shaking hands.

"All right, Herr Baumann? Sorry about that. We're trained to react fast, you know."

"So is a mousetrap. It's no indication of brain size."

"That's –"

"Don't that's-enough-of-that-Fraulein me. I'm leaving."

"We've still got a few questions about your statement."

"My what?"

"It won't take long."

"No, it won't."

The young punk led Max to another office, where inconsistencies in his fabricated evening with Annalie Schumacher were ironed out. He supposed they had checked with her, and that she must already know that he was under suspicion. It took slightly longer to clear up Max's activities in St Gallen, as he had absolutely no idea what they were on about, and suffered the indignity of having his fingerprints recorded like someone who has been coerced into appearing on *The Muppet Show*.

After he had signed the statements he threw the ballpoint pen contemptuously onto the desk.

"For your information," he said, "everyone in the village knows who is responsible for the attacks, so why you can't find out beats me."

"I wouldn't be so sure that we haven't."

"Then why drag me into it?"

"We received information that suggested that line of enquiry."

"What information?"

"That's confidential, Herr Baumann."

Max paled. Someone – someone in the village? – some nameless person, had denounced him. One of those he occasionally nodded to, even.

"You're not telling me that you'd be carrying on like this if I were a citizen."

"That's very unfair, Herr Baumann. We make no distinction."

"Huh."

When Max emerged into the watery sunshine and the wind-ruffled pansies and the parked cars, nose to tail, like elephants, he was trembling and cold. He stood on the step, belting his coat up, bereft of an instinct for what to do.

It was nearly eleven o'clock. No point in going back to the office, he would only arrive in time for lunch. Besides he wanted to decontaminate himself before returning to the haunts of Fraulein Schumacher, Frau Enge and his boss.

He frowned as he noticed Fraulein Pagliacci lolling against his BMW. The leathers on her moist haunches might leave a stain.

"You haven't been waiting for me all this time, have you?" he asked.

"Yes. Just wanted to make sure you're all right."

"Thank you. I'm perfectly all right."

"They didn't say anything more about me, did they? I don't suppose it was bugged, was it?"

"Of course not. I told you so."

"That's a relief."

"But I still think it would be best if you made a clean breast of it."

"That's easy for you to say. You worried about your wife, or something?"

"My wife?"

149

"You know – the blonde."

Max blushed. "No. Why should I be?"

"Well, I would be. With old Umberg right next door. In fact, I wondered if I ought to warn her."

"My wife is aware of the danger, thank you."

"Well anyway, my Dad had a talk with Umberg. Got a bit tough, you know. With any luck he'll take the hint and keep himself to himself in future."

"I thought you hadn't told your parents who it was?"

"Just my Dad. I can talk to him much better. Besides, somebody had to put an oar in, didn't they? I'm not stupid, despite your doubts on the subject. My Dad's good at that sort of thing."

"Yes, I can imagine."

The Fraulein's Dad was a morose gravel-pit operative who looked as if he strangled bulldogs to keep fit. Max was rather incredulous at the idea of his having a side cuddly enough to win the confidence of a sharp little tyke like Fraulein Pagliacci. He had also been robbed, he now realized, of a chance to reduce Herr Umberg to a tearful jelly himself, which would have given him the thrill of doing something useful for the community.

"I'm glad to hear it. But if there is any more trouble, there must be no more nonsense about covering up. Understand?"

She turned away. "You don't impress me, Herr Baumann. You're quite different out here, but in there I saw your knees knocking like billiard balls. You can't threaten me."

"I'm just advising you."

"Well don't bother. Ciao."

"Wait a minute." He could not have her spreading stories like that. He was alarmed by the appalling rudeness of her observations. He was sure that at her age he would have been far too polite to notice his elder's weak points. It went against the grain but he felt he had to sweet-talk her a little. He followed her towards the road and put a hand on her arm.

"Now don't be a silly young person. I'm just trying to give you some friendly advice."

"Well I don't need it."

"That's possible. I'm sorry if my manner offends you, but I have other things on my mind besides this absurd business – problems at work and so on, that a young person like yourself couldn't possibly imagine. If I appeared to be tense in there, that's the reason. It has nothing to do with this ridiculous investigation."

"Okay. Forget it."

"Just promise me that if you hear of any more trouble you will at least let me try to persuade you to co-operate with the police."

Fraulein Pagliacci grinned. "And how would you do that?"

"I don't know yet."

"Tell you what, I'll give you a clue. Take me down to Möwenpick and buy me a Swiss Chocolate Doodle, and I'm yours."

"I beg your pardon?"

"I'm hungry. I've been upset, too, you know. I need a treat to calm my nerves."

"Well why don't you go home and read a magazine?"

"Eh? Is that what you'd do? Oh, go on. Let's go."

"You're a very changeable young person. I don't understand you."

"Will you stop calling me a young person!"

"I'm sorry. But you are one, so why should it upset you?"

"You make it sound like a cut of meat."

"Do I? I'm sorry."

"Oh come on, you silly old fart. We'll just get there before the rush."

She took him by the arm and steered him back to the car.

It was as well that she was in such a chatty mood and could entertain herself, for Max needed all his energy to cope with the humiliation of escorting this monstrously juvenile bikie for an ice cream. He calculated that he would be in her presence for at least another hour and a quarter, and could only be grateful that the venue she had chosen was one where he was the least likely to run into any acquaintances. Having no children, he was unaware that most of his acquaintances took theirs for a Swiss Chocolate Doodle every Sunday. As it was, he was stiff with repulsion as he followed Fraulein Pagliacci into the popular roadhouse, his eyes darting about for signs of people collapsing with laughter over their Hawaian Pineapple Burgers at the sight of him.

He led Fraulein Pagliacci to a shady booth where the table was decorated with the plastic flag of Möwenpick Enterprises. He toyed with a black tea while she pored over the selection of lurid sundaes and chattered on about her Christmas holiday with relatives in Calabria. When the Doodle came he interrupted the flow to give her a lecture about the body's sugar-insulin chemistry and the artificial craving for carbohydrates promoted by lipoprotein lipase in those who foolishly tried to correct overeating by dieting, and suggested that she could well have a genetic deficiency of serotonin if Swiss Chocolate Doodles were a regular part of her diet, because besides making people crave chocolate sundaes it could account for her highly nervous behaviour.

When he had finished she told him about her dishy Uncle Mario, who was a policeman and had been present at the arrest of Paul Getty's grandson's kidnappers. Max stopped trying to make conversation. Talking to her was like being forced to listen to the plot of *Dallas*.

He got up to put on his coat while Fraulein Pagliacci was still scooping the dregs out of her dish.

"How are you going to get home?" he enquired, as they emerged into the wind that whistled round the roadhouse. Like citadels of yore it was built on a promontory commanding the main road – a six-lane motorway in this case.

"Eh? Well, that's nice. I can hardly walk up the motorway, can I?"

"I'm afraid I can't take you. I've got to get back to work."

"Can't you even take me back into Winterthur?"

"It's out of my way."

"Charming. All right, if you're going to be like that I'll hitch and get murdered, probably. And don't forget you'll have been the last person to see me alive." She laughed. "The police are going to think that's just a bit too much of a coincidence, aren't they?"

"Oh, very well. I'll take you into Winterthur." Max was secretly relieved that she had pointed out this bizarre eventuality. As an added precaution he got out of the car with her when they reached the station and, in full view of a group of fascinated Japanese businessmen who would, he thought, be easy to trace in an emergency, he kissed her woolly-mittened hand and made an effort to smile. Fraulein Pagliacci stared and slowly blushed.

"No hard feelings, Fraulein."

"Better luck next time. Ciao."

Anxious to get back and catch up on the day's work, he triggered off a speed trap which immortalized the BMW's rear end on a photograph which the telltale flash warned him to expect a couple of days later, together with a demand for the fine, in true blackmailing style. He had accumulated so many of these photographs that he had started making them up into Christmas cards for his particular friends at the Elks. He did not have that many particular friends, so another photograph was a major irritation.

He stopped at a kiosk to buy two packets of chocolate peanuts in lieu of lunch and ate them in the car. He knew they would give him heartburn, but he was so hungry he could not resist. He recalled that there were several essential B vitamins in peanuts.

Everyone was out to lunch when he got back to the office. Annalie had left a message on his desk that she was terribly busy at the moment, but would meet him in the foyer at 5 o'clock. It was just as well. He needed to immerse himself in work for an hour or two, to be in the right frame of mind for his meeting with his boss, Herr Waldvogel, at four. It would probably be a difficult meeting. The glory in which he had basked since landing the Polish pumping stations contract was beginning to fade. A couple of important prospective orders that Max was in pursuit of had fallen through, mainly, according to Max, as a result of Herr Waldvogel's inflexible pricing policy, and according to Herr Waldvogel as a result of leaks of said policy from Max's office. Herr Waldvogel seemed insufficiently aware of the frustrations of trying to sell multi-million dollar equipment to bankrupt governments. If only he could be transferred to the Middle East he would be sure of a turn-around, besides the suntan and the excuse to stay away longer.

He did a few callisthenics exercises before getting down to work, but was interrupted by Frau Enge as soon as she came back from lunch. "Herr Baumann, your appointment is here, Frau Berkeley."

"Who?"

"An American lady."

"I haven't got time to see her now."

"But she did make an appointment, Herr Baumann. She's come from Zürich."

"Oh very well."

"And Herr Baumann, you will remember to see Herr Waldvogel at four, won't you?"

"Christ. When am I supposed to get some work done? I'm off to Hungary in the morning."

"I think you'd better see Herr Waldvogel before you go."

"All right, I'm not deaf."

BJ was hovering behind Frau Enge. She assessed the incipient rejection situation and quickly stepped into the room and shook hands with Max.

"Hello, Max. It's good of you to see me. Don't worry, this won't take long. I realize I should probably have gone straight to your boss, but as I'm so friendly with Kirstin I thought it would be appropriate to approach you first. I have a lot of respect for Kirstin. She has a sensational body."

Max stared at her.

"I guess you've forgotten why I'm here," continued BJ. "Well, I can make things real short. Here, this is our company." She laid on the desk the glossy brochure showing on the cover a collage of shirt-sleeved young wasp executives in dynamic huddles on, around or near a computer outlet. Max did not even glance at it.

BJ already felt herself beginning to panic in the face of his mesmerizing coldness. She avoided looking at him as she talked.

"As you see from the brochure, we offer a number of analytical services, but it would help me a lot if you could give me a brief outline of your operations here. I understand this is the diesel department."

She looked around. There was not even a photograph of a generating station to brighten the place up.

"And you handle the East European market. Our company has unusually good access to information in the communist bloc. I think maybe we could be a real help on the market penetration problems over there."

Max glanced down at the brochure and briefly looked through it. BJ was slightly encouraged.

After a moment's silence Max said, "Frau Berkeley, I am telling you only one thing. I do not want that you are seeing my wife any more now. I want that you do not get in touch with her again."

"I beg your pardon?" BJ blinked and twitched her head. "I don't believe this. What are you saying?"

"My wife is a rather weak person and she should not be associating with persons like you. It does not help her cope with her life."

"She is not a weak person! You're crazy. And anyway, what do you mean, persons like me? You know nothing about me."

"I am not having to know about you. I only have to know the influence of you on my wife."

"What influence?"

"Before she is knowing you she was quite happy. Now she is making difficulties all the time and is not happy. You are not good for her."

"Now listen. Now you just listen." BJ was so shocked she could hardly speak. "In the first place, I hardly know your wife. I've met her a couple of times to talk and that's it. Second of all, you have absolutely no right – no right whatever, to tell me who I may or may not see. Third of all, if Kirstin is going through an identity crisis it's pure coincidence that I happened to come along at the same time. And anyway what the shit kind of relationship do you have that you think you can control her like this? It's bizarre – it – it's sick. Truly, I think you're sick. You should get professional counselling. If my husband behaved like this I'd leave him at once."

"Lucky man."

"Now listen." BJ rose, clenching her fist on the desk. "Now you listen. I get it. I'm not going to allow you to provoke me, but I tell you something, I only have to tell my husband about this and I tell you he

154

weighs around two hundred fifty pounds and he's in excellent shape I only have to tell him about this and you'd better watch out I tell you."

"This is, of course, typical. You think you can come in and do a man's job and you get into difficulties and are at once threatening me with your husband. Even Kirstin would not presume to do this."

"Well she probably knows better than to go on a fool's errand."

Max stood up. "What are you saying, please?"

"What I'm saying is, that as long as Kirstin is fool enough to stay married to you, you're entitled to come down on her as hard as you like, if she'll take it. But don't try it on me, that's all. I'll go on seeing Kirstin if I wish, and there's nothing you can do about it."

"We shall see."

"Are you threatening me? Oh now really. Don't bother, okay? Just don't bother. I'll go now. I can see I'm wasting my time. Thanks for letting me come out here for nothing. Thanks a lot. You're missing something, you know. This isn't some crackpot encyclopedia outfit that's going out of business in a couple of months. It's you people over here who are going to go out of business if you don't catch on to this kind of technology and I'll enjoy watching it, you're all so fucking smug over here."

"You are deceiving yourself, Frau Berkeley. We already have this kind of technology."

"And the data to go with it? Don't tell me a crummy outfit like this has people all over the world servicing data."

"We don't need to know everything that is going on all over the world. Everyone all over the world knows about us, that is the point."

"Everyone who runs a diesel engine, maybe, but what's the point of that if they aren't buying them? I know this department's running at a loss, don't put on a show for me."

"I suppose you think you could turn that around." They had both resumed their seats.

"Yes, as a matter of fact, I might just be able to do that. I think I know enough about sales work to do that."

"And diesel engines? Do you know enough about that, too?"

"That's irrelevant. Anyone can be trained to use a slide rule."

Max smiled. He leaned back with his hands in his pockets. "So now you are threatening me. You think you can take over my job."

"No. All I'm saying is, I wouldn't be so complacent about it if I were you. I mean, with the kind of services we offer, and a reasonable knowledge of the product, I would be able to perform your function perfectly well. Okay, laugh. I know you have to have three years of college to sell chestnuts here, but that doesn't mean it's necessary."

"Is this the way you normally sell your product, Mrs Berkeley?"

"No. Normally I deal with reasonable people who appreciate what I'm doing." She put the brochures back in her briefcase and stood up.

"So you have a lot of success in Switzerland?"

"Not as much as I'd hoped. But that's okay. One never does. Frankly I attribute that to the poor quality decision-making skills in the people in key positions over here. They're so shit scared of making a mistake, nobody can make up their minds about anything."

Max nodded. "It is good of you to try and help."

"Well, you know the new religion – America helps those who help themselves. One can only do so much."

"Are you sure you are correctly analysing your low sales, Mrs Berkeley?"

"What do you mean?"

"You are blaming the ignorance of the customer, not yourself."

"I've thought about that, actually. But the fact is all customers are ignorant. And I did real well back in the States, so what am I supposed to think?"

"Perhaps you should do something about your appearance."

"My what!" BJ fell back on the chair.

"Your appearance. You know, you are looking rather old-fashioned – the hair lacquer, and this little necktie, and the suit – like a British Airways cabin attendant. Perhaps it creates not a good impression."

"Why you – you – you – How dare you criticize my appearance! I've been praised from coast to coast for my dress sense!"

"By men who wear checkered trousers?" Max smiled.

BJ stood up again and picked up her case, desperate to get out and past the secretary before the tears flowed. "I don't think we can have anything else to say to each other, Herr Baumann. Good day."

"Goodbye, Mrs Berkeley. And please remember what I say to you about my wife."

"Ditto my husband," she managed to gasp before slamming out of the room.

Max tried to return to his calculations as if nothing had happened. He considered that he had dealt with Frau Berkeley as he had intended to. But what with the police, the peanuts and the slight unpleasantness of the interview, he could not concentrate as usual. He needed a change of scene. He packed up his papers for the Hungarian trip. Frau Enge was on the phone. He muttered something about an acupuncture appointment and, ignoring her frantic gesticulations, left the building and drove to Zürich.

# CHAPTER

# TEN

WHEN MAX got to Zürich he remembered that he had arranged to meet Annalie Schumacher at five. It was now twenty past. Too late to phone. One did not expect a girl like that to wait more than five minutes.

Cursing, he walked towards the Niederdorf. It was crowded. Women with toddlers in pushchairs jostled with prostitutes in thigh-length boots and the oriental businessmen in their wake. The fast-food outlets and pizzerias were peppered among sex shops and porn cinemas in an equal mix with shops selling model railways, Art Deco lamps and umbrellas.

Max went into a bar for a drink. He ordered a Campari or two and sat in a corner, feeling condescending about the lonely flotsam that made up the bar's clientèle. Then he noticed the girl behind the bar smiling at him in a pitying, motherly kind of way. Infuriated, he got up and went out, leaving his third Campari half-finished.

It was still only six-thirty. No good going home at the height of the rush hour. There seemed only two alternatives – go into a homemade pasta shop and buy some tortellini, or watch a striptease. He went and bought the tortellini. Then he came out and went into a striptease. He ordered a large whisky and watched someone called Sharon La Vérité go through a routine with a lot of nun's veils, with a black man with a whip dressed up as an ayatollah. He felt himself aroused, not by the girl, who was skinny and blonde and reminded him of Kirstin, but by the thought of what those lucky bastards could do to their women if they wanted to. He ordered some more whisky. What would he not give to be able to ship off B.J. Berkeley and Fraulein Pagliacci and even the super-smooth Annalie Schumacher for a fortnight's behavioural correction in a Teheran jail. He did not wait for the next act, but decided to leave while he was still enjoying himself.

Before he even got out of the car in his garage, he was aware of noises that indicated a party was going on in his living-room. He walked quickly up the garden path to the front door. Just as he put his key into the lock a muffled voice in the shadows bade him good evening. Max jumped and turned round. He pulled aside the strands of weeping willow under which a creature wearing a gas-mask over a ghost's costume was standing. It carried a machine-gun in hands enclosed in the plastic gloves doctors use to probe the bum. From the yearning expression of the bloodshot eyes behind the gas-mask Max could tell that it wanted a beer, but he did not even stop to shake the plastic hand.

Looking through into the living-room as he hung up his coat he could see Kirstin running around with a five-litre thermos jug, pouring coffee for the soldiers who were not drinking Max's best Löwenbrau beer. She was flushed and laughing and there was a lot of loud ill-at-ease jollity. The floor and furniture were littered with dirty plates and greasy food tins and the odd crumpled paper napkin stamped with a view of Olde Winterthur.

He was just about to go in, when he was distracted by the noise of running water from the shower room by the front door. He went to investigate. There was a naked young man drying himself on Max's monogrammed towel, and the smell of his favourite nettle shampoo hung in the steam.

"Oh. Good evening, Herr Baumann."

The man held out his hand. Max only looked at it.

"What are you doing here?"

"Having a shower, sir."

"After what?"

"After about a week, actually. How do you mean?"

"Do you normally leave the door unlocked?"

"Yes, I do, as a matter of fact. Sorry. Field mentality. But I did ask your wife's permission. You know what it's like – you get to smell like a goat cheese after a week in the field."

"After something else as well, perhaps."

"Sorry? Good grief, I hope you're not suspecting your wife of anything improper, sir. With the whole company in the living-room!"

"I suppose you're not that careless."

"Certainly not, sir. I'd come back later, sir."

Max slammed the door shut.

Kirstin was standing near the door, talking to what looked like a fifteen-year-old recruit who was blushing up to and through his curly hair.

"Hello, Max. You are so late. Did you have a good day?"

"Yes thank you. There is a man in the shower."

"Yes. He asked. I told him it was all right. He is their officer, you see."

"I call it damned effrontery asking you such a thing. Did he ask you at the end of a bayonet? I suppose you didn't have the guts to refuse."

"Oh but Max," she lowered her voice, "it is so unpleasant for someone of that class to feel unwashed." She tried to manoeuvre him back into the hall, but he would not budge. The jollity had dropped to a perfunctory fuzz of conversation, so that the imminent row could be heard by all. One discreet soldier got up and went out to alert the lieutenant to the situation. "You know it's customary to be a bit hospitable to the army."

"You don't have to turn the place into a public bar, do you? I don't suppose they've offered to pay for those drinks."

"Have you been drinking, Max?"

"Apple juice," he assured her.

"Please don't make a fuss now. Let's talk about it later." One or two of the soldiers had begun to fumble in their pockets for small change. "They will think you are resentful because you are a foreigner."

"Oh, I see. Foreigners have to be twice as nice, is that it? I come home and find a naked man in the shower and a bunch of camouflaged drunks turning your husband's living-room into a den of thieves and I'm supposed to like it, am I? I suppose the furniture is lent, not given."

"Max, you shouldn't just quote the Bible in anger." She was afraid he would go through the room overturning ashtrays. "If you want them to leave I will tell the lieutenant."

"Stay where you are. He's probably just applying my Eau Sauvage body freshener."

"Oh yes. Could you please –" She turned to the fifteen-year-old.

The young soldier stood up, swallowing hard and clutching a half-eaten white sausage in his right hand. His face glowed like a night light.

"My friends," he said, "please forgive me for speaking, but I feel I must."

A groan of anticipation issued from some of the soldiers. They started to pack up their things.

"What?" said Max.

"Herr Baumann, your wife kindly asked us into her home –"

"My home."

"Er, yes, your home, because we were all tired and cold, but I would just remind you that there is someone else here tonight."

"There is? Who?"

"Jesus."

"Jesus?" Max looked astonished, and instinctively glanced around for telltale golden footprints. "Where?"

"I don't mean in the flesh, naturally," smiled the young man. "Except insofar as we are all members of His body."

"Which bit are you?"

"Max, please be respectful!" Kirstin's hand unconsciously closed over the paperweight.

"It's all right, Frau Baumann, I understand your husband's anger. I just thought it might help to remind him that Jesus is always in our midst. If we thought about that all the time we would behave a bit differently, don't you think?"

"It would make for some wild parties."

"Jesus is not against wholesome fun."

"Neither am I, but I don't include getting drunk at my expense in that category."

"Come now, Herr Baumann, they're not really drunk. And anyway, would you begrudge Jesus a beer?"

"No. He made it, you lot just drink it."

"But that's the way He intended it. Jesus said that whatever you give to someone else, you give to Him."

"Is there anything else He'd like?"

"No, except that He might like us to kneel down together and give Him thanks for your hospitality."

"Never mind Him. What about thanking me?"

"Come, Herr Baumann –"

He knelt, trying to pull Max down beside him. Kirstin was already squatting.

Just then the lieutenant appeared, pink and fragrant in his camouflage, the glasses steaming up a little in the slightly cooler air of the living-room.

"All right, Padre, you can get on your feet now. My apologies, Herr

Baumann. I've told him not to go around pestering civilians. He's been all right up to now."

"He doesn't bother me in the least, but I don't think he should be allowed to use the army to spread the gospel."

"Absolutely."

"It brings God into disrepute."

"Well, that's a bit unfair. Armies generally do."

"He could have caused my wife permanent emotional damage."

"I doubt it. He's actually quite harmless. But we've got to get moving now, anyway."

"Good."

"Come along, lads."

Most of the soldiers had already gone outside. The young "padre", still smiling seraphically, shook Max and Kirstin by the hand and called for God's blessing on their house.

Max shut the door behind them and went to open the window in the shower room before going back to Kirstin. She was clearing up the mess, her head well down so that her hair veiled her face.

Max flopped into an armchair and watched her.

"I suppose you're pissed off because I broke up the party."

"It wasn't a party, Max."

"I suppose you're pissed off because I came home at all."

"Max, shall I make you some fresh coffee?"

"Why?"

"Because you're repeating yourself."

"So what?"

"Well, I think you're drunk."

"I am not."

"All right."

He watched both of her in silence for a few minutes. Then he said, "I suppose you're pissed off because I buggered up your chances of getting pregnant. Just think of all the little heroes you could have squeezed out of that lot."

"What? Max, don't be ridiculous. You know me well enough to realize I'd never even think of such a thing."

"Oh do I? Do I? I think perhaps I don't know you at all."

"What do you mean?"

"Nothing. Well what are you pissed off about, then?"

"If you must know, I'm upset because you were so rude to that young man. You shouldn't make fun of religion, Max. God knows, life is hard enough without trying to destroy beliefs that make it tolerable for people."

161

"You're so sanctimonious, it's sickening. If God knows so much, don't forget He knows what you're up to when you're not sitting here knitting pot-holders."

"What am I up to?"

"God knows."

"What are you talking about, Max?" She finally stopped bustling and sat nervously on the edge of the sofa.

"Trying to get yourself pregnant all over the damn village, like a damned poodle. I tell you I've had enough of you trying to make me feel guilty about it all the time. I tell you, as long as you are married to me there are going to be no children, Kirstin. Is that clear?"

"I heard you." Her mouth trembled.

"There you go, trying to make me feel guilty again. Trying to be pathetic again. A pathetic little goodie-goodie, that's all you are for me, aren't you? But when my back's turned you're as horny as a poodle straight out of the jungle, but not for me, oh no. God I've had enough of you whingeing, squealing, smiling, hypocritical horny women. Do you know what I'd like to do to the lot of you?" He leant forward. "I'd like to tie you all up and dangle you over boiling mud and beat you with live wires."

"Good God! Max!"

"I would. Do you know why I'm not going to?"

"No."

"Because I'm too pissed."

"Thank goodness."

"I'll compromise and rape you."

"Oh good."

"Don't want you to die with any ambitions unfulfilled."

"No."

"Go on, get upstairs. Go on. Immediately. Go on."

"All right. Are you coming?"

"Of course I'm bloody coming."

Kirstin solicitously guided his stumbling feet up to the bedroom.

162

# CHAPTER

# ELEVEN

THE snows of December, January and February seemed to have put a stop to raping activities in Eglikon. The impending snows of March, April and May, when they began to overlap with the mosquito season, promised another few months respite, although according to BJ, who called Kirstin regularly with rape news from Zürich, bad weather had little influence on the loins of the econo-socially oppressed.

Often, when Kirstin was up in the bedroom, she would pause from dusting the bedsprings and go to the window and peer worriedly through a chink in the nets at the Umbergs' house and downhill to the silent huddle of the village, which gave off a greyish glimmer in the snow-decked valley.

In the interminable hours between Max getting up at five and coming home in the evening there was plenty of time to gaze out of the window, and to reflect how easy it would be for a rapist to waylay the female resident of his choice: everybody did everything at the same time, and with the help of even moderately powerful field glasses it would be a simple matter to pick a time and a victim.

At least Max was ruled out. Neither of them had had any more visits from the police. And his attempts at so-called rape on the night he came home drunk had clearly demonstrated his unsuitability for the work. He had tried to stick it everywhere from her armpit to the crack between the divans and she had finally had to roll him over and do it herself.

That had been a couple of weeks ago and very little had happened since. Everyone was reluctant to get their cars out while the roads were icy. *La Vie en Eglikon* had come to a standstill. Kirstin was quite relieved. It gave her jaws a rest from smiling, and the weather was making her very tired, so that after lunch she would go up to her bedroom and spend the long twilit afternoons falling asleep over a book or her temperature charts. They never showed any change. It was so depressing, sleep seemed an increasingly comfortable element.

One afternoon the bedside telephone rang, startling her awake.

"Hello. Baumann."

"Good afternoon, Frau Baumann. I hope I am not disturbing you."

"No, not at all."

It was a cultivated, twinkling female voice that spoke, as if it were accustomed to selling amazing new products by telephone.

"Who is speaking please?"

"Ah. If you don't mind, I would rather not say. In view of what I have to tell you I think it is best."

"What do you have to tell me?"

"Perhaps you know already. Did you know that your husband is having an affair, Frau Baumann?"

"No."

"Ah. I'm sorry to be the one to tell you, but I thought perhaps you didn't. I have always thought that was so terrible, when the wife is the last to find out. Frau Baumann? Frau Baumann, are you still there?"

"Yes."

"You're all right?"

"Yes. How do you know my husband is having an affair?"

"The woman is a friend of mine. Don't worry, my sources are impeccable, I'm not making it up. You know last month when your husband went to a very hush-hush meeting in Novosibirsk?"

"Yes."

"My friend went with him. That was when it began to get serious."

"How do you know? There might be many reasons for going to Novosibirsk."

"Name one. You are a strange person, Frau Baumann. I tell you, Novosibirsk in winter, it's like one of those circles of hell in the Paradiso, you know. Not exactly first choice for a getaway weekend."

"You are speaking from experience?"

"I? No, no. I am just telling you what my friend told me."

"Then perhaps nothing happened. Just going to Novosibirsk with someone for a hush-hush meeting – it seems far from conclusive evidence to me."

"Well what does it matter where it was?"

"Quite a lot. If you had said Martinique, or Macau, it would have banished all doubts."

"Frau Baumann, I am not a travel agent, I'm just trying to tell you a simple fact. Do I have to be more specific? They are lovers. Aren't you glad to know that?"

"I don't know that. And I don't see how you can either. Even if your friend told you that, it may not be true."

"Why on earth would she make it up? Do you think it's something to boast about? It wasn't all that difficult, you know. Your husband is like a cigarette machine when it comes to sex – a child could operate him."

"Did your friend tell you that, too?"

"Yes."

"And is she in love with him?"

"No, not any more."

"You seem to be a mind-reader as well as a rat."

"Now just control yourself, Frau Baumann. I am only acting for the best. My friend is hoping to get married soon, and the affair with your husband will have run its course, but nevertheless, in your position I would be grateful that somebody had told me what was going on."

"Perhaps you would like to be in my position. It's you, isn't it? There is no friend, is there? Perhaps it is my husband you are hoping to marry, is it? Well, I tell you, you can have him, and I wish you joy of his back to you in the mornings and in the evenings and his constant criticizing and putting you down making you feel like an incontinent dog leaving messes all over the place and saying such ugly things to you my God if you knew some of the things he's said to me of course he doesn't realize how hurtful he is but you'll remember and don't think you can trap him with children because he'd rather give up sex altogether children make messes too you know you'll just shrivel up and die after a few years but your body will still be walking around grinning like a catfish and people will be so sorry for you you'll want to hit them on the mouth but Christ almighty that's nothing to what I'll do to you if I ever get my hands on you do you hear how dare you phone me in my own home with your dirty revelations about my husband how dare you even if it's true how do you think it feels to be tied down and forced to watch your lover screwing someone else well that's what it amounts to isn't it I had to listen to you didn't I I didn't have any choice did I I tell you I'll kill you if I ever catch up with you you filthy interfering obscene disgusting person why don't you mind your own business why don't you kill yourself hello – hello? Are you there? Are you there?"

But for an unknown time she had been speaking to an anonymous buzz.

Kirstin put the receiver down and sat on the side of the bed, shaking. Then she crawled under the duvet and stared at the phone, hardly daring to move in case she set off any secondary eruptions.

It was not that the idea of Max having an affair was so surprising, but the fact of his having one put out all hope. It was not as if he would be torn apart by conflicting loyalties. The marriage was finished.

The snow blundered against the window again, trying to pile up and obscure the house. When she considered the choices open to her, the prospect of being buried alive in the warmth of her bed was not unwelcome. She foresaw a life of perpetual baby-sitting. Furthermore, she supposed she would have to get a job, as a front, to mask the essential pointlessness of her existence. Whatever she decided to do she would be starting the run-in to death.

She decided to call Geraldine, who usually managed to put things into a humorous, if sometimes vacuous, perspective.

The phone rang for a long time before Geraldine answered it.

"Hello, Geraldine. Did I wake you up?"

"Yes."

"Oh, I'm sorry."

"Well in that case, if you ring off now I can still get back to sleep."

"Listen, I am not disturbing you for nutting, Geraldine. But someting terrible has happened."

"Really? What a relief. I was beginning to think that everyone was dead. What?"

"I was having an anonymous telephone call."

"How utterly thrilling. Do you have any idea who it was?"

"No. Do you know what she is telling me?"

"Actually, no."

"She telephoned exactly to tell me zat Max is having an affair."

"Ah. Well I can't say I'm surprised, my dear. It's not me, if that's what you're wondering."

"No, of course not. I tink it was the woman herself. She said her friend was ze woman, but she is knowing so much about it, like ze scenery of Novosibirsk. I was not believing her."

"Good thinking, Watson. Yes, that's quite likely. On the other hand, people are so public-spirited around here I daresay you'll be hearing from all her friends in time. Did I tell you that one of our friendly neighbours informed the police that Peter washed the car on Sundays?"

"Really? Zis is terrible."

"It's like the French Revolution, isn't it? They should have official denunciation boxes outside the post office."

"Yes, but it was not only that ting about his mistress that upset me, Geraldine. I don't know what happened to me, but I suddenly was becoming so angry and hysterical, I shouted terribly at this woman, and I am telling her she should be killing herself, and so, and really bad tings. I am not knowing how I could do zat, now."

"Well what's wrong with that? It's a shattering thing to tell anyone. I'm not surprised you lost your temper, for once. I just wish I'd been there to see it."

"Oh Geraldine, you never take anyting serious."

"Well what do you want me to say? You don't seem particularly upset about the news, so what is there to get serious about?"

"But don't you tink it is an offence to deliver abuse on ze telephone?"

"Don't be so wet, Kirstin. It can't be worse than making anonymous telephone calls. Honestly, I'm sorry, but that's so typical of you, it's so irritating. Some unknown creep phones you to give you some very nasty information, and you end up feeling guilty because you reacted as any normal person would. I wish you'd have a bit of gumption sometimes."

"Tank you."

"Well, honestly, Kirstin. I'm not surprised Max gets frustrated sometimes. Why don't you go and get a job, or something? You'll probably find you get pregnant quite easily if you stop sitting up there brooding about it."

"Yes, BJ."

"Eh? I'm not BJ."

"You are sounding just like her."

"Am I? Well BJ talks quite a lot of sense sometimes, you know, if you can filter it through all that regurgitated tripe about sexual awareness and noble car bombers and whatnot. We both know that's what she'd advise you to do, don't we?"

"I suppose so. You tink I should be like her and devote my life to ze sale of consuming durables?"

Geraldine laughed. "It's no better or worse than devoting your life to not selling consuming durables. Listen, I'm not being much help, am I? I'm sorry, I'm always bad-tempered when I wake up. Why don't you come over?"

"No, tank you. I am disturbing you too much already, I tink."

"Now don't be a dog in the manger, love. I know for a fact you can't possibly have anything to do. Wednesdays is one of Max's nights out, isn't it?"

"Yes, but –"

"But me no buts. Didn't you ever suspect anything with his being out in the evenings so much?"

"No. He is never spending much time at home."

"Oh Lord. Well, I can understand your feeling sorry for yourself, but let's face it, there is a positive aspect to all this. You want children and Max doesn't. It's high time you got out of the marriage while you're young enough to meet someone else who would suit you better. It could be a blessing in disguise."

"But Geraldine, I love Max."

"How can you? Honestly, you're so impractical. You're throwing your life away on that man, and he'll probably leave you when you're fifty and marry a twenty-five-year-old and have four children."

"Do you really tink so?"

"Well it does happen, Kirstin. He'll have his citizenship by then. You must start thinking about the future, or you'll just drift through life embroidering bags to put onions in and –"

Kirstin quietly put the receiver down. She had obviously caught Geraldine at a bad moment, when she was unable to disguise her real opinion with her usual crackly banter. It was really no higher than Max's. He must have been right, that she had been cultivating Kirstin all along for the sake of the baby-sitting. And to think that she had reproached BJ for her attitude to Geraldine. Kirstin was tempted to call BJ for the sake of hearing the note of respectful allegiance in her voice. But that would be self-indulgent and passive. Instead, she got the paper and started looking through the Situations Vacant column.

For the next few weeks Kirstin avoided Geraldine and concentrated on looking for a job. She was tantalized by an advertisement for female crane operators in the assembly shop of Humbel Brothers. She rang BJ for advice. BJ thought that if she had a driver's licence there should be no problem, and strongly urged Kirstin to apply.

She did, but when the day came for the interview she had to stay at home for the washing machine repair man.

Herr Waldvogel summoned Max to his presence as soon as he got back to the office after his trip to Hungary. He immediately sensed trouble from the way Herr Waldvogel ostentatiously rummaged through his filing cabinet for the first few minutes after Max entered the room. Herr Waldvogel was a short, jittery man, normally no match for Max's towering condescension, but on this occasion he evidently felt more comfortable keeping Max standing.

"Nice of you to spare me a moment," he snapped. "I wasted two hours for you the last time. I even tried calling you at home, but there was no reply."

"I'm sorry. I – I forgot." Max paled. Now he remembered that he had stood Herr Waldvogel up on the afternoon he had gone into Zürich. It was the same occasion on which he had forgotten an appointment with Annalie Schumacher, also. The demon Age bared its toothless grin. He began to sweat a little.

"What was it you wanted to see me about so urgently, Herr Waldvogel?"

"This." He turned round and handed Max the telex from Poland.

Max read it in silence. The sweat turned to full-scale collywobbles. Herr Waldvogel handed him the accompanying letter, in which the change of the comradely mind was attributed to social disturbances and consequent changes in government policy.

"As you may know, Max, we already have people out there, and the first consignment is ready for shipment."

"Yes."

"Is that all you've got to say?"

"What can I say?"

"Well, this is marvellous, Max." Herr Waldvogel sat down at his desk. "First you bugger off before I can tell you, and when I do, you act as though I'd just given you a tram ticket. I don't know why I bothered."

"It's a serious blow, of course."

"Serious blow! It's the equivalent of a 500 megaton bomb, Max. You handled the sale, you should know how much we're going to lose."

"True. But I don't see that I'm responsible for their political problems."

"No downpayment, of course. You'll have to work out the penalty clause. If you've got time. You're not exactly overloaded with paperwork at the moment, are you?"

Max said nothing. It was more dignified to allow Herr Waldvogel to relieve himself of his spleen uninterrupted.

"Of course," Herr Waldvogel continued, "I realize it isn't entirely your fault."

"I don't see that it's my fault at all."

"Perhaps not directly. But there hasn't been much coming in since, has there Max? You've been resting on your laurels, a bit. That's exactly the attitude we cannot afford in these difficult times."

Max inwardly goggled at the description of his recent schedule as "resting", but Herr Waldvogel was clearly not in a logical mood.

"I don't want to alarm you, Max. I'm very fond of Kirstin and your job is certainly secure as long as orders keep coming. But no longer. Do I make myself clear?"

"Perfectly."

"Right." He rustled some papers. "We're all in the same boat, Max. I'm not indispensable either."

Too true, thought Max.

"Perhaps you should take Kirstin along with you sometimes. You've got no kids, have you? She's a charming young woman. She might open a few doors."

And close others, Max reflected. What a preposterous idea. He would as soon take a favourite teddy along.

"Well, I'm off to Singapore on Thursday, Max. Please get this business tidied up by the time I get back."

"Is that all?"

"Yes. No. This is for you, I believe." He took the postcard from Elena out of his desk. "No comment, Max. You understand? But we don't want the company involved in any unavoidable scandal. We've got enough genuine problems. And as Kirstin's uncle I cannot but be concerned at the idea of your mucking about behind her back, Max. If you want to change partners, do it honourably. No one will think the worse of you for that."

"What do you think of the tie I'm wearing?"

"Eh? All right, Max, no need to get uppity. That's all."

Max returned to his office, fulminating at the tendency of his friends and acquaintances to refer to Kirstin all the time. He normally never thought about her when he was not at home: it was highly perverse of others to do so.

# CHAPTER

# TWELVE

WHEN the time came for Kirstin's unpaid working holiday in Bergün, she did not rush off like a prisoner starting parole as she had been wont to do. Following her quarrel with Geraldine she had re-examined some of her other relationships with women, and that with her bossy Cousin Daniela had come in for the most revision. It had been a good arrangement when Cousin Daniela's children were very young and Kirstin had gone sledging and skiing with them all day while Cousin Daniela was churning out liver and rösti for the millions. But now the children did not need supervision, and one day two years before Daniela had drawn Kirstin into the family snuggery on the first floor of the hotel, elaborately closed the door and obliged her to have an intimate chat about the future. Both of them had smiled till they ached throughout, but the upshot was that Kirstin had outlived her usefulness as a babysitter and if she intended to go on occupying a guest room at the height of the season she had better earn it waiting at table.

As she walked down from Bergün station towards the village Kirstin looked around her in ambiguous mood. The sky was gem-quality blue, and the sun burned off ledges and drifts and hills of dazzling snow. The houses and trees were laden with such huge gobs of it the whole village looked as though it had been dipped upside down in cartoon ice-cream. Brightly coloured skiers and about ten thousand children with sledges swarmed over the snow, and the air was full of the squeals of women and children being agreeably murdered. It was a familiar, much-loved sight to Kirstin, but as it was the last time she intended to come nostalgia for it was already tainting her pleasure.

Cousin Daniela was napping after lunch when Kirstin arrived at the hotel, and there was no one at reception, so she went straight to her room and unpacked.

Kirstin especially liked the old building when it was quiet like this. It was a big old chalet, the wood now black, and the uneven floors and crooked windows were buckling under the weight of snow on the roof. When it was quiet the ghosts of its former inhabitants seemed to swill out of the corners: men who had proudly fathered their children, women who made their own cheese and who did not have to get onto the school board, or take a turn as president of the ladies' gymnastic union, to feel that they were useful members of the community. Kirstin smiled sadly at the thought of the ennobling simplicity of their ancestors' lives as she fitted the wide-angle lens on her Olympus OM-4.

She hooked the regrettable nylon nets onto the rod and focused her camera onto the people in the main street below. The bed on which she sat pitched quaintly towards the low window; there was scarcely room for anything else. She was very excited by a frame of two little girls in green coats and woolly hats standing together at the corner of a painted house in Anker-like artlessness, bending their heads over something that one of them had picked up out of the snow. When they had moved on she put the camera down on the bed to put a jacket on and she had just turned back towards the window when a snowball hurtled through it and thwacked her right between the eyes. For a moment she was paralysed with shock, blinking through the gritty, cold clusters of snow that clung to her face. Then she leapt up and leant out of the window. The obvious culprits – two young boys – were dodging in and out of a doorway opposite, waiting for the reaction.

"You little vandals! You could have broken something. You wait till I see your mother!"

The boys put their thumbs in their ears and waggled their hands. "You-can't-catch-me-nanny nanny boo boos!" Then they took off on their plastic sledges, crashing downhill into the legs of pedestrians.

Kirstin stared after them, shocked. She recognized the boys as Stefan and Joachim Huber, the doctor's two youngest.

Like a light fizzling up a fusewire, the sight of the two boys ripped up to the stunning conclusion that the doctor must be in Bergün. The Frau Doktor too, unfortunately, but – correction – now that she had her priorities right the presence of either of them was of no significance to her whatsover.

As she tore on her boots and coat she marvelled at the fact of her pronouncements having actually influenced the movements of the family Huber. It was awe-inspiring, as if she had discovered the power to bend spoons. She clattered down the steps and outside just as Cousin Daniela emerged from her room, groomed for the evening, exclaiming with disapproval as Kirstin flew past her.

The Huber boys had gone some way further down the street. Number three was with them too. She quickly went round to the hotel ski room and took a sledge and followed them downhill at high speed, passed them and ended up at the crossroads. Then she got up and pulled the sledge back up the hill towards them. She smiled broadly at eight-year-old Stefan, whose face remained a deliberate blank.

"Why, hello. Stefan, isn't it? Baumann."

"Hello, Frau Baumann."

"That was naughty of you to throw the snowball, wasn't it?"

"Yes."

"I won't tell your mother if you promise not to do it again."

"Okay."

"Are you all here?"

"No. Christian and Michael have gone with the school."

"Have you been here long?"

"No, just today."

"I see." She also saw that young Stefan felt himself skewered to the spot by her attentions and was aching to get away. "Well, I hope you have a good time. Are you staying somewhere nice?"

"Just there – at the Weisses Kreuz."

"How convenient." It was indeed. She would have to go near it every time she went to the shop, the station or the swimming pool.

That seemed to be all she could accomplish by accosting young Stefan, but she heard his name called and looked round.

There on the steps of the Weisses Kreuz, his muscles lightly swelling a pale blue polo-neck sweater and white padded jerkin, photo-grey glasses dark against the glare of the snow, was Dr Huber. He had come out to look for the boys. For a moment their eyes met, with difficulty through their sunglasses, and to Kirstin's jangling imagination on the doctor's face was a look of unpleasant surprise, as if her own presence in Bergün had not been understood when she recommended the place, so that he could have had a chance to weigh it in the balance with the good points. But the moment was soon over, and the doctor cantered down the steps to shake her hand.

"Hello, Frau Baumann, so, you see we took your advice. Here we are."

"Yes. That's quite amazing, Herr Doktor. I had quite forgotten – honestly."

"Oh? It wasn't a joke, was it?"

"No, no. I'm sure you will like it. Are you here for a week?"

"Yes, unfortunately, just the week. You know what they used to say in the old days – a tooth for every child. Well, now it's a week's holiday."

"Now, I am sure you are joking, Herr Doktor."

"Are you? Well, well. Why don't you come in for a drink just for a moment? I'm sure my wife would like a chat since you know the place so well."

"Well, I'm not sure –" She looked at Stefan as the barometer of the outlook should she accept the offer, but he was happily stuffing snow down his brother's neck.

"After all, what else is there to do until dinner-time?"

"Perhaps just a mint tea."

"Yuch. Do you know there are tannins in mint tea that have been linked to cancer of the oesophagus?"

"No, I didn't. Are you sure?"

"I beg your pardon? I hope you're not trying to teach me my job, Frau Baumann."

"Certainly not. But I never know when you are serious, Herr Doktor."

"Always. We're sitting through here."

He led her into a snug, smoke-filled ethnic dining-room, heavily panelled and decorated with artily primitive motifs of the Graubunden ram. Frau Huber, recognizable for her athletic build and practical fuzz of blonde hair, was sitting underneath one of them, looking towards the door.

Her very appearance struck caution into Kirstin: large-boned and upright as a young pine tree, high cheekbones and bold blue eyes, Kirstin could well imagine her in former times manning the barricades of Eglikon against the barbarian. She seemed genuinely pleased to see Kirstin, and as she never did at home Kirstin assumed it was her rôle as Familiar Face that the Frau Doktor was reacting to.

"It's so nice to see a familiar face," said Frau Huber, beaming. "Do sit down, Frau Baumann."

"Thank you."

The doctor went off to order Kirstin a glass of mineral water. The Frau Doktor started telling Kirstin how difficult it had been to persuade 'Enki' – presumably the doctor – to come away for the sport week, and how pleased she had been when he suggested it himself at last. There followed detailed information on the trying stress situations that Stefan, Remo and Joachim were going through at school. Christian and Michael were also in stress situations at school, it seemed, but they were old enough to go with their class. It crossed Kristin's mind to suggest that, in the circumstances, it might have been better if those two had come with the family as well, but she did not say anything as she was too busy churning over the fact that the doctor had apparently not told his wife that she had given him the idea of coming to Bergün.

The doctor came back with Kirstin's water and they all raised their glasses. Kirstin was anxious to give the impression that she had been lending her ear with total abandon to Frau Huber during his absence.

"I don't know how you manage to stay so calm and cheerful, Frau Huber, with the children so much under stress. Doesn't it affect you?"

"Oh well, they all have to go through it some time. It wouldn't help if I went running down to the school every time they got into difficulties. They have to learn to fend for themselves."

"At six months in our family," remarked the doctor, raising his beer.

Kirstin smiled, but ignored the remark. It presumably referred to Frau Huber's hyperactivity in the local community – church council, toddlers' swimming instruction, doll-making, gymnastics and secretary to the Beautiful Eglikon society were only the activities that Kirstin knew about. There were probably others. And despite it all, she was a model of streamlined vigour. She was such a remarkable doctor's wife that the remains of Kirstin's fantasies about the doctor were ground into the dust. She could use a bit of lipstick now that age was beginning to drain the raspberries from her lips, but her remarkableness was undimmed.

It was no strain to talk to Frau Huber, so long as one stuck to the subject of Christian, Michael, Joachim, Remo and Stefan. Or perhaps it was that their combined energy field inevitably sucked the conversation towards them. At first the doctor leant forward eagerly, at the ready to join in, but after a while he sat back and drank his beer, keeping his eyes downcast except when he looked up at new arrivals.

Kirstin began to feel uncomfortable. The steady twitch of the doctor's jaw suggested repressed tension. He looked rather pathetic, trying to appear to be enjoying himself while being totally excluded from the conversation. Kirstin tried to close the triangle to him with a stream of concerned smiles, but he did not respond.

Eventually Frau Huber's attention was drawn along the path of Kirstin's, and she started to smile at the doctor too, in a half-hearted way, as at a polite child.

"Are you sure you ought to be drinking so much beer, sweetheart?" she said. "Isn't it bad for your rheumatism?"

"I'll worry about my rheumatism, thank you dear." He summoned the waitress to order another.

"Poor Enki," she said to Kirstin, "he's always so busy at home he finds it rather difficult to relax at first."

"I can understand that. Don't you? You're a very busy person, too, aren't you?"

"Yes, of course. But you know, with so many children the holiday can be more tiring than staying at home."

"Then why are you always so keen to go, my love?" asked the doctor.

"Just for the change, really. And it's good for the children. It's nice not to have to cook for seven people twice a day."

"Most people would regard that as a full-time job in itself," said Kirstin. "You have amazing energy, Frau Huber."

"It comes and goes. I try to keep fit, of course. Frankly, I think the more you do the more energy you have. Actually it's Enki I'm worried about more than myself. He doesn't seem to be as keen on sport as he used to be, do you, sweetheart?"

"Don't I?"

Frau Huber laughed, uncomfortably, sensing the doctor's mood. "He also seems to have got a bit coy about answering a straight question. It must be the Change, don't you think so, Frau Baumann?"

"Not yet, surely. I mean, I would have thought the doctor was far too young –"

"He's forty-four. Most men usually go over the top around fifty, don't they? But it depends on the individual. I would say Enki was just about ready for a small mid-life crisis. He's done an awful lot, you know, he used to be with the Olympic team before we came to Eglikon, and men are lucky to live past eighty, so he's definitely on the wrong side of the hump."

Frau Huber laughed, and Kirstin laughed, but only to hide her rising panic. She was appalled at the condescending tone in which Frau Huber talked about her husband to his face, and squirmed with anxiety to change the subject.

"My grandfather lived to be ninety-four," she said.

"Really?"

"Yes. He went swimming every day until he was ninety-two."

"Now that's a good idea, Enki. Why don't you go swimming while I'm away with the boys? Is there a pool?"

"Yes, quite a nice one."

"He can't ski at the moment, you know, because of his knee."

"Yes, I know."

"Perhaps you wouldn't mind going with him the first time, Frau Baumann? Do you have time? I'd be much easier in my mind if I thought he was enjoying himself while we were all skiing. It's such a shame, he used to be so good. And then he'd be occupied and won't get fidgety. Yes, that's a very good idea, don't you think so, Enki?"

"Brilliant. Has Frau Baumann agreed to it? A minor point."

"Yes, of course," said Kirstin, preparing to leave. "I'd do anything – I mean, I really like swimming." She felt the charge from the doctor's tense body prising her out of her seat. "But I really must go now."

"Then why don't you pick him up here after breakfast, Frau Baumann? All right, Enki?"

"All right."


Kirstin slept badly. She was too hot in bed and threw the duvet off to lie with one foot on the window sill, listening to the sounds of intoxicated après-skiers returning to their hotels. The tiny room was lit from the street lamps, and because it was so small and the bed so near the window, she had the feeling of being always on the point of falling out of it, bed and all. She assumed that was why she could not sleep, being accustomed to king-size comfort and rural blackout at night. And although the doctor's image was embedded in concrete in her mind's eye, she struggled like a medieval saint against reviving her sexual fantasies about him. She was tormented by the memory of BJ advising her to try it with someone completely different. The thought of being close to the doctor's almost naked body in the morning produced a sensation as of dewy lotus blossoms opening and closing with wild schlurps in her lower abdomen.


Punctually at thirty seconds past ten she arrived at the Weisses Kreuz. The porch was full of skiers preparing to leave for the morning's sport, clumping around in their cement-filled plastic boots. Kirstin looked for the doctor in the parlour where they had been the day before, and found him reading the paper over the rubble of his family's breakfast. He got up readily when she came in, and steered her outside again through the crowded entrance hall.

Once beyond the main square they found themselves virtually alone: the skiers were all going in the opposite direction. Already the gentle slopes to the left of the village were spotted with midgets hurtling down at great speed, and straggly rows of small beginners with their teachers. It was hot in the sun, and they had not gone far when the doctor took off his padded jerkin. It was such an omen of things to come that a chill passed through Kirstin's body. They made small talk about the delightful painted decorations on the houses they passed.

"Isn't it a pity," said Kirstin, "that it's only here in the mountains that the houses are so pretty. The mountains are so beautiful anyway. It's down where we live that one really needs the colour and decoration like this. It's so grey for so long down there."

"Yes, it is. But perhaps the contrast would be too painful. Depression is pretty rife as it is, if my patients are anything to go by. Ah. Excuse me." He stepped aside to make way for a large brown hen that was hogging the middle of the narrow street, jerkily sinking up to the nethers in snow, to her obvious disgust. "Do you often get depressed, Frau Baumann? You've never said so, that I recall."

"Oh well. Sometimes. Things are a bit difficult just now. But it doesn't matter. If I don't get pregnant I think I will get a job."

"You're depressed about not getting pregnant? I can't think why."

Kirstin laughed. "It's all very well for you to be sarcastic. You have a wonderful family."

"Hmm."

"And your wife is so capable. She must be an excellent mother."

"She is. To all of us."

"Now there you go being serious again, Herr Doktor."

Kirstin cursed herself for bringing up the subject of Frau Huber. She had a numbing premonition that the doctor was about to tell her that his wife did not understand him. From what she had seen it was perfectly true.

"I am always serious when I talk about my wife, which is never, as a matter of fact. But I will agree with you that she is a remarkable woman."

"Yes. I envy her her confidence. She could take on anything."

"Women with a meal ticket for life generally are pretty confident. Five meal tickets in her case."

"Oh Herr Doktor, that's not fair, is it? She works so hard."

"She does."

"I think perhaps we should not be talking about your wife."

"All right. Let's talk about your husband, then."

"Oh. Why?"

"Well, it changes the subject. You implied that things weren't going too well. I am your doctor, remember. You can trust me if you need someone to talk to."

"I don't know. Look we're here now. Oh dear, which one is it?"

They had stopped by a deserted children's play area in an open space between a number of white residential buildings. They looked so much alike she could not remember which one housed the swimming pool.

"I suppose he's got a girlfriend," mused the doctor, looking around without interest.

"How did you know that?" Kirstin was startled and stared at him.

He laughed. "It was just a guess. I hardly know anyone who doesn't."

"That can't be true. But you are right. I got an anonymous telephone call just before I came away."

"Nasty. Did you report it to the police?"

"No, we've had enough of the police. They suspected Max of doing the rapes in the village, you know."

"How ridiculous. He's not the type at all."

"Nor are you, but there are those who think you are the guilty party."

The doctor gave a shout of laughter. "Really?" He pinioned Kirstin's arms behind her. "Were you one of them, Frau Baumann?"

"Stop it! No, I wasn't. At least not up to now I wasn't."

He let go of her. "It could explain why you seem so nervous."

"Do I? I don't know why that is. Well, to tell you the truth –"

"Yes, please always tell me the truth."

"I thought your wife had rather pushed you into this. I wasn't sure if you really wanted to."

He put a hand through her arm. "Let's just get on with it, shall we? We agreed not to talk about my wife."

"All right. I remember where it is now. It's through that archway."

Kirstin led the way into a small entrance hall with notice boards and a turnstile. A window was open into the office where a young man was typing at a table. Doctor Huber took out his wallet in masterful fashion and motioned Kirstin to stand aside.

"We'd like to swim, please. How much?"

"Do you want a ticket for the week? There probably won't be anyone here from tomorrow."

"Yes, please."

179

He paid for the tickets and they went through to the changing cubicles, and after some banter about choosing a nice one they locked themselves into adjacent cubicles and started to change. It reminded Kirstin of undressing behind the shower curtain in the doctor's surgery, and a revenge fantasy where the doctor was forced to lie on his back with his legs in the air like a beetle while she examined his private parts made her blush in the dark. She leaned down to look at his feet. They were solid and squatly toed like the Statue of Liberty; the little toe on the left twitched rhythmically.

The doctor was ready and showered first, and when Kirstin emerged it was to the mighty plop of his body entering the water. That was a relief: she had not looked forward to having to survey each other curiously beforehand, as in the joke about the Protestant and the Catholic. There was no one else in the pool, and only a cleaning lady dreamily pushed a floorcloth around the tiles.

Kirstin sat on the edge for a moment and splashed her feet, watching the doctor's powerful body ploughing channels through the water. It looked as though a combine harvester had gone berserk in the pool. He was really a powerful swimmer. It was therefore something of a surprise when, coming back to the shallow end, he heaved himself out and lay face down gasping for breath.

"Jesus, I'm knackered," he panted. "I used to do fifty lengths in the Hallenbad."

"Well, you're the doctor, as you keep reminding me. You should know better than to show off like that."

"I was not showing off. I was trying to kill myself."

"Oh dear. Are you serious? You don't have a bad heart, do you?"

"I do now."

"You are only out of condition. Your wife was right."

"Why do you keep talking about my wife, Frau Baumann? Are you in love with her?"

Kirstin laughed and catapulted into the pool. She managed twenty lengths with a struggle, but she had not swum for some time either, and she was glad to yield the pool to the doctor again while she sat on the side and got her breath back. This time he strolled the water with a leisurely backstroke.

"Want a race?" he called from the deep end.

"Oh sure. With whom?"

"I'll keep my hands behind my back."

"You are determined to kill yourself."

"Well come in again anyway. It's not good to sit around in between."

"But it's so warm and sunny here. I'll come in again in a minute."

The sun streamed through the glass wall, gilding the intimate quiet around the pool. The cleaning lady had gone and the only sounds were the doctor's leisurely stroking the water and the squeals and shouts of children whizzing down the ski slope just beyond the building. Kirstin shut her eyes and turned her face towards the sun. A dreamlike suspension of reality was operating, with its fragile tension of timelessness and imminent disruption. She tried to think about Max, but the effort was flooded out by the dazzling warmth and ease of her body – abruptly doused by being pulled by the ankles into the water. The doctor had escaped, submarine fashion, by the time she spluttered to the surface. They swam up and down the pool for a while until Kirstin was breathless. She got out and dried herself and lay down on the floor near the window. Her legs had barely got her there, and she was rather frightened by the powerful squelches of the heart that beat upwards against her throat. But when the doctor came and lay down beside her it never occurred to her to mention it. She merely breathed deeply, trying out Max's favourite theory about bending the body to the will.

"Ah, that's what I needed," sighed the doctor, flexing his feet up and down on the floor. "A week of this and I'll be back on form."

"How's your knee?"

"All right. Shall we come again this afternoon?"

"If you don't mind I think it would be a bit much for me."

"All right. What shall we do then?"

"Won't your family be around?"

"No they won't. They'll be getting their money's worth until at least four-thirty."

"We could take the train up to Preda and come down on the sledge. Or go for a walk. The woods are nice up there."

"Whatever you say, nurse."

"I could never be a nurse. I'm not efficient enough."

They lay in silence for a while. Out of the corner of her eye Kirstin observed the doctor discreetly consulting his waterproof Omega. Then he lay still again. Until his large, dexterous hand crawled over like a friendly spider to rest on hers. Kirstin held her breath. A small gesture, but she had not been aware of so many barriers being swept aside at once since President Nixon went to China. For a moment they lay quietly, the doctor firmly holding her hand. But then, whether the Omega was urging him to take action, or on some more naturally urgent impulse, the doctor leant up on his elbow and began to stroke her hair, moving it away from her face.

181

"You have the most beautiful hair I have ever seen," he said.

Kirstin could not speak, but she rolled over into an attitude of naive enticement, just noticing, before he hauled himself on top of her, how much younger he looked without his glasses. For some minutes they lay locked in a devouring embrace, their teeth occasionally crunching in the frenzy to get at each other's innermost parts. Through the doctor's swimming trunks Kirstin could feel his penis, like a hot cucumber, burning a channel in her thigh. She pulled her face away.

"Somebody might come in," she said.

"You'd rather not be caught in the act?"

"It's not just that, but –"

He bore down on her again, but she struggled to get up. Apart from the high risk of someone coming in, she could not help imagining the more remote, but ghastly, possibility that Stefan, Joachim or Remo might crash off the ski slope and through the plate-glass wall. The doctor sensed her unease. Hiding his modesty with the towels he steered her towards the shower cubicles. He pressed her up against the side of the cubicle and helped her off with her damp swimsuit, which had begun to steam. Then he turned her round so that her warm body was pressed to the cold wall. They were almost the same height. He held a towel over her mouth so that she could gently scream into its slightly chlorinated folds.

Only a matter of seconds later a chattering family of four came in. The doctor and Kirstin quickly separated, showered and went to get dressed.

When Kirstin was ready she brushed her long hair under the drier and found that her hand was shaking. It was hard to tell if it was delayed shock or a result of overtaxing her muscles. The doctor was combing his hair in front of the mirror on the other side of the room. It seemed an almost more intimate act to witness than what had gone on in the shower.

They moved towards the exit simultaneously. The doctor put an arm round her shoulder and smiled. When they were outside he said, "By the way, don't worry about getting pregnant. I've been to the pound."

"I should love to get pregnant."

"You have such a delicious body. Why do you want to muck it up having babies?"

"That's not the primary object – mucking up the body, I mean. Is it inevitable?"

"Probably not in your case."

Impulsively she stopped and hugged him.

"Hey, steady on. Save it for this afternoon."

"Sorry. I'm just not used to – Oh, I don't know how to describe it."

"I don't like the idea of elaborate deception, but a scandal would be bad for the children."

"Of course. We'd better keep the deception simple."

"You make it sound very trivial. You're not one of those nymphomaniac baby-doll types, are you?"

"Heavens, no. Don't misunderstand me, but I thought, all things considered, it would be better not to get too serious."

"But I've already told you, Frau Baumann, I am always serious."

In practice it was eerily simple to carry off the deception. No one was interested. They went separately to the pool in the mornings and the station in the afternoons, from where they rode up to Preda and went off into the woods to find a secluded clearing in the trees to make love, with the aid of a groundsheet and air mattress that the doctor had specially purchased. The proceedings were occasionally interrupted by air farting out of the mattress; the doctor had not wanted to buy a really good one as he already had several at home from the camping trip to Norway. She wanted to tease him about being suspiciously unreckless for a man in love, but then she was not at all sure that he was in love. Time was so short they tended to let their bodies do the talking, and when they did talk it was nearly always about her, or Christian, Michael, Stefan, Joachim and Remo. Kirstin did not even have to feel guilty about his wife as, from what the doctor said, Frau Huber seemed to be conniving at the arrangement, being of the opinion that it was a good thing for him to sow a few wild oats in a strictly controlled situation. The doctor likened it to applying leeches to his libido as a precautionary measure.

Afterwards he would turn away from her and grab her arm to wrap round his neck while he dozed off, like a child with his favourite teddy. Kirstin never slept. She lay awkwardly while her arm went to sleep and tried to think about what was happening. The doctor had dropped enough hints that he would like to make their relationship permanent, she could not avoid considering it. But even assuming that her own marriage was doomed, there was the redoubtable Frau Huber and then Christian, Michael, Stefan, Joachim and Remo. The doctor's five sons stood like a regiment of foot between them and dreams of starting again. No wonder he wanted to put her off having children as he could not have any more himself. And as they only had a week it was no longer surprising that he had been ready for action from the first moment. She wryly remembered him consulting his watch before touching her hand, lest the programme should get behind schedule.

It worried her. When she had fantasized about him it was in a world in which Frau Huber had discreetly died in a car crash, not one in which she would pursue them with alternate threats of suicide and cut-throat lawyers, who would anyway beggar him twice a week for daring to walk out on his irreproachable family. But if the doctor's hints were to be believed, for her sake he was prepared to face financial ruin and public scandal, separation from his family and everything that was familiar. And yet they were still almost strangers. It was unreal. She imagined telling a delighted BJ, and hearing BJ's opinion – that there would be something seriously wrong with the doctor if, at forty-five-ish, he did not jump at the chance to walk out on Frau Huber and five pre-teenage sons for a near-virginal blonde playmate with her own money.

She dreaded having to pour cold water on his speculations about permanent change. He was full of what Kirstin considered mad schemes for breaking up the family and yet hanging on to the children, and talked of having them on alternate weeks, or every weekday for a month and then every weekend for a month, and other variations. It was like trying to solve the Rubik cube. She tried to persuade him that he would be lucky to get them once a month for a day. The idea of all those wopping boys lumbering back and forth between their parents like mad mammoths seemed to sum up the farcical nature of the whole project. If they were in stress situations at school now, they would surely blow their fuses under such conditions. And setting aside the possibility of the doctor's leaving his family, Kirstin did not see how they could continue the relationship back in Eglikon. The field glasses would be trained on them from every window and there was nowhere they could discreetly meet. Hardly in the woods, as here. Even assuming it had stopped snowing in Eglikon, the woods there were always shady and cold and any tryst would be at risk of interruption by the forestry department, illegal mopeds, parties from the riding school and *Jack der Bauchaufschnittler*. And under Max's nose, too. It was not that she felt guilty – having come to the conclusion that adultery, like religion, was there because it fulfilled a need – but because she could not bring herself to make a fool of Max. *Noli Max Tangere*.

At the interval in the film Michael did not want to go into the foyer, but BJ had only eaten a kilo of peaches and a square metre of rhubarb flan all day, and besides being hungry she considered her restraint had earned her an ice-cream cone.

Michael reluctantly joined the crush round the ice-cream counter and BJ took herself to a quiet corner by the cigarette machine to wait for him. She was feeling somewhat nauseous but was reluctant to attribute it to the harrowing scenes that had preceded the interval. In view of her political philosophy she considered that she ought to be able to remain objective in the face of carnage, brutality and sadism. It was an underground Bolivian film about a group of peasants struggling to hack a living from rocky soil while being pestered by bandits called The Glorious Way, who threatened to machete the peasants' children if they helped another lot of bandits called The People's Hope – who actually did machete their children when they co-operated with The Glorious Way. The first half had ended with a group of government troops disguised as The People's Hope ripping out the stomach of a mother-to-be, and it was at this point that BJ's hunger had started to make her feel nauseous.

When Michael brought the cone she opened the wrapper with care, making little noises of eager delight.

"Would you like some French fries with that?" said Michael.

"Not right now. Perhaps later."

"Are you sure you're eating the right diet for a pregnant woman?"

"Let's talk about something else, okay? The only way I can get through this is to pretend it isn't happening."

"Poor kid. You ought to have gone back to the States to get rid of it."

"Oh, that's fantastic. When I first told you about it you were going on all the time about what a great thing it was and being positive about life, and stuff."

"I still think that, but I am feeling sorry for the kid, now. You cannot pretend it isn't happening when it is already born."

"I'll deal with it somehow." She was gnawing her way down into the cone, smacking her lips. "Actually, I've already decided, I'll just have to get someone to look after it during the day, so that I can go on working. And then Philip can get up and feed it during the night. That way I'd practically never see it, and Philip would get to feel good about being a better parent than me."

"I hope at least you are going to a doctor."

"Of course, Michael. I'm not irresponsible."

"I am impressed that you have given up smoking. That is very responsible, I must say."

"Don't bother. It wasn't my idea, but my obstetrician more or less

185

said he didn't want to be responsible for the pregnancy if I didn't quit. He's actually quite a fascist. That's probably why I'm attracted to him."

"I don't understand you, BJ. How can you be attracted by a fascist? I thought you are supposed to be so radical? Look at this film you have dragged me to see."

"Aren't you enjoying the film?" This was a disappointment. It had been such a triumph to get him there, and she had chosen the film carefully because she considered it was at his level, having won a basketful of golden vegetables and fruit at festivals around the world, and dealing as it did with humanity at its most interestingly crude.

"What is there to enjoy? A lot of starving peasants butchering each other. One knows that happens, I don't see the point to pay for seeing the actual blood."

"Yes, I must say it was somewhat explicit."

"And look at the people here. They are all peasants anyway. People who should see a film like this never go to the cinema."

BJ looked around. The foyer was full of young women in baggy smocks and flat sandals and scruffy men in Indian shirts and necklaces. Michael himself was wearing elegant cream trousers and a matching cotton and silk Italian knit.

She smiled. "I guess you feel somewhat out of place. Don't feel badly. There are a couple of guys over there who must feel even more conspicuous. They look like KGB flatfoots to me." She indicated a couple of portly middle-aged men in dark single-breasted suits who were standing together not saying much, drinking orange juice from disposable beakers. Michael glanced at them but did not comment. "I guess this kind of film is regulation viewing for those guys. Right up their street."

"There you go being American again. Why do you have to think that the Russians do not respect human life? It's so stupid."

"Now don't get mad. I only mean it must make them feel good to be reminded that there are fresh frontiers for the revolution, that's all."

"Well those people need a revolution. Are the Americans the only ones who are allowed to have had one?"

"Oh-oh. You're going to get round to El Salvador any minute."

"Yes, I am. I happen to know someone who was killed over there."

"Well I'm truly sorry about that, Michael, but don't take it out on me. But the fact is, if the Russians have friendly governments on our doorstep they'll start broadcasting all kinds of seductive stuff to our kids. You know the way they do it – five minutes 1940's pop music, two minutes documentary about comradely irrigation schemes in grateful underdeveloped countries. They'd only have to make Lenin look sort of like the Reverend Moon and they'd have gotten a real foothold in the psychology of the country."

"Oh well, if Americans are really so stupid I guess it doesn't matter what happens to them."

"Thank you, Michael. I may remind you that you wouldn't be standing here today if – Oh. Hi."

The two men in suits were passing them on their way back into the auditorium and had stopped to say good evening, smiling and nodding.

BJ stared after them. "Do you know those guys, then?"

"No. They must have mistaken me for someone else."

"But didn't one of them call you 'Misha'? That's a short form of Michael, isn't it?"

"I didn't hear that. Anyhow, I do not know them at all."

"Okay, okay." Michael was clearly lying. Given that his mainstream Germanic looks could have led to mistaken identity, she was quite sure that one of the men had called him 'Misha', and that that must mean that there was a degree of intimacy between them. Sexual, of course.

"By the way," said Michael, "are you still going to work? Whenever I call you're out."

"Oh yeah. As a matter of fact I'm phasing out the data sales job. I've found it impossible to develop a sound market base in the face of the blatant misogynism among business people over here. I've applied for a few jobs."

"Such as?"

"Well I've applied for one job as a marine engineer."

Michael's body slumped against the cigarette machine.

"But BJ, I thought your major was in Visual Arts."

"It was. But one has to be flexible." She laughed at his open-mouthed disbelief. "It's easy to get any kind of job if you put yourself over right. It all comes down to sales technique, Michael."

"But BJ, do you have any idea what a marine engineer does?"

"Sure. And the fact is I find heavy machinery extremely erotic."

Michael slumped again.

"By the way, do you realize the second half started about ten minutes ago?"

"Yes. Listen, would you mind if we go and have a drink instead? I think I got the message in the first half."

"Okay. I'm sorry you don't like it. I was so pleased you came, Michael. I thought you'd been avoiding me since we went to St

187

Gallen. Whenever I come over to sleep with you, you always have company. Or so you say. You never introduce me. Why don't you want me to meet them? Are you ashamed of me?"

"Perhaps I am ashamed of the company."

"That's what I figured."

If he was in the habit of bedding his porcine Russian chums it was no wonder he wanted to keep it quiet.

She tagged along happily after him to the nearest bar.


The Hubers were going home on Sunday, and on Saturday afternoon the doctor had promised to go down the sledge run with the boys, so Saturday morning was their last chance for him and Kirstin to meet.

High grey clouds had moved in over their clearing and they had to keep their anoraks on because of the cold. They lay face to face with their goose-pimpled legs entwined. The doctor had been trying to persuade her to meet him in Zürich after they got home, or Schaffhausen, or Appenzell – anywhere. It was so tempting, she was not even sure why she did not agree to it.

The doctor sighed. "I sometimes have the feeling I'm talking to a phon-o-mat. It's pretty depressing, you know."

"But I do get depressed when you talk like this. I just can't see it working. It will all get so complicated."

"I don't understand you. How can you make love to someone every day for a week and be so cold-blooded about it?"

"I'm not cold-blooded. Far from it. I don't want to break six hearts all at once. Please let's talk about something else."

"No. When are we going to get another chance to talk?"

He sat up on his elbow and rested his hand on her abdomen, which emerged from the anorak like a lollipop stick.

"So that's it. We just get back into our boxes and pretend nothing's happened."

"Don't keep trying to make me feel guilty. I can't break up your family. You can't make the world flat, you just can't."

"You don't love me enough to take the risk. You're only interested in my body."

She gave an exasperated shout, between laughing and crying.

"By the way," he said, "are you feeling all right? You haven't had a period?"

"No."

"What's your temperature?"

"Around 38."

"You could be pregnant, you know. I can't be sure, but it's worth checking."

Kirstin sat up slowly. "Oh no. You couldn't tell after a week, surely?"

"Don't be silly. It would be at least two months."

"It's not possible. My God, I don't believe it. Did you feel it? Is it a girl or a boy?"

"Don't get so excited. It isn't certain."

"How can I help getting excited? Nothing else matters to me – nothing. How soon can I find out?"

"Take a urine sample to a chemist. They'll tell you in a couple of hours."

"Let's go. I can't do anything till I find out."

"There's no rush. You have to take the sample first thing in the morning after you get up."

"Oh no. Tomorrow's Sunday. I'll have to wait two days."

"Hard cheese."

He was still lying propped up on his elbow, watching dismally as Kirstin's legs crunched and sank into the crusted snow in her rush to get dressed. The tone of his voice made her stop and look up. His body was slumped into a paradigm of rejection. She finished dressing and sank onto her knees on the mattress.

"Don't say anything," he said, after a longish silence.

"Ernst, what can I say? I didn't mean to hurt your feelings. But you do know how important this is to me, don't you? It's different for you, you've got five children already, and anyway it's always different for a man. You don't know how awful it is for a woman to be infertile."

"Yes I do. I watch *Dallas*."

"Surely you know from your patients –"

"Sure." He sat up. "Come on. We'll miss the train if we don't go now."

Kirstin took his arm as they walked down to the station. It was an effort to keep the bounce out of her step and fall in with his mood of dejection. She also had a sense of loss, but for what had been, not for what might have been. And there was something about the virtual sulk that the doctor had assumed that was hardening a core of self-protection in her. She could see that his motives where she was concerned were entirely selfish. Fair enough. As BJ maintained, true unselfishness was a contradiction in terms. But she had had enough of filling spaces in other people's lives. It was time to fill up the spaces in her own.

As the train approached Bergün again the doctor made an effort to perk up. He gave her some practical advice on how to take the urine sample.

"And if it's positive," he said, "you'd better go to an obstetrician for the pregnancy. I'll write down the name for you. Dr Kaiser. You may have heard of him."

"Yes. He's known as Bluebeard among the ladies. Does it have to be him?"

"He's extremely competent." He was also well known for reducing his patients to pulp if they voiced anxiety about their pain, lumps or issues of blood.

"I don't see why I can't go to you."

"I'd rather not."

Kirstin was disappointed, but accepted that it was the price she had to pay for preferring babies to lovers. She was aware that many men regarded children primarily as competition for the mother's lap. At least it was a competition that Max would not enter. She was surprised to find herself looking forward to telling him, rather than dreading his rage. Perhaps it had to do with the experience of being prized, if not above rubies, at least above Frau Huber, Christian, Michael, Joachim, Stefan and Remo.

The area around the Weisses Kreuz was choked with arriving and departing skiers. Trying to enter the hotel was like some ghastly medieval game where the object was to reach the door without being beheaded by an adult swivelling his skis into the neck, or castrated by a child doing the same thing to the groin. The doctor protectively ushered Kirstin into the hotel in front of him. Kirstin was glad that it was such an unsuitable atmosphere for heavy farewells.

They were to go to the parlour, so that Kirstin could say goodbye to Frau Huber. Before going in the doctor drew her aside.

"Listen, Kirstin – Well, I just hope you get what you want. And that it is what you want."

"Thank you. I –"

"You can't say the same to me, so please don't say anything. But let me know what happens, eh?"

"Of course."

"And for Christ's sake screw the top of the bottle on properly or it will spill all over your handbag."

# CHAPTER

# THIRTEEN

To mark Kirstin's thirtieth birthday BJ had bought her a gift worthy of her body and class. It was a rug from Russian Turkestan, about four feet by two, in several sludgy shades of rust and blue. It had been marked down from 5,300 francs to 4,730.

Kirstin was able to accurately price and appreciate the gift. She was embarrassed and overwhelmed by BJ's generosity, although not quite as overwhelmed as BJ had expected. There was something, BJ thought, of the practised air of royal gratitude, of the Queen of England on a foreign tour, warmly amazed by the presentation of a water-buffalo. Either Kirstin was accustomed to lavish gifts, or she assumed all Americans had money, whereas BJ had had a nightmarish week wiring her father for a loan to fill the gap in the bank account before Philip noticed it. Nevertheless BJ could not fault Kirstin's reaction on technical grounds. Every detail was picked on for comment, until there was nothing more to be said and Kirstin could not keep off the subject of her pregnancy. BJ was irritated. She resented her own badly enough: it compounded the humiliation to be expected to carry on the baby/knitting/shitty diaper junk conversations that traditionally went with it. The relationship she had envisaged with Kirstin had been of such a very different order.

Everything was changing. She even noticed that after receiving her gift Kirstin became much more attentive than she had been before. It saddened BJ somewhat, this less-than-regal susceptibility to the glamour of supposed wealth. But it made an agreeable change. She was anyway anxious to keep in touch with Kirstin, to know if there had been repercussions from BJ's letter about Max to the police. Since dashing it off in the heat of anger, she had been increasingly haunted by the possibility that it might be traced back to her, and the consequences from the police and, more dreadfully, from Max.

There was plenty of time to brood since she had run down the PIS job, and her lethargy was aggravated by an April heatwave. She envisaged a summer fattening up on the sofa with her feet up sixteen hours a day, convinced that her exquisite legs would be riddled with varicose veins the minute she stood up.

She had taken to sighing a lot in Philip's presence, and wondering why he never noticed. In her heart she was dying to share the awful truth with him, but since their row it had become harder and harder to say anything of any significance to each other.

It was not difficult to fill the day. The time not taken up by her few business and social contacts was equally divided by light housework, working out, and collapsing on the sofa with *Sexual Fantasies of Embryos*. It was no wonder that all American housewives were on drink or drugs or seeking oblivion in soap operas.

When she woke up, woozy and disorientated at five o'clock in the afternoon, the isolation, the pointlessness of life without work was crushing. She never knew where she would get the energy to fix dinner, and only the urge to go to the ice-box and get a large dish of pistachio ice cream and a peanut-butter sandwich could stir her into action. She consoled herself with the thought that it was a good thing to have drunk the gall of homemaking, in case she should ever be tempted to relax her career imperatives in the future. She rarely saw Michael except on the few occasions when he hung his washing out or fetched it in.

Under the circumstances it was hard to plaster over the cracks in her malaise brought about by the prospect of social contact with Kirstin and Geraldine, although their occasional lunches made for some sort of pattern. In tones of heavy sarcasm she complained to Philip that the coffee mornings had started and that it would be baby showers next, hoping that he would ask her what she was getting at. But he only remarked that she need not go if she did not want to.

It seemed to BJ that Philip was changing, too. He did not make love to her any more, but that was okay, because of course she had never really enjoyed it, and as they had never resolved their quarrel it was to be expected. More irritating was the fact that whenever he did start to communicate it was in the form of aggressive questioning of BJ's basic values, like the moral superiority of drop-outs. And he had reduced by almost fifty pounds, which was annoying at a time when BJ was gaining three pounds a week.

Before leaving for the next lunch appointment BJ bathed, massaged, powdered and painted herself with grim seriousness, seeking escape from her doom in the meshes of artifice.

Geraldine was not pregnant. In fact she was as thin as a deckchair and looked remarkably good, despite the pink-a-dink lipstick and pink sprigged muslin dress which she apparently thought appropriate for the occasion.

BJ congratulated her on her improved appearance as they sat down at the terraced restaurant, which was built out into the river like a bandstand. BJ thought that Kirstin had also gotten thinner. By the time they had got over the introductory remarks about the fact they could see the Alps, and ordered a bottle of white wine and some Black Forest Gateau, they were all sweltering hot under the bare branches.

"I guess we shouldn't really be drinking this stuff," said BJ, taking a swig of the St Saphorin. She had noticed a couple of tubby men in pale suits, of some slit-eyed, bottle-brush-haired Asiatic origin, slumped on their table over glasses of beer, rolling their heads and blinking at her like giant pandas. She supposed that in this city of skeletal women her now plumped-up flesh looked longingly attractive to them.

"Perhaps I should get really fat," she thought out loud. "I guess there's nothing essentially ugly about fat. It sort of reduces you to a kind of slavery to your body that could actually be quite erotic."

"You certainly come from the right country for fulfilling that dream," said Geraldine. "When we were in Florida everyone kept asking if we were so thin because Europe still had food shortages after the war. It's all we could do to dissuade them from air-lifting food parcels."

"Oh? When were you in Florida, Geraldine?"

"About nine years ago. I got pregnant in a motel in Talahassie. It always happens on holiday, doesn't it?"

"Not in my case. Unless you call my enforced detention in Switzerland a holiday."

"You're looking forward to going home, I take it?"

"Yeah." BJ grabbed her wine glass, caught unawares by a lump in the throat. "Well Kirstin, and how's life on the farm? How's your doctor?"

193

A raspberry ripple flooded up Kirstin's face. "Fine, as far as I know. I have not seen him for a long time." Nor had she ever found the right moment to tell BJ about the Bergün interlude.

"How's Max taken the news about the kid?"

"I have not told him yet."

Geraldine and BJ silently raised their eyebrows.

"That's perfectly understandable," said BJ. "It will probably bring on a miscarriage. I wish I could say the same about telling Philip."

"Now, BJ, don't exaggerate," said Geraldine. "I know you didn't plan this, but you'll be glad later."

"Don't patronize me, Geraldine, I'm not in the mood."

Geraldine pursed her lips and drank some more wine. Kirstin glanced at her watch.

There was an embarrassing silence. Geraldine noticed that BJ was on the verge of tears. She assumed a breezy tone.

"Well I thought having babies was very exciting. You never know what's going to conk out next."

Silence resumed.

BJ gulped. "Shall we just – go – now?"

"No, no," said Kirstin. She put a hand on BJ's arm. "Listen, we must be able to being honest wiv each other wivout making offences, yes?"

"Yes, apart from the grammar."

"Oh dear. It is so hot I think my brain is smelting."

"Don't worry, love," said Geraldine, "it's the same with me. My English is atrocious these days. I've been away so long I couldn't tell you the difference between litotes and fish and chips. I listen to the radio just to keep in touch, but it's a mixed blessing, you know how improving the Beeb likes to be. Oh dear, the other day, for example. Guitar Workshop followed by Atrocities of the Cultural Revolution. It was just revolting. I couldn't tell you all the things they did. I was cooking liver as well."

"Like what?" said BJ.

"Oh I'd rather not say. You'd both be sick."

"Why?"

"Well it was so awful. What they did to women. You know. Their breasts."

"What?"

"I can't remember the details."

"Please try."

"Go on."

"No."

"Please."

"No!"

"Spoilsport."

Kirstin and Geraldine laughed.

"Honestly, BJ," said Geraldine, "you go too far."

"No I don't. You had all the fun of hearing the details, but you deny it to us. That's real mean."

"Actually, you're right," said Geraldine. "Only this morning I hid a copy of *Newsweek* from the children because it had pictures of those criminals in India who had their eyes gouged out. And as soon as they were out of the house I read the article down to the small print."

"Exactly. Actually," said BJ, looking at Geraldine with new respect, "you're not the sort of person I'd have expected to make an admission like that. That's – that's good."

"I'm not a complete dead loss," said Geraldine.

"No, I can see that."

"I suppose it's just sex."

"Sure. Though I like animal violence better. You know, I saw a public TV special once, about elks – or moose – something with horns. The camera lingered on these two animals killing each other – all in awed silence, of course, just the crunch of antlers – because, I mean, this is Nature, right kids? And we all know animals are nicer than people, right? So whatever animals do is okay, and what's even better is, it's okay for us to watch it in slow motion. It was really funny."

"Have you ever," said Geraldine, "watched a slug eating a live worm? I have. For about an hour, just to illustrate your point."

"Did it turn you on?"

"No, but that's because my apparatus clapped out several years ago."

"Jesus, are you serious? You mean you don't have orgasms any more?"

"Well, let me see. I think I had one in 1978, but ever since then I've been too tired."

"Jesus. Does that always happen after you have a kid? I never thought of that."

"Oh, don't take my word for it. The English aren't a very sensuous race, you know. Stiff upper clitoris, and all that."

"I'd better check that out," said BJ, her mood darkening after the lift it had received while talking about violence. "Listen, if I didn't have an orgasm every day I'd get sick. Most of the women I know in the States are the same way."

195

"How do you know that? Do you normally talk about that sort of thing when you're sober? I thought it must be the wine."

"Huh? Of course not. In the States people talk openly about everything these days. There's been a real change in the climate the last few years."

"How appalling. You mean people at dinner parties ask you when you last had an orgasm? I thought it was bad enough being asked how much you earn."

"Well that's – as usual – somewhat exaggerated." BJ smiled. "What I mean is, people are real honest about their bodies."

"But what about people who don't want to know?"

"They don't have to tune in."

"You mean this goes on on television too?"

"Sure. It's healthy. Everything is discussed right there in your living-room – calmly, scientifically –" She made a calm, scientific gesture. "And what it means is, there are no embarrassing diseases any more. You get really somewhat prominent people in the community coming forward and admitting they've got herpes, or whatever. Well sometimes they're blacked out so they can't be recognized, but what I mean is, you don't have to feel like a leper any more just because you've got some freak thing wrong with you. Like, just before I left I was watching a discussion programme about how to get the best out of anal intercourse, and there was another one about new surgical procedures for reconstructing a penis. It's highly informative and – sort of – mature, and it makes you realize the world is full of people with hairy breasts or VD, or whatever, and I think that's healthy."

"How do you reconstruct a penis?" asked Geraldine, fascinated.

"I don't know, I wasn't really listening."

"Please," said Kirstin, "I am not understanding."

"Sorry, love," said Geraldine. "We're being very rude. When did you last have an orgasm?"

"Oh. I don't remember."

"It must have been a good one," said Geraldine, laughing at the blush that had sprung to Kirstin's face.

"You seem to have a lot of hot flushes, Kirstin," said BJ kindly. "Is that the pregnancy?"

"I tink so, yes."

"I've noticed that too. Are you taking anything for it?"

"No. I think it is only because I am very stressed until I am telling Max."

"Then why not tell him?" said Geraldine. "I'll stand outside with the tranquillizer darts."

196

"Tank you, but I would rather be alone."

"You're right about the stress thing," said BJ. "Putting it off doesn't solve the problem. But Philip's acting somewhat strangely at the moment. Sort of not noticing things. I sometimes think I could go the whole nine months and he still wouldn't catch on."

"Does he look – diffferent?" said Geraldine.

"He's reduced quite a bit."

"Cherchez la femme."

BJ had not done French in school so the inference passed her by. And her attention had been caught by what looked like Michael and a woman walking along the opposite bank of the river. She quickly put on her glasses to get a better look and sat anxiously scanning the distant figures.

Kirstin frowned at Geraldine. "Not Philip also?" she said.

Geraldine shrugged. "Why not? He's nice." She looked to see if BJ was still distracted and lowered her voice. "He's actually much more attractive than she implies. A bit – massive – you know, but very civilized. Godzilla after five years of prep. school. He has that air of the gentle beast which personally I find very attractive."

"Oh dear," said Kirstin. "Zat would be terrible unfortunate."

"It's just speculation. There's probably nothing in it."

BJ turned back to them with a sigh and took off her glasses. "I'm sure that was Michael," she said. "Absolutely sure."

"Any reason why it shouldn't be?" asked Geraldine.

"He was with a woman. That's – that's somewhat disturbing."

"It seems natural enough to me. Are you surprised because you thought he was homosexual?"

"Not entirely. He sleeps with women on an individual basis, I'm sure."

"Then what's funny about it?"

"I just wouldn't have expected to see him walking around town with one."

"It seems slightly less incriminating than sleeping with them," said Geraldine.

But BJ was chewing her lips and frowning into the distance and was clearly not able to discuss the nature of the turmoil she had been thrown into. She had automatically dismissed Kirstin and Geraldine as unqualified to make the slightest comment on Michael.

Geraldine tried a number of unrelated conversational ploys to re-engage BJ's attention, but to no avail. Frustrated by her failure to do so, she peremptorily summoned the waitress for the bill.

"Will you walk to the station with us, BJ?" she asked.

197

"Okay."

They strolled over to the Bahnhofstrasse, which was bright and animated with the rich and suntanned, and a representative selection of their inferiors. They were obliged to stop for an extended family of Africans in tribal finery who were spilling out of a black Cadillac and into a bank. The chauffeur was anxiously gathering up fly-swats and shopping bags from the car.

Kirstin and Geraldine smiled and were pleased by the sight of the exuberant black party, but BJ looked on with faint enthusiasm.

"Wasn't that nice?" said Geraldine, as the last cheeky black child skipped into the bank in the wake of the billowing Liberty prints.

"In what way?" said BJ.

"Well – you know – seeing them lord it over everyone for a change."

"I guess it depends how many tribes they massacred to get here."

"Are you implying they're still savages? I wouldn't have thought you were a racist, BJ."

"I'm not. You were the one who thought it was cute seeing a black family get out of a Cadillac. My prejudices are not based on colour at all."

Geraldine drew breath in speechless confusion, and quickened their pace until they reached the subway entry into the station.

"We still have a little time," said Kirstin to BJ. "Will you have a coffee wiv us?"

"No thank you," said BJ. "I have some thinking to do. I think I'll just go back down the Niederdorf."

She crossed over the tramlines, heading for the area where she had seen Michael and the woman. She walked all the way back to the lake, criss-crossing through the side streets, peering into shops and cafés and even poking her head nervously into strip joints and gaming halls.

When she reached the bridge at Bellevue she was exhausted. She went down to the edge of the water where the pleasure ships were berthed and slumped onto a concrete slab. Her attention was briefly caught by a couple of lily-white sunbathers stretched out on a jetty. But it was not her quarry and she subsided again, took out an open packet of stale cigarettes and began to chainsmoke them, gazing across the water, lost in thought.

After what seemed to her like several hours, but was actually forty minutes, she stood up, and abruptly sat down again. Her heart squelched wildly and she thought she would pass out. A man who was passing stopped to offer assistance and BJ, grateful and frightened, permitted him to help her walk slowly to the tram station. He insisted on staying to see her into the tram, and by the time it came she had recovered enough to obtain a fair amount of personal information about him. He was Swiss, of an Italian mother who had been having an affair with a Jewish building magnate for the last twenty years. He himself managed a body shop, specializing in procuring technical experts for Third World projects, and he was married to a Swiss-American woman whom he suspected of sleeping with his younger brother who was living with them while he finished his studies in bio-chemistry. No children. BJ decided he was really quite cute, and managed to scribble his name and telephone number on the cigarette packet while climbing aboard the tram.

The acquisition of this data package distracted her for a while, but it was not long before dejection and dread returned. To reach the office where Philip worked she had to change trams, and as the next one shunted up the Bahnhofstrasse towards her, associations of tumbrils and pogrom specials came with it. Sitting by the lake she had faced the truth that she must tell Philip about the kid, that planning on other relationships only heightened the poignancy of her impotence at the present time, and that the kid should start out in life with two parents, at least till around eighteen months when it could begin to take care of itself. BJ felt herself weighed down with Wagnerian-type heroism as a result of this decision, and at the same time she felt that physically and emotionally she had never approached Philip at a lower ebb.


The interior of the building where Philip worked was classically arched and cool, updated with cushioned vinyl and sparsely decorated with notice boards and glass cases containing models of the molecular wonders of the world. When BJ knocked at the door of Philip's office there was no reply. She opened it and went in.

At first glance she could have been looking at a storeroom in a wax museum. Philip sat motionless at his desk, one arm resting on it, contemplating his blotter. Leaning against a filing cabinet was the graduate student who had handed over the key to their apartment. At that time she had been swathed in scarves and raincoat, but in jeans and a Save-the-Trees T-shirt her appearance was startling. Her features were strongly chiselled, of a jutting sensuality that suggested Elvis Presley in repose, her well-proportioned muscular limbs were grafted onto a tiny Mr Universe waist. BJ's admiration was instantly and ungrudgingly activated.

"Hi," she said, sinking into a padded leather chair that let out a slight fart on impact. "You have a sensational body."

"I do? Thanks." She half-smiled, colouring a little. Her voice was low and steady.

"This is Prunelle Baker, BJ," said Philip. "You've met."

"Yes. Hi," repeated BJ. "You're a grad. student?"

"Yes, I am." She glanced at Philip as she spoke. "I guess I'd better be going."

"Okay," said BJ. "Bye, Prunelle. You must come by for dinner some time."

"Thanks."

BJ's eyes lingered on Prunelle's rear as she left the office. "Truly sensational," she remarked wearily. "Boy, am I glad you're in. When you didn't answer I was afraid you'd gone already."

"We were talking."

"I'm sorry. Did I interrupt anything important?"

"It can wait. I didn't expect it to be you, BJ. It's so long since you've come by the office."

"Well, we do see each other at home."

"So what's different about today?"

"Oh. Well –" Her heart had started to flap eagles' wings again, and she leant forward with her head in her hands.

"Is anything wrong, BJ?" For the first time he spoke with a slight intonation in his voice. "Are you sick?"

"No. No, I'm okay now." She sat up and smoothed her hair and laughed. "Actually I'm pregnant." Then she burst into tears.

Philip passed her a man-sized paper tissue. "I thought so. How long?"

"About four months."

"He was silent for a while and then he said, "I see."

BJ tried to smile. She was puzzled. The dam was taking longer to burst than she had anticipated.

"Am I the father?"

"Are you – Well, of course, Philip. It's since we came to Switzerland. I haven't been to bed with anyone since we came to Switzerland. It's been a total bust from that point of view."

"I see. I just wondered why you took so long to tell me."

"I wanted to be sure. I knew you'd get all excited about it and then –"

"I see." He resumed contemplating his blotter, but with a frown.

BJ gave a short laugh. "Well," she said, "you certainly aren't reacting the way I expected."

"What did you expect, BJ?"

She shrugged. "I don't know. I thought you always wanted kids."

200

It was a struggle to keep the tears out of her voice.

"I did."

"You did? You mean you've changed your mind? That's great. Terrific. What a time to tell me."

"I didn't plan it like this."

"Neither did I."

There was an agonized silence. BJ did not trust herself to speak.

Philip finally leant back in his chair and clasped his hands together. When he spoke his tone was professional, breaking bad news to an eager student.

"The fact is, BJ, that at the time I was keen to have kids the dynamics of our relationship were very different from what they are now. I honestly thought of our marriage as a lifetime commitment. I kinda assumed that around thirty, thirty-five, you'd see things a bit differently, maybe." He paused, from force of habit, to give her a chance to produce a statistical challenge, but BJ was silent. "That didn't happen."

BJ looked up, about to remind him that she was only thirty-one. But she decided not to bother. If Philip was being unscientific he had clearly moved out of the realms of objective to that of personal truth, at whose doors logic and statistics beat in vain. She knew what was coming. She concentrated on being able to hear her sentence with dignified indifference.

"The fact is, BJ, over the last few months – Well, you know yourself we haven't been getting along." He paused for objections again, with the same result. "The question of whether or not to have kids was irrelevant. I just haven't thought about it. What I have been thinking about, very seriously, is whether or not we still have a marriage." Silence. "And I have to say that I really don't think we do any more. I think this trip has shown up too many weaknesses in our relationship."

"And what did you have in mind to do about it?"

"I think we should live apart for a while."

"Uh-huh. And the kid? What about the kid?"

"Don't worry, I'll see you have an adequate settlement."

"A settlement. Oh-oh. Are you thinking of legal tie-ups already?"

"BJ, I wish to God you weren't pregnant, but the fact is I'd already made my decision."

"And the kid makes no difference? Huh?" She leaned towards him, her fist clenched on the desk, but she could not again draw his attention from the blotter. She leapt up. "You fucking bastard! How could you desert your own kid? It isn't even born yet!"

"Look, I haven't had time to think about this, but surely it's better to make a clean break before a relationship is established. If you want we could stay together until it's born, but I think it would only make things more difficult."

BJ stared at him, her breath coming in short, incredulous gasps. "You mean you're planning on a divorce? Like, now? Like, that's it? Just pull the plug out and no discussion. I can't believe this. We can't get divorced, Philip – we're married! What about our relationship? You can't just write it off like that after eight years. Why does it have to be so final?"

Philip shifted in his seat and began to look uncomfortable. BJ sat down again.

"Wait a minute," she said. "There can only be one reason you want a divorce so fast. So you can be free to re-marry, right?" Silence. "Or at least free." Philip took his glasses off and rubbed his eyes and put them back on again. "Your friend with the body wouldn't have anything to do with it, by any chance?"

"What friend?"

"That girl who was in here – Prune something."

"Okay, BJ, don't try and get smart about it. If you want to know, yes, she does have something to do with it. But not everything. I would never have started a relationship with her if things had been good between us."

"So. You've slept with her already."

"That's none of your business, BJ."

"Huh! That's cool."

"It's the way you've always wanted it, BJ."

"True. That's somewhat irrelevant, anyway. I guess there have been others. But I guess Prune is special. You think you're in love with her, do you?"

"I'm sorry, BJ, I can't discuss her with you."

"But it's probably okay to discuss me with her."

"Not at all. I've told her what's appropriate, of course."

"And what is appropriate? Go on, tell me. Just what do you consider the salient points of the situation?"

"You really want to know what I told her?"

"Yes."

"Well, I told her that I considered you had married me for my social position and the prospects attached to it and that you accepted all the benefits arising from the marriage without accepting any personal commitment."

BJ gasped. "You didn't! Philip, that's total crap!"

"That's the way I see it."

"What personal commitment are you talking about? Having kids? Well, I'm having one. What do you mean by that? We always did things together. Of course, we maintained our freedom as individuals –"

"No. You maintained it, BJ. I always wanted you to myself, but you insisted on spreading yourself around." He looked at her directly, a tremor of emotion breaking through.

"Well of course I did, at my age. How could I promise to give up sex in the prime of life? Before the prime of life, even, when I married you. Are you saying that's all there was to it? Nothing else to be taken into consideration except this medieval fidelity thing? We had a decent, civilized, practical relationship."

"A medieval one."

"Huh? But Philip, we enjoyed it that way, didn't we?"

"You made the best of a bad job, yes. I told you I considered your motives were entirely self-interest."

"Oh come on. You make it sound like you picked me out of the gutter and gave me my first bath. I admit your family has class, and I was probably somewhat influenced by that, but it would take more than that to lure me into a crummy cat-food empire if I didn't have strong personal motivations too. On a strictly commercial basis I can tell you I had much more attractive offers. Remember that guy Pierre who was caretaker of the Church of Divine Bran, or whatever it was called?"

"The Church of Bio-ethnic Divinity."

"Right. Well he was crazy about me, and his family were in petro-chemicals. They had an outfit that makes Uncle Remus look like a garage sale."

"So what you're saying is, you didn't sell yourself to the highest bidder. It doesn't alter the fact, BJ, that I've always had this feeling you married me for other than emotional reasons."

"Of course I did. That doesn't mean there weren't emotional reasons too."

"I've never seen much evidence of that."

"Oh, what's the point of going into all that? People get married for one reason, and they stay married for other reasons. Like the kid. Who's going to look after the kid?"

"Don't you want to?"

"No." She started crying. "I wanted to get rid of it, if you must know, but this country's so backward you can't bribe anyone for an abortion."

"I don't think you can have tried hard enough. It can be done."

"But why should it? I didn't know you were going to be such a rat as to walk out on me at a time like this."

"Aren't you just jealous because you can't walk out? I gather you're all for it, but as you can't you're determined that I won't either."

"Right. The only way I can get rid of it is to kill myself."

"Is that a threat, BJ?"

"No Philip. It's a statement of fact."

"That's the way things are, BJ. Nature hasn't evolved to accommodate women like you yet."

"That's not true. There's a water bird called the jacana where the female runs off with someone else after the birth and leaves the father to bring up the chicks."

"BJ, you cannot model your behaviour on that of a little-known water bird."

"Oh, where does rational argument get you anyway? God, I'm so exhausted. You have no idea how exhausted I am."

"Have you been drinking, BJ? You look flushed."

"I had a little wine, that's all. It's so fucking hot."

"I should go home and lie down. We can discuss this later."

"No. From what you've been saying there's nothing to discuss."

"Then what do you want to do?"

"I want to go home. I just want to go home. I can't stand this anymore."

"To the States?" BJ nodded, gulps of tears shaking her. "Perhaps that would be the best thing. Here, don't go on like that. It's bad for the baby." He put out a hand to her but she hit it away.

"Don't patronize me." She got up. "I'm . . . going . . . back to the apartment now."

"I'll come up in about an hour."

"No, Philip. Don't come – unless – you – mean – to stay."

"How's that?"

"Listen, if we're going to – split up – let's do it now. Right now. I don't want to see you again, okay? Except in court. You think about it. Talk to Prune, talk to anyone you want, but please don't come back to the apartment unless you intend to stay with me."

"I can't make a decision as quickly as that."

"You said you'd already made it. You said yourself putting it off would only make things worse."

"Sure, but –"

"But you want to wait till you've got your new nest feathered? Oh no. Sorry. If you're going to fuck up my life like this you're going to have to put up with some inconvenience."

"I didn't want to fuck up your life, BJ. Be fair. As far as I knew you had several options, any of which would have been a fair exchange for our marriage."

"That was before the kid. I have no options now. None."

"Well I'm sorry. If the kid had been here a year ago this would never have happened."

"Well I'll tell him that, Philip. I'll tell him he ballsed up his opening move. He must have my brains and your feet."

"BJ –"

"Goodbye, Philip." She moved towards the door.

Philip stood up, gripped by an afterthought. "What are you going to call him?"

" 'Reject'." She slammed out.

# CHAPTER

# FOURTEEN

HERR Waldvogel's preening jollity following the success of his Singapore trip was almost more than Max could bear. He had bounced into Max's office virtually flourishing order forms. Steel clamps closed round those portions of Max's brain that were ordering him to feed Herr Waldvogel into the shredder. Herr Waldvogel had not only got an order from a pirate radio station for two turbo-charged engines, but he had sold a stationary generator to a "crazy coolie" he met in a massage parlour who was setting up a plant to turn manure into methane gas. Max had frowned and looked disapproving. Herr Waldvogel was irritated.

"All right, there's no need to look at me like that. We're in sales, not education. And I've stirred up some interest in the uniflow scavenged engines too, Max." These were the white hope of the department. "Now what I want to know is, do you think you're up to following through on this? As we've already discussed, your record lately has been pretty pathetic, hasn't it Max?"

"I cannot turn straw into gold. If you want to exchange territories I think the figures would speak for themselves."

"I thought you might take that line. And of course there is some truth in that, Max. But –" He screwed up his face and scratched his head. "You've got to inspire more confidence, Max. Trust. Warmth. Do you know what I mean? You've got to be relaxed, but alert, persuasive without being intimidating."

"Like you?"

"Well I get the results, don't I? Your taking umbrage won't help." He sat down. "Look, is there anything bothering you? Personal problems, that sort of thing."

"Certainly not."

"All right." Herr Waldvogel got up again with knee-jerk speed, as if retrieving a toe from boiling water. "I've had my say. I'll give you this project, Max, as a trial. It could be your territory has gone stale on you. We'll see. How's your English? We'll arrange a refresher course if you like."

"All right."

"By the way, did you clear up the matter with your friend in Prague?"

"I . . . I'm just ignoring it."

"You can start a clean slate with the new territory, Max. No scandal, all right? Head Office is getting a bit worried about our image, with the rise of fundamentalism and whathaveyou."

"Are they planning to introduce the Sharia into the office by any chance?"

"Look, I'm just trying to give you some friendly advice."

It was a struggle for Max to remain seated after Herr Waldvogel had left the room. His loathing for the man conflicted with a relief almost amounting to gratitude for the opportunity Herr Waldvogel was giving him to move into the Far East, at present the Captain's table of sales areas.

It would be a good idea if he immediately established with Annalie Schumacher her willingness to participate in his renewal, especially if Humbel Brothers was looking into the moral fibre of its employees. Herr Waldvogel would take Kirstin's side, of course, so the sooner the unpleasantness was over, the better. Unfortunately Annalie was away on holiday.

Theirs was a curiously unbalanced affair. He now had difficulty reconstructing the scene in the Xerox room where it had all started, perhaps because, afterwards, he was reluctant to remember that it was Annalie who had suggested they have sex. He preferred to think of it as some mysterious process of natural selection. She had certainly personified his female counterpart, that is, the ultimately desirable today's woman, with her tight fashion breeches and aggressive rise through Spare Parts. Her suggestion had so surprised him he could have been felled to the ground and robbed, but he had remained outwardly cool and quickly adjusted to the arrangement.

But one reason he was now anxious to consolidate his position was that for some weeks there had been no position. And then she had gone on holiday without telling him. He looked at his watch and counted the days until she would be back.

When BJ got home to the apartment she sliced a cucumber and lay in a horse-chestnut bath with the slices plastered over her face, contemplating the possibility of never getting out again.

The image of Prunelle Baker lolling against the filing cabinet with the relaxed confidence of the all-in wrestler bestrode her imagination. It was of course perfectly natural that Philip should have lain down with this Attila of grad. students. Their bodies complemented each other exactly. It would have been like two Great Gates of Kiev coming upon each other on a crowded beach.

But the attendant prospect of Philip and her cleaving to each other through the rest of their lives, and BJ's life, of Philip's transferring his allegiance, his person, possessions, his tentacles in the cat-food industry, his aristocratic family, the beach house in Maine, his knowledge of things like the insides of air conditioners and starting stick-shift automobiles without an ignition key, and laying all these things at Prunelle Baker's feet – this was a prospect that momentarily bereft BJ of the will to live. She now knew that even if she were not pregnant and unable to work, life without Philip would be intolerably difficult and unpleasant, at least for as long as it took to establish a new relationship. Her failure to interpret the signs Philip had thrown in her path like concrete slabs disgusted her. She should have become suspicious the first time he left his dinner roll on the side. It was shattering to realize that she had been unable to use her unique perceptions of sexual dynamics to shift her own traditionally blinkered perspective.

Her watch was on a chair by the bath. 7.07. The water had gone cold. She flipped the drain open with her toe, let some out and filled it up with hot. She tried to work out the earliest possible time that his return could be expected. Assuming that his program would include a long soul session with Prune, dinner, and perhaps some lonely pacing about the indifferent metropolis, the earliest possible deadline would be 10.30. She thought she might expire of nervous tension long before. If she at least knew her fate she could swing into healing action. But until then she must endure this death-cell drama that paralysed her in the face of any activity at all, even, after a while, re-filling the bath. She lay in the cold water sighing and sobbing, shifting from one side to the other, seeking the comfort of the relatively warm air on her body.

Then she felt something strange going on in her lower abdomen, as if a hamster had got in and was nosing around for the exit. Breathless, she removed one cucumber slice and squinted down at her abdomen. There was a tiny pulse under the skin. She experienced a slight flutter of excitement. At least it was a highly active, dominating-type personality if it was kicking around already. Like herself. She got out of the bath to see if it would still work while she was walking around, but it did not. The temporary distraction roused her sufficiently to get her to the ice-box and two peanut butter sandwiches and half a congealed apricot cobbler.

Once they were eaten she put on her robe and padded round the apartment picking things up and putting them down again, staring out of the window at Michael's apartment, flinging herself on the sofa and leaping up again after thirty seconds. She took all the books off the shelves and threw them on the floor. In the process of kicking them around a bit, another slug of despair hit her. They were all Philip's books. If he went the shelves would be bare, apart from *Sexual Fantasies of Embryos* and a few paperback best sellers.

She sat down on the pile and flipped through a couple of volumes. Inside *Convexity in the Theory of Lattice Gases* she came upon a Photomat strip of Prunelle Baker, her jaw clenched in an uneasy smile, eyes popping into the flash.

BJ's heart stopped for a second as she picked up the photo. Its presence in the apartment seemed to add a whole new dimension of finality to the affair. It might have been there for months, and its concealment seemed to invest it with the sinister threat of a voodoo doll. It brought home to BJ, as nothing else, the seriousness of the relationship between Philip and this leonine female. It was all very well to sleep with someone, even to talk of marrying them, but to possess their likeness was a semi-official procedure that made subsequent official ones more natural and more likely.

A leaden resignation descended, which wiped out all but the faintest flutter of hope. She thought back on the scene in Philip's office, hoping to recall some evidence that Philip was painfully torn between conflicting loyalties, which would allow of the possibility that her case would be considered. But the evidence was all the other way: he had shown no guilt about leaving her or the kid, he had seemed to have been storing up enabling resentment against her for years, he had asked her what she intended to call the kid – the most telling detail of all for someone whose own dynasty pre-dated the harnessing of electricity.

She had lost. It was only a question of surviving the hours that would end with the conclusive proof that she had lost.

Grimly satisfied that Philip would be left to foot the bill, she telephoned her mother in Malden, Massachussetts, and in an unpunctuated torrent of misery told her mother everything, ignoring her shocked attempts to interrupt. When her narrative had brought her up to the moment she picked up the phone she paused and asked her mother what she should do.

"Honey, I just don't know what to say. I'm just so shocked. You'd better come home right away." She paused. "This is going to kill your father."

"It may kill me, Mother."

"No, no, don't say that, Bernice, that's wicked talk, honey."

"Well as usual your instincts are trying to make me feel guilty."

"No I'm not, honey. Now don't be ugly, let's talk about this quietly. I only mean it's going to be a terrible blow for your father."

"So what do you expect me to do about it? Make it not true? Don't you think I'd do that if I could? Who the fuck is this happening to, anyhow? It's not happening to Dad, it's happening to me. He's had his life."

"That's awful hard, Bernice. He's a good man. He loves you so."

"Christ. I can't stand this. Goodbye, Mother."

BJ slammed down the receiver and went into the kitchen to make coffee, anticipating a vigil. She took an unopened packet of chocolate cookies back into the living-room and stationed herself at the telephone with her address book.

A thundering swag of grassy bombs dropped from Pinot Gloire's rear as Kirstin entered the stall to groom him for the last time. She was touched: it showed how excited he was to see her. It had been so long since she had been able to ride him that he had started to eat his own droppings in protest, and now there was the fear of miscarriage to be considered, so it had been expedient to sell him on several counts. Max had only commented that it was certainly high time she started divesting herself of emotional props. As a mark of approval for this first attempt to strengthen her character he had offered to remove the dinner dishes onto the kitchen table for her to do later, so that she could get down to the stable before it got dark.

In the field behind her house sticks marking the dimensions of the new properties bent before the wind. Their sinister skeletal outlines produced a feeling of stifled panic. She wished they would put up the houses ready-made, instead of forcing one to witness the heaping of brick after brick upon the individual will.

The May evening was cold, the clouds lined with a steely sheen, and the wind buffeted incoming groups of swallows over the sprouting maize fields. As she walked down from her house the wind flattened the skin across her bones and ripped away curses from those struggling to lay plastic sheeting over the seedbeds of early lettuce and spinach.

It was a relief to get into the steaming stall. There were stalls for three horses but two were empty, and Pinot occupied the one farthest from the door. As she fetched his feed and began to sweep up the sodden straw a martin nesting in the corner staged a noisy display of threatening swoops through the open door. Kirstin could hear the tiny chatter of its young, no doubt affected by their parent's agitation and the booming wind. She felt on edge herself, and Pinot was bucking and snorting more than usual.

It was a while before she realized that she was being watched, that the bird was dive-bombing a shadowy figure outside the door. The wind was raging over a profound silence now. She moved fearfully towards the door.

"Who's there? Is anybody there?"

The man stepped into the stall, closing the lower door behind him. It was Herr Umberg. His bulk blocked out the light so that she could not clearly see his face, but half-sounds of nervous movement came from it. He was breathing noisily.

Kirstin stood beside Pinot, clutching a curry comb out in front of her in a defensive pose.

"I've n-nearly f-finished Herr Um-m-mberg," she stuttered. Her jaw was vibrating independently.

Still he said nothing, but moved a bit closer towards her, his hands dangling at his sides.

"I – I'm g-going n-now." She could feel her mouth rolling with the painful effort of the deaf and dumb.

"Not yet, eh? Not yet."

"N-no – d-don't – t-touch – m-me –"

He took her by both wrists and pulled her out of the stall and up against the back wall. They struggled. Kirstin tried to pull her mouth away from the malodorous weight of his body pressed up against her face. He began to pull at her trousers. She tried to remember the karate blows that Max had once demonstrated, but the sight of Herr Umberg's dripping nostrils pressed up to her cheek made her want to vomit, even if she had been able to twist a hand free from Herr Umberg's grasp.

"Just let me – just let me –" he mumbled, his stained cheeks flapping.

"N-no Herr Umm-b-berg I'm p-p-pregnat – d-don't t-touch –"

"No you're not, Frau. Everyone knows you can't have any –"

"B-but its t-t-true – p-please –"

"You're just saying that – just let me – please –"

The gate of Pinot's stall was open. As they struggled the horse backed out, stamping and tossing his head. Herr Umberg had grasped her pubis. Kirstin screamed. Herr Umberg looked round as the horse's flank blundered against him. He let go of Kirstin with one hand and tried to push the horse away, but the animal was beginning to panic, and just as she managed to get one hand off her arm Pinot's thrashing hoof crunched onto Herr Umberg's foot, and as he staggered away another kick got his shinbone. He stumbled over towards the door and fell on the floor, something oozing from his mouth, but whether blood or sick Kirstin could not tell.

Pinot stood still, as if to work out why it had suddenly gone quiet. Kirstin went to him unsteadily and managed to pull him back into the stall and tie him up. She put her arms round his neck and buried her face in his mane. He quietened down and nonchalantly studied his hooves. Then she noticed that her trousers were still round her knees and she pulled them up, looking over to where Herr Umberg lay groaning on the floor.

Hugging her stomach as if something had fallen out, she limped over to him. He was a truly sickening sight, the flabby, lumpen body, dripping eyes and nose, the chattering teeth blunted and stained, like the horse's. He looked up at her, and put a trembling hand to his face, as if afraid she might hit him. Kirstin thought she was going to faint and quickly lay down, but in that position the lurch of nausea jack-knifed through her. She jumped up and just made it over to the pile of dung. Then she went and sat down against the wall.

For a while neither of them spoke. Herr Umberg groaned and sobbed and held his leg: Kirstin stared past him, wondering if she could escape without his touching her.

Then she said, "I should call an ambulance for you. Your leg." Her mouth was still stiff.

"No! I don't want to be taken away. A-ah!"

"All right."

"It'd kill my wife, Frau Baumann, see. You won't give me away, eh? I don't know what sets me off."

Perhaps he had been watching the same educational programme about child prostitution that Max had been curled up in front of when she left.

"Your leg isn't broken?"

"I don't know. Too bad he didn't aim a bit higher. I should be shot, eh? A-ah!"

"Pinot never did like men. You must stop this, Herr Umberg. You should go to the doctor. It would be completely confidential. He could arrange treatment."

"He's just a boy. What does he know? You think I should give myself up? I've thought about it. But then, what would happen to the wife?"

He gave her a suspiciously straight look. Kirstin scarcely credited his audacity, but he seemed to be hinting that she was the obvious candidate.

"You've got a big house," he remarked.

"Haven't you any nieces – or cousins?"

"No."

He must be lying, thought Kirstin. But she could understand why. She would certainly never entrust Max to the care of her relations.

"Anyhow," he said, "I couldn't get this treatment without it all coming out. I'd have to go to prison. I couldn't stand it."

"But you may have to anyway."

"Why – you wouldn't say anything, would you?"

"No. But Fraulein Pagliacci – she might still go to the police. Didn't you wonder why she hasn't already?"

"I asked her not to. I've known her since she was a baby, you know. Used to take her up on the tractor all the time."

"Herr Umberg you are – adrift. You're just not thinking straight any more. You're definitely sick. What started all this? Are you worrying about something?"

"Of course. I never stop worrying. Who does?"

"About this Roggenburger business, I suppose. Was that it?"

"Perhaps. You think I should go to some psychiatrist chap and talk about my mum and dad?"

"I don't know about your mum and dad, but you could talk about the fucking road."

"Would he let me dig it up?"

"Well – no."

"That's what I feel like doing sometimes. Just going out with a pick-axe and smashing things. I do. I frighten myself, sometimes, I get so choked up. They'd really fix me then, wouldn't they? Ow!"

"Yes."

"So what are we going to do about it? Talk?"

"No. I see. But promise you'll go to the doctor. If you do I won't say anything."

"All right."

Kirstin hurriedly stepped over him and opened the door of the stall. Herr Umberg started blubbering again.

"Sorry, Frau, sorry. I'm so ashamed."

"Well, I'll telephone in a few days to see you've gone to the doctor."

"Don't worry. I'll go."

"Goodnight, then."

Kirstin went to summon help from the proprietor of the stable, glossing over what Herr Umberg had been doing at the time of the accident.

As Kirstin walked wearily home past Geraldine's house she longed to go in and be fussed over and comforted. The thing that Geraldine had so dreaded had come to pass. She should have been the first to know. But it was nearly nine o'clock, after which time only burglars were permitted to call. She could see Peter washing dishes in the kitchen. She wondered that Geraldine had gone to bed already.

BJ's telephone marathon brought her little joy. Her acquaintances in Zürich consisted mainly of members of the American Women's Club, whose Bonwit Taylored exteriors concealed bottomless pits of sympathy for a young compatriot in trouble. She received so many offers of help that she began to feel uncomfortably awash in the milk of human kindness. What was needed was someone who would pour some clarifying acid on the situation, and her thoughts turned naturally to Geraldine.

The phone was picked up immediately by Peter. Geraldine was in bed and he was reluctant to get her up. BJ hinted strongly at a life-or-death emergency, and after ten minutes Geraldine came to the phone. BJ had completely forgotten the cloud under which they had parted in the afternoon, but Geraldine had not, and her reaction to BJ's news was as invigoratingly blunt as BJ could have wished. In fact it was so little shock-horrored that BJ wondered if Geraldine had known about Philip and Prune all along. Geraldine denied this.

"I'm just not surprised, that's all," she said. "These days it's getting so that you can predict a man's mid-life crisis almost to the day. It all started with the publication of a Ladybird book called *Fuck It Up Yourself*."

"You think that's all it is?"

"Probably. Well, who cares? If he's gone, he's gone."

"Thanks. You think I shouldn't even try to get him back?"

"I shouldn't try rushing out and having your hair done, or buying black leather undies and trying to lure him back that way."

214

"That never actually occurred to me. I was thinking of something more logistical."

"But what can you really do, BJ? You'll just have to defend your own interests as best you can. What I mean is, it's really Philip's crisis. I don't suppose you've changed that much, and he liked you the way you are for long enough. I mean, most people shouldn't be expected to put up with you for more than a week, but at one time he signed on for life."

"Thank you, Geraldine. Is this supposed to be cheering me up?"

"Yes, as a matter of fact. It's meant as a compliment."

"I'm not sure I appreciate it, but go on."

"Well you know you can be very provoking, BJ. You just like to stir things up for the sake of it, don't you?"

"I don't consider stirring up stagnant ponds to be an anti-social act."

"Well, goodnight. You see what I mean? No, you don't. I'm only saying that Philip's feeling for you must have been absolutely monolithic at one time to have overshadowed all the logical objections to living with someone as nerve-racking as you are. And that being the case, I suspect that most of it is still standing, he's just going through his self-awareness blitz. What's the bird like?"

"I'm sorry?"

"The other woman. What's she like?"

"She's sort of – devastating, actually. Sensational body – sort of athletic, like those guys on Greek vases. Somewhat asexual, as a matter of fact, but – wow – extremely sensuous."

"Never mind her body. What's she like?"

"How do you mean?"

"Well, her character, and so on. I mean, if she's pushing thirty and anxious to get onto a pension scheme she might be unscrupulous and go for the kill. Philip's quite a sound prospect financially, isn't he?"

"Yes, but only you would think of that, Geraldine. That stuff went out with whalebone corsets. This woman's body is her pension, anyhow. I bet she never even thinks about money."

"Perhaps not. The desire for security goes a lot deeper than thought. And there are other types of security. I presume she isn't married."

"No."

"And with no children she wouldn't have much of a conscience about the baby."

"Nor does Philip. I must admit that really bothers me. You know, I always thought Philip had this old-fashioned code of honour thing, you know, that kind of aristocratic East Coast sense of inherited responsibility."

"The coast is irrelevant. He's at sea."

"Right."

"I can understand your confusion. At times like this it's easy to see why society had to stamp out personal revenge. Do you feel you'd happily spend the rest of your life in gaol for the pleasure of knifing him?"

"Frankly, no. I'd rather see him live to pay for it."

"Same thing."

"I don't just mean money."

"No. You're not feeling suicidal yourself?"

"No, I guess not. I'm too anxious to know what happens to me."

"That's good. I suppose you'll go back to the States."

"Yes. I'll see about it first thing in the morning."

"That might be the best thing. But listen, come down once before you go, will you? I'd like to see you before . . . before you go."

"Okay. Thanks, Geraldine. You're okay. I'm sorry if I've been somewhat too honest at times."

Geraldine laughed. "Never regret what you can't change, fruit-gum. Chin up."

"Okay. Thanks."

BJ put the phone down and sat back smiling at Geraldine's obsession with security, but feeling better for her no-nonsense support. It was really too bad that Geraldine had been sold on the happy slave package, probably before she had had a chance to experience an alternative lifestyle. BJ had learnt from Kirstin that Geraldine had been a nurse in the army for several years before getting married, which seemed an almost laughable ritualization of her need for the reassurance of confining bonds: a more sheltered life than that of the army would be hard to imagine.

It was 11.43. Philip was not coming home. Her heart bellowed with exhaustion. She leant her head on her arms on the desk, and, rather in crumbling submission to oblivion than because Philip had not come, she let out a few shaky sobs.

When she woke up it was 2.04. A desperate, shameful voice suggested that perhaps Philip had come in while she was asleep and gone to bed without disturbing her. Rigor mortis had seized her limbs and shoulders, but she winced her way quickly into the bedroom. It was empty. BJ was too tired to feel anything except the pain in her arms and legs. She cleaned her teeth and got into bed, but could not

216

sleep, although exhaustion was dragging her head into the pillow as into a vortex.

But when she became aware of noises in the apartment it was in a state of coming round after anaesthesia, so she must have slept. She had not closed the drapes, and by the light of the street lamp she could make out the tip-toeing bulk of Philip as he got undressed. She rolled onto her face as he sat on the edge of the bed to take his shoes off. Somewhat atypically he got into bed minus his MIT nightshirt.

Philip lay with his back to her. He sighed deeply. BJ was fuzzily aware of a profound sense of loss that slumped the contours of his large frame into a pathetic pose. Hesitantly she put her hand on the saddle of flesh between his shoulder and hip. His inertia was palpable. She removed her hand and moved away from him. She was still just sufficiently conscious to be glad that tomorrow would be different from the one she had imagined. She would begin consolidating her position in earnest. As Scarlett O'Hara always put it, tomorrow was another day. That was such a self-evident remark, it was curious that it seemed to mean something. She would have to be careful not to provoke Philip into the classic "Frankly, my dear, I don't give a damn." In Zürich there was always plenty of fog for him to walk off into. Was Rhett Butler the guy who said that thing about holding truths to be self-evident, she wondered as she fell into a slugged sleep, and a dream in which the sea rose and formed itself into towering images of Philip which threatened to crash down onto the fragile boat in which she was rowing her baby to Australia.

# CHAPTER

# FIFTEEN

THE NEXT morning Kirstin discovered that she was bleeding and went immediately to the obstetrician. She dropped her copy of *Annabelle* as he strode past the waiting-room. He had dyed his grey hair American senator blue. The other women in the room, who had already recovered from the shock, giggled.

"Love," muttered her neighbour out of the corner of her mouth.

When her turn came he gave her a thorough examination, including breasts, patted her foot and helped her tenderly off the slab. He smiled.

Kirstin goggled. He was like the wolf in Grandmother's nightcap.

"Now I want you to go home to bed and stay there until the bleeding stops. Try not to have any hysterical female fits. Just relax. Read some magazines. It doesn't look too serious."

But being in possession of this relatively good news, Kirstin no longer felt like going to bed. She called in on Geraldine on the way home.

The wind of the night before had left the landscape motionless with exhaustion under a warm sun. Geraldine's garden, where the weeds were now 1.30 metres tall, was breathlessly still. There was something uncanny about it. Then Kirstin realized what it was. There was no litter of bicycles and three-wheeled Donald Ducks and plastic wheelbarrows. And for the first time the shovels and moulds in the sandpit had been tidied into a basket.

Kirstin walked with slow dread up to the door. It was open. She could hear noises in the kitchen and smell fried onions. From the door she could see the two girls sitting at the dining-table. There was nothing on the table except a vase of lily-of-the-valley, its mournful smell filling the room. Rachel leaned forward, swinging her legs. Claudia lolled on her elbow sucking her thumb. They looked as if they were waiting for their parents to take them to the airport. They did not react when Kirstin came in.

"Hello, girls. Where's your mother?"

"In hospital," said Rachel.

"Oh no. What's the matter?"

"Don't know."

"She's ill," said Claudia. She got up listlessly and went to the piano. Her stubby fingers rippled like pig's teats over the keys.

"Where's the baby?" said Kirstin.

"Asleep."

A woman whom Kirstin dimly recognized came out of the kitchen. She was wearing a floral overall and had a distinctly proprietorial air.

"Hello. I'm Frau Beck. Peter's sister."

"Yes. Hello. What's the matter with Geraldine?"

"She had to go in for tests." Her eyes worked hard to convey some other meaning. "Yesterday. Peter asked me to pop over and see to the children until – everything is all right again."

"It's not serious is it? She didn't tell me she was ill."

"Oh, we're hoping, you know. Will you stay for lunch, Frau Baumann?"

"No, thank you. You have enough to do."

"Please." There were tears in her eyes.

"All right."

"Good. Rachel, lay the table, there's a good girl. Perhaps you'd help me serve up, Frau Baumann?"

"Of course." Kirstin followed her into the kitchen.

"You didn't know then?" said Frau Beck. She spoke through the cloud of steam that rose from a landslip of wholewheat macaroni she was tipping into a sieve.

"No. What is the matter with her?"

Frau Beck grinned. "Cancer of the pancreas they think."

Kirstin leant against the counter, feeling faint. "No. Not Geraldine. Why didn't she tell me? I don't understand."

"They weren't sure for a long time. They told her it was constipation to start with. You know what doctors are like."

"They wouldn't deliberately mislead her, would they?"

219

"Who knows? But she'd been a nurse, you know. I think she guessed all the time."

"Oh Geraldine, how terrible. I can't believe it. I can't. Why didn't she tell me?"

"It's the children, you see, isn't it? That's the thing."

Frau Beck's breezy air had dropped away. They hugged each other, crying silently, afraid the children would hear.

"Thank goodness they've got a l-loving father," said Kirstin, patting the short figure in her arms, staring out of the window through a wall of tears.

"They'll be all right. I'll do what I can."

But Kirstin's mind had already escaped to a future where her own loving care of the motherless children would prompt Peter to offer her a permanent alternative to her present situation. She ground her teeth and dug her fingers hard into Frau Beck's flesh, trying to obliterate the savage wantonness of her imagination. Frau Beck released herself.

"Well, well, we mustn't keep talking as if she's buried already. Nothing's certain. I wonder if you'd mind baby-sitting this afternoon while I go and visit her?"

"Of course."

BJ was somewhat relieved that the old man's attack on Kirstin would give them all something to talk about during visiting hours. Kirstin had mentioned it in passing when she called to inform her of Geraldine's illness. BJ considered that Kirstin was probably over-reacting to Geraldine's condition – the lowered voice, hints of tragedy in the offing and so forth. Geraldine would probably recover, and if she did not, well – She was someone who had resolutely eschewed conditioning her body, she was not entirely blameless.

BJ had never been admitted to hospital and they gave her extremely bad vibes. To her they reeked of formaldehyde, and she imagined great tubs of it in the basement, waiting to receive the bodies. It was the more sinister with every attempt of today's hospital to disguise the grisly business going on there with parlour palms and day-rooms.

Geraldine was in a spacious room with six beds, two of which were empty. The other three were occupied by old ladies with their teeth out. Two sat bolt upright and glowered through bulging lenses at incoming visitors. The other lay on her side jangling drips and drainage tubes and moaning. Geraldine was next to the window. She had a book open on her lap, but was looking out of the window. The Venetian blinds slatted the sunlight over her white bed, but her cheeks and the inevitable pink-a-dink lipstick glowed.

"Hi," said BJ, relieved that she looked normal. "You're looking good, Geraldine. Really quite good."

Geraldine lolled her head to look at BJ. "Hello." She smiled. "You're in town tonight, then."

"Well, actually – Oh, never mind. How are you feeling?"

"Terrific. Hello, Kirstin."

"Hello." Kirstin kissed her on both cheeks and gave her the flowers she was carrying.

"Wow. Agapanthus. You didn't get those in the car park."

"No, they only had this type of thing," said BJ, handing over some gaudy mixed tulips.

Geraldine laughed. "Thank you, thank you. Could you stick them all in the sink. They'll wilt lying in the sun."

Kirstin went off with the flowers and BJ drew up a cavernous red armchair. "Just say if you're getting tired," she said. "You look sort of sleepy. Are you okay?"

"Yes fine. We've just had lunch."

"What are they doing to you here?"

"Oh, X-rays and things. Drugs. You know. I'm not sure, really."

"Listen, I probably shouldn't say this –"

"But it wouldn't be you if you didn't. Go ahead."

"I just wanted to say I hope you don't fall for the chemotherapy crap. The side-effects are gross. Totally gross. I'd never let them do that to me."

"I'm not sure what they're giving me."

"Uh-huh." BJ perceived from the soporific expression on Geraldine's face and the tendency of her eyes to roll shut unless she was actually speaking that she was even less up to a rational conversation than usual. When Kirstin returned to the bedside BJ asked her to tell them about the scene with Herr Umberg. Geraldine did not know about it and paid relatively close attention, blinking back oblivion as she listened.

"So," said BJ when Kirstin had finished, "you told him you wouldn't go to the police. That was a dumb move, Kirstin."

"Why?"

"The risk factor. See, there's an element of cunning in his behavior that's worked for him up to now. He chose a complete stranger when it was dark, and in daylight two females he knew well, so that he could appeal to them to protect him. But the pattern must be broken soon, and when the police get hold of him they'll be asking you some pretty uncomfortable questions."

"But how are zey knowing of ze attack?"

"Okay. So what? The guy's a health hazard. He's better off out of the way."

"I agree," mumbled Geraldine. "Shop him."

"But I promised not to."

"He had no right to extract a promise like that," said BJ. In any other country you could probably get away with it, but over here – If they get Interpol onto you to retrieve parking fines, I don't like to think what they'd do to someone who deliberately concealed a crime."

Geraldine nodded sleepily. "She's right, you know. You're going to involve Max in it, too."

"I did not tell him."

"You didn't! Well, stone the crows. Don't you tell him anything? You might as well be married to a wee-wee doll." Her eyes closed again.

"Didn't he notice that you were somewhat distrait?" asked BJ.

"No. I had just said farewell to ze horse. He tink it is zat. Oh dear, now I do not know what to do."

"Yes you do," said BJ, "we've just told you. Listen, most criminals have wives, but we don't suspend the legal system out of consideration for them."

"But BJ, you I am surprised to hear say this. I thought you do not hold crime to be wrong."

"I don't, in the usual moral sense. Morality is just deified expediency. In this case the expedient thing to do is to go to the police."

"Ay, ay, ay. I am tinking this is all finished now."

"It will be if you take my advice. Listen, they probably won't do anything drastic – maybe a suspended sentence conditional on getting treatment. Don't you think so, Geraldine?"

"Um? Oh, yes. Well, the maximum for rape is only about ten days, isn't it?"

"Ssh!" Kirstin looked nervously round at an evidently English-speaking visitor at the next bed who had shown interest in Geraldine's remark. She was one of three pear-shaped ladies whose temptation to eavesdrop was more than they could be expected to resist. Their old lady was still as rigid as a firedog and nobody at their bed had said anything for a quarter of an hour. "Sorry, but I tink we are being overheard."

"You look awful," said Geraldine, still with her eyes closed. "Is Max behaving himself?"

"Yes. I have not heard anyting more from zat woman."

"You must eat something, Kirstin, or you'll end up in here."

"I have so many worries. It has been so far a terrible year for me."

"Me too," mumbled Geraldine. "Aquarius must have been in Marks and Spencers."

"I told Philip about the kid," said BJ, smiling broadly. She avoided looking at Geraldine.

"And what did he say?" asked Kirstin.

"Oh he was ecstatic. Just ecstatic. Listen, I think we'd better be going. There are some more people waiting to see you, Geraldine."

"Oh bugger. Say I'm ill."

"Shall I?" said Kirstin.

"No. Just my joke. Well, goodbye, you two. Thanks for the flowers."

Kirstin kissed her and went to talk to the waiting visitors, whom she knew.

"Well," said BJ, "I guess we should shake hands, Geraldine. I don't know if we'll be seeing each other again."

"I thought you said I looked good?"

"Yes, you do. Quite rosy-cheeked, actually."

"The nightdress must be reflecting."

"It's a pretty color. I like those ruffle things round the neck."

"Thanks. It is nice, isn't it? The sort of thing Princess Di would wear for elevenses."

"I only meant I'm going back to the States next week. I don't know if I'll have time to come again. I'm sure you'll do okay. You seem to be in somewhat good humor, anyhow."

"Humour is the last sense to go."

"Oh."

"You know, the thing I dread more than death is the Mother and Daughter Choir coming round the bed and singing 'How Green was my Valley', or equivalent."

"Yeah. Right."

"Is everything all right now? With Philip."

"Oh sure. Sure. No problem." BJ took her hand and held it for a moment. "Goodbye, Geraldine. I hope you pull through this okay."

"Thanks. And I wish you luck when your time comes." Geraldine half-closed her eyes. " 'Be kind to Capn' Butler, Scarlett.' "

"Excuse me?"

But Geraldine seemed to be asleep. BJ studied her small crumpled features and shook her head.

Kirstin was waiting in the corridor.

"It's kinda sad," said BJ. "I think her mind's going. She was almost delirious at times."

"She is heavily drugged, I tink."

"Oh, is that it? It's so hard to tell with Geraldine."

Max was not due home for dinner that evening, but he had forgotten his track suit and had called in to collect it. As he was at home he took a shower. Kirstin followed him into the bathroom and told him about Herr Umberg while he washed. For some moments the massage spray and vigorous friction of the sisal mitt on Max's torso were the only sounds.

"When did all this happen?" he asked.

"Last Tuesday."

"Why didn't you tell me sooner?"

"I didn't want to involve you, Max."

"In what way? You're not making this up, are you Kirstin?"

"No. Why should I?"

"Hysteria sometimes manifests itself in that way."

"I am not hysterical. Ask Herr Umberg if you don't believe me."

"All right. But what do you mean about involving me?"

"Well, I promised Herr Umberg I would not go to the police if he went to the doctor to get help. But Geraldine thinks I should go. Now I need your advice. I don't know what to do anymore."

"You want me to tell you to go to the police, so that you can transfer your bad conscience to me? By the way, the towels are hard again. Do I have to start leaving little notes around the place?"

Kirstin did not say anything.

"I'm sorry, but I've known about Herr Umberg for some time. He's an old man, Kirstin. You'll be old, too, one day. I think it's better settled on a personal level, within the village."

"What do you mean?"

"Community action. There are one or two people round here who would help me sort out Herr Umberg, if necessary."

Kirstin's thoughts staggered between the fate of Peter Abelard and the vengeance of the Ku Klux Klan. She felt faint.

Max pulled back the shower curtain. He wiped the excess water from his limbs in a gesture learned from his underwater hockey colleagues. "I dare say it can wait a day or two if he's just had a blow-out. I can't do anything tonight, we're playing Wülflingen."

It was not possible to get an appointment with Herr Schulthess until 2 o'clock in the afternoon, by which time Kirstin's bowels had

224

run dry. When not on the toilet she paced about the house, turning away from mirrors: the refraction seemed to have been tampered with to make her look like a length of chewing gum. She could not eat. She did not even dare take a little wine to calm her nerves, afraid that the baby would start spinning like a tombola.

Herr Schulthess did not seem surprised to see her. He sat her down and rummaged in the drawer for a pencil.

"Now what's the problem, Frau Baumann? Have you got something to tell me?"

"Actually I suppose I've got a confession to make."

"Oh? That's not what I was expecting."

"Confession is the wrong word."

"Have you been attacked?"

"Yes."

"Just a minute, Frau Baumann. I'll get someone to –"

"No, wait. Please let me explain."

"What's the matter? It's not your husband, is it?"

"Oh no."

"Herr Umberg?"

"How did you know?"

"In a place this size you don't have to be Hercule Poirot to narrow down the suspects."

"Then why is he still walking around?"

"Lack of evidence. Now you can give it to us. What's the matter, Frau Baumann? You look a bit queasy."

"I'm all right. I didn't realize –"

"We were so hot off the mark? It wasn't that difficult. Rather an unusual case. If people want to protect someone, they usually don't report the crime. But in this case that was the biggest clue, see? People are odd, don't you think?"

"No."

"I see. Well now, Frau Baumann, are you ready to make a statement? I'll call a car."

"No, I'm not."

"You're not?" Herr Schulthess, who had got up, sat down again. "Are you trying to tell me this is a private visit? Look, don't you start that as well. I'm getting bloody tired of people round here speaking with forked tongue. If you go to the police it's because you want to see some action, right? Whether you realize it or not. Eh?"

"Perhaps."

"Then what did you expect to happen?"

"Look, do you have to arrest him and all that official procedure?

225

Couldn't you deal with the matter privately? Get him into a home, or something like that? You see, he's got a sick wife."

Herr Schulthess looked flabbergasted. "Frau Baumann, the criminal police are involved now, anyhow. I have no leeway in the matter at all. You can't have the police deciding each case on individual merit, they'd never be free from charges of corruption and bribery and whatnot, would they?"

"I suppose so."

"Look, I can appreciate that you're upset about this business. But don't worry, I'm sure your reputation will go before you. I don't think you need worry that you'll get a rough ride."

"I beg your pardon?"

"Well, you don't have to say anything to me, of course, but I'm assuming there's nothing in your past that would be likely to discredit you as a witness?"

"As a witness?"

"Well, naturally you'll have to give evidence."

"Oh."

"You see, as you're the party's neighbour, there might be some suspicion that you had it in for him, for some reason. Say you had plans to cut off his view with an in-law apartment over the garage, and only Herr Umberg's objections stood between you and the cement-mixer. You'd have to be prepared for accusations that you wanted him out of the way. Now all that's unpleasant, I know."

"No, it wasn't that at all."

"Well, I can guess what it is, then. I know all ladies must worry in a case like this that the defence will start probing into their private life, and find out how many men she's slept with, and the old man will find out and all hell will break loose. Don't think me impertinent, but I'm sure you're all right on that score, eh? No skeletons? Because if there are, I would make sure that your story and that of the other parties coincide. All right?"

An image of Doktor Huber's face, grim and resigned on leaving the divorce court, as it would appear splashed all over *Blick*, flickered before her mind as Kirstin slumped into a dead faint on Herr Schulthess's desk.

It was 4.30 before Kirstin left Herr Schulthess's office. He offered a car to take her home, but she had to call in at the shop for fabric conditioner for Max's towels and insisted that she was well enough to walk. He accompanied her outside the building.

"How long has he got?" asked Kirstin, despondently.

"Don't worry about him, Frau Baumann. We're not savages, you know."

"No, I suppose not."

"I wish I could convince you."

The Volg supermarket was busy. Kirstin stood listlessly behind a growing line of women at the cash desk. At the head of the queue a woman was treating the cashier to a shrill tirade against some man not present. The cashier and the other women around smiled as though dealing with the mentally subnormal. Kirstin paid no attention, until the woman turned round and she recognized Frau Doktor Huber. When she had finally had her say and gone, the cashier and the women standing near her rolled their eyes and shook their heads.

"Always thought she was a bit unstable," said one. "Hyperactive. Do you know she knitted curtains for every room in that house?"

"She didn't!"

"She did."

"And she put the fence up by herself," added another woman.

"She's terribly fussy. They all have to wear overshoes in the house. Even the doctor."

"No wonder he's had enough. Where's he living?"

"I've no idea. In the consulting-room, probably. It's very awkward, with the practice right in the house. Of course, she won't move out."

"Apparently it's awful up there now. She keeps coming into the practice and shouting at him in front of everybody. Poor man. It's bound to affect his concentration."

"It certainly does. My neighbour went in about her varicose veins and he pumped her ears out. Of course she didn't say anything, as it was the first time it happened, but it can't go on, can it?"

"No, of course not. Imagine if he'd started examining her breasts!"

"Oh there's some that would like it," remarked a jolly woman with forked teeth, over the riot of laughter. "I've heard there's a younger woman involved, as usual."

"Never. Not the doctor."

"Anyone we know?"

"I've no idea."

"Disgraceful. He'll lose his patients."

"Rubbish. I should think he'd double them. Didn't you read about that sect leader who was gaoled for having sex with fourteen-year-olds? When he got out there were women of all ages queuing to join up."

"I don't want to listen to this filth," piped up a tiny old lady at the back of the queue. "Pay for your sardines and get a move on, you vultures."

"Sorry, I'm sure."

There was more rolling of eyes, but the queue started moving again.

Kirstin staggered outside and sat down on the wall surrounding the car-park. She was trembling. Since returning from Bergün she had had no contact with the doctor, and had assumed that the daily demands of his work, and the living tapestry of Christian, Michael, Joachim, Stefan and Remo had driven all thoughts of her into their rightful place in the mind's floppy disk.

But supposing he had made no contact because he thought she might take him more seriously if he went through the purification of divorce and desertion first? Kirstin had already forgotten the disabling agonies of infatuation, but there were enough examples in the papers of great men losing their kingdoms for a crumpet to remind her that one should never underestimate its force.

She was dumbfounded by the rubble of shattered lives that was building up around her: Herr Umberg, Frau Umberg, the doctor, his wife, their five children, even their future wives and families might suffer if the Hubers broke up. What worried her was how Frau Huber had got to know of the affair, if indeed she did. Unless the binoculars of Joachim, Stefan or Remo had been trained on them from the shadow of the forest.

Kirstin noticed the slumped figure of Fraulein Schupisser over by the post office, waiting for the bus. Fraulein Schupisser was looking towards her and her expression of suspicious curiosity, and something about the way she clutched at her bag, suggested that she was barely restraining herself from coming over. Kirstin made a non-committal gesture of recognition and Fraulein Schupisser at once ambled up to her.

"Good evening, Frau Baumann. Are you all right?"

"Yes, thank you."

"You should lie flat on your back, you know. It might be the uterus pressing against the spinal nerve."

"How did you know?"

"Everyone knows."

Fraulein Schupisser's face was silently working with repressed torment.

"Isn't that your bus, Fraulein?"

"It doesn't matter. I'll get the next one."

"Oh."

"Frau Baumann, I didn't know you were pregnant, you see. Otherwise I wouldn't have done it."

"Done what, Fraulein Schupisser?"

"Pardon?"

"What have you done that concerns me?"

"Didn't your husband say anything about the letter?"

"No."

"Excuse me, that's my bus."

She ran off to catch it, waddling from the knees only, like a nun.

Kirstin started on the long plod up the hill to her house, and to the opening scene of the inevitable parting from Max. If Fraulein Schupisser knew about the pregnancy, there was no reason but to suppose that Max was the only person in the village who did not. As if summoned to play his part, Max's BMW hove alongside as she walked up the hill. He frowned when he saw the vapid grin on her face as she sank into the front seat and groped for the seat belt.

"Where have you been?"

"To the police, Max. I decided to tell them about Herr Umberg after all. I'll have to go to court, you know, to give evidence. Perhaps you will too. I hope you don't mind."

"Of course I mind. I've wasted enough time on this business already. Why do you think I told you not to report it?"

"Because I thought you wanted to get some of your squash friends along to beat him up?"

"Have you been drinking, Kirstin?"

"No. Why?"

"Well what could have put such an asinine idea into your head?" He drew up outside the garage and applied the handbrake with conscious drama. "I only wanted to spare us the disagreeable business of getting involved in a court case. Do you realize they'll ask you things like, 'Was your jodhpur zip open or closed at the time of the assault, Frau Baumann?' "

"I don't wear jodhpurs."

"Even so, they'll try to prove that you're a deranged nymphomaniac housewife who preys on arthritic old men for kicks."

"Which is what you think."

"You really are exasperating, Kirstin. Why did you ask for my advice if you didn't intend to take it?"

"I'm making a scrapbook."

"What? Listen, Kirstin, this can't go on. You know that, don't you?"

"Yes, I do."

229

"A man likes to come home to a little mental, as well as physical, comfort."

"Well of course."

"But when I come home I feel as if my day is just beginning."

"Just like a working wife. Oh dear."

"I've tried to pretend it's otherwise, but you just don't seem to be able to come to terms with the realities of your situation, Kirstin. I've tried to help."

"It wasn't my fault it got run over."

"I've come to the conclusion you don't want to be helped. It's wearing me out, Kirstin. I'm completely exhausted by the strain of it all." His body assumed a heart-wrenching slump.

"Yes, you will find it much less tiring to do everything yourself."

"I see. Well, your failure to see the problem has been a stumbling block all along. Hello, they haven't come for him yet then."

"What?"

Max was looking in the rear-view mirror. "Herr Umberg has just gone past."

"Oh shit. Let's go for a drive, Max. I don't want to go into the house until he's gone."

"We may have to camp overnight. How do you know when they're coming?" He sighed and started up the engine. "You see. You started all this and now you can't face the consequences."

"I thought Herr Umberg started it. Or whatever it was that started Herr Umberg. I don't think it's so odd that I don't want to see him taken away. It's not everyone who eats meat that would want to visit an abattoir."

"I was at an abattoir in Budapest only the other day, and I can assure you that the employees there take as much pride in their work as artists, or chocolate manufacturers."

"But I don't take as much pride in their work."

"Then you should become a vegetarian."

"As a matter of fact I intend to. That's one of the things I'll do when I'm on my own."

"I see. Are we going anywhere in particular?"

"Let's go somewhere where there are no people."

"Gone off them, have you? Don't tell me you're going to become a hermit as well as a vegetarian."

They drove in silence across hills and through several villages until the fields levelled out again near the German border. Max abruptly turned the car down a dirt road towards the thick clotted line of trees that marked the course of the river Thur. They lurched at speed through the trees and finally turned off again into a clearing that jutted onto the beach. On either side they had a clear view up and down the river. The wide pebble beach was pitted with charred stone circles, some of them still smoking from the fires of recent fry-ups. It looked as though Napoleon's army had spent the night there.

For Kirstin the place had more recent historical significance. In the early days of their marriage, before Max had taken up hang-gliding, they used to come here on Sundays for barbecues with their friends. She wondered what instinct had led him to the spot, or whether it was just the usual unpremeditated insult.

Max attempted a sardonic smile. "How will we know when the coast is clear? Should we ring up Frau Umberg and ask?"

"I would prefer never to go back."

"Please don't start crying, Kirstin. It doesn't achieve anything."

"Oh shut up, Max. Just shut up. I'm so tired of your fucking condescension."

"I see. So this is it, is it?"

She nodded.

"All right. Fine. If that's what you want."

Kirstin yelped and started chewing her knuckles.

"Well if that isn't what you want, what do you want?"

"Of course it's not what I want. But I'm pregnant, so I thought we might as well break up sooner as later."

"I thought as much."

"Naturally."

"Not from your appearance, which points to anorexia nervosa, but you seem to have gone to pieces completely in the last few months. So, you finally brought it off. With whom?"

"Don't be insulting, Max. You don't honestly think I would pass off another man's child on you, do you?"

"Your anxiety to turf me out of the nest before it arrives does suggest something like that, yes."

"It's just the timing. I know you don't want children, I know I agreed not to have any, and I know you've been having an affair with someone at work, so —"

"Just wait a minute, will you. What affair are you talking about?"

"How many have there been?"

"How did you find out about it?"

"I got an anonymous telephone call."

"Did you find out who from?"

"No. But I think it was the woman herself. She was very business-like."

Max smiled. That was Annalie, all right.

"Did she say anything else?"

"I don't remember, exactly. She said you had gone to Novosibirsk with this woman. And she claimed it would soon be over."

"It doesn't seem very likely, does it? If she took the trouble to tell you what was going on."

"No."

"So you think we ought to separate for a while."

"About twenty-five years, at least."

"You seem to be taking a rather facetious attitude to the matter, Kirstin. I hope your good humour is not based on the idea that you can use the information you have about my affairs in court."

"I am not in a good humour, Max."

"Because if you did have any ideas like that I warn you that I would not hesitate to retaliate."

"What do you mean?"

"When I asked you who the father was, it wasn't just the cry of the wounded stallion, you know. I know all about the good doctor."

"What? What do you know?"

"Enough."

"How?"

"That's not important. You'll find out in court if you try and pin anything on me."

"Oh no, Max, please! You couldn't drag him into it. Think of his family."

"I am. And his reputation. I daresay I could lodge a formal complaint with his professional overlords."

"No, Max, no. Even you couldn't be so despicable, surely."

"Thank you."

"Anyway, you could never prove it. I don't believe you could. There were no witnesses. I'm sure there weren't." She started chewing her thumb. If only she could have got hold of Stefan, Joachim and Remo and held their heads under a cold tap until they talked. Everyone must know what had happened at Bergün. And they had been naive enough to imagine that no one had noticed. There might be photographs waiting in some vault under the Bahnhofstrasse for the moment when they would be brought forth in triumph, like an axe. Where had those hidden cameras been?

"So, you don't deny it then."

Kirstin shook her head and started crying.

"Well, that's it, then. You know, if this hadn't happened I might even have overcome my objections to the child. But it's out of the question now. How do I know there haven't been others? If there was one aspect of our marriage about which I had no complaints it was your loyalty, Kirstin. But if that was a failure – well –"

"You rat, Max. How despicable you are. You drive me to desperation and then accuse me of being weak. It's not fair. All right, I slept with him. He's a kind, unselfish man and I wish to God I had someone like that, but if you think he's left his wife because of me you're mistaken, and so will he be."

"Has he left her? I didn't know that."

"Well I didn't encourage him to. I think it's terrible. I'm sure it's not because of me, I wouldn't hear of it. Oh anyway it would never work. I'm sure he only wants me because my body is in mint condition. Men are all the same – so selfish."

"Kirstin you are covering yourself with ambiguity, you're almost invisible. I think we had better go home."

"All right. But I'm walking." She opened the car door and put one foot out. Max grabbed her arm and tried to pull her back in.

"Don't be so self-pitying, Kirstin. You're in no condition to walk so far. Get back in the car."

"No. Let go of me."

She pulled herself free and stumbled towards the path. Max watched her from the car and when she was clear he backed up and drove off, but stopped before turning into the main road and got out. He leaned on the car, watching her wobble out of the wood. When she was within hearing distance he shouted at her.

"I'll walk. Don't be so selfish, Kirstin. You know how much you despise the trend. Think of the baby."

He walked off down the main road and began to thumb a ride. By the time Kirstin reached the car he had disappeared into the cabin of a Yugoslavian container lorry.

# CHAPTER

# SIXTEEN

FOLLOWING Kirstin's revelations, Max was more than ever anxious for Annalie to come back from holiday, and triumphant when she called and invited him to lunch.

"Let's go in my car," she said. She was smiling and looked sensational. Her skin was tanned after the holiday, and she wore a sleeveless white dress with flouncy skirt and bits of lace all over it.

"We'll go somewhere quiet," she informed him, hitching up the frills to leave her legs the freer to push pedals. She was positively twinkling with excitement, no doubt the consequence of seeing him again after three weeks enforced inactivity in the Seychelles.

Or was it? There was something pent-up about her zest that not his modesty alone suggested might have another cause. Promotion, perhaps. Max registered mixed emotions. On the one hand it would mean a bigger joint income to finance their co-habitation: on the other, if Annalie were to get too obsessed with her career it would amount almost to a *ménage à trois*, and the immediate benefits to himself as compared to his present situation would be less pronounced. He could not concentrate on the conversation, although normally the problem of disproving liability for a cracked driving pinion would have riveted his attention.

The chosen venue was a castle with a pleasant terrace restaurant, and a view over distant kilometres of fields and wooded hills. Max smiled attentively as Annalie chattered on, but he had no appetite and distressed her by ordering a sausage salad.

"Is that all you're having, Max? This is my treat, you know. Are you sure you wouldn't like something more substantial?"

"No thank you. I rarely eat a big lunch, as you know. It reduces my efficiency in the afternoons."

"That wasn't my impression, Max," she smiled coyly. "You were always marvellous in the afternoons."

Although she looked at him tenderly and squeezed his hand in grateful remembrance, her words produced a chill of foreboding. Was this some kind of Last Supper? Had she invited him out in order to sweeten the pill of rejection? If so, her naivety was stunning. And sickening. He suddenly became so agitated that he did not even bother to lower his voice.

"Are you trying to tell me something, Annalie? Because if so just please have the guts to say it. Whatever it is, there's no need to soften me up with second-rate food first. What's on your mind?"

Annalie's face crumpled. He noticed that when she frowned her skin was quite furrowed.

"But surely, Max, we have had such a nice relationship I don't need an excuse to ask you out, do I?"

"Well, do you?"

"No. I really wanted to invite you, Max."

"And you have nothing to tell me? Your references to our so-called relationship have suddenly swung into the past tense. Just co-incidence?"

"No." Annalie closed the knife and fork over her uneaten vol-au-vent and chips. "But please don't be angry that I invited you, Max. I really did want to anyway."

"Apart from what? You are officially terminating our relationship, are you? Well, you started it, so I suppose that's your privilege."

"Don't be angry, Max. It's not because of you, or because I have changed my feelings about you, it really isn't." The soft, pampered hand again sought his, but did not find it. It retreated to the water glass. "I've always thought you were terribly attractive, Max, and I still do."

"Then what has changed?"

"Well – our relationship could never have been permanent. You're married – and I would like to be too. That's all."

"You're getting married?"

"Yes." She smiled again. "My fiancé is an old school friend, Max. He's a nuclear physicist and he's been working in California for six years. We were lovers before that, actually, but nothing serious."

"That seems to be your style."

"Please, Max. Anyway, he suddenly wrote to me about six months ago, and he came home at Christmas. He wants to settle down, you see. He has had many affairs, like me, you see, but now he wants to get married and have a family. And so do I, of course."

"Of course." Max was furious. Would the day never come when women stopped having babies?

"Why yes. I am thirty-four, now. I can't leave it much longer. Well now I don't have to. Oh he's such a wonderful person, Max. I wish you would meet him. He has matured so much since he's been abroad. He is so considerate, he enjoys just ordinary things so much. He doesn't need to be entertained all the time."

"That will leave you up a creek rather, won't it?" He would have liked to take hold of the springing arc of triumph in her voice and ram it into the ground.

She looked down at her folded hands on the table. "I find it very relaxing." Try as she would to maintain a solemn air, she could not stop her face from expressing her thoughts.

"Well," said Max. "So that's that. I really don't know why you had to go to all this trouble to tell me that. It's very sexist, Annalie. Just the sort of thing your average boss would do when seeing off a used secretary."

"Is it?" Annalie looked mortified. "I didn't mean it like that. I appreciated you, Max, I really did. I couldn't just send you a memo and leave it at that."

"Why not? You're exaggerating the significance of the affair rather, aren't you? I thought it was petering out even before you put it into historical prose. I was quite prepared. There was no need to stage it somewhere where I couldn't break down and beg you to change your mind. As you can see, I'm not at all upset."

"Oh. Good."

"I've no doubt you're doing the right thing. I assume you will go to California and do it."

"Yes. For a few years, anyway."

"Splendid. Please don't keep sending me postcards." Shades of Elena the receptionist passed before him.

"All right. Are you sure you wouldn't feel better about it if you met him, Max? I'm sure you could be friends."

"No thank you. I suppose he's waiting in the car-park."

"No."

"And just because I may seem a bit irritated don't assume it's

236

because of your news. I'm irritated by this pointless exercise." He indicated the terrace restaurant in general. "Our relationship would have been over soon enough, anyway. My wife is expecting. I'm not entirely unprincipled."

"Really?" Annalie's reaction was not the geyser of sympathetic rapture he anticipated. "That's wonderful, Max." She spoke without conviction. "Congratulations. What made you change your mind?"

"Oh, well . . . it's a woman's birthright, I suppose. There's nothing much else Kirstin can do. It will keep her occupied."

"Now that's not fair, Max. I'm sure there's a lot of things Kirstin could do. You're just pretending. You must be bursting with excitement."

Max stared at her. "As you wish."

Annalie sighed and looked wistfully into the distance. "So. The future is very exciting for both of us, isn't it?" She forced a smile. "When is the baby due?"

"I'm not sure. September I think."

"My favourite month."

For a moment she held her bright smile, but then Max was obliged to watch in horror as it crumbled into a howl.

"Annalie, why on earth are you crying?"

"I don't know." She cried some more. "I – hic – don't know."

Max looked around nervously to see how difficult it would be to shepherd her out of the place without attracting attention.

"Do pull yourself together. We'd better get back to the office."

She nodded. "I'm sorry. I'm all right."

"I thought you were so happy?"

"So did I."

"Then what's the matter?"

"I don't know."

"Christ. I give up."

He summoned the waitress and paid the bill, then marshalled Annalie back to the Datsun Cherry and took the wheel himself. Annalie sat mute in the passenger seat, her face averted.

When they got back to the office car-park she had managed to cheer up a bit.

"I'm sorry, Max. I don't know what happened. I'm all right now."

"Good."

"May I tell people about the baby? I mean, it will be here before you know it, it won't do any harm to let people know, will it?"

"Oh very well. Not that it's anybody else's business."

"No, but people like to know that sort of thing. It's a common denominator, Max."

"You mean, they like to hear the chains rattle."

"Would you like me to invite you to the wedding?"

"In what capacity? We're not exactly in the same department. Unless it's the done thing these days to invite all one's ex-lays."

"No, it isn't. But thank you for doing your best to banish my regrets." She took the car key from him with a stiff, snappy movement.

"I don't have the faintest idea what you're on about half the time, Annalie. What are you angry about now?"

She only laughed and walked quickly into the building. A gust of wind banged up her skirt just as she opened the door, revealing her neat dancer's legs, knock-kneed for modesty. Max was caught unawares by a twinge of tenderness towards her. Annalie's silence in the car had allowed him to mull over the incident. There was the possibility that it was just pre-menstrual tension, a condition that seemed to afflict women for three weeks out of four. But her dramatic depression on learning of Kirstin's pregnancy could only mean that she was jealous. She was still sufficiently steeped in the mistress mentality to be jealous of the legitimate aspirations of his spouse. This was very cheering.

But why had she thought the situation hopeless? Simply because he was married? Perhaps she had ethical objections to divorce: there were still a few who considered it immoral if both parties were in good health. He spent the rest of the afternoon in fruitful calculations.

His good mood did not last. Although he admitted to himself that there was a largeish element of relief in knowing that there was to be no future with Annalie Schumacher after she had revealed her emotional dependance, it was hardly appropriate to share the good news with Kirstin, who now asked him at least twice a day when he was going to move out, and in between kept demanding to know the name of his lawyer and whether or not he wanted to share the wedding presents.

It was clear that they could not rationally discuss their future until Kirstin was in a calmer frame of mind, that meant until after the birth. Her anxiety for a divorce was highly irritating, especially as Annalie had done such a good job of spreading the news about the baby round the office. Soppy grins spread like a rash through huddles of employees at his approach, not only in the office, but right through the assembly works. It was infuriating not to be able to explain his position to the lower orders, but when bolder members started murmuring congratulations he seized the opportunity to implant the idea that it was all a mistake. "I'm away so much, I don't even have enough time for my wife, let alone a child," he would say, in grieved tones. He found people agreeing with him, which was further cause for annoyance.

Herr Waldvogel was the most put out by Max's declining to join in the euphoria over the coming event. A father of three himself, he bounced into Max's office as soon as he heard the news, extending his hand to Max as if to welcome him to the human race.

"I think perhaps we have the clue to what's been bothering you lately, do we Max? You and Kirstin have been married quite some time, haven't you? Of course, in view of your immigrant status I can see why you'd want to start a family. It all helps. You were worried about the old vacuum pump, were you?"

Max fixed Herr Waldvogel with his hooded cobra glare, but Herr Waldvogel was not about to be put off. He had recently decided that Max's hostility was a front for an extremely sensitive and shy personality ill at ease in conversations unrelated to ships' engines.

"This is just what you need to give you a new lease of life, my friend. Couldn't be better. You'll have something to work for, you see. There'll be some point to it all."

"I have always seen some point to my life. The child was my wife's idea, not mine."

"It usually is, old chap, believe me. But you'll cave in like the rest of us when the time comes. That's just nature, you see, keeping things in equilibrium."

"I thought nature was our servant these days, not our master."

"Damn it, Max, I hope you're not taking this line with Kirstin. An expectant mother is supposed to keep calm and cheerful, you know."

"She's perfectly calm."

"I think you need a break, Max. You're obsessed with work. You're losing sight of people, you know."

"I wish I could. They're being continually thrust up my nose. I take it you're not complaining about my devotion to duty any more."

"No, of course not. But I have to say, Max, that you're a very difficult man to get on with. If you weren't so good at your job you wouldn't last five minutes."

"Then I'd better get on with it, hadn't I?"

Herr Waldvogel snorted and went back to his office. Max as a captive audience for the dammed-up flood of anecdotes on tantrums and teething gels had been, he thought, unfairly snatched from him.

Herr Waldvogel was hurt, and resolved not to waste his breath trying to be friendly with Max any more. Max's attitude to family life, although based on ignorance, succeeded in casting its value into doubt.

The scrubbed-up smiling faces of his Stefan, his Claudia, his Andrea, gazed trustingly up at him from a photograph on the desk. On a normal day he would not give them a moment's thought, but now he did glance at the photograph once or twice. He felt they had been spat upon.

But mixed up with the indignation this aroused in him were seeds of doubt as to his real feelings towards them. There were days when it would be nice to go home to a quiet, tidy house, and be sure that one could eat supper without being strafed in the cross-fire of sibling rivalry. And only that morning his eldest daughter, who was fourteen, had called him a complacent old fart who knew nothing about sex and was only interested in food.

He had known there would be sticky patches, but going through it was like having one's foot shot off as opposed to merely reading about it. It hurt. It produced secondary symptoms like shock and dis-orientation. Only a steely resistance to agreeing with Max about anything not produced by the company kept him from wondering whether Max might be right. He was full of disquiet, and vague alarm, and could not concentrate on the tender for nine trunk-piston engines that only that morning had had for him all the fun ingredients of a video game. He put down his pencil and headed for the soothing enormities of the assembly room.

Max was pleased to note that word had got round. In a couple of days the rash of grins had cleared up, and his impending fatherhood was no longer referred to. He had even got Kirstin to stop referring to it, and had managed to convey to her that if she did so he might agree to remain at his post until she was over the worst. She was so wrapped up in Geraldine and her family that she accepted without protest, or even comment, that they postpone taking decisions about their own future.

Kirstin was spending so much time at the hospital, visiting Geraldine, that she did not even think of it as a coincidence that the contractions started there. At first she did not realize what was happening. She went for a walk in the garden and sat down on a shaded bench watching the coming and going of stunned patients and busy-busy white-coated staff in the shadow of the tower block. A general paralysis had taken over her emotions, as well as that part of her body that was not in the rhythmic embrace of white-hot irons. With each wave of pain she gripped the edge of the bench, but made no sound. Then she felt her legs saturated with warm wetness that the breeze quickly cooled. She did not look down, but hobbled towards the building.

The doctor in charge was one of those long-haired, earth-shoed, people-loving, life-enhancing types that Max instinctively loathed. He went around touching people, Max noticed. He even laid a hand on Max's arm as they shook hands, in what was presumably meant as a Brotherhood of Man gesture.

By the time Max got to the delivery room it was all over, but Kirstin was still being cleaned up. She seemed surprised to see him. Max was aware that he appeared more tight-lipped than he actually felt. The shock of receiving a call from the hospital at work was bad enough, but the sight that met his eyes slammed shut all remaining hatches like a submarine preparing to descend. The white linen was smeared and soaked with blood in brown, red and yellow stains. Kirstin lay with her soiled legs sagging open, her sweat-darkened hair stuck to her face and breasts. All around were gleaming dishes to put parts of the body in, long-handled scissors and scalpels, instruments for cutting and clipping and sucking and tugging at flaps of flesh. Max swallowed hard and kept his eyes riveted on Kirstin's face, trying not to inhale the terrifying smells.

They exchanged a few words about the difficulties Max had encountered by-passing the roadworks in the centre of town. He asked her if she were all right, and she said she was fine. Then she burst into tears and turned her head away. The hairy doctor noticed that Max was at a loss and suggested they go outside for a chat.

After the near-embrace and a few words of heartfelt sympathy the doctor put his hands jauntily in his trouser pockets.

"I expect this has come as a nasty shock, Herr Baumann. One can generally assume one's troubles are over by the fifth month. I expect you'd already started fixing gates on the stairs, hadn't you?"

"No."

"Well, no, perhaps not. But still, psychologically you'd be getting geared up for the great day, I know. It's bound to take a while to adjust. Your wife may well be depressed for a while. You too, I dare say, but try to disguise your own disappointment as much as possible. Keep her spirits up, if you can. Well –" He again squeezed Max's unresponsive arm just about the elbow, possibly to feel for the pulse, as Max was standing like a waxwork, with his eye fixed on the fire extinguisher behind the doctor's head. "What I wanted to say, Herr Baumann, is that, as far as we can tell at the moment, there doesn't seem to be any organic reason for the miscarriage. There's no obvious structural defect. Has your wife been ill lately?"

"No."

"Has she been under an unusual stress?"

"No."

"I see. Well, she seems in rather poor condition – her blood count is extremely low, for example. But there's probably no reason why she shouldn't have a healthy child one of these days. The best thing is not to worry about it. Think positive. You know, I used to live next door to a woman who lost her first child just like this and went on to have eight magnificent specimens afterwards."

"Christ."

Max followed him back into the delivery room. It never occurred to him to kiss Kirstin, but he squeezed her hand and frowned in what he hoped was a positive manner. She yelped and passed out. He looked down. He had been so intent on not taking his eyes from her face that he had failed to notice the large needle stuck into her arm from the infusion. A nurse tut-tutted and hurried over to put it back in.

It seemed both callous and foolish to go back to the office, as Herr Waldvogel had told him to take the rest of the day off. Instead Max drove up to Constance, had a cup of coffee and drove back home. It was not the first time he had spent the night alone in the house, but the first time it had happened following the death, so to speak, of one of its occupants. He imagined that a funereal pall lay over the house, the more noticeable for the arrested cycle of daily trivia that everywhere met his eye. When Kirstin went away alone she always left the house as orderly as a waiting-room, but as her absence was unexpected there was a trail of unfinished business through the house – geranium cuttings drying on the bathroom window sill, sculptured mounds of ironing standing on the board, the shower curtains flapping on the clothes line.

Max longed to cry out in protest to someone at the inconvenience of it all. And the inconvenience did not stop at the shower curtains. How was he going to conduct himself around the office in view of this turn of events? He poured himself a beer and took it and some cheese and bread into the dining alcove. He had done such a good job registering his complaints about the expected birth that he felt downright frustrated now the cause of his complaints had been removed. He could hardly look pleased: people would expect a more solemn line.

Neither did he now have any cause to chafe in the bonds of marriage: as there was to be no child they could separate with a clear conscience.

But the prospect of eating bread and cheese in an over-priced studio apartment every night no longer struck him as a step up, as it had before Annalie Schumacher announced her engagement. He looked around at the house in uncomprehending confusion, anger rising. It was, of course, entirely Kirstin's fault that she had lost the baby and put him in this untenable position. If she had taken proper care of herself instead of slaving over another man's family, and above all if she had not got herself attacked by Herr Umberg, she would not have lost it. He realized that he had already formulated objections to every aspect of child behaviour up to the age of twenty-five, together with appropriate pre-emptive strikes. He had to admit that he had been looking forward to showing the world how these things should be done.

# CHAPTER

# SEVENTEEN

THERE were no seats available on Swissair flights to Boston for more than two weeks after the showdown with Philip. BJ had become mildly paranoid about, among other things, air safety since she became pregnant, and considered that the national airline of a society which washed and re-used its plastic bags was likely to be the most trustworthy carrier. In the meantime she packed, took the doormats to the cleaners, polished the washing machine and carried the mattresses into the garden for a sun bath.

Philip was subdued, but co-operative. He made a point of coming home early for dinner, and she responded by preparing something like their old familiar gourmet feasts: stuffed quails with blackcurrant sauce, braised pork with bourbon and prunes.

BJ deflected Philip's attempts to discuss what had happened: she was harnessing her emotional reserves for the farewell with Michael. He had no idea that she was going back to the States early, and would be extremely distressed, perhaps even angry.

Her suspicions about his female associate had been confirmed. She had several times seen him with a stunning figurine with long black hair parted in the middle, like a ballerina's, and slightly oriental features. The woman's skin was white, her body skinny and supple. She looked sensational in moth-eaten Persian lamb coats and, in warmer weather, battle fatigues.

There was a child attached to this intriguing creature, a boy of about seven or eight, also of a weird and exotic appearance, dressed in totally inappropriate Mothercare polyesters. BJ assumed that this woman was the source of Michael's insights into childbirth. The first time she had seen mother and child leaving Michael's house had been a moment of sickening alarm and jealousy. It rocked her assumption that he was ninety per cent homosexual. The remaining ten per cent, she perfectly realized, would not go that far. But Michael's friendship with this other woman seemed to be a sufficiently regular and important arrangement as to force a reassessment of his sexual preferences. BJ was still sore from the humiliation of Prunelle Baker's existence: it was imperative that she find out the exact nature of Michael's relationship with the Woman.

She chose a time – 9.30 on a Tuesday morning – when she could be reasonably sure he was at home alone. If he were not up, so much the better. They could have their conversation in bed.

When she rang the bell there was no reply for a long time. She rang again, and finally he looked out of the window to see who it was.

"Oh, it's you, BJ. Can you come back some other time. I'm –" he made a gesture into the apartment "– busy."

BJ grinned. "Are you taking a shower? Let me hold something for you. I have to see you now, Michael. I have something terribly important to tell you."

Michael looked at her for a moment.

"Okay, come in."

BJ waddled triumphantly up the stairs after him, but when she saw the Child sitting at the table eating coconut yoghurt, and two other used place settings, she was dismayed.

"This is Georg," said Michael. "He doesn't speak English."

Georg looked at BJ without interest. BJ quickly absorbed the salient points of his slender body, the doleful expression of the eyes, the shaggy, silky hair.

"He's gorgeous," she said, and smiled weakly at Michael. "Is he the attraction? I mean, I know you have this thing with his mother, but –"

"What? What are you saying, BJ?" Michael was flushed. "Have you really got such a filthy mind that you think –"

"Okay, relax Michael." She put a hand on his arm. "Forget I said it. It was foolish. I wouldn't expect you to admit it. May I sit down?"

"I suppose so."

"There wouldn't be any coffee left, would there?"

"I'll see."

"Thanks a lot. Is his mother here, too? I couldn't help counting the egg cups."

"Yes. She is dressing."

"That's pretty cool, Michael. I mean screwing the mother in one room and the kid watching TV in the other. Oh, you don't have TV. Well, what else do they do? Read comics?"

"What do you suggest as an alternative? Should she leave him by himself all night in their apartment? That is not my idea of morality."

"I only said it was cool, Michael. I didn't say it was wrong. You know me, I admire cool."

"In my opinion, one should not do anything one would be embarrassed to tell to a child. And if that is the case one should always tell it to them."

"That's quite puritanical in its way, Michael. But I think you are."

"Very perceptive, BJ. Then why are you always trying to seduce me? Here's your coffee."

"Oh I don't count sex. Like, I know you don't believe in marriage, but if you were living with someone you'd expect them to go into purdah."

"Yes, probably."

"Are you – er – thinking of living with this lady?"

"Perhaps. It would be more convenient. We work together on translations. She is Russian."

"Ah! That explains it. I couldn't quite place her. You seem to know a lot of Russians, Michael."

"No, not really. Listen, I'll just go and tell Galina you're here."

"In case she walks in in the nude? Oh really, Michael, you see, you are puritanical. Okay, go ahead."

BJ seated herself by the window and looked over towards her own apartment. There did not seem much point in trying to talk to Georg, who was just cutting his fourth slice of the hand-hewn bird-seed bread that Michael preferred.

When Michael came back into the room he was followed by the Woman. Close to, she was even more phenomenal than BJ had imagined. Her long eyes were a mottled grey-green, her ears tiny and yet studded in several places with gold knobs, her teeth small and even, like a row of pearls behind a wide, thin mouth. And the body, of course. She wore black trousers and a blouse with devastating effect. Her waist was so narrow it was a wonder to BJ how she managed to fit all her bodily organs down it.

"Hi," said BJ, swallowing hard on the gall of self-loathing that choked her as she looked at the Woman. "You have a very unusual body. Just terrific. You look so breakable, it's wild. A real turn-on. I'm jealous, that's the truth."

"This is Galina, BJ," said Michael. "You have to speak slowly, her English is not so good."

"Sorry. Well, are we all going to sit down? Well, now, Galina, what do you do?"

The Woman was sitting upright with her hands folded in her lap, smiling. "I . . . um . . ."

"She's a physicist," said Michael. "By training."

"Oh?" BJ was astonished. "That's wonderful. Is that what you do over here?"

"No," Michael answered again. "She works as a laboratory assistant. Can you imagine? They do not recognize her qualifications over here."

"Is she a Nobel prizewinner or something?"

"No. Just a PhD. That's all. Like your husband."

"Now Michael, are you getting going on your anti-imperialism spiel?"

Michael shrugged and began to clear the table around Georg. Galina jumped up to help him, but he firmly directed her back to her seat.

"So, you're a physicist, Galina?" pursued BJ.

"Yes, I am a physicist."

Galina's pliant smile and willowy frame reminded BJ of someone. Kirstin. But it was curious that in Galina's case the submissive seraglio image had been kept up in tandem with really tough achievements, like the doctorate, sexual freedom and, presumably, voluntary exile from Mother Russia. She could see the attraction for someone like Michael, whom inertia would surely drag into the grave unless he was continually bounced from the bizarre to the erotic to the revolutionary without dropping back into the normal in between.

"My husband is a physicist," said BJ. "Perhaps Michael already told you."

"No, he has not told me."

Galina did not stop smiling, but her English By Radio habit of echoing the preceding phrase gave no clue as to whether she knew what she was saying.

"I live next door," said BJ.

"Ah, yes. You live next door."

Hard to tell. "Do you help Michael with his translations?"

"Yes, I help Michael with his translations."

247

"That's fascinating. Yes, I can see why you'd think it was a good idea to move in together."

"It's mostly very boring stuff, isn't it, Galina? Instructions for fertilizer users and so on."

Michael had come over to sit beside Galina on the two-seater sofa, a new acquisition which boded ill to BJ. He put an arm along the back of the sofa behind her and seemed to have lapsed into a radically better mood. He blew cigarette smoke in a jaunty gesture towards the ceiling.

BJ, sitting alone on an upright chair facing them, felt uncomfortably like an inexperienced reporter. Michael was decidedly rubbing it in, looking at her from the comfort of the sofa with that luminous, blouse-opening smile that he knew sent columns of revolving desperation into her core. "I'll bet. I can just see you translating subversive literature up here in your five-star garret, Michael. You could even be a spy, with all your languages and all. I suppose there's no chance you'd tell me if you were?"

"No. No chance. But I told you, that stuff I do in Russian is very boring – just technical matters."

"I know. But you're such a mystery man, Michael. You deliberately sort of build up that image. Aren't you mixed up in anything the least bit subversive? It seems such a waste." She knew he responded to talk like this, that he liked to tease her with the great mystery of what he did when she wasn't around. "I'll bet you helped organize the riots last year. Your behaviour was highly suspicious, did you know that?"

"No. Don't say even you have fallen for that Communist plot nonsense, BJ. You are supposed to be on the other side, aren't you?"

"Oh well, just because I don't believe in political morality doesn't mean to say I don't think just about everybody is capable of dirty tricks. I mean, either there was a plot or there wasn't one. It's not a moral choice to believe in it or not."

Michael shrugged, conceding the point. Galina permitted herself a little sigh of tedium. Michael spoke to her in a low, bedroom voice. She smiled some more and got up.

"I go now. Goodbye."

"Do you have to go? Well, I guess it's real boring for you. Okay. You must come round and meet my husband. He'd be fascinated by you."

"Thank you, he will be fascinated by me."

"Right."

"Galina is going into town with Georg," Michael explained as she went in search of her son.

"Not on my account I hope."

"No, BJ. Actually the trip was already planned."

"That's too bad. I wanted to tell her I respond to her body as much as I do to yours, Michael. I'm outclassed, I admit it. But would you let me watch?"

Michael's face reflected the confusion of his mind as it ricocheted between the desire to either slap BJ's face or encourage her to reveal more of her flattering vision of his sexuality.

"You talk as if Galina were a prostitute, BJ. Don't you think she should be consulted?"

"Oh sure. I'm not proposing to spy on you without telling her. Aren't you being somewhat hypocritical, Michael? You and I don't have to be embarrassed about our sexuality, do we?"

"I am not embarrassed, BJ, but you see, Galina is someone who still thinks of sex as a very personal and private thing."

"Oh. She does? Okay. That's too bad, but I guess if you come from a society where it's considered normal to stand in line four hours for a tomato there probably isn't much scope for developing one's sexual awareness."

"That is quite right."

"I still think she should meet Philip, though. A Russian physicist. He'd be thrilled to death."

"No."

"Why not?"

"It would be very difficult for her, because of the language. There is really no point."

"Come on, Michael. They could communicate on the computer."

Michael shrugged and looked away.

"You're being funny, Michael. You're acting so protective about her. Are you afraid she and Philip will recognize each other right away, like quarks, and just nucleate before your eyes, or what?"

"No. But Philip is not interested to explain his work to others."

"Not to you, maybe. But that was because he saw you as a rival sexually. But I'm sure he'd love to talk to Galina."

"No."

"But his paper – he may want it translated some time. I know it's really important. It's appearing in July in the States, you know. He's real excited. I guess it will be read all over the world."

"Everyone who needs to read it will be able to do so in English I think."

249

"The Russians too? I had the impression language wasn't their strong point. Although actually that can't be true. Philip says it's quite common for some guy to publish a paper in the States and then lo and behold it turns up in Russian under another name. I mean, they don't even tamper with the punctuation."

"Academic piracy is a world-wide problem. It's not just the Russians."

"Well, that doesn't make it okay. Oh, now I know what you do. You go round the bookstores looking for titles that would sell like hot cakes in Sbrinsk, translate it and get the commission. Well, that fits. Wow, I envy you. What a cool way to make money."

"It's bloody hard work, I tell you. Translating science is no fun at all."

"So you do admit it?" She laughed.

"No, not at all. I told you, what I do is very dull."

"Well I'm sure Philip's paper would appear dull to you too, if you didn't understand it."

"At least it was short."

"I beg your pardon? What did you say? Sit down a minute, will you." Michael had stood up to go to the kitchen. "You mean 'is' short, don't you?"

"Yes. I don't know. What did I say?"

"Wait a minute. Wait, wait, wait. I don't feel good." BJ put her hands to her head. "I said – what did I say? Something like, it would be dull if you didn't understand it. And you said, 'At least it was short.' Right?"

"So, it was a little mistake."

BJ shook her head theatrically. She was pale. "No. You don't make mistakes like that, Michael. You must have had access to the manuscript, right?"

Michael shrugged. He looked amused.

"I think I'm going to throw up. I can't believe this. You've seen Philip's paper. How, Michael? My God, if Philip finds out – I guess you may have even translated it already. I guess you have. Have you? How did you get hold of it, Michael? Who gave it to you?"

"Nobody gave it to me."

"Then how did you get hold of it?"

He looked at her as if she were being a bit dense. "I took it, of course."

"You – took – it. No, this isn't happening. You took it? How? When?"

"When you were in St Gallen."

"What! Michael, you can't have – you can't – I think I'm going to pass out."

Michael sat up. "What's the matter, BJ? I thought you'd be amused."

"Amused? At your breaking and entering my home and stealing a personal, private document that my husband has been working on for three years? And for what, I'd like to know? What did you do with it? I don't even know what you'd want with a thing like that."

"Don't be silly, BJ. I wouldn't have taken it unless I already had a buyer."

"A buyer? A buyer! Jesus H. Christ, Michael, you're shameless! A buyer! You talk like it was a couple of pounds of hash or something. It's immoral, Michael. It's just disgusting."

Michael stared at her. "BJ, I tell you, if I had known you would be so upset I wouldn't have done it. But look, be honest. The way you talk about Philip – and your attitude to your marriage and so on – it's anyway so commercial. I didn't think honestly that you would mind."

"What has my marriage got to do with it? We're talking about what you've done. By any standards it's immoral."

"Why?"

"It's stealing."

"I didn't take anything."

"Oh come on –"

"Look, it's actually a compliment to Philip, isn't it?"

"But it's such a betrayal, Michael. After we invited you to dinner –"

Michael burst out laughing. "BJ you are ridiculous. You accuse me of betraying your husband because he invited you to dinner – although he left in the middle, I must remind you. And you betray him all the time, if you like. But that does not count, apparently."

"That's not the same thing. Philip and I have this understanding." Or did. It was true that he had subsequently claimed not to have understood. "I guess it was one of those Russian guys we saw at the movie?"

"No, actually it was another one."

"I don't believe this. You mean it's translated and could appear over there before Philip's? Oh my God." BJ started crying.

"I don't know what they will do with it. I think they are just curious to see everything of the Americans that they can get hold of. Why are you crying BJ? Please tell me."

"Why am I – huh – crying? Don't you – huh – know what this will – huh – mean to – huh – him? All that – huh – work. He was – huh – so excited. He was sure it was – huh going – huh – to make his – huh – career. Oh my – huh – God."

Michael began to look genuinely concerned. "Please calm yourself, BJ. I wish I had not told you."

"Then why – huh – did you?"

"Well – you almost worked it out anyway. And then I couldn't resist. I'm sorry, I really did not know you would be so upset."

"Why not, for Christ's sake? It's the lousiest trick I ever heard of. You used me, Michael. Like I was a love-lorn typist or something. It's disgusting."

"But you use Philip, if you like. What's the difference? You do not care for him."

"I never said I didn't care for him."

"But what you do say means the same thing."

"Michael, how can you say that? You know how it is. I don't go around pretending to have Hallmark Hall of Crap feelings that I don't have, but that doesn't mean I don't have any feelings at all. Why do people always think I have no feelings? I'm an extremely sensitive person, Michael."

"Sorry."

"My God. If Philip ever finds out he'll kill me."

"But you are blameless."

"Oh yeah? I only told you about it. I only introduced you into the house and let you get me out of the way while you broke in. Oh God, I'm going to throw up."

"Yes, I must admit that is why I did not tell you before. I did not expect you to be so upset, but I guessed that Philip would be a little angry perhaps. And he is –" he pretended to shiver "– such a gorilla. I would be scared to death to make him angry."

"Jesus, you're cool, Michael. Breaking and entering is a crime, you know. I could report you to the police. You just assumed I wouldn't because I'm in love with you."

"No, because it would mean telling Philip. And, excuse me, I did not break anything. You never even noticed."

"That's true. That's what makes it so horrible."

"BJ I am stunned. I thought you admired free criminal enterprise?"

"Not at the expense of one's friends."

"I'm sorry. But at that time we were not so friendly – as now. Were we?"

BJ looked at him sullenly. She was stunned herself. There was only one way to punish him, and that was not to tell him she was leaving.

252

She stood up with consciously foreboding mien.

"I have to go now, Michael. I have to lie down."

"As you wish, BJ."

She put a hand on his arm and looked deep into his eyes, trying to pierce through them to the heart.

"Promise me you'll never let Philip know about this. He'd kill me, he really would."

"Are you being crazy? It is me he would kill." He shuddered again. "I do not want to meet him down a dark alley some day. I have all reasons to be silent. And you know, it is not certain that it will be published. Philip will probably know nothing about it."

"I still think it's the rottenest thing I ever heard of."

"Then I still do not understand you. It was quite well paid, actually. Don't you even appreciate that side of it?"

"That's the worst thing of all! That makes it, like, total corruption. You don't even need the money."

"Nor do you, BJ. You could stay at home and let Philip support you. Why don't you?"

"Let's not get into that again."

BJ looked at him gravely. Then she put her hands around his neck and pressed his lips to hers. They stiffened slightly, like a stomach muscle under the stethoscope.

Michael came to the door with her. She did not say anything more and descended the stairs with conscious pathos, determined, Orpheus-like, not to look back.

But as she opened the front door she did look back. He smiled and waved. BJ crumbled and, crying and saying his name, she panted up the stairs again and flung her arms round him. He endured it as long as he could. Then he gently led her back down the stairs and, murmuring solicitudes, made sure she got out of the front gate.

As a result of his transfer to the Far East Max was so busy researching hot spots in Hong Kong that he did not have time to collect Kirstin for ten days.

Kirstin's mother had come to keep house, an arrangement that had been more greatly desired by the women than by Max, as it gave him no excuse not to spend every available moment at Kirstin's bedside, and he found it impossible to talk to her in hospital. If he sat down the great white bed rose above him like a catafalque. If he stood up he felt like the hospital chaplain.

For as long as she was in hospital Kirstin managed to be, if not cheerful, at least sanguine. The momentum of tragedy kept her afloat. But they were all dreading her return to the house.

The scene with Michael left BJ prostrate until the middle of the afternoon, when she suddenly remembered that she had intended to go downtown and pick up some ceremonial bamboo steaming-baskets she had seen when she had had no money on her.

Sharing the front of her mind with the steaming-baskets was an obsessive review of the scene with Michael, and its awful revelations. BJ had to admit that the main concern, more than moral outrage, was that Philip should not find out, and she went over and over the possible course of events from now on, to reassure herself that this could not happen. Even if the unlikely worst happened and the paper did appear in Russian, there was no possibility that he would suspect the truth. He would be much more likely to suspect that Michael had persuaded her to hand it over while they were in the throes of adulterous ecstasy.

Besides which, in her innocence, BJ had often drawn his attention to Michael's almost professional knowledge of Russian affairs, in the hope of impressing Philip with Michael's intellectual respectability. The only consolation was that everybody knew the Russians stole all their ideas, so that Philip's reputation might survive the scandal. She dreaded seeing Philip again, and starting the habit of searching his face and pronouncements for evidence that he had found out. It seemed ironic that of all the marital offences she had deliberately concealed from Philip none had given her a twinge of guilt, but this unintentional offence would torture her for years.

Max collected Kirstin from the hospital at ten in the morning, and her mother stayed at home to cook the lunch.

Kirstin was silent in the car, apart from a few comments about the flowers that had come into season since she went into hospital. As they drove past Herr Umberg's house she looked away. The Umbergs had disappeared more than a month before, and already the house was let to a rowdy family with four children. Not a word had been spoken about their departure, and the silence from the police had been deafening. It was as though the Umbergs had been discreetly transported from the planet. Behind the house the breeze-block outlines of the new buildings were rising on their ugly, churned-up lots.

It was a melancholy meal. Kirstin's mother was inhibited by Max at the best of times, but now almost every subject except foreign wars seemed to be too touchy. She had cleaned and tidied the house meticulously, removed all trace of human habitation. The sounds and gestures of their eating obtruded obscenely on the sanitized air. Kirstin forced down a morsel of noodles and a mouthful of camomile tea and, hotly urged by the others, went upstairs to rest.

Max brought her some more tea. She was looking glumly out of the window towards the Umbergs' house. Max followed her gaze.

"Now don't start brooding about them, Kirstin. You did everything you could."

"But it's so disturbing when people just disappear and nobody knows what's happened to them. It's like Stalin's Russia."

"That's a bit unfair. The postman might know. Well, if you've got everything you want I'll be off. Beat wants me to go canoeing with him."

"On the Rhine? Do be careful, Max, the current is so strong."

"Thank you, Kirstin, I am aware of that. I'm not going to be swimming upstream over a waterfall, you know. I'll wear a lifejacket if it will make you feel better."

"Yes, it would. Isn't life precious to you, Max?" Her voice trembled.

"Oh Christ, don't start again. Listen, you've really got to get a grip on yourself, Kirstin. I'm sorry to say this, but it's my opinion that you brought this miscarriage on yourself. Look at you. There's not enough flesh on you to spread on toast. If you want to have a successful pregnancy you must make more of an effort to keep fit. What was that?"

A missile of some sort had landed on the side of the house. Max went to the window. The squeals of the guilty parties could be heard from behind the forsythia next door.

"I'll soon put a stop to that," he muttered.

"Was it the children?"

"Yes. Four of them. Catholics, I suppose. Two's enough."

"But the population is shrinking, Max. The Swiss are going to die out in two hundred years."

"So be it. It's the price you'll have to pay for prodigal self-indulgence. Do you realize how much nuclear waste each of those children will cause to be produced in its lifetime?"

"No."

"One hundred cubic metres. Or thereabouts. Think about it. Two's enough."

★

255

In the end, the parting from Philip was much worse than BJ had anticipated.

She woke up on the day which she would see setting over the view from her in-law's beach house almost choking with elation. Everything apart from her nightdress and toilet articles had been packed the day before. There was nothing to do after breakfast except clean the john, disassembling the seat to get at the yuchy deposits underneath the hinge.

Still they arrived at the airport one and three quarter hours before take-off. Right up to passport control she looked around to see if it had been revealed to Michael in a dream that she was leaving, and by which flight. For a while she deluded herself that she sought him in fear, but by the time the chance was gone she knew it had been in hope.

Philip was relaxed in his favourite rôle of tour organizer. He even presented her tickets for her, and carried her boarding card as far as passport control. But there was still three quarters of an hour to kill. Philip suggested a drink, but BJ said she was reluctant to engage in valedictory rituals at this point. She would rather he had dumped her at the entrance and gone straight home, but feared that if she had said so it might have been correctly interpreted.

They paced about the gleaming concourse, and sat down outside a souvenir shop, watching Saudi ladies rummaging through the Heidi outfits.

"Have you thought any more about moving out of that apartment?" said BJ. "You're going to get pissed with housework."

"I told you, BJ, we have to honor the contract."

"What will you do after that? You'll still have a month. Where will you stay then?"

"I do not know. I might do what we planned to do anyway – travel. You know, do Europe."

"You mean you want to see more?"

"I'm sorry it's been such a bad experience for you, BJ."

"Actually one could get used to the place. In different circumstances I would consider making another attempt to bring about peaceful change. I kinda regard us as, like, Peace Corps volunteers – bringing aid to an underdeveloped country."

"And what have been your achievements so far?"

"What do you mean?"

"Let's see. You just about detonated our marriage. Both your best friends end up in hospital –"

"Pure coincidence."

"Are you sure? I seem to remember my father died shortly after a conversation with you."

"He had heart trouble. And what do you mean 'I' detonated our marriage?"

"If you hadn't gotten involved with Michael –"

"Okay, okay. Let's change the subject."

A family of four huge-eyed Turkish children skipped and strolled along after their demure mother, her face obscured by the traditional Hermes headscarf.

"You know," said BJ, "it seems funny leaving without knowing whether Geraldine – I mean if she's going to be okay. It's funny, I wouldn't give a shit if I never saw Geraldine again, but I'd sort of miss her if she was – well – rubbed out."

"I don't think that's funny. It's normal. You probably feel the same way about me."

"Philip, come on. I didn't mean that's just the way I feel. That's just the way one feels. You've gotten to taking everything so personally."

"We'll have to talk, BJ."

"Sure. You know it's a shame I wasn't around longer from Geraldine's point of view. I think she felt that too – that I could have helped her out of the mire."

"How can you be so sure she was in a mire? I thought your main complaint about her was that she was so contented."

"Ah, well she thought she was, of course. She'd brainwashed herself. But – like this cancer thing. I mean, that's an indicator, isn't it? I mean, it's well known that cancer is, like, the body expressing stress and anger and frustration and stuff."

"But that doesn't mean that everyone who has cancer is suppressing all those things."

"Not in every case, perhaps. But in Geraldine's case it fits, doesn't it? I mean, why else was she so aggressive with me?"

"Perhaps because you made it obvious you despised her."

"I did not. I always gave my opinion in a totally neutral manner."

Philip smiled. "You really think you could have got her tumours to recede? You should hang up your sign and make some money."

"Who knows? If I'd had longer to work on her and persuade her to break out of that creepy bovine homemaker syndrome. I mean, isn't it amazing that that kind of set-up is so common over here? It's even considered normal."

"You think she should be a bovine PhD student instead?"

"PhDs are just frills. No one really needs them. I don't have one.

It's self-determination I'm talking about. Not just caving in to other people's expectations."

Philip did not say anything.

"They're calling the flight. I'd better go," said BJ.

They walked back in silence to passport control. BJ turned to say goodbye before attempting to fight her way through the crowd of grief-stricken departees and their relations who were clogging up the entrance embracing each other. On the outskirts of the group were businessmen of various nationalities shaking a hearty and cheerful hand of their Swiss hosts. It was in this periphery that BJ instinctively stopped and turned to Philip with her brave, self-determined face on. After collapsing ignominiously in Michael's presence, she was on guard against the same thing happening with Philip in a public place. The last hour's conscious neutrality had, when the moment came, driven emotion down to dangerously high pressure. As they said goodbye the hot tears began to run down her swelling nose. Philip looked distressed and his hands twitched at his sides, but he did not touch her.

"Take care, BJ. Remember me to Mother."

"A picture would help. Ciao. See you – huh – in – huh – August."

"Here's your boarding card."

"Thanks."

She edged her way to the front of the line, got through, and walked to the top of the escalator. She turned once more with a wave and a sniff, and managed to descend facing front and not backwards as one or two of the retards did.

Down in the departure area she felt better. It was not long before she noticed that a middle-aged oriental businessman had become attached by a thread to her elbow in the duty-free shop. He wore an elegant dark blue cloth suit and gold cufflinks. BJ tried to play Grandmother's Footsteps on him, but whenever she swivelled round his gaze was just grazing her ear, and it was only then that he looked at her directly and laughed his silent oriental laugh.

She managed to shake him off in the stampede onto the plane, but it was no surprise when she looked up from her *Swissair Gazette* to see him putting his briefcase in the overhead rack and taking his seat next to her.

BJ looked out of the window towards the airport building, wondering if Philip had stayed to see take-off. It would be out of character for him, but for her it would be a final reassurance to see his shadowy, silent form, so recognizably like the RKO building, keeping vigil in the observation tower.

The cabin attendants were beginning their demonstration of the lifejackets and oxygen masks. A comic routine, BJ thought. It must take at least five minutes to find the thing, get it on, do the straps up, find the inflation tab, press the light, at the same time as holding the oxygen mask over your face and lining up in an orderly manner by the nearest exit, assuming that one was calm enough to consult the card showing where they were.

Sweat broke out on her face at the idea of imminent oblivion. It would be a not unwelcome development in some quarters: the ball and chain dropping from Philip's side at a stroke. A hypothetical scenario came to mind, where the husband in such a case would have planted a small bomb in her washbag. Not that it needed a bomb if a hairspray could do the same thing. There were probably several substances that a physicist would know about that might cause explosions on board. Something quite small, that could be slipped into a suitcase unnoticed . . .

BJ gave a short, mad laugh. The thing was ridiculous – wasn't it? For one thing, the security precautions were surely the most thorough known to man, why else was she flying Swissair? Quite apart from the absurdity of the notion that anyone as conventional as Philip would have the nerve to blow up over three hundred innocent people just to get rid of her when he could do it at no risk by more conventional means.

But however firmly she told that image of the lethal package to go away the scene continued to unfold – Philip returning to the office under a pre-determined plan to carry on exactly as normal – Prunelle silently joining him, an exchange of facial or other signals to indicate the successful plant – the surreptitious emergence of a transistor radio on which to wait announcement of the fatal crash –

BJ laughed out loud. She turned to her oriental admirer.

"Isn't it crazy the things you think of at this point?" she shouted above the Muzak, which was turned up to drown the screams of take-off. He laughed. "I was just thinking, if my husband wanted to get rid of me he could have planted a bomb. But I guess everyone else must be thinking something along the same lines."

His eyes popped open. "Your husband plant bomb?"

"No, no. Of course not. No, don't worry. I was just fantasizing."

"Good." He laughed. "Bombs no good."

"No."

"You okay?"

"No. I want to get off."

"Too late. We moving now. What you doing, madam?"

BJ had unbuckled her seatbelt and was pushing the button with the matchstick air hostess on. "I want to get off." She stood up, grasping the seat in front of her for support.

A stewardess sidled up to them. Her light grey eyes gave warning of merciless treatment for offending passengers.

"Please sit down, madam. We are preparing for take-off."

"Let me out. I want to get off."

"Are you sick? What is the problem, please?"

"I just want to get off. I've made a mistake."

"It is impossible, madam. Is this your first flight?"

"Of course not. How do you think I got here?"

"You must sit down, madam." She applied her bony, sun-tanned hand to BJ's shoulder and bore down with remarkable force. "You are disturbing the other passengers. I am bringing you something."

A steward had appeared at his colleague's elbow. They exchanged a few words in German, and he also told BJ to sit down. He promised that if she did so she would be allowed to visit the flight deck afterwards. The oriental businessman tugged at her arm.

"Just let me get off. Can't you call the control tower?"

"It is too late, madam. Sit!"

The plane had come to a stop. But as the command was issued it began its thundering gallop down the runway. BJ was thrown back into the seat, the stewardess lunged across to fasten her safety belt, and both attendants tottered to the back of the plane as it lifted its huge nose into the air.

BJ started to cry. Shortly after they were airborne the attendants came back.

"Is everything all right now, madam?"

"Oh – huh – sure. Everything's great."

"Would you please accept this with our compliments."

She took from her male colleague, now smiling, a tray on which was a small bottle of champagne substitute, two plastic glasses and two large pictorial chocolates, showing the covered bridge at Luzern and the entrance to the Gotthard tunnel.

BJ stopped crying and sat up like a hungry dog.

"Well – thank you. That's nice – that's nice. Thank you." She turned to her neighbour. "You'll join me?"

"Okay."

"Listen, I'm sorry. You must think I'm crazy. It's just that thinking about my husband made me realize I made a dumb move leaving just now. Cheers."

"Cheers. You got problems with husband?" His eyes sparkled.

"Who doesn't? Let's talk about you. Are you Japanese, by the way?"

"No, no. Chinese. Hong Kong."

"Ah. Sorry. I know one should always ask the other way round."

He laughed. "Okay."

BJ noticed that when not actually speaking to her, he would look politely at the back of the seat in front. Considering that he had so pointedly attached himself to her he was far from pushy. She ran an eye over his body. It was a standard-issue oriental body with few distinguishing features, a kind of Action Man body. Its aesthetic neutrality interested her. It provoked the question of how it would perform in a sexual situation which more sharply characterized bodies suggested for themselves.

"Do you mind me asking what line of business you're in?"

He laughed and drew back the sleeve of his jacket. There were three watches on it.

"Watches?" said BJ.

"Wight."

"Oh. I won't ask you what you've been doing in Switzerland, but I can guess."

"You in business too?" he asked.

"Sort of. We'll come to that. Are you going to Boston or Chicago?"

"Boston."

"I'm going to our beach house in Maine, but if you like I could come down town and show you around a couple of days."

"Wery good. Thank you wery much."

"That's okay." It would make a change from getting fat on mother-in-law's BLTs, and her morale was in the state where she could benefit from bedding a Chinese industrial pirate in no doubt luxurious surroundings.

"Where are you staying in Boston?" she asked.

"The Mewidian."

BJ had always wanted an excuse to patronize it.

"I suppose you're hoping to get into the market over there," she mused. "Have you done any feasibility studies?"

He shrugged. "A bit. But is expensive."

"Yeah, I know." She felt with her foot under the seat to make sure the briefcase containing the PIS material was still there.

BJ sat up, and the air of vocational reverence settled over her.

"I think," she said, "I have something that might interest you."